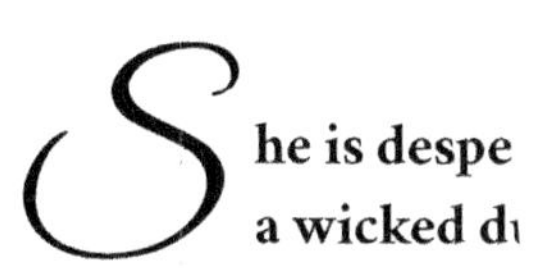

S he is despe ... ves her a wicked d...

Simon, the Duke o ... s house party, especially as her matchmaking hat is firmly in place. Attempting to atone for a misspent youth, Simon has become a sober, respected member of Parliament—and a hunted bachelor. His plan to avoid the minefield of ambitious mamas and their daughters is cast aside when he happens across a lady whose beauty is enhanced by her warmth and teasing tongue.

Miss Jessica Tremaine never forgot the kindness Simon showed her on a dark day when she was a young girl. Unexpectedly crossing paths once again, he assumes she's a lady's maid and not the girl from a troubled aristocratic family. It's clear he doesn't remember her, and for a time, she allows herself to dream of a future away from her despicable stepfather.

Simon learns of her deception and retreats to London to nurse what he suspects is a broken heart. When Jessica finds herself in London and in danger, she turns to the one man she trusts—even if he doesn't trust her.

Warning: Contains a lady in need of a knight-errant, a duke in need of a lady, and a deception that ignites a passion for the ages.

A DARING DECEPTION

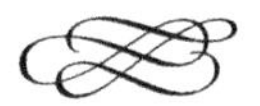

LAURA TRENTHAM

AUTHOR'S NOTE

When I started writing the Spies and Lovers series, I had no plan for how many books or who the main characters of each would be. This was my first foray into writing and I jumped in blind with two characters, Lily and Gray, and soon after Rafe and Minerva.

My plan was for the third book to be Simon and Jessica's book, and I would have a completed trilogy. But then Maxwell stepped onto the page in A Brazen Bargain, and I became obsessed with the surly Scot. And then Marcus and Delilah came as a couple, and I began to wonder how they got together in the first place. And then... Well, you get the picture.

I've ended up with a series that jumps around in time because of the poor timing of my characters and when they walk into my head. Lol!

Next up will be a spin-off series from Spies and Lovers called Laws of Attraction, and you will meet the first hero Damien Northcutt in A Daring Deception!

Every book in the series is a standalone story, but here's a list to help keep the timeline straight.

An Indecent Invitation, Gray and Lily, Spring 1812

A Brazen Bargain, Minerva and Rafe, Fall 1812

A Reckless Redemption, Maxwell and Bryn, Winter 1813

A Sinful Surrender, Marcus and Delilah, Spring 1812

A Wicked Wedding, Cole and Diana, Winter 1813

A Daring Deception, Simon and Jessica, Summer 1820

A Scandalous Secret, Garrick and Victoria, Winter 1814

ALSO BY LAURA TRENTHAM

Historical Romance

Spies and Lovers

An Indecent Invitation Book 1

A Brazen Bargain, Book 2

A Reckless Redemption, Book 3

A Sinful Surrender, Book 4

A Wicked Wedding, Book 5

A Daring Deception, Book 6

A Scandalous Secret, Book 7

Spies and Lovers Boxset

CONTEMPORARY ROMANCE

Sweet Home Alabama Novels

Slow and Steady Rush, Book 1

Caught Up in the Touch, Book 2

Melting Into You, Book 3

Christmas in the Cop Car, Novella 3.5

The Sweet Home Alabama Collection

. . .

Highland, Georgia Novels

A Highlander Walks Into a Bar, Book 1
A Highlander in a Pickup, Book 2
A Highlander is Coming to Town, Book 3

Heart of a Hero Novels

The Military Wife
An Everyday Hero

Cottonbloom Novels

Kiss Me That Way, Book 1
Then He Kissed Me, Book 2
Till I Kissed You, Book 3

Christmas in the Cop Car, Novella 3.5
Light Up the Night, Novella 3.75

Leave the Night On, Book 4
When the Stars Come Out, Book 5
Set the Night on Fire, Book 6

Fieldstones Adventure Novellas by Leah Trent

An Impetuous Interlude, Fieldstones Adventure Book 1
A Naughty Notion, Fieldstones Adventure Book 2
A Mysterious Masquerade, Fieldstones Adventure Book 3
A Dangerous Desire, Fieldstones Adventure Book 4
The Fieldstones Adventures Boxset

I love to hear from readers! Come find me:

Laura@LauraTrentham.com
www.LauraTrentham.com
Sign up for Laura's Newsletter
Join Laura's Facebook Squad

Are you interested in receiving a FREE book?!

Join my newsletter! There will be links in your Welcome Email for TWO free books!

Sign up for Laura's Newsletter

PROLOGUE

England, Winter 1813

It was an uncomfortable, frigid day for travel. The steel-gray clouds closing in on them had precipitated an early stop for the evening. At first glance, their hired carriage appeared well-heeled with its red velvet interior and glossy black paint. It had certainly cost an eye-popping amount of coins to hire, but the springs were shot, the wheels were deformed, and the interior smelled musty with the overtones of rotten vegetables.

The mention of the inadequacies had inflamed her stepfather's ire and earned Jessica a hard pinch. Although she'd done her best not to give Goforth the satisfaction of seeing her pain, a small cry had escaped and made him smile. Any suggestion he was not the cleverest, bravest, and best would lead to less-than-pleasant consequences.

She stepped into the inn and rubbed her still-throbbing arm. Now that Goforth's back was turned, the urge to stick her tongue out was almost too much to control. But she was attempting to act more ladylike. Although fourteen, she still preferred short skirts and playing catch me if you can with the children in their Pennsylvania village rather than taking tea and quietly embroidering pillows.

Her mother drew Blake, Jessica's younger brother, closer while Jessica stepped farther into the inn. Burning peat filled the room with a soft veil of smoke. The scent was earthy and foreign but not unpleasant.

"Your two finest rooms, sir. If you have any that qualify as such." Goforth's booming voice scraped Jessica's nerves.

A pall fell over the occupants of the common room as they turned their disapproving gazes toward her family. Her cheeks burned with embarrassment. Her mother kept Blake tucked to her front and while drawing an arm around Jessica's waist and squeezing. Was her mother protecting or warning her?

Protection was all her mother had the strength to offer anymore. She no longer gave her children hope or optimism for the future. Goforth had ground both to dust.

Blake unexpectedly inheriting an earldom through their dead father's English ancestors had made Goforth alternately resentful and grasping. He too was an English immigrant, although with less illustrious bloodlines. Nevertheless, he thought he deserved the kind of luck that brought Blake, a mere child under his care, such wealth and power. While Goforth wasn't the cleverest of men, he was cunning enough to seize an opportunity.

Goforth recognized Blake's ascendancy could carry him to greater heights than an undisputed leader in their Pennsylvania village. Jessica worried their mother was not strong enough to protect Blake from her new husband's ambition, which was more dangerous than his wrath.

The innkeeper was a soft-spoken man with a lined face and halo of thick white hair. He tried to assure Goforth he would have the best rooms possible, but Goforth made a dismissive sound. Red burnished the innkeeper's cheeks, and his mouth narrowed. It was obvious Goforth was testing the man's usually jolly disposition. A young boy was tasked with showing them to their rooms.

"Wait here while I assess the quality. I refuse to sleep with lice," Goforth said to her mother, but loud enough for everyone in the common room to hear. He stomped up the steps, rattling a series of bucolic watercolors lining the staircase.

Jessica shrugged her mother's arm off. "You should apologize to the innkeeper for his behavior, or we might find spittle in our dinner this evening."

Her mother's gaze darted up the stairs as she shook her head. "It's best not to try your father's patience."

"Stepfather."

"Please don't, Jessica. It's been a difficult journey, and you will only make things worse for yourself." In a smaller voice, her mother added, "And for all of us."

Goforth thumped his way back downstairs. "'Tis decent enough, I suppose. Quit hovering over the boy, Margaret."

Goforth grabbed Blake's arm and twisted him away from their mother. Blake made a sound of distress and reached out, but their mother lowered her face as if as long as she didn't see the pain in Blake's eyes, it didn't exist.

Jessica stepped between Blake and Goforth. "Leave him alone, you bully."

Goforth's lip curled. She braced for one of his insults but got the back of his hand across her cheek instead. Her ears rang from the blow. The pain would come, but for now she welcomed the fury. Straightening, she blinked away the sting of tears and set her chin, daring him to hit her again.

The stillness in the inn was so complete she could hear the crackle of the peat burning in the hearth. Goforth's shoulders tensed with readiness to deliver another slap.

"That's no way to treat a young lady." A man approached, drawing everyone's attention.

Jessica might legally be an earl's sister, but at heart she was merely a young woman from a small village in America. She had no experience with the class system that ruled Britain. Even so, she recognized a gentleman when she saw one.

The man moved with an arresting confidence. He wore power as well as he did the finely made greatcoat hanging from his broad shoulders. His hair was a burnished gold, his features even and handsome. He was older than she, but still young. Much younger and fitter than Goforth.

Her heart fluttered with something she'd thought had abandoned her forever. Hope.

"That's a sharp-tongued shrew, sir. She's no young lady." Goforth turned to face the man.

"Shrew or not, in these parts, hitting young women is beyond the pale," the man said with derision.

Jessica glanced at Goforth, gauging the likelihood of his turning his growing fury on the man.

But Goforth surprised her. His gaze took in the man's well-tailored clothes and aristocratic accent. Instead of hurling punches or insults, Goforth lips turned up into an ingratiating smile. Would the gentleman be fooled by the sudden change in attitude?

"My name's Edward Goforth, and we're on our way to Lipton, seeking the Penhaven estate. Do you know of it?"

"I do. What's your business there, may I ask?"

"Here's the new Lord Penhaven, right here in your midst."

"You?" The word came out on a bark of surprise.

"No, not me. My son, Blake Goforth, is the new Lord Penhaven." He gestured toward Blake, who had retreated back under their mother's arm.

"Blake Tremaine, not Goforth." Jessica's correction gained

her the gentleman's attention. His eyes were the blue of a summer sky, and the warmth of the sun burst through her.

"Since I married their mother, I don't see why they shouldn't take my name." Goforth addressed the gentleman, but he narrowed his eyes at Jessica, promising retribution.

"Because you're not our father." She wished Goforth would disappear from their lives forever through fair means or foul. It was a disturbing thought she couldn't mold into something more palatable.

"You impertinent little twit." Goforth raised his hand and stepped toward her.

She bobbed backward to avoid the blow, but nothing happened. The gentleman had grabbed Goforth's wrist and wrenched it away.

"I think not, Mr. Goforth." The man's voice was as cold as the wind whistling through the cracks around the door.

"And what authority do you have to stop me, whelp?"

"I'm the Duke of Bellingham, you arse. You can address me as Your Grace or not at all. If you insist on acting the boor, we'll call the local magistrate." The gentleman seemed to grow two inches with his anger.

What made the situation even more unbelievable was that his anger was on her behalf. Not even her mother had found the strength to stand up to Goforth. Bracing his legs apart, the duke cracked his knuckles and stretched his neck as she'd seen the village boys do before a brawl.

While she wasn't fluent in the aristocracy, even she knew a duke outranked an earl and dwarfed a mere mister. Apparently Goforth realized too and ceded the field.

"I'm terribly sorry, Your Grace. I suppose such things are better handled in private." Halfway up the staircase, he barked over his shoulder, "Margaret, come. With the children."

Her mother's shoulders were hunched in fear or embarrassment, or likely both. She followed like a dog given a command, pulling Blake along with her. She had been beautiful once, but Jessica could barely remember when.

Jessica didn't follow. She stared at the duke, trying to remember every line and angle of his face. He stepped closer, raised a hand slowly as if she might balk, and brushed a knuckle over her reddened cheek. "I'm sorry he hit you."

"Honestly, I deserved it. I'm awfully impertinent."

"No woman deserves to get hit. Don't ever convince yourself otherwise please." He glanced out the frosted window to see snowflakes floating down. "I'm only sorry I can't do more. I hope I didn't make things worse for you later. Unfortunately, I must ride on to attend to some business."

"Don't worry, Your Duke."

He smiled in a way that made her feel gauche, and she found herself nattering on.

"I'm a survivor. At least that's what my nana used to say. It was good to see someone other than me stand up to the lout. You've given me a bit of hope. Maybe things will be better here in England."

"What's your name?"

"Jessica Tremaine."

"You're American?"

"From Pennsylvania. What's your name?"

He tilted his head as if surprised by her question, but he finally said, "Simon. My name is Simon."

Simon took her small hand and bussed the back. "Well, Miss Jessica Tremaine from Pennsylvania, I wish you luck and good fortune here in England."

"Thank you. I believe I'll need all the luck I can get." She held her fisted hand against her chest and flew up the stairs, stopping in the shadows at the top to watch him.

He was halfway out the door when he paused. Her stomach swooped, hoping he might seek her out once more. Instead, after a whispered conversation, he slipped the innkeeper a few coins. With one last glance over his shoulder, he left with his greatcoat swirling around his black boots in a flurry of snowflakes.

Jessica leaned her head back against the wall and closed her eyes. Simon, the Duke of Bellingham. She would never forget his name or what he'd done for her this day. Never.

CHAPTER 1

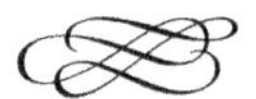

Summer 1820

Simon, the Duke of Bellingham, crouched behind a clump of young trees and scrubs as he battled a list of sundry emotions. At the forefront was chagrin at what his colleagues in Parliament, who respected his sober intellectualism arguing for the plight of beleaguered Londoners, would think of his current predicament.

A predicament he should extricate himself from immediately. The consequences of being caught ranged from life altering to embarrassing. Yet he was frozen. Utterly befuddled and absolutely flabbergasted.

A nearly naked woman was in the pond. *His* pond. Well, the pond at Wintermarsh, which was his sister and brother-in-law's estate, but he considered it his home as well. Even though he owned landholdings and a large town house in London, Wintermarsh was his refuge. *Usually.*

This particular morning had been trying. He had escaped to rail privately against the autumn house party his sister, Minerva, was planning. Simon had a terrible feeling she was planning the party for him. As in, he was the bait. He could already feel the noose tightening.

The guest list included a gaggle of eligible ladies in possession of bloodlines worthy of being a duchess. Minerva had denied the machinations with poorly faked innocence in her blue eyes. His sister was incorrigible and determined. A dangerous combination.

The woman in the pond distracted him from the impending nightmare of the house party. The wet shift she wore was translucent and clung to her curves. Her face was tilted up to the sky to catch the summer sun's heat, and the long dark strands of her hair danced above firmly rounded buttocks.

She held up sections of hair to hasten its drying, and he caught the tantalizing outline of the undercurve of her right breast. His imagination drew in the rest, including a rosy pebbled nipple pressing against the thin cotton shift.

His squatting position was becoming uncomfortable. So was the cockstand he was sporting. The thing had no sense of decorum. Where were the gentlemanly impulses he'd cultivated after a misspent youth? Apparently, they'd disintegrated at his feet like the leaf litter.

His gaze unerringly found its way back to the woman even as he was determined to scrape the remnants of his honor off the bottom of his boot and leave the lady in peace. Not taking his gaze off her, he rose, wincing at the protest from his cramped legs.

If only he could get a glimpse of her face. *Turn your head, my little nymph, turn,* he begged silently.

As if she heard him, she stilled and tilted her head like a wild creature sensing a predator.

And that's all he'd be to the young woman caught unawares in a vulnerable state. Shame welled up. If she was of a lower class, his power over her would be absolute. He had seen the powerlessness of women forced to sell their bodies and worse, their children, in order to survive London's slums. He refused to be the one to make life more difficult for this particular woman.

Resolute now, he took a step backward, smacking the crown of his head against a low limb. He let out a curse and dropped to his haunches to peer from between thick vines. The noise had spooked her.

The woman clamored to shore and pulled on a plain brown dress with buttons in the front. He watched her turn into an ordinary maid. No, not ordinary. No woman with her hair would ever be ordinary.

He caught a glimpse of her profile. A straight nose and high cheekbones were highlighted by a rosy complexion. Her mouth was turned down in worry, but he could imagine her lips tipped into a smile. Her eye color remained a mystery. One he wanted to solve.

Clutching a pair of half boots to her chest with one hand and lifting her dress nearly to her knees with the other, she took off in a barefooted run. He stepped out of the brush after she disappeared into a copse. She ran not toward Wintermarsh, but north. Was she a servant or the daughter of a crofter? She might even be another man's wife.

What could he do even if he did discover her identity? He couldn't pursue a servant or a country maid in any honorable fashion. At almost thirty, he was expected to wed a lady of impeccable breeding. He was merely a stud horse and his future wife a mare, and together they would need to produce healthy progeny to inherit the dukedom.

It rankled. His sister had made a love match. He often joked it was because of her state of happiness with Lord Rafe Drummond that he was forever finding fault with the young ladies thrust at him in London. Except he no longer found his situation amusing. While he didn't envy his sister her happiness, he despaired of ever achieving the same.

Minerva was two years his senior, but she'd been married nigh on eight years. Simon observed the sometimes tempestuous but always loving marriage his sister had made and found his every attempt to form a similar sort of bond impossible. He wanted a woman who would challenge him, surprise him, even set him back on his heels from time to time when he deserved to be put in his place.

The yearly crop of debutantes in London were too eager to please. If he declared the sky was green, they would readily agree. If he asked them to go jump in the lake, they'd ask from which bank. Minerva chided that he never gave the young ladies a proper chance. She tried to convince him the debutantes were intimidated by him and needed his encouragement to reveal their true natures. Perhaps she was right, but he couldn't summon the patience or will to court a single one.

More and more when Parliament was in session he found himself eschewing the whirlwind social life in favor of his clubs, where he could connect with political friends and foes alike. He also spent more and more time in the country, seeing to his estates and visiting Wintermarsh.

Still, once mounted on his horse, he found himself riding not toward Wintermarsh, but in the same direction as the woman. He kept the horse at a walk, fearing he would overtake and frighten her. Over a rise, he came to a stop. A large expanse of lawn with golden-tipped grasses led to a handsome manor house of red stone. The woman made her way through the field of gold, leaving a path of grass bending to her will, her hair streaming behind her in the breeze.

His heart skipped. She slowed to open a tall wrought iron gate at the edge of the kitchen gardens. Instead of rushing through the gate, she slowly turned and scanned the countryside. There was nowhere for him to hide this time.

As though sensing his discomfort, his horse chuffed, tossed his head, and sidestepped. The distance was too great to gauge her expression or for her to identify him. Still, their stares seemed to reach across the expanse like a cord being braided together. Simon's breathing grew shallower. She moved first, plunging through the gate, lost to him in the vines. Released from her spell, he took a deep breath and regained his sanity.

While he had never been to the estate, he knew where he was now. *Penhaven.* The estate was cursed, the line of Penhaven earls given to violence and madness. He also knew something of the man who served as proxy lord until the heir to the earldom reached his majority.

Mr. Edward Goforth was a pompous bully. He'd been elected to the House of Commons and relished the position of power. The man's mission focused on keeping the lower classes in their slums. Simon had done his best to ignore the inflammatory rhetoric coming from Goforth and his ilk, but it was becoming more difficult to ignore the raucous following he had gained.

Simon wheeled his horse around and galloped toward Wintermarsh. Who was the young woman? It wasn't Sunday, the typical half day given to servants. If not a servant, could she be a companion to the family or a poor relation? A more startling thought occurred to him. Could the woman have been Miss Tremaine? She'd been teetering on the edge of womanhood the last time their paths had crossed, and that had been years earlier. Surely she was well past twenty now.

As soon as the stables came into view, a portion of his frustration eased. Wintermarsh was special. He'd become a man here and grown close to the people who lived and worked at the estate and in Lipton. He was grateful Rafe and Minerva didn't mind him hanging about. He supposed the house party was his bill coming due.

He left his horse in Tom Donahue's capable hands and entered the house through the stately front door. His sister called his name from the study. He changed direction. Minerva sat at the desk, making notations in a large ledger.

His sister's marriage was unusual in many ways. One being the fact that Minerva managed the money she'd brought to the marriage as her dowry. She invested in business ventures that interested her, and the profits were funneled to various charities benefiting women and children.

"What have to say for yourself?" Minerva put down her quill and regarded him with a flinty expression.

How the devil did she know he'd been spying on a servant at their pond? To buy time to formulate a suitable excuse, he asked, "Whatever do you mean?"

"I mean, Simon, really! You gave Christopher a handful of sweets. Of course he ate every last one in record time and cast his accounts all over the rug. I should have sent for you to clean it up this morning."

He stifled his laugh of relief when her countenance didn't crack into an answering smile. "Terribly sorry. I did tell him to only eat two and save the rest. Perhaps you should teach him to count."

"He's only three, you bounder! You should know a child can't stop when faced with such temptation." Minerva cast him the *look,* and for a moment he was twenty again and began to wither slightly.

"Don't you dare look at me like that. I'm a grown man and a duke. Save it for Rafe or Christopher." Simon jabbed a finger at Minerva.

"Unfortunately, glaring doesn't work on Rafe. Never did." Minerva harrumphed, but it was good-natured. "How's your bill progressing?"

"Quite well. I'm hopeful I'll have the votes by year end." The bill would limit the age of chimney sweeps so children who weren't born into privilege like Christopher wouldn't be forced into servitude. "I'm working on a bill to improve the conditions in the workhouses as well, but the support has been lukewarm."

His efforts to get his fellow peers to look beyond the veil of their own contentment and bear witness to the suffering around them had produced only marginal successes. The wheel of justice moved at too slow a pace to suit him.

"That's excellent progress. Rafe and I are proud of you."

"It's just the beginning, I hope." Simon's throat tightened with emotion. His sister's praise was something he'd always strived for, and even as a man grown, he relished it.

Minerva bent her head back to her task, her golden hair, so like his own, shining in a shaft of sunlight. He meandered to the nearest shelf of books and ran his hand along the spines, gauging Minerva's reaction from the corners of his eyes. "I was wondering... Do you circulate socially with the family that inherited the Penhaven estate?"

"The mother passed away a handful of years ago. I attempted to befriend the daughter, Miss Tremaine, but she rebuffed my invitations. The son is quite charming, but green yet. As I understand, he's at Eton and not often home."

Simon plopped in the chair across from the desk and ran a finger over his lips. "That's too bad about the daughter. I met her once many years ago. Our interaction was brief, but she seemed full of fire and gumption."

"She seems to have never found her footing in Lipton, I'm afraid, and I'm not sure what Goforth's plans are for her with regard to a London season. If he doesn't present her soon, she'll be on the shelf."

"Do you know if Miss Tremaine has a companion or other female relation to help ease her entrance into society?"

"Not that I know of, but as I said, she has politely and firmly rebuffed my invitations, and to be frank, I haven't issued one in quite some time in case her stepfather gets wind of it and accepts for them both. Goforth has made no secret of the fact he would like an invitation to Wintermarsh to further our acquaintance."

"Goforth struts around London as if he's in line for prime minister, always lamenting the fact *he's* not the Earl of Penhaven." Simon didn't begrudge a man for attempting to better himself, but Goforth's methods included trampling those in his way. Soon after arriving in England, he had officially attained citizenship through his father and established himself as a force in politics.

"I don't doubt it. Why the sudden interest?" Minerva's curiosity was piqued and pointed.

"Goforth is turning into an annoying obstacle to my goals in Parliament."

"And?" Minerva raised a brow. She knew him too well.

Simon searched for something—anything—plausible. "Our paths rarely cross in social settings. I thought perhaps I could sway him if we met under more congenial circumstances."

"This has nothing to do with Miss Tremaine?" Minerva's attention homed in on him with an intensity that made him squirm.

"Of course not. It has been some time since our paths crossed, but I do feel sorry for her." He couldn't help his next question. He had to know. "I remember her as an attractive girl. Is her appearance pleasing?"

"Pleasing? It's hard to say, to be honest. All I've been able to ascertain about her looks is that she has brown hair and dresses abominably."

It was the barest of descriptors and could describe countless women, his mystery one included. "You mentioned her mother died some time ago. Does she have a companion? A poor relation, perhaps?"

"Not that I'm aware of, but I'm not in the know. I should have called upon her more often after her mother's death." More than sympathy weighed her words. Minerva understood what it was like to lose parents and be left adrift and floundering. As did he.

Simon shook off the melancholy of the past to focus on the present. Minerva's description of Miss Tremaine kept a spark of hope alive. The young lady in the pond had brown hair and wore an unflattering dress. He ignored inconvenient questions about why a lady would be bathing in a pond and why she was traipsing around the countryside unaccompanied.

With an enthusiasm he found uncomfortable, Minerva clasped her hands and smiled. "You'll be quite pleased by my guest list."

Simon managed to stop his eyes from rolling halfway around and assumed the bland expression he often wore during Parliamentary sessions.

Minerva listed off names and lineages of young ladies. Lady Anne and Lady Faith and Lady Something-or-other and her also-available cousin, Miss Whatsit.

"You should invite them." It popped out of him like the first steam from a teapot.

"I have invited them. Have you been listening to a word I've said?"

"I was referring to Goforth and Miss Tremaine."

"Are you quite serious?"

"It's the polite thing, is it not? Wintermarsh and Penhaven share a border. What will they think when they see the outings to Lipton and across the estate and know they weren't invited?"

Minerva regarded him like he'd sprouted horns. "It's neither here nor there. We're out of bedrooms."

"I'll sleep in the cottage." The brilliance of his plan was only now becoming clear. The cottage was both solution and escape. "I'll drag Damien along to stay with me. That will free up two rooms."

Minerva sat back and regarded him with bemusement. "Is this part of your political machinations?"

Simon seized on the explanation. "Indeed. I hope to convince Goforth as to the merits of my bill. While I may not be able to garner his support, I may be able to tone down his vociferous opposition."

"This has nothing to do with Miss Tremaine?"

"Of course not."

Minerva ignored his denial. "Because while Miss Tremaine is on the market, she is not at all your usual sort."

"As I stated clearly, the invitation has nothing to do with her." His sister's observation penetrated his defensiveness. "Wait. What's my usual sort?"

"Beautiful, buxom, and *not* a lady."

Simon flushed. While it was true he had enjoyed the favors of such women, he had eschewed such pursuits recently to concentrate on more serious matters. "You make Miss Tremaine sound like an ape-faced spinster. She can't be much past twenty."

Minerva puffed out a breath. "I hardly know what the poor chit looks like because she stares at her feet as if they may walk off without her and hides behind a cap more suited to a dowager."

"This party is a chance for you to gently influence her. Remember how difficult things were for us?"

Minerva stared at Simon for the longest time, and with some effort, he kept his face impassive. "Fine, but I'll let *you* inform Rafe he has to be polite to Goforth for a week."

Simon sat back with a smile of satisfaction.

Minerva returned to writing in the ledger. "And I wouldn't advise doing it during your fencing match."

That wiped the smile off Simon's face. He rose to take his leave but stopped in the doorway. "If you'll ready the invitation, I'll deliver it myself."

Minerva didn't look up. "I'll have it ready after nuncheon."

At worst, he had done a good turn by Miss Tremaine. Would

discovering the identity of the woman from the pond be a good turn or bad for him though? Considering the devilish part of him he'd tried to quash years ago was positively gleeful at the possibility, he decided it would be very bad indeed. Yet he was going to do it anyway.

CHAPTER 2

Miss Jessica Tremaine's heart had taken up a new cadence. It was as if the man on the hill had introduced her to a new dance that left her exhilarated and dizzy. Had he been spying on her at the pond? Had he followed her to the manor? Was he the man she'd dreamed about off and on for years? She shook her head to rein in her imagination.

What mattered was the man had not been her stepfather. That twist of fate would have been disastrous. Her years of imitating ugly wallpaper would be for naught if Goforth had spotted her out of her usual disguise. But she was fairly certain her stepfather would have confronted her immediately. Lying in wait was hardly his style. He was a slap-first, ask-questions-later sort of man.

She ran straight to her chambers on the third floor upon returning to Penhaven Manor, luckily not crossing paths with anyone. Once used by a governess, the room was spare but comfortable, and most importantly, it was as far away from her stepfather as she could credibly manage.

A schoolroom with dusty wooden blocks and a broken slate was connected by a door next to her bed. When sleep wouldn't come and she was feeling particularly melancholy, she would wander the abandoned room. Her brother had used it for two years before Goforth sent him to Eton after their mother's death. Dwelling on the wrenching pain of the day her brother left was enough to unsettle her.

The Penhaven estate had welcomed them on a blustery snowy day eight years earlier. She had been in awe of the size and opulence of the manor. For a brief moment, she'd been filled with a hope they would finally find the elusive happiness they'd lost since her father died.

Instead, tragedy had come to call and misery had moved in. There was nothing she could do but make the best of her bedfellows. Her goal was to make sure her brother, Blake, the ninth Earl of Penhaven, found contentment in his future.

In her room, she stared at herself in the distorted looking glass. Her cheeks were flushed, and her hair had dried in thick waves around her shoulders. The plain brown dress she wore clung to her damp chemise, outlining her body.

She barely recognized herself. A hint of the girl she'd once been lurked in the defiant flash of her eyes, but it hurt too much to see her again. She turned her back on her reflection, stripped naked, and proceeded to don her armor.

Not metal to stop the point of a sword from breaching her heart, but a more subtle protection. On top of her underthings, she tied padding around her waist to disguise her figure and slipped on a baggy, ill-fitting gray frock. She glanced toward the looking glass. A familiar figure emerged.

She finger combed her hair. It was clean and smelled sweet, and she couldn't bear to apply the grease she used to keep her stepfather uninterested in her prospects. Instead, she braided it and coiled it under a white mob cap more befitting a dowager than a young lady. Next, she applied a light coat of powder over her face to make her appear pale and sickly and paint to darken the undersides of her eyes.

Her stomach growled. Her stepfather was in residence, which meant remaining out of his purview whenever possible and acting gauche and uninteresting when she was required to keep him company.

The only two people she trusted in the house were Abby, a maid of all work who saw to Jessica when necessary, and Mrs. Hamish, the cook. The butler and the housekeeper traveled from the country to London with Goforth, and while they were polite enough, Jessica had little to do with either of them.

With her gaze on her feet, she made her way to the kitchen and poked her head around the jamb, relieved to see Mrs. Hamish sitting at the table eating a scone and reading a week-old discarded *London Times* with a pair of worn spectacles perched on the end of her nose. She was alone.

When Mrs. Hamish looked up, Jessica smiled, took a still warm scone for herself, and joined the cook on the bench seat.

"Aren't you a relief to my poor abused nose, little tiger," Mrs. Hamish said with a twinkle in her coal-black eyes.

"Breathe me in now, because I need some more of that grease to coat my hair before dinner. I fear if I plead sickness again, Goforth will call in a physician to bleed me."

"Ack, why must you go to such extremes? The way you frown and dress and scrape your hair under that atrocious cap are enough to deter the man. Not to mention the powders of a Drury Lane actress you insist upon using."

"If I wasn't so repugnant, he would have already bartered me off to one of his cronies for a vote."

Mrs. Hamish's normally kind face hardened. "It's disgraceful is what it is. He's your father."

"*Step*father." Even calling him that left a sour taste in Jessica's mouth the scone couldn't mask. In a softer voice, she said, "Mother will have been gone five years this autumn."

"I can scarcely believe it. I remember the day you arrived like it was yesterday. You were spitting fire and full of righteous indignation at anyone who tried to be kind to you. It's a wonder I didn't give up on you right then and there."

"I'm glad you didn't." Jessica craved a hug, but it wasn't the way things were done in England. "I was never meant to be an earl's sister. What an idiotic twist of fate. How much longer can I avoid Goforth's notice?"

"I don't know, lamb." Mrs. Hamish sounded more worried than reassuring, which in turn worried Jessica. Blake was still years away from gaining his majority and their freedom from Goforth.

The previous Lord Penhaven had been mad and a murderer and, most salient to Jessica's situation, had died without fathering an heir. The Penhaven bloodline had taken a circuitous route through her father to Blake.

Sometimes she imagined what her life would've been like if she had stayed in Pennsylvania. Would she be married to a handsome farmer with a babe on the way? Or would she have moved to the bustle of Philadelphia and worked as a shopgirl? Either way, her life would be moving forward. In England, she was stuck in a mire.

A knock on the door leading to the garden startled them both. Mrs. Hamish peeked out the window to the walk, then turned to Jessica with wide eyes. "It's a fine-looking gentleman."

She might as well have said a dragon was rapping on the door, looking for a maidenly sacrifice.

"A what?"

"A gentleman."

"What on earth could he want here?"

"Nothing good, I'd say. Go on with you." Mrs. Hamish shooed Jessica away with her apron. "I'll send him on his way forthwith."

Instead of retreating to the safety of her room, she crammed herself into a cupboard, squatting under a shelf of turnips and next to a sack of flour. The padding around her waist made it a tight fit. Her heart had assumed the rhythm of a now familiar dance. It couldn't be a coincidence she'd spotted a gentleman on the rise and now one had appeared on their doorstep. What did he want?

"Good afternoon, sir. What might I do for you?" The door was at an awkward angle and Jessica could see nothing, but Mrs. Hamish's usual no-nonsense Yorkshire brogue did not warm with a welcome.

"A good day to you to, madam. What is that delightful scent?" The man's voice was like a luxurious fleece-lined cloak, enveloping and warm.

"Buns fresh from the oven."

"You must be Mrs. Hamish."

"Indeed, I am." The tenor of Mrs. Hamish's voice indicated her pleasure at being recognized by name.

"Why, Mrs. Potts has been raving about your buns. Everyone at Wintermarsh is most grateful you were kind enough to pass along your recipe. They have become a favorite with Lady Drummond especially."

"That's very kind of you, sir."

Jessica rolled her eyes. The fastest way to Mrs. Hamish's heart was to compliment her baking. Mrs. Hamish stepped into view, gesturing for the man to enter. Her cheeks were apple red and her smile bright. She had the look of a schoolgirl talking to her beau. What sort of man could create such changes with a deft compliment?

The man stepped into Jessica's narrow line of sight. Suddenly she understood, the way a bird understood flying. It was instinctual. Primal. Her breath caught before she even had time to catalog everything that combined to make the man undeniably attractive.

He removed his hat and ran a hand through his golden hair, leaving it charmingly disheveled, as if that were his planned toilette all along. His smile was wide and white and exuded a warmth she was sure wasn't faked. From her squatting position, he seemed impossibly tall and broad.

Even more startling than his appeal was the fact the man was no stranger. It was him. The man from her dreams.

Simon Bellingham. His Grace. The duke. Her stomach clenched. She might be able to dismiss his charm and good looks as shallow in another man, but he had shown her a kindness years ago. A moment he had no doubt forgotten. A moment she would never forget.

She leaned forward to drink him in. The door of the cupboard creaked open another inch, and she pulled back into the shadows, but her gaze didn't waver.

He visited his sister and brother-in-law, Lord and Lady Drummond, fairly often if the talk around Lipton was to be believed. Jessica had never seen him, but then again, she avoided town and socializing.

Goforth had made it clear after their arrival in England that the girls she might have enjoyed spending time with—the daughters of the shopkeepers or farmers—were considered beneath their new station in life. The girls from gentry families had struck her as priggish and boring and had made fun of her accent and clothes. Resentment at being plopped into a foreign land had made her sensitive to their teasing, and she hadn't bothered to mend bridges once she was older and more mature. Her worries eclipsed what to wear to the next dance or hunting for a husband.

"I'm Simon, the Duke of Bellingham, by the way." His small bow was somehow deferential and self-depreciating at the same time.

Mrs. Hamish's blush spread, and she dropped into a wobbly curtsey. "Oh, Your Grace... I-I apologize... I didn't realize..."

"Please." The duke held up his hands and smiled a crooked little smile that did funny things to Jessica's stomach. "No need to stand on ceremony. I was on my way to see Mr. Goforth but was lured in by the delightful aroma coming from your kitchen. I wouldn't want to interrupt your duties."

Mrs. Hamish knew Jessica was hiding in the cupboard, so surely she wouldn't invite him inside and offer him—

"Pish! Come and sit. Have some tea and as many buns as you'd like." Mrs. Hamish bustled to gather a cup and saucer. A kettle of hot water always stood at the ready. They settled near Jessica's hiding place at the end of the rough wooden table across from one another and in profile to her.

Considering his illustrious title, he looked oddly at home in the kitchen with Mrs. Hamish. He took a bite of a bun, closed his eyes, and smiled. Delight shone from his face, and Mrs. Hamish's expression was beatific in her reflected pleasure. He finished the first bun in two bites, reached for another, and ate it just as quickly. After a third, he patted his belly.

"I have a weakness for sweets. I consider myself quite the connoisseur, and these rank in my five favorite buns. Nothing in London even compares."

Mrs. Hamish squirmed on the seat like a child given high marks from a demanding tutor. "I'll pack some in a basket for you. Would you like me to ring for the butler? He can escort you to the study straightaway if Mr. Goforth is expecting you."

Jessica mouthed a silent word of thanks. Cramps along her thighs and calves were making things deuced uncomfortable.

"I'm in no hurry. I don't actually have an appointment." The duke shifted, and a portion of his ease was overtaken by expectation. "Since I'm here, perhaps you can appease my curiosity. I came across a young woman this morning as I was riding. She was too far away for me to call a greeting, but she entered through the kitchens."

"Oh?" Mrs. Hamish rose and gathered his plate and teacup, the rattle of china transmitting her sudden discomfort. "What did the young lady look like?"

"Long chestnut hair. Trim figure. Dressed in a brown frock." His lips moved as if he had more to stay, but he only shrugged.

"What would you want with this young lady, Your Grace?" Mrs. Hamish's voice had lost its bemusement.

"When I spotted her, she was on Wintermarsh land. Quite a long way from here."

"I'll speak with the servants about wandering off the estate grounds. Do not trouble yourself further, whoever it was will be reprimanded."

"No! No need for that." The duke straightened. "Please. I didn't intend to cause trouble. The young lady is welcome to make use of the pond. It is seldom, if ever, frequented by Lord Drummond."

It was Jessica's turn to blush. He *had* seen her in a state of dishabille then. She'd nearly convinced herself she had imagined the prickly feeling of being watched. Dear Lord, she'd been nearly naked. Nearly wasn't as horrible as completely naked. Still, the cupboard was close to bursting into flames at the flare of her embarrassment.

"I thought perhaps it was Miss Tremaine?" Uncertainty stumbled in his question.

She could only stare at Mrs. Hamish with desperation. If she told him the truth, he might relay the information to her stepfather. And then what would happen? Nothing good.

"Certainly not. The girl you saw is a... maid. Miss Tremaine's maid. They resemble one another in height and coloring. That's who it was." The lie didn't exactly trip from Mrs. Hamish's tongue with confidence, but at least she hadn't told him the truth.

In fact, it was a stroke of accidental brilliance on Mrs. Hamish's part. Abby and Jessica did share the same coloring, and from a distance, they might even be mistaken for one another. How close of an inspection had the duke made of her in the lake? Close enough to draw him to the Penhaven kitchens to question the cook.

Had he found her attractive? Intriguing?

Her heart leaped and then promptly splatted into reality. Jessica touched the lace edge of her mobcap. What did it matter? The Duke of Bellingham wouldn't give her a second glance as Miss Tremaine.

"I suspected the woman might be a servant here." A hint of red burnished his high cheekbones. It only added to his appeal.

His features were similar to her memories but blunter and more masculine. Straight nose, strong jaw, blue eyes, thick blond hair. What she didn't remember was his body being so broad and muscular. The way he was sitting with his legs splayed wide accentuated the pull of buckskins over his hard thighs with no hint of the paunch that so many other men accrued with age.

He rose and fed the brim of his hat through his hands. "I don't suppose Miss Tremaine is home and receiving? I would like to renew our acquaintance."

Panic—or was that excitement?—shot through her.

"I don't believe she is receiving. She suffers from megrims, you see."

It had been Jessica's mother who'd suffered from the debilitating headaches, but she applauded Mrs. Hamish's quick thinking.

"That's quite unfortunate."

"Why don't I ring for—"

The duke stepped out of her range of vision. "Don't trouble yourself, Mrs. Hamish. I'll make my way around to the front. No need for anyone to know I stopped in the kitchens."

Mrs. Hamish tripped over her goodbyes and good wishes for the duke as the door opened and closed.

"You can come out now," Mrs. Hamish said after a few beats of silence.

Jessica groaned and levered herself out to sit on the floor and shake her legs. Pins and needles tingled along her calves and thighs.

Mrs. Hamish stood looking down, her hands planted on her hips. "Mark my words. This bodes trouble."

"How so? Thanks to your quick thinking, he believes the woman he saw at the pond is a maid. He won't pursue the issue further." Jessica grabbed the edge of the table and hauled herself up.

Mrs. Hamish barked a laugh. "You didn't see the look in his eyes. He won't give up so readily."

"Even if he pursues the matter, he will find no such maid."

"Unless he attempts to make contact with Miss Tremaine and discovers you are one and the same."

"That is highly unlikely. He'll see this"—Jessica gestured to her falsely stocky form—"and realize I am not the same woman. Even though I am."

"Nevertheless, you must refuse to see him if he calls again." Mrs. Hamish's voice took on the scolding tone of a mother. "And never return to that pond. If I'd known you were venturing so far from the estate, I would have cautioned against it. It's a wonder someone hasn't caught you before now."

Jessica had been going to the pond for years without spotting a single soul. There wouldn't be so many little red squirrels or antlered deer roaming freely if men had left their musty scent. She had always felt safe to shed her disguise and enjoy the wilds.

Her time at the pond cleansed her body and soul and provided her a peace she never found at the Penhaven estate. The thought of never returning drew tears, but she blinked them away. Tears had never changed her fortunes.

The duke would forget about her soon enough. Instead of relief, she only felt regret at what would never be.

CHAPTER 3

The spoon slipped from Jessica's numb fingers, splashing soup onto the starched white tablecloth. "A house party? And we are invited?"

Edward Goforth's smile somehow managed to make him look even more pompous than usual, which was quite the feat. His once handsome features had coarsened due to excess drink and rich foods. "Last week of September. I told you my star was rising. Speaking against the poverty laws has garnered attention, and now look what's happened. Excellent, excellent."

"But doesn't the duke support the poverty laws?" Jessica wouldn't admit to her stepfather that she pored over the *Times* for any mention of Simon. It was a habit she had maintained since their encounter so many years ago. Through the brief mentions in the papers and around Lipton, she had pieced together an indistinct picture of his life.

"The duke. Pah!" Goforth slammed his glass of wine down. "It's true he has made his opinion known, but there may be an opportunity to press my agenda with Lord Drummond and whomever else they have invited. I could turn the tide and gain favor. The connections could prove invaluable."

Jessica's appetite, always scarce when her stepfather was in residence, vanished entirely. She daubed at the soup stain on the tablecloth. "I'll remain here. I would only be a liability."

Goforth's grunt was one of agreement, and Jessica's shoulders slumped slightly, even if she couldn't pinpoint the direction of her emotions. Relief, yes. But it was tinged with something darker and less pure.

Goforth snapped his fingers, and the footman moved forward to clear their soup and serve the fish course. "I would leave you here, but Lady Drummond personally added a note requesting your attendance. Apparently, she is looking forward to bettering your acquaintance."

Bettering their acquaintance? That implied they were acquainted at all. Which they were not, beyond their paths crossing a handful of times over the years in Lipton. The few invitations Lady Drummond had issued early on had been declined with no small amount of regret. Jessica would have dearly loved a friend, especially one so close with the duke, but she couldn't risk the connection. The last invitation had been soon after her mother died.

What did the invitation mean after so long a time? Was Mrs. Hamish correct? Was this Simon's way of manipulating her into his sphere? No, not her. Her maid.

Goforth pointed a knife at her. "You are not to embarrass me. And it should go without saying, but you are to stay away from Bellingham."

The laugh that escaped her was one of disbelief. "The duke is not likely to spare me a second glance." Or at least he wouldn't after seeing her in her unfashionable frocks with her disguise fully in place.

"True enough. He is a man of refined tastes, but he might be inclined to use you to get to me. Nevertheless, there will be other gentlemen of means there, and you must look presentable. Dress appropriately, and for goodness' sake, have your maid wash your hair more often so you can get rid of that horrid mobcap." Goforth didn't bother to hide his disgust. "You act like you'll break out in hives if you are touched by water or soap."

Jessica tried not to smile at his assessment. He had been thoroughly fooled by the deception she had cultivated the past several years. Goforth had treated Jessica as a burden until her mother died. Then she had gone from useless girl to a pawn to be sacrificed for his advancement.

With help from Abby and Mrs. Hamish, she had used the cloak of her grief to gradually transform from a young woman who attracted appreciative glances from local lads to a woman gentlemen crossed the street to avoid. Her disguise was her only protection against Goforth and his machinations until her brother came of age. Five years seemed an impossible amount of time.

The rest of their dinner was an excruciating liturgy of Goforth's accomplishments and plans to cultivate alliances with the peers attending the house party. Jessica nodded and moved food around on her plate. The torture of the dinner finally ended, and Jessica made her escape.

She bypassed her room and stood at the base of the stone staircase that led to a small room at the top of the turret. At one time, it had been her favorite place. Exposed wooden beams overhead gave it a rustic feel, reminding her of their cozy house in America. She'd spent countless hours reading, daydreaming, and hiding from Goforth in the room. It had been her refuge.

Until her mother died.

Five years had passed since she'd climbed the steps and found her mother hanging from the rafters. She shuffled forward, but her feet grew leaden and wouldn't move another step. The shadows reached down the stairs toward her with the same black malevolence of a nightmare she couldn't escape.

Her vision narrowed, and her breathing quickened. She turned away and scuttled toward the opposite end of the corridor. A ladder led to a trapdoor in the ceiling. With clammy panic squeezing her lungs, she fumbled the latch open and cast the hinged door upward. Night air washed over her.

A platform with a rotting wooden railing awaited her. She could imagine some long-dead Penhaven earl using it to scout approaching armies. She held her skirts knee-high and clamored up the ladder to the platform. On her haunches, she took one deep breath after another until the panic receded.

The dew-wet stone was scented with all the years gone by and still stood. There was nothing she could do to change the past. The gentle breeze offered solace, and the starry night sky spread above her and made her problems feel insignificant.

She closed the trapdoor and lay on top of it to stare up at the pinpricks of light. Her father had enjoyed stargazing. His nattering about constellations had put her sleep many nights. If she closed her eyes, she could almost hear his deep voice tinged with an English accent.

The only constellation she recalled with clarity was the Plough. She traced the formation of stars with her finger, taking comfort in the fact her father had found the same stars when he was a child not so very far away from where she lay. And hundreds of years distant, someone would look up and trace the same shape.

Her mind calmed, and she was able to concentrate on her present predicament. The entire point of her charade was to deflect Goforth's plan of using her to his advantage, but her disguise would make her stand out as a curiosity among the fashionable ladies who would be in attendance. She needed to avoid attention as much as possible—good and bad.

And then there was Simon. He was a duke, and as out of reach as the stars above her. The moon inched toward its zenith, and Jessica shivered. A droplet of dew settled on her eyelash like a tear from the expanse. She wiped it away with the back of her fingers.

Her life stretched out before her, hopeless and lonely. Was it selfish to yearn for a sliver of good fortune? She wasn't naive enough to believe happiness could last forever, but what-ifs scrolled through her head. What if she came face-to-face with Simon, not as the pitiable Miss Tremaine, but as the maid with no brother or stepfather or complications? Someone who was bold. Someone she wanted to be.

She rubbed her face and got to her knees to open the trapdoor and descend back into the darkness of the manor, leaving her hopes and dreams for the universe to ponder.

THE NEXT WEEKS PASSED QUICKLY, and the heat of August faded into a cool September. The weather had been fine, and the carriage rattled through dry ruts on the approach to Wintermarsh. The seat of the Earls of Winder was not as sprawling or ancient as Penhaven Manor, but they teemed with life and welcome. Was it her imagination, or did joy seep from the mortar between the gray stones?

Footmen dressed in blue and gold livery unloaded a carriage that had arrived before them. Children ran around a manicured side lawn, playing a game of catch me if you can, their squeals of laughter adding to the merry atmosphere. Lord Drummond, in buckskin breeches, polished black boots, and a dark green frock coat, stood at the front, conversing with a tall man with black hair and an air of insouciance.

Simon—His Grace, she silently berated herself—was not present. Her relief was marked by bitter-tasting disappointment she had no right to. According to the gossip columns, the duke was a catch, and hostesses all over London vied to draw him to their functions. Speculation on when and whom he would wed to secure the ducal line had become more heated every season.

Most likely, he had forgotten all about the maid he'd spotted at a distance weeks earlier. And he probably had no recollection of the young girl he'd saved at the inn so many years ago. She was delusional to expect him to concern himself with her arrival in any way.

Their carriage rocked to a stop. Jessica smoothed a nervous hand down the skirts of her new dress. A tiny little smile tipped her lips before she battened down any spark of personality or humor.

Goforth had ordered her to commission new frocks for the house party. The fact he was willing to outlay the coin was proof enough of the party's importance in his mind. She and Mrs. Hamish had debated whether to pick drab fabrics that would not cause offense or draw attention, or the most heinous colors in order to incite disgust. After much thought, Jessica had picked two hideous fabrics and one plain gray more suitable for a governess or companion.

Out of weakness or hope, she wasn't sure which, she'd also packed the brown dress she wore when roaming the estate out of her disguise. Appropriate in cut and style for a servant, the dress was simple to put on and take off without any assistance.

The dress she'd chosen to arrive in was a shade of yellow that veered toward green and made her appear ready to cast up her accounts at any moment. If the color didn't scare everyone off, the severe cut, high neck, and absence of any decoration might. It looked like something a color-blind vicar had picked out for his daughter.

To complement her dress, she wore the most god-awful bonnet she could find in a clashing shade of blood red. She could see nothing that wasn't directly in her field of vision, but the excessive brim of the bonnet allowed her to avoid any curious gazes. Her outfit would set the tone for the week. If Goforth's plan was to barter her hand away to gain political clout, he could think again. She was prepared to embarrass them both.

As the footman offered a helpful hand out of the carriage, Jessica lifted her gaze to meet Rafe Drummond's startled eyes. The poor man was speechless, his mouth opening then snapping shut. She stifled a nervous, inappropriate giggle.

Finally, he turned his head and bellowed, "Minerva! Come greet *your* guests."

Jessica didn't miss the slight inflection in his voice. Had Lord Drummond not wanted them invited? Did Lady Drummond really want to better their acquaintance? The lady of Wintermarsh sashayed gracefully out the door, faltering slightly when she spotted Jessica. To her credit, her flash of dismay was brief. A smile warmed her classically beautiful features and made her welcome appear genuine.

Goforth's blustery laugh was loud, as if he too was nervous at being received by the Drummonds. "Fine place you have here. Not so big as Penhaven Manor though, is it? I stocked our lake recently. Do you have a stocked lake here? You should ride over, and I'll guide you fishing."

Jessica wanted to duck her head in a different kind of shame. Lady Drummond came to her rescue, neatly cutting herself into the conversation and looping an arm through Jessica's. "My dear Miss Tremaine. I'll have our housekeeper, Mrs. Devlin, show you to your room. I'm afraid the way things worked out you're not on the same floor as your father."

"*Step*father." The correction came out more harshly than intended. In a modulated monotone, she added, "That will be fine, Lady Drummond."

Although she had learned to mimic the aristocratic accent of an English lady, she preferred the familiarity of her American vowels and found even the gentry around Lipton more apt to dismiss and ignore her when she spoke with her native accent.

Lady Drummond stopped in the large entryway. The expanse of marble was warmed by a side table with autumnal flowers and an arrangement of books. Before she could step closer to examine the spines, Goforth and Lord Drummond entered. Lord Drummond cast a long-suffering look in his wife's direction. Lady Drummond motioned toward the study with a quick jerk of her chin.

The unspoken communication continued until Lord Drummond threw his hands up in surrender and offered Goforth a brandy in his study. He closed the door behind them and then popped his head back out like a jack-in-the-box, startling them both. "Send your bloody brother in here, Minerva."

The door shut with more force than was polite, and Lady Drummond shook her head. "That *man*. I apologize for his language. He's proved impossible to tame." The fond amusement made what might have been a complaint from another woman come out sounding rather lovely from Lady Drummond.

Jessica fidgeted with her reticule, not having to fake discomfort or shyness. She'd never attended a house party. In fact, she had never been invited to one. Abby, her maid, who was trailing discreetly behind her, appeared just as overwhelmed.

Servants bustled by and other guests meandered through the entry, tossing them curious looks. Lady Drummond looked around and hummed. "Our housekeeper must be occupied elsewhere, so allow me to show you to your room. However, if you should need anything during your stay with us, Mrs. Devlin will be happy to help you. William will bring your trunk and your maid can unpack."

Jessica followed Lady Drummond up the stairs. The blue silk dress she wore was expertly cut and sewn and complimented her figure and complexion. Her blond hair had been swept up in a loose chignon, and even though Jessica knew the Drummonds had a son, her figure was enviable.

A pang of longing brought a lump to Jessica's throat. She wanted to look beautiful and stylish, but even more, she wanted to laugh and tease and have someone look at her the way Lord

Drummond looked at his wife. When her brother came into his own, she hoped to be able to drop her horrible guise. But that was still years away, and by then, she would be well and truly on the shelf.

Lady Drummond led her into a room decorated in shades of buttery yellow and rich gold. Her yellow-green dress was even more of an abomination against the sunny backdrop of the room. Before she could stop herself, she smiled at Lady Drummond. "It's lovely."

Lady Drummond cocked her head, her gaze turning speculative. Jessica silently cursed herself and compressed her lips back into a thin, frowning line. She must do a better job at maintaining her disguise. One slip in front of Goforth could prove disastrous.

"Yes, it is quite lovely. Normally, my brother stays here."

"Oh. Is he not planning to attend the party for the duration?" Perhaps business in London or at one of his many estates had called him away. She felt strangely bereft. Even if she planned to tuck herself in convenient corners, she hadn't been this close to him since their one pivotal interaction. She didn't count her subterfuge in Mrs. Hamish's kitchen.

"Never fear, I've given him no quarter. He will stay and entertain us for the week," Lady Drummond said casually, but her piercing eyes searched for answers to unasked questions. "However, given we have a full house, he is staying elsewhere on the estate."

"I hope he hasn't been put to any trouble on my account." Simon had given up his room for her. Her stomach swooped before she clipped its wings. She doubted the duke had even known who would be staying in his usual room. "I'll be certain to thank him for his kindness."

"I have the feeling he will extend his gratitude to you first," Minerva said dryly. "You have offered him a means of escape."

Knowing her bonnet was an effective defense, Jessica turned

her head before she was tempted to query Lady Drummond more about Simon. It would be unseemly and reveal too much interest.

The footman clattered into the room and deposited her trunk on the rug in front of the wardrobe. Abby followed and stood quietly to the side of the door.

"I look forward to getting to know you better, Miss Tremaine. I'll leave you to get settled and rest. Join us in the drawing room at six for drinks and to meet the other guests before dinner." With that, Lady Drummond swept out of the room with the footman trailing her.

Abby closed the door behind them, and Jessica's shoulders slumped. Even though she'd been kind, warm even, Lady Drummond was too clever and observant for Jessica's peace of mind. With luck, the house party would keep Lady Drummond too busy to focus on one insignificant guest, but it was clear Jessica would need to tread very carefully.

CHAPTER 4

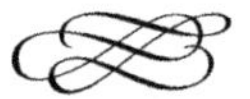

Simon dodged the bustling staff in the kitchen, grabbed a tart from the tray Mrs. Potts had left out to cool, and retreated down the hallway leading to the dining area. His mistake was focusing on the treat in his hand and not what was around the corner. Someone grabbed the sleeve of his jacket and yanked him into the butler's pantry.

"Where in the devil have you been?" Rafe's whisper came from between clenched teeth. "Minerva made me entertain Goforth. It was a good half hour before I could escape the mushroom."

Instead of offering apologies, Simon took a bite of the apple tart and chewed, rather enjoying watching Rafe's ire rise even higher. "That's not very egalitarian of you. Don't you admire his grasping, climbing charisma? I find it rather charming myself." A lie, of course.

"I had not planned on enjoying this blasted house party anyway, but with that bounder here, I'm likely to go queer in the attic. *You* are the one who insisted we invite them, so *you* can be the one to entertain him from this moment forward."

"Did his stepdaughter arrive with him?"

"She did." Rafe's gaze dropped to examine the stone floor underfoot with an unwarranted intensity.

"And her maid? Did you see her?"

"I didn't pay any attention to what servants they brought along. Don't most women bring someone to do their hair and such?" Rafe gave Simon a funny look.

Simon could think of no plausible reason to explain his interest, so instead he asked, "What is Miss Tremaine like?"

"Very... yellow."

Simon blinked a few times. He'd never heard a woman described as a color. "Yellow happens to be my favorite color."

Rafe hummed and gave an exaggerated shudder. "Not this yellow. It was ghastly."

"What was she like aside from the ghastly dress?"

"I have no idea. Her bonnet reminded me of horse blinders, if they were a devilish red with ruffles. If she spoke, I couldn't hear her over Goforth's blustering. By the time I recovered my senses, Minerva had taken her in hand and shown her to her room."

Regret at his impetuous invitation rose. Not only had he subjected Rafe to Goforth, but Miss Tremaine would be subjected to possible humiliation from the other guests. "Perhaps the chit simply lacks feminine influence. Minerva is the very picture of elegance. She could offer advice on colors and patterns and such."

"Feel free to take that up with your sister. I'll not be the go-between." Smiling rather maliciously, Rafe added, "Speaking of, I've made sure Bertie placed you across from Goforth and next to the daughter at dinner tonight."

Distaste at the thought of entertaining Goforth soured the tart in his stomach. He wasn't usually one to make hay over his title, but desperate times and all that. "I'm a duke. I should be sitting at your right."

"'Should be' is the crucial phrase. Anyway, I want to discuss something with Damien, so he's sitting next to me. I see you all the time." Rafe had never been one to follow the dictates of society.

Arguing would prove useless, so Simon merely inclined his head. "As you wish."

Rafe gave him a narrow-eyed, suspicious glance before stalking from the pantry and out the side entrance. The man was beating a hasty retreat, which considering his reputation for bravery, spoke volumes.

Simon wished he'd seen Goforth and Miss Tremaine and their entourage arrive. No matter how many times he told himself to forget the maid, he couldn't erase the indelible image of her in the pond. He'd gone into Lipton several times, loitering at the inn, trying to catch sight of her again, sure he would recognize the woman from any distance, but he hadn't spotted her.

Already dressed for the evening's entertainments, he wandered into the drawing room to find Damien Northcutt sprawled in the corner of a settee, his head lolled back, dozing. Simon kicked at his friend's boots on his way to the sideboard. Damien snorted himself awake and blinked up at Simon.

"Long night?" Simon raised an eyebrow.

"Long week." Damien stretched before resuming his lounge like a big cat.

"Has it to do with a woman or with work?"

Damien's smile was wolfish. "Both, actually."

"Who's your latest conquest?"

"Parsom's widow. She's quite an attractive piece of goods. Although it was less a conquest and more an out-and-out surrender on my part. She pursued me all season. I finally got bored enough to accept her offer." Not even a hint of true affection colored his voice.

"Will Widow Parsom be the one to tame you?" Simon asked

sarcastically, knowing full well it would be a cold day in hell a woman brought Damien to heel.

He barked a laugh. "I was glad of this charming little party to put some distance between us. She was already dropping hints after three nights in my bed. Can you imagine?"

Looking Damien up and down, Simon said seriously, "Actually, no, I can't. I don't understand why ladies pant after you. Even more puzzling is why they keep coming back time and again begging for a mere pat of affection. The poor debutantes are alternately terrified and fascinated by you every season."

Damien waggled his brows. "I work hard to cultivate a bit of fear in the young and innocent. I hardly want to become an object of *their* desire, not that their mamas would allow it. I'm extremely bad ton if ton at all."

"There are plenty who would accept your money even though you're a bastard." Simon chuckled to lessen the sting of the truth. "I meant that in both the figurative and literal sense."

Damien accepted the brandy Simon poured for him with aplomb, not animus. "I'm only here to make you look more shining and golden by comparison. As if you need my help. I'm going to start calling you Saint Simon."

Simon quaffed his drink and huffed. "If you only knew how far off the mark you are."

Damien straightened, and the mask of nonchalance fell away under his curiosity. "Do tell. Does this unsaintly behavior have something to do with inviting Goforth? Are you planning to garrote him in the night?"

"Don't be ridiculous. And what have you heard about my invitation?"

"Drummond cornered me on my arrival for an interrogation. If I had known why you were set on Goforth's attendance, I would have cracked, by the way. Drummond is positively terrifying when he sets his mind to it. Are you planning to sway Goforth to your way of thinking?"

"That seems like an impossibility."

Damien ran a finger over his lower lip and regarded Simon. While Damien projected an air of insouciance, underneath was an intellect and ambition that equaled Simon's. While their approach to societal change was vastly different, their goals aligned. Their friendship had remained unshakable since their first meeting at Eton. Simon a duke and Damien the bastard son of one.

"Surely this has nothing to do with the daughter? I saw her on their arrival. She's not your usual taste." Damien took a sip of his brandy but didn't look away from Simon, who felt himself being stripped and evaluated as if he were sitting across from Damien at a card table. The man was ruthless in the pursuit of money.

Even with Damien, Simon didn't feel comfortable revealing his true reason for the invitation. "I met Miss Tremaine soon after she arrived in England. She was quite the spitfire then. Goforth has kept her cloistered since, and I can't help but feel a bit sorry for her. It was only polite to issue an invitation as the Penhaven estate sits not five miles away."

Thankfully, Damien's too-perceptive gaze shifted to the window where the sun cast brilliant colors as it fell toward the horizon. "Your sister has assembled a veritable buffet of young innocents for you this week. If I weren't so amused at the thought of you being hunted like a fox, I'd feel rather sorry for you."

"It's rather horrific, isn't it? I promised I'd keep an open mind, but if you see me dragged into the garden, please come save me." Simon was only half joking. He could imagine a scheming mama encouraging her offspring to lure him into a compromising situation so he would be obligated to extend an offer. Manipulation and lies were not solid foundations for marriage.

Further conversation was cut short as Rafe and Minerva,

along with a handful of guests, arrived in the drawing room. Drinks were poured, and tongues loosened. Three young ladies —one with black hair, one brown, and one blond—cornered him, tittering about the latest fashions and the opera. Besides their coloring, there was nothing to distinguish one from another.

Even if he had an opinion—which he didn't—he could hardly get a word in edgewise. They moved on to discuss the other young ladies in attendance, wrapping veiled insinuations and insults in backhanded compliments.

Minerva would no doubt chide him about being ungracious and judgmental, and as usual, she would be right. Yet he couldn't help feeling an almost primal urge to escape. Simon kept an eye on the door, debating his chances.

Goforth strutted into the room and greeted Rafe with a grating, boisterous laugh. Simon almost overlooked the drab figure who edged into the room on his heels and inched along the wall.

He was beset by equal amounts of shock and pity. The Jessica Tremaine he recalled was nothing like the young woman whose shoulders slumped and mouth turned down, making her appear older than he knew she was. Her hair was scraped back from her face and covered in a cap that would have looked more at home on a dowager matron of eighty instead of a young unmarried miss of twenty.

Her face was sickly pale against the dark brown of her gown, which was severe and hung on her square frame. It was the sort of dress a woman wore to dig a large hole or dust an abandoned house. He dithered over what to do. Miss Tremaine was here by his invitation, even if she didn't realize it. Guilt assailed him. He had invited her for the most selfish and dishonorable reasons. His prurient interest in her maid must be quashed.

The young ladies who had trapped him turned their arrows upon one another. Simon excused himself from the three furies and sidled toward the corner Miss Tremaine had tucked herself into. She was worrying a loose string along the edge of her dingy lace gloves and didn't notice his approach.

He stopped a few feet away and cleared his throat. Her head popped up, surprise widening her eyes and smoothing away her frown. In a blink, her expression resumed its wary anxiousness, her eyes and mouth downcast, but for a moment, she had struck him as… not pretty perhaps, but not as unappealing as he was given to believe.

"Good evening, Miss Tremaine." Simon sidled a bit closer. Unlike the other young women in attendance, she didn't appear at all enthusiastic at his attentions, which was a welcome change from the usual fawning and made her more interesting rather than less. "I hope I'm not interrupting?"

"It seems you've caught me between being overrun with guests seeking my regard." While her voice bore the hallmarks of an American accent, it was flavored with an indistinct English lilt.

But it was her dry sarcasm that was wholly unexpected. A genuine laugh sneaked out of him before he stifled it with a clearing of his throat. "I hope you're finding everything to your liking at Wintermarsh."

She tilted her head and scanned the room as if evaluating every person and piece of furniture. "Indeed. It is a very welcoming house. Happiness resides here."

Simon was taken aback. His question had been polite small talk. Instead, she had answered with a truth he felt in his bones as well. "I have always thought so too. Perhaps that's why I find myself spending as much time here as my own estates."

"Lady Drummond informed me you relinquished your usual chamber for me. It's a lovely room, thank you."

"Think nothing of it."

Silence followed. Usually, he left it to the young ladies to drive the conversation, but Miss Tremaine seemed content with the quiet between them.

Oddly, he found himself wanting to natter on. "What sorts of things interest you?"

"Interest me?" Another flash of surprise animated her face. "Nothing."

"Nothing at all? Do you paint or embroider?"

"Neither. I find needlework tedious and have no talent with the brush."

"Do you play the pianoforte?"

She flinched as if the question hurt. "I used to, but my stepfather rid the manor of our pianoforte some time ago."

A story scrolled untold behind her answer. One he wanted to hear but was sure she would never tell him. "There's an excellent one here. Minerva has a musical evening planned. You should entertain the group."

"I'm sure the other ladies will be eager to demonstrate their skills."

"Then I would be honored if you would favor me with a tune one afternoon."

"Goodness, no. I only ever played for my mother." Her voice hitched with emotion, and Simon regretted his insistence had caused her any grief.

His brief recollection of her mother was of a wan woman who had been pretty yet beaten down by life's circumstances. Many women he met in Whitechapel and Seven Dials had the same haunted, exhausted look in their eyes. Given the nature of her husband, Simon wasn't surprised.

Simon flicked his attention to Edward Goforth. The man had cornered Mr. Comstock, who was an offshoot of a titled family but much wealthier. Goforth's cheeks were ruddy from the drink. Comstock looked around as if seeking an escape after only a few minutes.

Living with Goforth day in and day out must be hell. It

would crush anyone's spirit. Forcing a merry tone, he leaned in conspiratorially. "I've sat through performances that made the alley cats wail. You would do your mother proud, I'm sure."

She jerked away. Had he been too familiar and caused offense? As he opened his mouth to apologize, she asked, "Have you been eating peppermints?"

He smiled at the unexpectedness of her question. "I have. I actually brought them for my nephew, but I learned the hard way to dole them out one by one or else he'll sick up on my sister's favorite rug. I can commiserate with his gluttony. My weakness for sweets is legendary."

Her slight laugh was husky and attractive. "My father loved his peppermints. I would crawl up on his lap at night while he told me stories before bed. It's my favorite memory of him."

Simon reached into his jacket and offered her a peppermint. "Here. Take one."

Like she was a starved dog being offered kindness for the first time, she hesitated with her hand halfway to his. Slowly, so as not to scare her off, he inched the treat closer. Careful not to touch him, she took the candy and popped it into her mouth. Her eyes closed, and her lips tipped into a smile. She had traveled into her memories.

With her pallid, sickly complexion, she would never qualify as a beauty among the ton's finest. Yet something in her expression spoke to him.

"My parents died when I was young." He surprised himself with the admission.

"How young?"

"I was seven."

"Do you miss them?"

How to answer? When they had been alive, he'd only seen them on their occasional visits to the nursery. They had been beautiful distant strangers. "I miss the lack of memories of them. I have nothing to revisit. Does that sound odd?"

"Not at all." Severity tightened her features, and he felt suddenly exposed and vulnerable.

No matter the pity she inspired, he would do well to remember she was the relation of his political enemy and any weakness could be used against him.

He performed a small bow and excused himself. She merely nodded and retreated farther into her corner, if it was possible. Troubled, he made his way toward his sister and drew her aside.

"Have you made everyone's acquaintance, or do you require an introduction?" Minerva smiled and nodded at one of the guests behind him.

"I interpret that to mean the acquaintance of the available ladies present. I was lucky enough to be cornered for a scintillating discussion of where ladies' waistlines will fall at the new season."

"Some may need a bit of polish, but they will mature. Any one of the ladies here would make a fine matrimonial option."

Simon rolled his eyes. "I see you aren't even attempting to disguise your ambition to see me married off."

Minerva transferred her full attention to him and lay her hand on his arm. "I want you to be happy. That's all."

The sincerity in her eyes was enough to make his resentment dissipate even if he didn't approve of her methods. "I will marry when I'm ready and not before."

"And that will be…?"

"When I find what you and Rafe have." A moment of doubt assailed him. What if he never found anything resembling love? What if he was forced to accept a marriage of convenience?

Minerva squeezed his arm, her expression somewhere between hope and pity.

Simon cleared his throat and changed the subject. "I welcomed Miss Tremaine."

Minerva's gaze darted over his shoulder toward Jessica's

corner. "She seems a sweet but painfully awkward young lady with horrendous fashion sense."

While awkward was certainly apt, he wasn't so sure sweet was the correct descriptor. Their conversation had proved to be unusually profound, and the young lady had an acerbic bite he rather enjoyed. "I worry she'll be ignored and bullied by the other ladies."

"I'll not allow it." Minerva on the warpath could wither the prime minister. The only man she was unable to intimidate was her husband. "Oh dear. You'd better rescue Rafe before he plants a fist between Goforth's eyes."

Simon quickly stepped toward Rafe and Goforth. Rafe shot him a dirty look that promised retribution the next time they sparred and stalked off without a by-your-leave.

Goforth stared at his retreat. "I say, I was in the middle of advising Drummond about a more efficient way to manage Wintermarsh. There's no reason for him to support the rabble on small plots of land. They should be pushed out to make more room for stock."

"He seems to be managing things adequately." While Rafe was forward thinking in terms of investments and estate management, he was also traditional in his beliefs of caring for those under his domain. Simon forced a lightness he did not feel into his voice. "Let's not speak of politics or business this evening."

Goforth looked put out at the suggestion, making clear his plan to use the house party to make alliances. Simon had invited the fox into the henhouse.

"What do you wish to speak of? Ton gossip?" Goforth sniffed dismissively.

It had been clear when their paths crossed in the halls of Westminster that Goforth remembered their first meeting. Simon had used his title and youthful bravado to protect Jessica and humiliate Goforth. The man had not forgotten nor forgiven the slight. His poorly veiled disdain bordered on hatred, and Simon could honestly say the feeling was mutual.

"Speaking of the ton… Will Miss Tremaine be making her debut this season?" Simon asked.

"Why do you want to know?" Goforth rocked his feet farther apart and his bull-like shoulders seemed to stretch his jacket seams.

"Merely curious."

Goforth narrowed his eyes. "I've been considering it. She'll be too long in the tooth if I wait much longer, and it's time for her to make an advantageous match."

Of course, Goforth meant politically advantageous to him. Simon couldn't imagine he cared about his stepdaughter's feelings or well-being.

"That would not include you, of course," Goforth added with a maliciousness that wasn't often displayed so nakedly in Simon's social circles. A facade of manners and breeding often kept such impulses at bay.

While Simon hadn't meant his curiosity to reflect a romantic interest in Miss Tremaine, he couldn't deny himself the opportunity to needle Goforth. "Surely that is for her to decide."

Simon and Goforth stared one another down and might have continued the contest all evening if the dinner bell hadn't rung.

Goforth harrumphed and stalked off. Unfortunately, Simon knew something Goforth did not. They would be seated across from one another at dinner and could continue glaring at one another through the many courses. It was enough to make his stomach turn. Simon contemplated how angry Minerva would be if he and Goforth engaged in fisticuffs before the second course had arrived.

The mental picture of Minerva withering Goforth with her *look* lightened Simon's mood enough to make him smile as he joined the line of guests for dinner. If he paid extra attention to

Miss Tremaine, he could raise her profile with the other ladies and keep Minerva's dinner violence free.

The party arranged itself in the proper hierarchy to proceed into the dining room. He stepped out of the front of the line and swooped in to offer Miss Tremaine his arm. "May I escort you in to dinner?"

CHAPTER 5

Jessica stared at Simon's arm as if he were offering a powder keg for her to light. Her acceptance would be explosive. Not only did her stepfather detest the duke, but she had intercepted more than one green-eyed glare from other young ladies while she and Simon had conversed. And now, inexplicably, for a second time, he had sought her out. His attention threatened to upend her goal of being mistaken with the wall coverings.

Examining herself in the looking glass earlier had confirmed she looked utterly dreadful. The white face powder, the flesh-colored greasepaint she'd used to blot out all color on her cheeks and lips, and the kohl she'd dotted under her eyes combined to make her look sickly. And that wasn't even taking into account her cap, her dress, the way she tucked her chin back to make it look weak, and the perpetual frown she did her best to maintain.

Although she couldn't deny a tiny part of her squirmed with pleasure whenever he was near, he must have ulterior motives. Was he in search of her "maid," or was he using her as a political pawn to get to her stepfather? She must remain on guard against either possibility.

"Th-thank you." She laid her hand lightly on his forearm. Her dingy lace glove was an abomination next to the snowy-white cuff shooting from the sleeve of his dark blue jacket. His clothes had been expertly tailored to accommodate the width of his shoulders and lean torso. She clamped an arm around her padded waist, knowing the contrast they must present.

The awkwardness only grew when he showed her to her seat and she discovered they had been seated next to one another. Her stepfather was directly across the table, his stare piercing. She dropped her gaze to her lap.

The conversation flowed around her as if she were a rock in the middle of a babbling brook. Socializing with the array of urbane, witty people gathered for the house party was like being thrown in the deep side of the lake in a heavy skirt while holding an anchor and expected to swim.

In addition to the unmarried misses accompanied by their families, there was also a gentleman espousing steam locomotion as the next great advancement for civilization and a sea captain regaling the table with stories of his travels around the world. Everyone seemed leaps and bounds beyond her in experience and worldliness.

Goforth hadn't deigned to spend the coin to present her in London, and Jessica had eschewed all social functions in Lipton. Only now did she realize how isolated she was. Whose fault was it? While she wanted to lay the blame at Goforth's feet, she had been happy enough to hide away and nurse her grievances.

A more practical matter garnered her thoughts. The number of forks, knives, and spoons in varying sizes lying with military precision around her plate was dizzying. Would they all be required during one paltry meal? Footmen approached with tureens of soup, ready to ladle. She thanked the man after he finished filling her bowl, drawing several raised brows from around the table.

Sinking a bit lower in her seat, she waited until the woman seated across the table picked up a spoon and then mimicked her. As long as she kept her mouth shut and paid attention, she should make it out of dinner without being thoroughly humiliated.

Goforth's loud, indelicate diatribe against the laziness of the poor drowned out the conversation around the table. Count on her dear stepfather to provide her humiliation.

Simon stared at Goforth with naked disdain. The animosity between the two men roiled below the surface but might erupt at any moment, shattering the social construct that usually kept such anger contained.

She cleared her throat and posed the same questions he'd presented to her earlier. "What are your interests, Your Grace?"

He shrugged. "Riding, fencing, shooting. Typical pursuits of a London dandy."

She guffawed just as she was sipping from her spoon, causing her to sputter and draw curious gazes. Simon offered her a water goblet. Once she had herself under control, she murmured an apology, hoping her powder was thick enough to counteract the heat in her cheeks.

"I must know what I said that was so humorous though." He cast a half smile in her direction. His primal appeal turned her knees to water. "Was it the fencing or the shooting?"

Was he flirting with her? That made no sense. This must be how society worked. A volley of charisma and charm. Unfortunately, witty retorts were not in her repertoire. "It was the dandy part. Based on the books I've read, you aren't one."

"Ah, so you do have interests. What sort of books do you read?" He nodded at the footman who replaced the soup course with fish.

"The Penhaven library is extensive, and I've used my pin

money to send for the latest novels from London." She poked at the flaky fish, unable to take more than a few bites. "I find a good story keeps me company."

"Are you lonely in the country?" Simon asked. "Why not ask your stepfather to present you?"

She was terribly, horribly lonely, but a London debut would only make things worse for her. "I enjoy the country. Do you enjoy reading for pleasure?"

"I'm afraid all I get to read these days are bills for Parliament."

The rest of dinner was spent discussing the state of Parliament and the plight of the poor. Simon's intentions were to be commended, but as long as men like her stepfather were allowed even a modicum of power, the oppressed would remain that way. Goforth needed to grind as many people as possible under his bootheel to make himself bigger.

Dinner ended with the serving of an apple torte. Lady Drummond was the first to rise. The rustling of the rest of the party following suit was accompanied by an increased murmur of conversation. Simon favored Jessica with a smile and inclination of his head before moving around the table to join the gentlemen at the sideboard. She smoothed her skirts and trailed the other ladies out of the dining room.

Jessica slowed. If she was to escape, she had to make a move. Her move consisted of one step toward the stairs before Lady Drummond looped an arm through hers and smiled warmly even as her blue eyes were coolly assessing.

"You aren't considering retiring so early, I hope? The gentlemen plan to go shooting at dawn, but the ladies aren't expected to rise at such an ungodly hour."

"It's been a most stimulating day, and I feel a megrim coming on." While not true at the moment, it would be if she were forced to spend an hour exposed in the drawing room.

"Of course we want you feeling bright on the morrow. You

can choose to accompany some of the ladies into Lipton or remain here for gossip, cards, and a walk through the gardens. Sleep well." Lady Drummond favored her with one of her assessing smiles before entering the drawing room.

Nerves planted roots in her belly. Jessica kept her pace sedate until she was sure she was out of sight, and then she scurried to her room. Abby, who had been napping in the armchair with her feet up, started awake. "Were everybody fooled, my lady?"

"I think so." Jessica refused to dwell on Simon and his unexpected attentions. One glance in the looking glass reaffirmed her opinion that he had ulterior motives for inviting her and Goforth. A woman like her didn't merit the sort of attention he had heaped upon her this evening.

She pulled the mobcap off, and Abby got to work unpinning her hair and washing out the color she used to make her hair look darker and dank at her hairline.

Once her hair was clean, Jessica washed her face in the basin of tepid water, scrubbing off the powder and grease. She patted her face dry and stared at her reflection, feeling a shot of relief at seeing herself. One day she feared her disguise would no longer be a deceit but reality.

Abby braided her hair and helped her out of the gray monstrosity of a gown. "Are you ready for your night rail, miss?"

"Yes." Once she was dressed, Jessica, said, "I won't need you until morning. Thank you, Abby."

Abby left and closed the door softly behind her. Jessica took a deep breath and stretched her jaw. It was sore from trying to make her chin appear weak. The evening had proved more challenging than she'd anticipated. She could only hope any curiosity had been appeased and Simon would transfer his attention to one of the lovely, accomplished debutantes vying for a smidgeon of his regard.

She pushed the window open. The night air was cool and refreshing. Light spilled out from the floors below and cast a glow among the tangle of shrubbery and flowers. Laughter overlay the patter of someone playing pianoforte. It sounded… fun.

A pang reverberated in her chest. She couldn't put her finger on what she felt. Annoyance, yes. Resentment, of course. But also something more insidious. *Longing.*

She had long ago accepted her situation, but that didn't mean her anger and grief had vanished. She'd merely learned to tame and channel her emotions.

Simon had asked her what her interests were, no doubt expecting them to mirror other young ladies. What if she'd answered truthfully? She spent her days keeping herself from being beaten or bartered or worse. Her overarching interest was to ensure her brother was safe and protected. And last but not least, she spent hours imagining a painful revenge against Goforth.

What would Simon's reaction have been? Shock? Disgust? Or would he have been outraged on her behalf like he'd been years ago at the inn? Having someone care enough about her to protect her was a dream she dared not contemplate.

Jessica was used to being alone. She wasn't used to feeling lonely.

She closed the window and the draperies to block out the noise and lay on her bed. She turned her head and smelled the pillow, her heart kicking a quicker rhythm against her ribs. Could she detect the faint scent of peppermint? She groaned and pulled the pillow over her face. Sleep would not conquer her restlessness.

Surrendering, Jessica rose, slipped off her night rail, and retrieved a chemise and the simple dress she wore to blend in with maids, shopgirls, and farmers' daughters in Lipton. Unlike a lady's gown, it was simple to put on and take off herself and didn't require stays. After wrapping one of her mother's shawls around her shoulders, she checked the hall. Finding it empty, she slipped out of her room toward the servants' stairway.

Abby had described the lay of the house after they'd arrived. The parts no lord or lady would be interested in. At a house party of this size, Jessica counted on the fact no one would question a maid they didn't recognize.

And she was right. She nodded at a harried-looking footman in the servants' hallway, but he only nodded back and went about his duties. She was outside in a matter of moments and slipping around the back to the gardens below her window.

She had only sought fresh air and a view of the stars, but she lingered at the edge of light and darkness, half hidden by a tall evergreen and with an unobstructed view of the merrymaking in the drawing room.

When her gaze landed on Simon, she admitted her lie. This was exactly what she had planned to do when she left her room. Ladies surrounded him like a pack of hunting dogs cornering their prey. All of them were young and pretty. It was obvious Lady Drummond had planned the house party with the intention of finding her brother a wife. Who would it be?

A few minutes of self-torture followed as Jessica pictured each woman on Simon's arm. What was she doing? It was foolish to wish for something that would never be. She forced herself away from the scene and wandered until she found a stone bench under a trellis covered in vines. She gathered her shawl closer around her shoulders. Burying her nose in the folds, she took a deep breath, but nothing of her mother remained.

A duet of male voices had her perching on the edge of the seat, debating whether to hide or flee. She froze when she recognized Simon's voice.

"Thank you for your timely intervention." Amusement and exasperation in equal measures colored his voice.

"You know how dangerous darkened gardens are for the innocent." The tease in his male companion's deep voice hinted at a long friendship.

"This was only the first night. How desperate are the young misses and their mamas going to be by the end of the week?"

"Desperate enough that you will need a chaperone more than they will."

"Are you available to squire me around and protect me from all the lovely ladies?" Simon's laugh was a deep-chested rumble that made Jessica's stomach take flight.

"Lovely? They are calculating and greedy. They want your title and your money. The fact you aren't seventy and have your hair and teeth adds to your appeal. Mark my words. You will be caught in the parson's mousetrap before the week is out."

"That is a revolting thought. No man would want to marry under such circumstances. There would be no trust." Simon's tone was one of horror.

"Marriage isn't about trust or respect and certainly not love. It's about procreation for your dukedom. Your wife merely needs to possess the correct lineage for breeding."

"Good Lord, that's cynical, Damien." Silence fell between the two men.

Mr. Damien Northcutt. She'd overheard two ladies tittering over him in the drawing room before dinner. He was a gambler and investor and considered very bad ton, yet the ladies had been breathless with fascination and not disgust. Jessica found his dark looks handsome, yet cold and hard like obsidian and the twist of his mouth cynical and guarded. It was odd to think of him and the honorable duke as close friends, but it was obvious that's what they were.

The scent of cheroots wafted to her. "My sister married for love, you know," Simon said idly.

"Is that why you haven't picked a chit and wed and bedded her yet? Are you waiting for *love*?" The man imbued the word with dripping derision. "Your sister and Lord Drummond are a rarity among the ton, and you know it."

"Yes, I know." Simon's voice was heavy.

Jessica wanted to reassure him, but she couldn't. Partly because revealing herself would be idiotic, but mostly because she agreed with Damien. After all, love had killed her mother.

Her mother hadn't needed to remarry. She had been left a widow of comfortable means, but she had succumbed to Edward Goforth's charms and wed him as soon as her mourning had been cast off. Loving a man had been her weakness and downfall.

Goforth had been handsome in a brawny, overblown sort of way. He'd had a healthy, ruddy complexion and strong features. He'd also been arrogant and never let her mother state an opinion or even ask a question. The family had quickly learned what the consequences were for defying Edward Goforth—a harsh pinch, a hard push, a swift backhand.

Blake possessed their mother's sensitive nature, with feelings that were easily trampled. Although it had broken Jessica's heart, the only way to keep Blake safe had been to see him sent away. She'd planted seeds and tended them carefully, finally making Goforth think it was his idea that Blake should attend the finest of schools, Eton. Although she missed her brother desperately, she was relieved he'd escaped Goforth's brutality.

Her mother had not been so lucky. While Goforth hadn't committed murder, Jessica blamed him for her mother's death just the same.

"So Miss Tremaine..."

Her name coming from Damien made her heart stumble. For a moment, she thought she'd been discovered, but Simon answered before true panic set in. "What about her?"

"She commanded much of your attention this evening." Although it was a statement, it was clear Damien expected a response.

"Yes." The pause was charged. "To my shame, she is here by my invitation."

"Is she a pawn in a nefarious plan you've hatched against Goforth?" Damien's voice was idle, but Jessica sensed an underlying attentiveness to his manner.

"Good God, no. Nothing like that." Another meaningful pause. "I'm not using her. At least, I didn't intend to use her, but I suppose I am in a way."

"You are speaking in riddles. What is your intention with the lady?"

"Put plainly, I have no intentions with regard to the lady. Her maid, on the other hand..."

Damien's laugh was incredulous. "You are pursuing a servant?"

Simon shushed him. "No. I absolutely am not. That would be dastardly."

"If you were to take her against her will and abandon her, yes."

"I would never do such a thing." Simon's very real outrage soothed her slightly.

"I know," Damien said with a surety that offered further comfort to her. "Will you seek this fair maid out?"

"I shouldn't."

"Probably not. But as you didn't offer a definite no, my guess is you will find her before the week is out." When Simon didn't offer any denial, Damien asked, "How did you meet?"

"We haven't. Not really. I saw her from a distance in the pond at the edge of the property while riding this summer."

"Ah, so she is a siren then. Let's hope she's not bent on your destruction."

"It's madness, I know."

"A madness instigated by your cock. It happens to the best of us, Your Grace." Amusement bubbled from the words.

"Don't you start calling me that too." The testiness in Simon's voice at the use of his title intrigued Jessica.

A heel ground on the graveled path. "If we don't return, your sister is bound to let the hounds loose to drag you back."

"Thank the gods we're not staying in the house."

"Indeed. I would have to clear your bed of young ladies who accidently found themselves in the wrong room every night." Damien's mocking laughter faded into nothing as they made their way back to the house.

Chaos brewed inside her. Would Simon, the Duke of Bellingham, seek out a simple maid? Would he attempt to seduce her? The thought sent a shiver through her. Not fear, but something akin to anticipation, which was madness.

Jessica considered her options. The maid in his imagination didn't exist. If Simon looked hard enough, he would find Abby. While her maid favored Jessica in height and hair color, Abby would be scared witless to talk to a duke. He would soon forget about the "maid" he'd spied upon and marry one of the suitable young ladies in his path. Or...

No. There was no "or" that didn't lead to her ruination.

She rose and meandered to the edge of the gardens to stare out over the manicured lawn and the woods beyond. The nearly full moon peeked over the line of trees, sending fingers of silvery light toward her. On her left, she spied the bank of a large pond through tall grass, and in the distance stood rows of apple trees, the branches heavy with fruit yet to be harvested.

The air was redolent with autumnal scents. Fruits, leaves, and the faint hint of smoke. She was comforted, and for a moment she allowed herself to remember her life before her father died. She'd had a home full of love once, but that future felt as out of reach and impossible as a duke.

CHAPTER 6

Simon poured himself a second brandy. He could blame no one but himself for Goforth's irritating presence, but by God, the ladies Minerva had invited were positively rabid. They were due a long chat about boundaries. It was time to turn the tables and lecture her for once. Minerva needed to tame them, or he would mount a protest and remain cloistered at the cottage in the woods with Damien, a pack of cards, and several bottles of brandy.

Rafe dropped into the chair behind the desk of his study. "Thank goodness for the early outing tomorrow. I wasn't sure how much more I could stomach. And this was only the first evening. Did you know your sister wanted to extend the party to a fortnight?"

"I suppose you put your foot down and refused her." Simon propped his shoulder against the window sill and made a teasing growly noise.

"Putting my foot down with Minerva usually results in an injury of some sort to my ego." Rafe rolled his eyes. "If you must know, I charmed her into a change of plans."

Charming was not the first word to spring to mind when

describing Rafe Drummond. Intimidating. Courageous. Savage. As an agent of the Crown during the Napoleonic War, Rafe had acquired more than his share of scars, both physical and emotional. It made him a complicated, yet fascinating man. The best Simon had ever known, and a true match for Minerva.

"When are Gray and Lily expected?" Simon asked idly. Recently knighted, Sir Gray Masterson and Lady Lily, Rafe's sister, were stuck in London because of Gray's work for the Crown.

"Not soon enough," Rafe grumbled. "Tomorrow or the next day, I think. The Wyndams will join us tomorrow unless Marcus has a horse ready to foal."

Lord and Lady Wyndam lived in a centuries-old castle a few hours ride from Wintermarsh. Simon had purchased several horses from Wyndam's stables. The man had grown his reputation for breeding and training the finest horseflesh in England.

Simon took a sip and stared out at the rising full moon. It cast an ephemeral light across the gardens as if a portal between the human and fae worlds had opened for a blink of time. Movement at the edge of his vision drew his gaze back to earth. A woman limned in moonlight sent his heart into a lope. Was fate giving him a nudge? Simon drained his glass and strode toward the door.

"Where are you headed with the devil on your heels?" Rafe asked.

"I forgot I have an assignation to keep." At Rafe's speculative, sardonic brow lift, Simon hastened to add, "With Damien. I promised him a drink and hand of cards."

Rafe half rose. "That sounds like the perfect antidote to a trying evening. I'll join you."

"No!"

Rafe's eyes widened.

Simon modulated his tone and smiled as he backed toward

the door. "Damien and I will be heading to the cottage, and I'm sure Minerva would prefer you join her. In bed."

Simon shuddered at the implication he was forced to make, but it had the intended effect. A definite gleam entered Rafe's eyes. Simon exited before Rafe could question him further. Even as he bolted out of the double doors leading to the gardens, he berated himself. Hadn't he decided not to pursue the maid? It probably wasn't even her. In fact, it was madness to hope it was her. Nevertheless, a mad hope made his chest tighten.

He trotted to where he'd seen movement but found no one. His imagination had played a cruel trick. The soft hum of an unfamiliar tune carried on the slight breeze. He cocked his ear and followed like a rat to the Pied Piper. Luck was with him. Whether the luck would prove to be of the good or bad variety had yet to be determined.

A woman stood at the entrance to a bower. Her face was tilted toward the light as if she were a moonflower, her beauty blooming at night. Although the shadows were deep, a frisson of awareness shot through his body.

It was her. He had never been more sure of anything.

The woman had haunted his dreams far too many nights for him not to recognize her. He shuffled forward, expecting her to vanish like a mirage any second. The scuff of his shoes on the graveled path drew her head around, and she retreated into the shadows of the vines reaching overhead to form an arch.

He held his hands up in mock surrender. "I'm sorry for startling you, miss. I mean you no harm."

"It seems to me that's exactly what a man bent on taking advantage of a woman would declare." Her accent would not have been out of place at a ton ball.

Simon opened his mouth to respond with reassurances and then closed it. She didn't sound frightened. Quite the opposite, in fact. If he had to put a name to her tone, he would call it teasing.

"I'm harmless, I swear." He put his hand over his heart in a pledge he wasn't sure was even true. At least where she was concerned.

"A man let loose in a darkened garden is not a man to be trusted, sir."

He squinted to see her better but didn't dare move closer. The last thing he wanted was to scare her off. Why did he feel like a callow youth going courting for the first time? He assumed this was how one felt when calling upon a lady one admired. He'd never had to deal with an infestation of butterflies on this scale.

"My name is Simon." He was loath to mention his title, not wanting deference to drown the unexpected ease between them.

"I know who you are." She didn't sound the least bit intimidated or deferent. "You spied on me."

Heat rushed through him. Not the desire he'd battled while watching her at the pond, but acute embarrassment. He barely kept himself from squirming. His knee-jerk reaction was to lie and deny any knowledge of what she was referring to, but he was a man grown and had learned the hard way to own his missteps.

"I assure you it wasn't intentional. I heard a noise and suspected a poacher, but when I drew closer, I could see..." The image of her rising from the water in a wet, diaphanous chemise outlining her body flashed in his mind.

He was considered a skilled orator and enjoyed debating all comers on a variety of issues on the Parliament floor, but in this moment, his dexterity with words abandoned him without a backward glance. "Your clothes. I mean, your *lack* of clothes. The point being I realized you weren't a poacher."

"No, I was merely enjoying the supposed solitude."

He fought the urge to squirm at her accusatory tone. "Not to put a fine point to it, but you were on Wintermarsh land."

"Does that give you the right to claim *jus primae noctis*?"

The use of the old Latin phrase by a lady's maid surprised him. Her recognition of his power over her was sobering. "Of course not. I merely want to warn you to be careful."

"I've swum in that pond for years without ever seeing anyone. Until you."

"Technically, you didn't see me either. My clumsiness gave me away."

"You followed me."

"Yes. I was curious."

"And here you are once more." She raised her chin in an unspoken question.

"My curiosity has yet to be appeased." He took a chance and joined her under the arch of vines, dipping his head to clear the low-hanging yellow trumpet flowers beginning to wilt with the arrival of cooler weather.

He cursed the darkness, wanting to study every angle and curve of her. Her cheekbones cast darker shadows, and a stubborn chin highlighted the softness of her full lips. Her almond-shaped eyes bridged a straight nose.

It was too dark to judge the color of her eyes or her complexion. Her dark hair was long and loosely braided, the thick rope hanging over her shoulder and tied with a ragged red ribbon probably cast off from her mistress. The loose dress hid the decadent curves etched in his memory.

She favored her mistress in a vague way he couldn't put his finger on. Was it her height or coloring or something less tangible? Unfortunately for Miss Tremaine, her maid was the prettier of the two even in her drab servant's attire.

"You are bound to be disappointed. I'm not interesting." Her voice held a warning he ignored.

"Let me be the judge of that. Would you like to take a stroll?" He gestured toward the moonlit lawn.

"No. I shouldn't even be in the gardens."

"Will Miss Tremaine chastise you? Is she kind or cruel?"

The woman under the bower turned away to strip the leaves from the closest vine. "I suppose she can be both protective and vengeful."

Simon tried to picture the sallow-faced, meek Miss Tremaine as a Valkyrie meting out justice, but he couldn't. "Is she kind to you though?"

"She is."

"How long have you been her maid?"

"Quite a long time now."

Simon did some quick sums. The woman before him couldn't be more than twenty, but girls as young as twelve entered service as scullery maids. Lady's maids in particular often formed a close attachment to their employers. "Are you close with your mistress?"

"You could say we're almost inseparable." The woman's wry smile warmed the darkness like the embers of a fire.

"May I ask your name?"

The smile faded, and she tilted her head, silent for too many of his thumping heartbeats. "Abby Blackwell."

"Miss Blackwell. It is a pleasure to make your acquaintance." He performed a small bow.

"And yours as well, Your Grace."

"No. Call me Simon." It was much too familiar, but his need to hear his given name tripping off her tongue was unexplainable.

"Simon." Her husky whisper sent a shiver through him. Of pleasure, yes, but also of premonition. Or was it foreboding?

"What brought you to Penhaven to be a lady's maid?"

"My mother died." Pain hid poorly behind her brief explanation.

"What of your father?"

"A fever took Papa long ago," she said softly.

"Did sickness claim your mother?"

"She died of a broken heart." A rawness in her voice spoke to him beyond her words. If he wasn't already tiptoeing along the line of gentlemanly behavior, he would be tempted to offer a very ungentlemanly comfort.

"Do you have any siblings?"

"A younger brother." Miss Blackwell tugged her shawl tighter around her. "He is away and safe."

"Safe from what?"

She worried her bottom lip. "Why do you want to know?"

She didn't trust him, and why should she, considering the manner of their meeting? "I merely wish to know you better."

"But why?"

It was his turn to gauge his trust in her. After the foibles of his youth, he had been discreet and careful with his associations. He had many acquaintances and political allies, but few true friends. This woman was a stranger, and yet…

"I haven't been able to stop thinking about you. The invitation issued to Mr. Goforth and Miss Tremaine was no accident."

Her intake of breath was audible. "They were invited because of me?"

"Does my admission make me sound daft?" He wasn't sure what to expect. Laughter? A slap in the face? Neither came. She was silent and watching in a way that had him tripping over his words. "I realize it is untoward of me to pursue you based on nothing more than an indiscreet moment, but something instinctual draws me to you."

"Is that what gentlemen call their baser needs? Their *instincts*?"

He reddened and was thankful for the dark he'd cursed not five minutes earlier. "I'll admit to a physical attraction. I could attempt to have you through seduction or coercion, but I don't want to hurt you, Miss Blackwell."

The silence lengthened, but this time he waited it out.

"It's my guardian."

"Pardon?"

"My guardian is not a good man." Her voice was a whisper, as if speaking his name might summon him like a demon.

"Is he why you are in service?" It would explain why her accent and demeanor were as ladylike as any of the debutantes.

There was a slight hesitation before she nodded.

Simon's hands drew into fists, and he linked them behind his back to hide his aggression from her. Would she think him odd if he asked for her guardian's direction? "I'm glad you and your brother are safe from his clutches."

"I'm a survivor. Or so Mrs. Hamish tells me."

A faint disturbance fluttered in the recesses of his mind, but it remained elusive. "I met Mrs. Hamish when I delivered the invitation to Goforth."

"She warned me about you." Warmth curled through her voice like the first flame of a fire. "Told me I should avoid you at all costs because I might not survive you."

"I'm not as dangerous as all that. I've found the best sort of people are survivors."

"What sort of hardships have you survived? Too many estates? Too many servants to manage? How taxing for you." Sarcasm dripped from her questions. Far from being offended, he was pleased at her jab. Not many were brave enough to take him to task.

And he supposed he deserved a measure of castigation from where she sat on the social hierarchy, especially if she'd taken a tumble. "It's true I've never had to worry about money, but my life has not always been easy. My parents died when I was young. It was a harsh, lonely existence for many years."

"I'm sorry. I shouldn't have assumed." She shuffled closer

and raised her hand as if to offer comfort. Before she could retreat, he captured her hand in his.

Skin against skin, their hands rasped and grappled until their fingers were linked.

"No need to apologize. I was lucky to have my sister, Minerva. She is older and as protective as you are with your brother."

"You have your own estates, yet you choose to spend a great deal of time at Wintermarsh. Why?"

For a moment, he wondered at how she knew where he spent his time, but he supposed gossip made the rounds in Lipton much the same way it did in London, which was to say like wildfire.

"Wintermarsh saw me through trying times. I find peace here. It's true I own other estates, but I call none of them home." He ran a hand through his hair. "That sounds sickeningly dramatic."

"No, it makes perfect sense. No matter how long I reside there, Penhaven will never be my *home*. A house is where you sleep and work, but a home is where your heart resides, no matter where you are."

Simon swallowed past the lump in his throat. She'd managed to express exactly how he felt about Wintermarsh. "Exactly so, Miss Blackwell," he managed to whisper.

His physical attraction to Miss Blackwell had been simple and crude. Faced with the woman before him, he was humbled and ashamed. She was a woman of feeling and depth.

"Did you lose your parents together?" Her change of subject was welcome.

"Yes. In a highway robbery. Mother refused to part with her jewelry, and both she and Father were shot. The irony was the jewels were paste. I don't know if she didn't want anyone to find out they were paste or was arrogant enough to believe herself above such lawlessness."

"That's shocking. I'm so sorry."

Simon shrugged. "It was long ago. My memories are vague."

She hadn't pulled her hand away from his, and he grew bold, caressing the back with his thumb. Between her accent and her use of Latin, it was clear she was gently born, and her current situation was driven by unfortunate circumstances.

"We're quite similar, you and I," he said.

Her throaty laugh was the sun peeping from behind dark clouds with the promise of fairer weather. "Yes, so similar. Except you're a wealthy duke with the world at your feet, and I'm a poor maid toiling away at a country house."

He smiled with an ease he hadn't felt in too long. "Our positions are different, but in our hearts, where it counts, we are similar."

She tugged her hand free and took a step away from him. A weak shaft of moonlight illuminated the right side of her face. He caught his breath. The shadows and light emphasized the sharp cut of her cheekbone and line of her jaw. Only her lips were soft, like the petals of a flower.

"This has been diverting, but I must be getting back." She took a step away from him.

He barely stopped himself from reaching for her. "I must see you again. Do you have any free time during the day?"

Miss Blackwell wore a troubled frown, but she didn't immediately deny him.

Simon was ready to beg if necessary. Never had he felt this sort of impatience to spend time with a woman before. "Please, Miss Blackwell."

"Not during the day, no." She took a half dozen steps and then turned back to him. "But my mistress retires early, and my nights are free."

His heart, which had briefly stopped, thumped hard. He proffered a small bow. "I am at your disposal."

"I fear Mrs. Hamish is in the right. She said the gleam in

your eye boded nothing good for me." Miss Blackwell's statement landed somewhere between accusing and defiant.

Simon supposed he could promise not to touch her, but he wasn't sure it was a promise he could keep. "Meet me at the garden's edge tomorrow evening, and we'll walk and talk."

"Only walk and talk?" she asked with narrowed eyes.

"My word as a gentleman, I will not seduce you." He let a few beats of silence fall before a tease crowded out his seriousness. "However, I will not ask the same promise of you, Miss Blackwell. If you wish to seduce me, I shall not cry foul."

As he hoped, a smile, quick and true, flashed over her face. "Only in your dreams, Your Grace."

"With a certainty, Miss Blackwell." He caught her hand and pressed a kiss to the back. Her fingers spasmed and gripped his fingers tighter, but he dared not press his luck further. He released her hand and inclined his head. "Until tomorrow evening."

And with that, she took flight, disappearing around a manicured hedge.

He stood there and felt like pinching himself. She was real. It hadn't been a dream, had it? No. She had surpassed the limits of his imagination. What would their next night together bring? Anticipation burned through him. First though, he had to navigate another day with ladies he already knew he would never marry.

CHAPTER 7

The beauty of the gardens barely registered as Jessica made her escape. Her heart still pounded from the kiss he'd laid on her hand, and she examined it curiously, expecting to find it transformed somehow. But no, it was still just her hand.

She was playing a dangerous game. Not only did she not have prior experience, but she didn't understand the rules. Simon, on the other hand, seemed vastly experienced and accustomed to winning. Could she trust his word?

Likely not. Except deep in his beguiling blue eyes she recognized a kindred soul and felt herself relaxing with him as if he truly did understand her. Even more astonishing was the fact she had flirted with him. Or at least, she thought that's what their teasing comprised. Thank goodness she had the wits to switch to a purely English accent. He hadn't seemed to question her identity.

But there was a problem. A big one. Lies did not come easily, and she'd found herself skating too close to the truth.

Her mother *had* died of a broken heart. Why else would she have put a noose around her neck and killed herself? Goforth had told everyone she had died of a quick illness, and she'd never heard anyone doubt his story. Even the magistrate had agreed. How greased were that gentleman's palms?

She pulled her mother's shawl tighter around her shoulders, a poor substitution for a hug. What she wouldn't give to be able to ask her mother for advice. Would her mother encourage her recklessness, or would she more likely berate Jessica's foolish decision to meet Simon again? A spring of tears made her snuffle, and she slowed to a walk.

Light still shone from the drawing room. She couldn't risk bumping into any of the house party guests and being recognized in the light of a dozen candles. She was already playing with fire by deceiving Simon.

Bypassing the main entrances, she made her way around to the kitchen door. The long wooden table was scattered with servants gathered for their own meal. Abby wasn't among them. Laughter and chatter filled the room. It was cozy and welcoming. Besides Mrs. Hamish, the Penhaven servants weren't a merry lot. Jessica wasn't sure whether to attribute the gloom to the house itself or its master.

A middle-aged woman holding a pot of stew bustled over. "Come on in with you, girl. No need to be shy. You're just in time to get some food."

Jessica allowed herself to be bundled to an empty space at the table. The cook set an earthenware bowl in front of her and ladled in a good portion of warm stew. The rich scent triggered her salivary glands. She'd been too self-conscious and uncomfortable to eat much at dinner. Her bowl was empty in no time.

"What's your name, girl, and who do you belong to?" The cook plopped down next to her, wiping her brow on her apron.

"I'm Abby Blackwell, ma'am, and here with Miss Tremaine." The lie flowed a bit easier off her tongue when not facing Simon.

The woman cocked her head. "Are you now? Welcome to

Wintermarsh. Not often we get folks from the Penhaven estate over here. I'm Mrs. Potts, the cook."

"Mrs. Hamish has complimented your skill in the kitchen many times." A gleam in Mrs. Potts's eyes had the back of Jessica's neck heating. Did Mrs. Potts know the real Abby Blackwell? It was possible they'd met in Lipton on errands.

"Mrs. Hamish is an extraordinary cook herself," Mrs. Potts said evenly.

The wash of panic receded when no accusation was forthcoming. With an enthusiasm born of relief, she said, "That was the best stew I've ever had."

Mrs. Potts's cheeks turned apple red with pleasure. "Tell Mrs. Hamish her tart recipe has become a favorite. Especially with Master Simon."

The opening was too tempting for Jessica not to step through. She forced the eagerness out of her tone lest Mrs. Potts suspect something Jessica wasn't ready to admit even to herself. "I saw His Grace in the entry hall earlier. He's very handsome."

"He's a scamp, he is. Too charming for his own good, I'd say, but a good man nevertheless." Mrs. Potts leaned closer. "Is Mr. Goforth really as overbearing as I've heard?"

"He's even worse," Jessica whispered.

Mrs. Potts made a sound of commiseration. "I count my lucky stars to be working at Wintermarsh."

"I find Lord Drummond rather intimidating."

"That man is all bluster. You'll never find a kinder employer in these parts." She clapped her hands on the table and rose. "Listen to me gossiping. Mrs. Devlin will clap my ear if she hears."

It was obvious by her tone, the cook wasn't actually worried about being disciplined by the housekeeper.

"May I take some warm water to my mistress?" Jessica asked.

"With all the comings and goings, I'm keeping a pot over the fire, so help yourself anytime your mistress requires it. The boys will need warning if she requests a bath, so keep that in mind." Mrs. Potts turned back to a bowl of rising dough. "You're welcome to come down and eat with everyone whenever you like."

Jessica carefully ladled the steaming water into a basin and headed to her room. Her belly was full and so was her heart, even as she attempted to quash the anticipation of seeing Simon again tomorrow.

~

NOT FOR THE FIRST TIME, but perhaps the most piquantly, Jessica felt a true abhorrence to the part she was committed to playing. She efficiently applied the powder and dotted dark greasepaint she'd acquired from a caravan of actors two years earlier under her eyes. Abby tied extra padding to her waist and hips.

Next came a tight, uncomfortable bun covered with a cap of dingy lace on her crown. It was natural to thin her lips in displeasure at her appearance. Today she'd chosen a severe gray dress that buttoned up her neck. She looked like a dreary rain cloud out to ruin everyone's fun.

Hopefully, the men were still out shooting and she could put in an obligatory morning with the ladies before retreating to her room for a "nap." Tramping down the stairs with a purposefully unladylike gait, she drew the attention of the two women chatting in the entry hall.

Lady Drummond tipped her head and regarded Jessica with an expression somewhere between pity and curiosity. The matron standing at Lady Drummond's side spared Jessica a disdainful glance before making her way into the drawing room. Females chattered like magpies inside.

"Have you decided to join the young ladies for a trip into Lipton?" Lady Drummond raised a brow, but otherwise betrayed little of what she was thinking.

"I believe I will remain here for the morning." Jessica tried to keep her expression equally as blank, but she felt a bit like she was a novice playing cards with a shark.

"May I ask you a personal question?"

Jessica swallowed and nodded, dread rising in her throat.

"Have you considered wearing jewel tones instead of shades of gray?" Lady Drummond pursed her lips as her gaze swept over Jessica from head to toe.

The question triggered both intense relief and embarrassment. Jessica feared her powder couldn't conceal her blush. "I like my dress."

Of course, it was a lie. Jessica hated everything about what she was wearing.

Lady Drummond's eyes widened, and she slipped closer to touch Jessica's forearm. "Oh dear. That was unforgivably rude of me. Rafe tells me all the time that I can't talk to my lady friends as I talk to him. I've grown used to being able to say exactly what I think."

Jessica attempted to imagine such a reality. She had grown used to hiding her true thoughts from everyone, even her brother. "You are very lucky, my lady."

"Indeed, I am." Lady Drummond bit her lip in a show of what Jessica could only assume was unusual uncertainty. "Please don't take offense. I marched Rafe's sister straight to a modiste her first season for an entirely new wardrobe from the stockings up. I would be thrilled to help you choose an array of flattering patterns and fabrics."

"New dresses are quite unnecessary. Browns and grays are perfectly acceptable for the type of life I lead here in the country."

Minerva raised her eyebrows. "You'll need new dresses for your London debut."

"I do not want a debut. I plan to rusticate at Penhaven for the season as usual."

Lady Drummond clucked her tongue. "I'm not sure your father will be willing to honor your plans. He mentioned last night after you made your excuses that you will make your London debut this spring."

Shock sent her thoughts into a whirl, and all she could choke out was, "He's *not* my father."

Lady Drummond looked taken aback by the vehemence driving the words. Jessica had to get a handle on her feelings before Lady Drummond became even more suspicious.

"I have spoken out of turn, and I apologize. You and he need to discuss your future. But my offer to help you have a successful launch in London remains open. I remember how difficult my first season was without the steady hand of a mother. I would be pleased to sponsor you." Under Lady Drummond's cool sophistication lurked a surprising well of kindness.

But Jessica couldn't afford to accept. "Thank you, but that will be unnecessary."

"No need to decide now. Come and break your fast. The tea should be hot." Minerva guided her into the morning room. Four young ladies milled about, pulling on pelisses and gloves while waiting for the carriages to take them into Lipton.

The ladies murmured greetings to Lady Drummond. Jessica took a step to the side to disentangle herself from her hostess's sphere.

A woman entered the morning room, untying her bonnet and setting it on the back of a chair. Her sparkling green eyes hinted at a wry humor, and Jessica had to stop herself from smiling at the new arrival.

"Delilah! When did you and Marcus arrive?" Lady Drummond stepped forward to take the woman's hands and buss her cheek.

"Just now. Marcus woke at a cursed early hour and decided he wanted to join the hunt. I rode on, and the carriage is following with the bags and children. They are quite beside themselves with excitement. Your nursery may not survive." Delilah's laugh was warm and contagious.

Jessica pressed her lips tightly together. She couldn't let her guard down for a second around these two ladies.

"I don't believe I've had the pleasure." Delilah looked Jessica up and down. Not with a scathing, insulting gaze but with a curious good humor. It was almost as though the woman could see through her drabness to what was hidden.

Minerva performed the introductions. "Lady Wyndam, this is Miss Jessica Tremaine from the Penhaven estate."

"Oh, you are our neighbor. How delightful to finally make your acquaintance. I was so sorry to hear of your mother's passing." The sympathy in Delilah's brown eyes appeared sincere.

"Thank you. It was a difficult loss."

A stark silence settled in the void. It was easier to manage her loneliness when not confronted with it. Jessica glanced over her shoulder toward the door. Could she retreat to her room for the rest of the day? Before she could move, Delilah looped her arm through Jessica's and led her to a settee.

"Marcus and I rarely go to London, but we attend most of the country dances in Lipton. They are great fun. Why I haven't I seen you at any?" Delilah sat and patted the cushion.

Minerva perched on the other side. To refuse would be to insult, so Jessica sank between the two ladies, outflanked and on the defensive. "I enjoy my solitude."

"Miss Tremaine has not come out into society yet, but her stepfather informed me last night he expects her to make her bow this season in London." Minerva leaned forward to address Delilah.

Delilah clapped her hands. "How exciting! My first season was a complete and utter *disaster*."

A surprised huff of laughter escaped before Jessica could stop it. Delilah grinned back, but Minerva's half smile was more speculative.

Maintaining her facade outside her normal environment was more difficult than Jessica imagined. How much harder would it be under the glare of the ton? "My stepfather has not informed me of any plans."

"I read the papers. Mr. Goforth is a commoner with aspirations. He will attempt to maneuver a match that will benefit him. My papa is a cit and held similar hopes for me." Delilah's grin faded into pensiveness.

"It worked, did it not? You married an earl," Jessica said crisply.

"A penniless Irish peer with very little to recommend him," Delilah said wryly.

Jessica tried to quickly rearrange her preconceptions. "Your father was against the match?"

"Vehemently. He cut me off and refused to sign over my dowry. Marcus and I married by special license." Delilah didn't seem tortured by her decision.

"And you harbor no regrets?"

"Not a single one. Jumping through that window was the best decision of my life."

Jessica was unfamiliar with the particular turn of phrase, but she understood the sentiments well enough. A combination of desperation and dread tightened her chest. Jessica looked back and forth at Delilah and Minerva. Her own worry sneaked through her defenses. "I don't want to be bartered away for my stepfather's gain."

"Of course, you don't." A combination of indignation and commiseration warmed Delilah's voice. It was becoming increasing difficult not to confess *everything*. Was this what having a sister or friend felt like? Delilah continued, "If you're brave enough and bold enough, you can make your own path. Isn't that right, Minerva?"

"Quite so." Minerva answered in the crisp tones of a general used to giving orders. "But in order to mount a counteroffensive, you need more weapons in your arsenal, else you'll find yourself a pawn sacrificed for the good of the king."

"Are you suggesting I carry a knife or pistol in my reticule?" Jessica was only half jesting.

Delilah laughed. Although Minerva smiled, her eyes held no mirth. "Men use knives, pistols, and fists. Women use charm, beauty, and brains. One is no more powerful than the other if wielded correctly."

"I'm not charming. Or beautiful," Jessica said flatly.

Minerva shrugged. "Charm can be learned, and much of beauty is outer trappings. All you would require would be a more flattering wardrobe and a new hairstyle. You are already in possession of the most important weapon—brains."

Delilah reached across and took Minerva's hand so Jessica was corralled. "We should help her."

"I can't accept your help." It was the same denial she'd issued earlier, but it emerged weaker under the care and curiosity of the two ladies.

"Of course, you can," Delilah said. "Anyway, Minerva loves nothing more than a project."

"It doesn't matter, because I'm not going to London." Jessica's declaration was ruined by a wobble in her voice.

The contempt and mockery flung in her direction had stopped bothering her long ago. In fact, the cruel arrows aimed with precision by Goforth meant she was not worthy of becoming his pawn.

Kindness was proving to be her undoing. She blinked to clear the telling sting of tears. Her last tears had been born of grief. These were accompanied by a warmth she couldn't afford to feel.

"Your stepfather has final say over your plans. That is the way of things unfortunately." Minerva paused and tilted her head. "However, we can help you achieve *your* goals, not his."

"Why are you doing this?"

"I should have offered my assistance after your mother passed." Minerva's usually steady gaze skittered away with her shrug. "Plus it would please my brother."

The weight of an anvil pressed on Jessica's lungs, leaving her breathless. "Why would His Grace deign to worry over me? We've barely been acquainted a day."

"Oh. I was given to understand your paths crossed many years ago. Is that not true?"

Jessica opened her mouth then closed it. The fact he remembered at all, much less had mentioned their first meeting to his sister, sent the butterflies in her stomach into a frenzy.

"No. It is true." Jessica looked her hands. "He feels sorry for me, doesn't he?"

His attention the night before in the drawing room and at dinner made more sense now. She wasn't quite sure how to feel about the realization, but she couldn't deny the disappointment.

"This is a story I haven't heard, and it sounds intriguing." Delilah's smile was warm and encouraging.

Friends had been plentiful during her childhood in America, and Jessica had had her mother to confide in as well. Everything had changed with their change of fortunes. While they were rich in land and coin, she was poorer in friends and spirit.

With the two ladies staring at her, Jessica found herself speaking of the day she kept close to her heart. "Our paths crossed at an inn soon after I arrived from America. I was young and hadn't yet learned to guard my tongue. My stepfather was not forgiving of my impudence. His Grace intervened. I've never forgotten his kindness, but I am surprised to learn he remembered me at all."

The two women exchanged a glance Jessica wasn't sure how to interpret. Lady Drummond transferred her pointed gaze to Jessica, who couldn't help but wither slightly under its intensity. "How did Goforth make you pay for your impudent tongue?"

Jessica swallowed. "The usual way, I suppose."

Delilah touched the back of Jessica's hand, and it was only then she realized she'd drawn them into fists. "What is the usual way with your stepfather?"

Jessica knew better than to answer with the truth. She had allowed the conversation to dig too close to the truth. She stood. "I believe I'll take a turn in your garden, Lady Drummond. If you'll excuse me."

CHAPTER 8

The young women had returned from their visit to Lipton and were playing charades in the drawing room. Simon intended to bypass the merriment and make his way to the nursery to play with his nephew and the other children. He'd promised Christopher a game of blind man's bluff.

He made it past the drawing room without being spotted and let out a held breath, lengthening his stride. His focus was on the stairs and freedom, which is why he didn't notice the hand snagging him by the shoulder of his jacket until it yanked him through the study door.

"Christ almighty!" he yelled.

"Keep it down, you dirty blighter," Rafe said in a menacing voice as he closed the door and stood in front of it like a Newgate prison guard.

A vastly amused Wyndam stood at the mantel sipping a brandy, and Lady Wyndam and Minerva occupied two armchairs, drinking port.

Rafe poked Simon in the chest. "*You* did this to me. What have I ever done besides steer you down an honorable path? And this is the thanks I get? Don't forget I still remember how to garrote a man in under thirty seconds. I'm tempted to employ my expertise on both you and Goforth. Why did you want him invited if you weren't going to court him for his support?"

It was true, Rafe possessed skills that had made him one of the Crown's foremost spies during the wars with Napoleon. But his gruff, intimidating exterior hid a big heart. Rafe would never purposefully hurt anyone unless he was protecting those he cared about. Simon counted himself lucky to be on that list.

"Am I to assume you were stuck entertaining him?" Simon asked idly even as Rafe fisted his neckcloth into a wad of linen.

"This morning on the hunt and at luncheon. I only just escaped, and not a moment too soon."

Minerva raised her brows and fixed Simon with a glare. "When Goforth offered to instruct Rafe on his investments, I thought a murder was imminent. I'm not sure what the devil is going on with you, but I *am* sure it has nothing to do with Goforth. What is your interest in Miss Tremaine?"

"You could have any one of the most beautiful women in the ton," Rafe said incredulously.

Rafe spoke the absolute truth. Yet his tone jarred Simon's nerves. Miss Tremaine might not be a diamond of the first water, but she had shown more depth of feeling than any of the other ladies present. "There's more to someone than the way they look. I should think *you* of all people would realize that."

Rafe's hand loosened around Simon's jacket, leaving crease marks. His features slid into a more contemplative cast. He glanced toward Minerva. "It seems you were correct, Minerva."

Simon silently cursed himself roundly. He'd been played by two masters. "I'm not interested in wedding Miss Tremaine. However, I can't help but feel sorry for her. Having Goforth as a stepfather must be a nightmare."

"Indeed, it must be," Lady Wyndam said darkly, adding her

glare to the others already aimed in his direction. "Which is why something must be done."

Feeling set upon by all angles, Simon crossed his arms over his chest and tilted his chin toward Lord Wyndam. "What have you to add, my lord?"

Wyndam threw up his hands in mock surrender. "Don't throw your daggers at me, old boy. I'm here merely for the brandy."

Simon harrumphed, but the shot of humor dissipated a good portion of the tension. A brandy sounded like a fine idea. He moved to the sideboard and poured himself a finger's worth. "Obviously, a plan has been hatched, or I wouldn't have been summoned as abruptly as I was."

"Delilah and I had a most interesting discussion with Miss Tremaine this morning. Her stepfather is planning her debut during the spring season. From what he has insinuated, it seems he is anxious to make an advantageous match—for him." The disgust at men's machinations was clear in Minerva's tone.

Imagining the painfully awkward Miss Tremaine at the mercy of the ton and Goforth provoked sympathy pains in Simon. "This party has been difficult enough. The ton will eat her alive."

"Indeed. I can't in good conscience allow the poor girl to enter a ballroom, or any other room for that matter, dressed as she is now. She's a walking disaster."

"Too true," Delilah seconded with a shake of her head.

"Perhaps you could drop a discreet word in Goforth's ear about her need for a sponsor," Rafe said.

"She doesn't need a sponsor; she needs a fairy godmother." Delilah exchanged a wry glance with Minerva.

Minerva tapped her chin, her lips tipping into the flash of a smile. "The situation isn't dire enough to require magical intervention. She merely needs a guide through the minefield of society."

"She has a rather fine bone structure," Delilah said. "A proper-fitting dress and stays would show her figure to its finest, and a new hairstyle would not be amiss either. A good lady's maid would go a long way to improving her looks."

"There's nothing wrong with her maid." The words shot out before Simon could even consider the damage. He tempered his voice. "I mean, I'm sure her maid is skilled. It seems to me Miss Tremaine is doing her best to hide any positive attributes."

Delilah's eyes widened. "Your brother has a point, Minerva. I wonder if she is deliberately downplaying her appearance to avoid being seen as a valuable bartering piece by her stepfather."

"Interesting theory." Minerva rose and paced. "If true, her resistance to any offer of help on our parts makes more sense."

Relieved his slip of the tongue had not gained Minerva's notice, Simon kept his tone even. "Goforth would not hesitate to leverage any advantage to his cause with no thought to Miss Tremaine's feelings on the matter of marriage."

Minerva stopped to pour herself another glass. "The complications mount."

"Perhaps it's not our place to interfere in another family's business," Simon said.

Minerva whirled around, her skirts swishing. "And where would we be if that had been Rafe's attitude all those years ago?"

Simon opened his mouth and then closed it, his gaze skating to the tips of his boots. He didn't want to imagine the path of his life if Rafe hadn't inserted himself in their business, even if it had been most unwelcome at the time.

"How can I help?" Simon glanced up at his sister in time to catch her satisfied smile.

"I'm not sure yet, but Miss Tremaine obviously holds you in high esteem."

"She said that?"

"She told us a bit of your meeting many years ago. You made

quite an impression." Delilah twisted around in her chair to gaze up at him.

The light dusting of freckles and her guileless brown eyes gave her a suggestion of youthful innocence. Considering Lord and Lady Wyndam had met over a dead body and eventually caught the murderer, Delilah was not a woman to be underestimated.

"Miss Tremaine certainly made an indelible impression on me that day. She was a girl of spirit. I pity what has happened to her now," Simon said.

"If we're correct in our assumptions, she doesn't want or require your pity," Delilah said lightly.

"Which means we will need to be delicate in our overtures." Minerva regained her seat. "If we can make her presentable, she can make a good match and get out from under Goforth's thumb."

"Unless Goforth barters her away for votes first," Rafe said darkly. "I wouldn't put anything past the man. He has attempted to turn me against Simon. The brazenness is breathtaking."

"Then we will need to be even more brazen and smarter. It shouldn't be *that* difficult," Delilah said pertly before leaning over to discuss the particulars with Minerva.

Simon joined Wyndam and Rafe at the mantel. "How likely are their schemes to end in disaster?"

Wyndam's eyes crinkled with the smile he aimed toward his wife. "I pity Goforth. He's used to charging straight at his opponents. He won't even see those two coming."

Rafe shook his head with a similar affectionate smile on his face. "Minerva will have him retreating to lick his wounds before the house party has concluded. It will be lovely to watch."

An ache spread from Simon's chest to hollow out his stomach. Would he ever find a woman who inspired such devotion and admiration? His mind went immediately to Miss Blackwell.

Had he found her? Perhaps, but his future could not include

marriage to Miss Blackwell. Even with the uncertainty, the anticipation of seeing her that evening quickened his blood and filled his heart with gladness and hope.

~

SIMON WAS ONCE AGAIN SEATED by Miss Tremaine at dinner. Damien shot him a look of sympathy from across the table, but Simon didn't mind. Miss Tremaine was one of the few women not in pursuit of his hand, and she was surprisingly easy to converse with.

She was, however, difficult to look at this evening. Her dress was yellow, which was a favorite color of his. But not this yellow. It was a mustardy yellow that would make any woman look a sallow, sick mess.

Delilah's speculation about Miss Tremaine deliberating attempting to look unappealing had him inspecting her closer. Her torso was rectangular and distinctly unfeminine and didn't match her lithe neck and narrow shoulders. Could she be wearing artificial padding instead of stays? It wasn't unheard of. Gentlemen often padded the shoulders of their jackets to appear more manly. It was difficult to judge her hair as it was pulled under a wretched-looking cap a decade or more out of style.

Delilah was correct about Miss Tremaine's high cheekbones though. A fine brow peeked out from under the lace edge of her cap, and her nose was pert and attractive. In contrast, her lips were colorless and drawn into a thin line, and dark circles stood out in her pale face.

He cleared his throat. "You're looking lovely tonight, Miss Tremaine."

"Thank you, Your Grace. I had this dress commissioned for just such an auspicious occasion." While her voice was flat, the baleful glance she shot him before taking up her soup spoon was full of dark humor.

He was becoming more and more convinced her appearance was indeed deliberately unappealing. "I'm surprised you have retained your American accent all these years."

When she didn't answer immediately, he glanced over to see her spoon frozen midway between the bowl and her mouth, a myriad of emotions lying across her face. "I apologize. We can discuss something less—"

"No, I don't wish to discuss the weather or hunting or horseflesh. Your question merely took me by surprise, Your Grace. Generally, no one is interested in my life before coming to England, and my stepfather does his best to ignore our American roots. It is a dirty little secret."

"Since the end of the war, relations are less strained between our two countries. I hope you haven't faced rudeness. After all, your brother is a peer."

"I don't believe my birthplace is what invites rudeness." While she spoke matter-of-factly, a fair measure of hurt feelings were obvious.

"Allow me to apologize."

Her laugh was throaty and unexpected and niggled something in his memory. "You have not been rude, and as much as you wish to, you can't take responsibility for everyone less fortunate than you."

He bristled slightly. "If it is within my power to shift the arc of justice, then shouldn't I do everything to see it done?"

She continued to delicately sip her soup, letting the silence between them crescendo before finally saying, "It isn't wrong. It is admirable." She put her spoon down and tapped her mouth with her napkin. "But your type of justice doesn't move swiftly enough."

"How so?"

"You are attempting to change society through its laws, but men like my stepfather will continue to thwart you until you must compromise your vision to see any good done."

She had distilled his fears into an arrow of truth that pierced his hope. His appetite gone, he pushed his bowl away. An attentive footman cleared the half-finished bowl. "What do you suggest I do? Give up and become a profligate rake like so many of my peers?"

"Of course not. But don't be surprised if the people grow impatient and rise up to change their own circumstances."

The service of the next course interrupted their conversation. Simon mulled over her opinion. The end of the Napoleonic Wars had seen England enter an economic slump. The corn laws had only exacerbated the problem. Tensions had come to a head the previous fall in Manchester. Dubbed the Peterloo Massacre, the insurrection had driven Parliament to crack down on reformists. Simon had vehemently opposed the acts, but to no avail.

With a crusted fish staring up at him, Simon put his fork down. "I suppose, being American, you have a unique perspective about the common people rising up."

She shrugged, the yellow ribbon decorating the cap sleeves of her dress fluttering. The ribbon itself was a pretty shade and contrasted with the ghastly color of her gown, but what was more interesting was the slenderness of her arm and delicateness of her wrist. It seemed obvious now that Miss Tremaine was in hiding.

"I suppose I do have an independent streak. I'm not sure I can attribute it to my American birth or simply being my father's daughter." Her lips tipped slightly up before thinning once more.

"He was a rebel?"

"He left England with little coin and a dream of owning his own farm. It took a few years of hard work, but we lived a comfortable life." She gestured around them with a shake of her head. "Nothing like this, of course, but I never wanted for anything as a child."

"I suppose it was quite a shock to arrive at Penhaven."

"The notion of a house with more servants than family members still seems ridiculous."

"English society is built on remnants of the feudal system. The villages rely on jobs in the big houses."

"There were no estates in my village. Everyone worked together and supported one another if a family fell into difficulties." Her brows drew downward and cast shadows both seen and unseen across her features.

"Did your family fall into difficulties after your father passed?" He kept his voice low, although as loudly as Goforth was discoursing to the entire table, the man would remain oblivious.

She toyed with her fork, drawing his attention to her hands. They were delicately formed and graceful without the dingy gloves to conceal them.

"Mother didn't want for coin, but company, and Goforth was there to offer his support." Her bitterness made his stomach turn in sympathy.

"He married your mother for her money?" It was a common enough occurrence in the ton. Simon counted himself lucky to not be burdened with the debt so many of his peers struggled with.

She gave a shake of her head. "I was young and wasn't privy to the secrets of their marriage. They were happy enough for a time, but not for long. It was only when we arrived here that Goforth got his first taste of what social standing will buy in terms of power and influence."

Goforth's booming laugh had her cringing, her shoulders curling inward as if she could protect herself.

Simon took a sip of his wine and searched for something less serious to discuss. "Surely you have enjoyed having servants tend to your needs just a little."

At that precise moment, the footman cleared their plates and replaced them with another plate with a selection of meat.

"I find having a barrage of men and women who will never be my friends more uncomfortable than enjoyable. In fact—please don't laugh—but I had thought to help cook the family meals on our arrival."

"Say you didn't!" Simon tossed his head back with a hearty laugh, drawing nearby eyes. "I'm sorry, I can't help but imagine the reaction."

Miss Tremaine covered an answering smile with her hand. He had the urge to draw it away. "The servants stared at me as I collected flour and sugar from the larder. Mrs. Hamish pulled me aside and explained that it wasn't at all the thing for a lady to do, and the servants would take it as a grave insult. I was humiliated."

Her overstep had been egregious and would have lost her respect among the servants who had their own social hierarchy. "Were you ever forgiven?"

"Mrs. Hamish smoothed things over as much as possible. She has always been kind."

The opening she provided was too tempting to deny. "I hope your lady's maid is a loyal and kind servant as well."

Miss Tremaine fumbled her knife, the clatter quieting the conversation around them for a few long seconds. Once the murmur of voices picked up, she said softly, "Abby has been good to me."

"How long has she been in your employ?"

"Quite some time." Her attention was on moving her food around her plate before fixing him with a narrowed glance. "Why are you interested in my maid, Your Grace?"

His mind blanked for a long, embarrassing moment.

CHAPTER 9

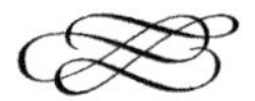

Of course, Jessica was well aware of why he was interested in her *maid*. Still, she was curious as to what excuse he might produce. Plus, she rather enjoyed making a duke squirm. And was that a flush coasting up his neck and into his cheeks?

After stuttering out a few inane words, he said, "I know my sister's maid offers much support to her, and I hope you enjoy the same."

"Indeed. Abby is most supportive. It's kind of you to be so interested in my well-being." Jessica was teasing him, yet with an unexpectedly bitter bite.

Simon speared a piece of succulent pork and stuffed his mouth, precluding further conversation.

Meeting the duke again as Miss Blackwell would be foolish. No, beyond foolish. It would be idiotic. Nothing good could come of their association. And Simon's not-so-subtle probing only reinforced the logic. His interest in her as a maid could only be prurient.

From this moment forward, Jessica planned to be as bland and uninteresting as a baby's first pudding. Already she had intercepted too many curious glances from Lady Drummond. Their conversation earlier in the day had cut too close to the truth.

Dinner came to an end. Once again, the men would remain in the dining area and gathered where footmen were laying out decanters, sharing jokes and companionably discussing the fate of the world.

The ladies were filing out in twos and threes and headed to the drawing room where ratafia and gossip would be served. With her gaze on Goforth, Jessica sidled to the door and slipped out with a sigh of relief. The solitude of her room beckoned.

The ambush was unexpected and came with a smile. Lady Drummond linked her arm through Jessica's and steered her away from the staircase with surprising strength. There was no escape without seeming churlish and rude.

"The servants must take their dinner, so there is no use retreating to your room with no maid to see to you. Come and enjoy a glass of spirits." Lady Drummond deposited her on a settee in the middle of the room and pressed a glass into her hand. "Drink and be merry, my dear."

Lady Drummond clinked their glasses and sipped, her stance relaxed in the corner of the settee as she watched the younger ladies flitter around, exchanging whispers and giggles. Were they laughing at Jessica? She tightened her grip on the delicate stem of the crystal glass and sipped to cover her discomfiture.

The sweet spirits hit her empty stomach and zipped straight to her head, fuzzing her thoughts. Before she realized it, her glass was empty and Lady Drummond was refilling it from a decanter on the nearby side table. She smiled her thanks at Lady Drummond before she realized what she was doing and resumed frowning.

A group of three young ladies gathered close by, chattering about dresses, desirable peers on the mart, and whispered speculation on the marriage bed. They compared notes on employing a fan flirtatiously, talking a gentleman into a garden, and obtaining a kiss. Two young women even discussed a current on-dit involving a viscount and his mistress.

"I'm not sure your eyes could get any bigger, Miss Tremaine. Are you scandalized?" Lady Drummond's question was rife with amusement, but it wasn't malicious.

Taking yet another ill-advised sip from her glass, Jessica schooled her face and voice. Her plan was already going awry. "Certainly not."

But she was rather scandalized. The trials life had set in her path had matured her beyond her years in some ways and left her woefully unprepared in others. Through circumstance and choice, Jessica had cloistered herself at Penhaven and eschewed the social circles available to her. If Lady Drummond was correct, Jessica would soon be thrown from the shallows into the deep end and would be expected to save herself in London's upcoming season.

Lady Wyndam joined them on the settee and shook her head. "Several of the young ladies are tittering about Mr. Northcutt. I fear they will learn the hard way he is not a house cat but a panther."

"Oh dear. I'll have Rafe drop a warning in his ear. I pity any young lady who attempts to tame him," Lady Drummond said.

"And Miss Danforth seems to have set her cap for your brother. She seems quite determined to catch him."

All three of them shifted their gazes to where Miss Danforth held court in the corner of the room. She was everything Jessica was not. Self-assured, well turned out, and lovely. Her blond hair was smooth and shiny with perfectly coiled curls at her ears to frame pretty features. If her eyes were a tad too sharp and her pout held a touch of malice, she would be forgiven as soon as anyone heard her tinkling laugh. She would be an admirable match for a duke.

"Wouldn't Mr. Northcutt be honor bound to make an offer

as a gentleman if he were caught in a compromising situation?" Jessica asked to distract herself from the feeling of loss she had no right to. Simon was not hers and never would be.

"Mr. Northcutt is no gentleman." Lady Drummond spoke with equal parts affection and warning.

Jessica felt like she was missing something obvious. "Why was he invited then?"

"Northcutt and Simon have been well acquainted since they attended Eton together, but they have grown especially close the past several years. He is a frequent guest." Minerva gestured dismissively with her glass. "Anyway, Rafe cares not if a man is titled or politically connected. He is interested in interesting men. Preferably ones with a head for investments."

"If he has the connections and wealth, why isn't he welcomed into polite society?" Jessica felt dense.

Lady Wyndam leaned in closer. "It's hardly for polite discussion, but when have I ever been polite? Mr. Northcutt is the by-blow of the Duke of Lonsdale. Unacknowledged of course, but the resemblance is uncanny."

"I wonder if Northcutt plays up the resemblance to annoy Lonsdale," Lady Drummond said.

"He is brash enough to do it." Lady Wyndam's voice dropped into more conspiratorial tones. "As charming as he can be, he's rather hard, isn't he? Besides your brother, I'm not sure he gives a jot about another human being besides himself."

"He is jaded and dangerous and deliciously handsome." At Lady Wyndam's surprised laugh, Lady Drummond schooled her features into a mask of pure innocence. "I may be a married woman quite in love with my husband, but I do have a pair of perfectly fine eyes."

Jessica covered her mouth to hide a smile. She couldn't help herself. Against her better judgment, she liked both Lady Drummond and Lady Wyndam. The warm friendship between the two ladies made her feel wistful and strangely covetous.

The gentlemen arrived and brought with them a boisterous energy. The ladies preened and put themselves on display like birds attempting to attract mates. Simon and Damien Northcutt entered together, their heads close in conversation. Mr. Northcutt was as dark as Simon was fair. Both were handsome, but it was Simon who held Jessica's attention.

Miss Danforth inserted herself between the two men, a hand on each one of them as if claiming them both as hers. The too-sweet ratafia churned in Jessica's stomach until she thought she might be sick. She stood, ready to make excuses, when she caught sight of her distorted reflection in the long window to the gardens.

A shabby young lady on the path to spinsterhood stared back at her. The longer she disguised herself behind the padding and the powder and the horrid dresses, the more she began to resemble the persona she had adopted. In a decade, there would be no need for disguises to appear worn and unattractive.

Lady Drummond and Lady Wyndam had shifted away to greet their husbands. Neither of them noticed when she slipped out of the drawing room door. She bounded up the stairs with less decorum than a girl fresh from the schoolroom. As soon as the door was closed behind her, she stripped away the trappings of her facade as if they were on fire.

The real Abby had been dozing in the armchair by the unlit grate and jumped up to help unfasten the back of her horrid yellow gown while Jessica pulled the pins holding the frumpy mobcap in place. Panic overcame her when one of the pins tangled in her hair. A sob broke out of her throat.

"Whatever has happened, miss?" Abby took over unpinning Jessica's hair with gentler hands.

Jessica stepped out of the dress and shucked her dingy chemise off while she was at it. She was naked now except for her stockings, and she huddled into herself with her back to the mirror. Abby draped a dressing gown over her hunched shoulders.

"Nothing in particular happened. I just… hate being me." Jessica washed the powder and kohl off her face in the basin of cool clean water. She stretched her jaw and rubbed her lips together.

"I'm sorry, miss." Abby steered her to the seat in front of a table with a small looking glass on top and gently worked the tangles out of her hair.

"How was your evening? Did anyone question you too closely?" Jessica asked.

"No one. With so many extra servants in the house, it was easy enough to slip in and out of the kitchen for dinner. The girl in my room is after one of the valets and pays me no mind." Abby brushed Jessica's hair until the copper highlights crackled in the candlelight and braided the mass with deft fingers.

Finally, a familiar face stared back at Jessica from the looking glass. She wasn't old and haggard. Not yet, anyway. But the future felt inevitable. Actually, she would be lucky to be a spinster and not married off to some horrid man Goforth chose for her.

"Would you like your night rail, miss?" Abby hovered, obviously worried.

Jessica forced a calm she didn't feel into her voice. "You can leave it on the bed, Abby, thank you. I won't need you again until morning."

"Very good, miss." Abby softly closed the door behind her.

The snick of the door triggered something in Jessica. Or had she made the decision when she watched Miss Danforth simpering at Simon in the drawing room? Jessica rose and pulled out the brown dress she'd worn the night before and a clean chemise. Her slippers were too delicate for a servant, but if Simon was astute enough to notice her slippers, then the game would be up for other reasons.

She pinched color into her cheeks and smiled at herself in the looking glass before groaning. She was a fool. An imbecile. Idiotic. Reckless. She was also young and alive and wanted Simon to look at her like he had in the garden the evening before. She wanted to touch his arm and flutter her lashes at him like Miss Danforth had done.

She hesitated only a moment before stepping through her door. This would be the last time she would pretend to be her own maid. A last stolen evening.

She stopped at the bottom of the stairs, lucky no one had spotted her. Laughter and conversation poured from the drawing room. She could hardly exit through the front door, but slipping through the kitchen carried its own risks.

Goforth strode out of the drawing room with an older gentleman. As if her antipathy was a noxious scent, he swung around to look in her direction.

She darted down the servants' hallway toward the kitchen, expecting to feel the devil's breath on her neck. Daring a glance over her shoulder, she could see nothing but shadows. She collided with a hard, warm body.

"Steady there, lass." The man's voice was warm and friendly.

She grabbed hold of his bare forearms to catch her balance. "I'm so sorry. Did I hurt you?"

"A slip of a girl like you injure an ox like me? Don't think so, sweeting." A charmingly lopsided grin complimented the man's ruddy, handsome face and laborer's thick shoulders.

His shirtsleeves were rolled up to his elbows, and his scent was hay and horses, not unpleasant, but a change from the pomades and perfumes of the guests. She dropped his arms and cupped her own elbows across her body.

"I was just—"

"I'm Henry Mitchell. I didn't notice you at dinner. And I would have if you'd been there. I suppose your mistress has kept you busy. There are still some of Mrs. Potts's meat pasties if you're hungry."

She was going to answer in the negative, but having been too distracted and nervous to eat at dinner, her stomach betrayed her and growled. She blushed, but Henry only laughed heartily and herded her toward the kitchen, commandeering her a pasty and mug of cool ale.

Most of the servants had cleared out of the kitchens to prepare for their nightly duties. Henry sat next to her on the bench but leaning back and bracing his elbows on the table. "What's your name?"

"Abby Blackwell." The lie was coming easier which was worrisome in and of itself.

"Who is your mistress?"

"Miss Jessica Tremaine." She needed to change the subject. What did men enjoy talking about? The answer, of course, was themselves. "Are you a member of the household, or do you belong to someone at the party?"

"I belong to Wintermarsh. I mostly work in the stables, but I've been commandeered to work the house for the party."

She devoured the pasty and licked her fingers clean. Henry was watching her with a gleam that made her slightly uncomfortable.

She popped up. "I must go."

"Must you?" He rose, blocking her exit, and crooked his arm. "I shall escort you. Where are you headed?"

"That's not necessary, Mr. Mitchell."

He threw his head back with a laugh. "Listen to you talking to me like I'm a toff. I'm just Henry."

Mrs. Potts bustled in from the larder with a sack of flour, the scullery maid on her heels. "Get on with you, Henry, and quit bothering the poor girl. Mrs. Devlin requires your services in the dining room."

Henry performed a mock bow, touched his forelock, and retreated.

Mrs. Potts set her baking items on the counter and wiped her forehead with the back of her arm. "He's harmless enough, but it'd be best not to follow him into any darkened corners for he's likely to steal a kiss, Miss Blackwell."

Jessica blinked in consternation. "From me, you mean?"

Mrs. Potts's eyes twinkled when she smiled. "From a new, pretty maid? Indeed he would. And the blighter is charming enough that you might just be tempted to give him one freely. Can I get you anything?"

"No. I had a pasty. It was delicious."

"Good, good." Clearly distracted, the cook turned away to begin preparing dough for rising.

Jessica slipped out the kitchen door and slunk along the side of the house, keeping in the shadows. Her encounter with Henry Mitchell had been both flattering and alarming. As Miss Tremaine, she was overlooked by men, but as Miss Blackwell, she had been noticed by a duke and a servant. Even Mrs. Potts had complimented her.

A tiny flame ignited in her chest. One she tried to extinguish for it would only serve to underscore how cold and lonely her life was. If Lady Drummond was correct, Goforth would force her to make her debut in London in the spring. Could she use the actor's makeup to mimic getting boils on her face? Imagining Goforth's impotent fury summoned a smile.

Her lips quivered and fell. Not so impotent. He could make her suffer in a myriad of ways, both physical and emotional. She worried less for herself than for Blake. Shaking the thoughts out of her head, she focused on the here and now. She was not a lady, with more problems than she could defend herself against, but a simple lady's maid.

The edge of the gardens came into sight, and her heart skipped. Voices stilled her feet. A man and a woman. Figures came into view around a yew tree sculpted to resemble a wild hare. It was Simon and the lovely Miss Danforth.

Jessica had been living in a world of fantasy. Miss Danforth not only possessed beauty but the connections necessary to make a marriage with the duke. As Miss Blackwell, she was a nobody.

Nobodies still possessed a heart and feelings. She did an about-face, prepared to dart through the kitchens and retreat to her room. Henry Mitchell stepped out of the kitchen door, blocking her escape in that direction.

Her options were to stay as still and silent as possible and hopefully pass for a topiary or to seek refuge in the stables. There was an expanse of lawn and gravel to traverse, but waiting for either Simon or Henry to discover her was alternately humiliating and terrifying.

She fisted her skirts and took off toward the stables like a bird in flight, not stopping until she'd ducked under the eaves. Deep in the stable, the sound of grooms settling the horses for the night could be heard, but there was no one in sight and she relaxed. As soon as Henry moved away from the kitchen door, she would return, but for now, she would wait and stay hidden.

The chuffs of the horses made her feel less lonely, and she shuffled to the nearest stall. A dark gray horse with a black mane clomped closer. She patted its neck and leaned in to rest her forehead against its soft mane, closing her eyes.

The crunch of grass and gravel underfoot had her hand tightening the horse's mane as she cracked her eyes open. The outline of a man filled the opening, the rising moon casting his features in shadow.

A sudden urge to mount the horse and ride until she left everything behind overtook her. Too bad she could neither saddle a horse nor ride one. With no other choice, she let go of the horse and turned to face her fears.

CHAPTER 10

Simon let out a slow breath, feeling as triumphant as if he'd caught a fairy. Which was exactly what she'd resembled as she scurried across the lawn before disappearing into the stables. Unfortunately, he hadn't been able to follow her immediately.

Miss Danforth's boldness wasn't a shock, but he'd been so focused on his meeting with Miss Blackwell he hadn't guarded against machinations, and she'd cornered him in the gardens without a chaperone. A dangerous situation.

His extrication had lacked politesse and finesse. In truth, he'd been rude, yet she hadn't seemed cowed. If anything, she seemed a young lady who enjoyed a challenge, which was what he'd proved himself to be.

Then he'd had another stumbling block to handle. Henry Mitchell had been as intent as Simon on reaching the stables. Was his target Miss Blackwell? The thought lit a green-hued fire in Simon's belly. He'd never been so grateful to be a duke and ordered Henry back to the house. The man's shoulders had rolled as if ready for a fight, but he'd backed down with a deep nod. Simon had made sure Henry was out of sight before continuing his pursuit.

His reward was standing in the shadows with her hand on a horse, her face tilted toward him in acknowledgment of his presence. The horse whinnied, but she offered no greeting.

"I feared you had abandoned me. I was beginning to despair." Keeping his voice light, Simon halved the distance between them. She took a small step backward, as skittish as a half-broken horse.

A hint of moonlight sneaked through the door, casting her in soft light and adding to the fae quality of their meeting. Her white chemise edged the bodice of the same brown dress she'd worn the night before. Her plaited hair hung over one shoulder with escaped tendrils waving around her face and neck.

"Miss Danforth offered comfort for your despair." The tartness in her voice gave him hope.

He took another step, and this time she held her ground. "She cornered me. Miss Danforth is an annoying gnat."

"That is a rather unkind thing to say. I've seen her. She's lovely." After a pause, she added softly, "You must choose one of those gnats to marry, Your Grace."

"I suppose I must. But not this evening or this week or even this year." He tipped his head. "You do not seem short of admirers, Miss Blackwell."

"What are talking about?"

"I intercepted Henry Mitchell headed this way on a mission."

She made a sound that did not reflect surprise. The odd frisson that heated his blood and drew his hands into fists could only be jealousy. He took another stalking step until a scant six inches separated them, and she had to tip her head back to maintain eye contact. He was used to fluttering lashes and averted eyes. No other woman besides his sister met his gaze with such boldness. A different sort of heat made his heart pound faster.

"Henry Mitchell has a bit of a reputation in Lipton. You should beware his intentions." His voice was rough with want and warning.

"I appreciate your purely honorable motive to protect my virtue, Your Grace." Her dripping sarcasm only fed his desire. Her tongue was sharp and able and, he imagined, skilled in a variety of pursuits.

"Don't call me Your Grace, I beg of you." While he would no doubt dream of her tongue doing salacious things to him, he was desperate for something simpler. He wanted to hear his given name roll off her tongue.

"Why not?"

"Because those ladies—Miss Danforth especially—don't know me. They don't care to know me. They only wish to be a duchess and become intimately involved with my bank account." He took a deep breath, a weight lifted from his chest with the unleashing of the truth. "I am merely a man, Miss Blackwell. One who is smitten with the woman standing before him in a stable."

Her intake of breath was swift, and she touched his chest with her fingertips. After his promises made in the garden the night before, he had resolved himself to not touch or hold or kiss her. The light pressure of her hand crumbled his good intentions.

He covered her hand with his and slipped them inside his jacket and waistcoat so her hand was over his heart with only the thin lawn of his shirt separating them.

"What shall I call you?" she asked huskily.

"Simon." In the word was a command for her to repeat it.

"Simon," she whispered.

Sensation skittered down his spine. Was it a premonition or simple pleasure? Either way, it was as electrifying as being struck by lightning. "May I use your given name?"

Her tongue darted over her lips, and her gaze dropped to

where her hand covered his heart. Surely, she could feel it trying to claw its way out to her. "You may call me Abby."

Laughter and conversation grew louder as two grooms made their way back up the wide aisle. Simon opened the stall door of the dark gray mare and pulled Jessica inside, shouldering the beast aside to reach the far corner. Luckily, the stall had been mucked recently, and fresh straw was underfoot, muffling their movements and sweetening the air.

Space was scarce. She notched herself into the corner, and Simon faced her, bracketing her with his hands on the stall walls. The moment veered intimate, and it was all he could do not to dip his face to hers and nuzzle the wave of hair at her temple. Could she sense the ties binding them ever closer?

"Do... Do you...?" The words emerged on her quickened breaths.

Did he want to kiss her? Lift her skirts? Lay her down in the hay and nestle between her legs? A resounding yes to the three most pertinent questions roiling in his head.

"Do you... enjoy riding?" The unexpected question left him reeling for an answer, and into the silence, she whispered, "Horses, I mean."

In turns confident and nervous, Miss Abby Blackwell was a delight. He could tell he held the upper hand in terms of experience, but he refused to hold it over her. That didn't mean he couldn't tease her.

"I do enjoy riding. Having that sort of power between your legs is heady stuff. And yourself?"

"I've never ridden. Papa promised to teach me, but he died before he could keep his promise."

Her wistfulness tugged at something inside him he'd thought he'd outgrown. He'd missed out on much childhood joy after his parents' deaths. The dukedom had weighed heavily on the shoulders of a seven-year-old.

"Would you like me to teach you to ride?"

"Yes, very much." The excitement in her voice dimmed. "I could not sneak away for such frivolity during the day. If I were caught..."

She needn't say more. A man like Goforth would sack her without a reference. "There's a clearing not far from here, and the full moon is nearly upon us. We could meet tomorrow evening after you've finished your duties. I'll saddle the gentlest horse in Drummond's stable and keep you on leads until you're comfortable."

She hesitated but finally nodded. "That is kind of you. Thank you, Simon."

Once again, a tingle traveled through him hearing his name on her lips. "It will be my pleasure."

"I don't understand this," she said softly.

He didn't pretend to misunderstand her meaning and dropped his forehead to hers. "I don't either. I wish—" He bit his lip.

"What? Tell me." She took hold of the edge of his waistcoat and tugged him closer.

"I wish I weren't a duke. Or you weren't a lady's maid."

"You wish we were equals."

Put like that, he felt lower than a worm. "We are equals in every way that's truly important. I suppose I wish things were easier. Clearer. Does that make sense?"

She chuffed a laugh, but it held no humor. "More than you realize. Things are muddled for me too, but there is one thing I know for certain."

"What's that?"

"I want you to kiss me. One kiss to remember." She tipped her head back in the sweetest offering he'd ever beheld.

Unable to deny either of them, he shifted closer, keeping his hands braced on either side of her, his lips moving within inches of hers. The horse chuffed and shuffled as if Simon's impatience was contagious.

He stopped himself. It was the most impressive exhibition of strength he'd ever demonstrated. Considering how often he'd been sparring with Rafe, the tremble in his biceps was unexplainable. "Hold on a moment. Do you forget I promised you last evening I wouldn't kiss you?"

"No. You promised not to seduce me. A kiss is merely... a kiss." She tugged her bottom lip between her teeth, releasing it agonizingly, arousingly, slowly.

"A kiss between us will never be merely a kiss. It will be a prelude to much more."

"All I can offer—all I can *afford*—to give you is a kiss, Your Grace."

"Then I accept, but you must be the one to kiss me. I will not be accused of taking advantage of you." Even as he said it, guilt niggled. He was a duke, and she a lady's maid. No matter who instigated a kiss, he was most definitely taking advantage of her. "And by God, call me Simon."

Abby pushed herself out of the corner and lay her hands against his chest. "Simon," she whispered.

Her touch was featherlight, yet it burned all his good intentions to ash. It was all he could do not to pull her body flush with his and take what he wanted more than anything in the world, yet like a trained horse, he waited for her signal.

One of her hands drifted up his chest to his shoulder, alighting only a moment to chart the dip and curve before continuing its trek to his nape. Now it was more than his biceps that quivered. A shudder went through him from scalp to toes. Her fingers threaded through his hair and tightened. She tugged his head down the same time she rose to meet him.

Her lips pressed softly against his and held still. A different sort of jolt went through him when he realized she didn't know what to do. Her kiss was all innocence. How had some young handsome footman not coaxed a kiss from her before now?

No one had kissed her. Possessiveness he had no right to had him smiling against her lips.

She pulled away slightly. "Am I doing it wrong?"

"Not wrong."

"Then why are you laughing at me?" The hurt in her voice arrowed into his chest and reverberated.

She tried to take a step to the side, but it was too late. The reflexes he had honed the past few years sparring and boxing with Rafe and Damien had him reacting with a swiftness that made her gasp. He pulled her close with an arm around her waist, notched his knee between her legs, and cupped her face with his other hand so she couldn't avert her face.

"Trust me, what I'm feeling has nothing to do with humor."

"Then what?"

She had been honest about what she could offer him—a kiss. What if he were honest about what he could offer her? A house and servants and his bed. She could hire her own lady's maid. He would squire her to the theater and the opera and even to functions that welcomed the demimonde.

No, such overtures during her first kiss would be untoward. She needed to understand a little of what sharing his bed would mean for her.

"I was merely marveling at the fact you've never been kissed." He touched his lips against hers once more, this time taking advantage of her gasp and sucking her bottom lip between his. The noise she made on her exhale was between a moan and a grunt of protest.

"H-how did you know?"

"May I show you?"

"So when the next duke comes calling, I'll know how to kiss him?" As off balance as he suspected she was, she still managed to inject more than a hint of spirit.

"Exactly so." He equaled the tease in her voice but vowed there would be no other man. Ever. She just didn't know it yet.

He slanted his mouth over hers, moving his lips in soft nips and suckles. Her arms weaved around his neck, and she melted into him with what was unmistakably a moan this time. He trailed his hand from her cheek across her arm to glide down her torso, his fingertips grazing the fullness of her breast. His cock, which had never possessed a sense of decorum around her, hardened to rival a marble statue.

He shifted his hips backward, but she followed him, not allowing an inch to separate them. It felt too bloody amazing to protest, and he rocked his hips against her.

Arousing, earth-shattering, life affirming, sweet—words couldn't do the kiss justice. It was made all the more potent as her needy lips moved over his. She mimicked him and nipped at his bottom lip. He stifled a groan.

"Did I hurt you?" Her lips never left his, and he felt more than heard the worry in her question.

"No, but you are driving me mad." He dipped his tongue between her lips, a reconnaissance to judge her reaction.

She recoiled for an instant, her wide eyes blinking into his before her lashes fluttered shut and she fused their mouths. This time, her tongue darted against his lips. He gladly allowed her access and deepened the kiss, his tongue making a more leisurely foray into her mouth.

Her hands turned frantic, slipping under his jacket and pushing it over his shoulders. He shrugged out of it and let it fall on the stable floor, not caring if it was trampled underfoot by man or horse.

He shuffled his hands through her hair, unplaiting the mass. Her hair was soft and wavy and tumbled halfway down her back. The picture of her nearly naked in the pond flashed into his mind. He cursed the shadows, wanting to see the sun spark in her hair and the pale beauty of her skin.

They swayed as if music played, and he shifted them until her back was against the stable wall and her soft breasts were crushed against his chest. She wore no stays, and he could feel the hard buds of her nipples through the silk of his waistcoat.

He trailed his hands up and down her body from the curves of her bottom and hips, through the dip of her waist, to the soft undersides of her breasts. His hard cock pressed into her belly. His body reacted to hers like a callow youth exposed to a woman's soft curves for the first time. Yet because he was experienced, he also recognized the firestorm of passion between them was unusual and not something to be taken lightly or for granted.

Her breaths came in gasps. She pulled on his cravat and shirt as if she were desperate for his skin. He could have her on her back with very little persuasion. He could sink his desperate cock inside her heat and ride them both to ecstasy. She wouldn't protest. In fact, she might even beg him for relief, for it was obvious she had no experience with the passion set ablaze inside her. His cock pulsed its wishes.

He would never forgive himself if he took advantage of her innocence. With effort, he reined in the desperation urging them on. She squirmed against him, her nails biting through his shirt. A half sob escaped her throat. He shushed her, still sipping on her lips but softer now, soothing.

"I know. I know," he murmured.

"What have you done to me?" She let her head loll against the wall, and he couldn't resist pressing a kiss against the quickened pulse in her neck.

"We could only build this fire together, sweetheart."

"It's not always like this?"

It had never been like this for him. Want and need and caring inextricably bound. "No, it's not always like this. We seem to be combustible."

A laugh full of bite came from her, but she didn't push him away. "That seems about right. Combustible with destruction to follow."

"It doesn't have to be that way." He tightened his hold, hugging her close and kissing her temple.

"How else could it possibly end, Your Grace?" Her formal address cracked the illusion of intimacy. The silence built, and she added, "I would be destroyed."

As a child, his parents had taken him and Minerva to the seaside. It had been a rare journey together as a family, and Simon had taken great delight in the new sights and smells. Even a hint of salty air jettisoned him back into that moment. Used to the placid waters of the lakes and streams on their estate, Simon had been eager to explore.

His father had encouraged him to swim in the ocean. Against the calls of Minerva, who wanted him to come back to the safety of the dunes on which she stood and watched, he'd ventured deeper and deeper into the water, feeling brave and indomitable. A wave had crashed into him, tumbling him this way and that until he didn't know up from down. He'd thought he might drown, but the wave suddenly spat him out onto the wet sand.

That's exactly how he felt right now. Reality tumbled him hither and yon and left him short of breath and not knowing what to do or say. He dropped his arms and took a step away, missing her already.

How could he reassure her when she was perfectly correct? As a duke and a man, he would walk away with his reputation untarnished and no complications. Miss Blackwell, on the other hand, would be ruined and left to deal with the consequences.

"I'm sorry." He wasn't sure what he was apologizing for, and then he compounded the moment with a lie. "It was merely a kiss, Miss Blackwell."

She sighed. He'd disappointed her somehow and barely stopped himself from apologizing again. Or falling to his knees and begging her for… What? Her body? Reckless. Her heart? Impossible.

"I must return to my room before I'm missed, sir." She sidled around the horse and out of sight. The soft snick of the stall felt like the slam of a door.

He was alone. For now. But he would see Miss Blackwell again. For in the buzzing aftermath, he understood, even if she didn't, that what they'd shared wasn't merely a kiss. It was a reckoning.

CHAPTER 11

Jessica pressed her hands against her cheeks and ran to the kitchen door. Her slippers were meant for the smooth floors of ballrooms, not an uneven lawn with roots and rocks. The ache in her feet was nothing compared to what was happening to her heart. What had she done?

It was merely a kiss.

Were all kisses so intense and hot? Did all kisses strip away inhibitions and sense? She didn't think it was merely a kiss, but then again, she had nothing to compare it with. Was she simply naive?

For a wild moment, she considered finding Henry Mitchell and testing her theory. Except she was already certain she wouldn't have to fight the urge to rip Henry's clothes off to get to his skin. Her body wouldn't buzz as if she'd downed a bottle of brandy.

She slipped into the kitchens. Mrs. Potts and two girls were kneading dough. The cook glanced up with a smile, which reversed itself upon seeing her. Before Jessica could make good her escape to hide under her covers, Mrs. Potts gave the dough one last punch before marching over and blocking the entrance to the servants' hallway, wiping her hands on her apron.

"Did that rascal Henry find you?" Her whisper was low but promised retribution to poor Henry.

"Uh, no. He didn't."

Mrs. Potts's eyes narrowed as if she didn't believe her. "What's happened?"

"Nothing. I'm fine. It's a fine night. Everything is—"

"Fine?" Sarcasm twisted Mrs. Potts's mouth, and she examined Jessica from head to toe.

Were Simon's handprints branded on her body? Was her heart tattooed with his name for all to see? It certainly felt that way.

Mrs. Potts's expression softened. "If nothing is truly amiss, you should get yourself up to bed."

Jessica nodded and didn't hesitate to make her headlong escape, too frantic to even care if anyone spotted her. She locked her door and plopped down at the dressing table. The looking glass revealed a girl—no, a woman—she barely recognized.

Her hair was tumbled around her shoulders, and her lips were swollen and red. Her eyes sparkled with shock and desire. Her breasts were overly sensitive, still begging for his touch. She wrapped her arms around herself and rocked. No wonder Mrs. Potts had questioned her. She looked tumbled.

But it was more complicated than that. She hadn't stood mute and let him kiss her. She had been as much the ravisher as the ravished. She had clawed at his clothes and put her tongue in his mouth. She covered her face and curled over.

He was a duke. A duke who thought she was a lady's maid. She had ravished and lied to a duke. Was that a hanging offense in England?

After stripping out of the brown dress, she crawled under the covers in her chemise. Restlessness invaded and pushed even the hope for sleep away. Tomorrow, she might not need to blacken the circles under her eyes.

Her embarrassment succumbed to her burning arousal. Under the covers and in the dark, she touched her lips, still tingling from memories of Simon's possession, and then skimmed her hands lower to her breasts. He hadn't taken full possession of them, but dear Lord, she'd wanted him to. The glancing caresses hadn't been enough to satisfy her.

She groaned, hugged a pillow close, and turned over. It was madness. There was no way her connection to Simon led anywhere but off a cliff. Continuing to meet him as Abby Blackwell would lead to her ruination. She was innocent but not stupid.

Her only option was to quit pretending and accept her life as it was. Lonely. Desperate. Painful.

When the veil of sleep claimed her, she dreamed about her mother. Not as she was during her final, terrible years under Goforth's thumb but as she'd been during the years with Jessica's father. Memories melded with hopes to paint a picture of happiness and peace. Yet when she awoke, she wasn't filled with warmth but dread. Her mother's happiness had been fleeting.

She needed to set aside the tantalizing pleasure Simon offered and concentrate on avenging her mother and destroying Goforth before he bartered her away and got his hands on Blake. A liaison with Simon was more than a distraction. It could ruin any opportunity she had to upend Goforth's plans for her brother. Her vow to protect Blake at all costs was one her soul couldn't afford to break.

Even if it cost her a chance at happiness.

She rolled out of bed, her wan appearance a boon for her disguise. A soft scratch at the door signaled the arrival of the real Abby Blackwell. Jessica let her in. The maid was looking fresh and well rested, her hair braided and pinned up, her cheeks rosy, her eyes bright. Her duties were much reduced at the house party.

"How was your evening, my lady?" Abby picked up the brown dress from the floor and shook it out with only a slight disapproving glance. She opened the wardrobe and hung the brown dress among the rainbow of dresses Jessica had brought for the party. A rainbow painted by a blind artist.

"It was fine." Jessica stifled a yawn and a small ironic laugh at the unconscious mirror of her words to the cook.

"Are you feeling well? You look..." Abby pursed her lips and averted her gaze.

"I didn't sleep well. That means less work for you."

Abby made a sound that didn't sound pleased. "Have you considered actually *trying*?"

"Trying what?" She sat at the dressing table, and Abby began scraping her hair back into the tightest bun imaginable. A headache was already invading her temples. Actually, it would be nice not to have to lie about not feeling well to retreat to her room.

"You are prettier than any of those other ladies. If you married well, you could leave Penhaven and your stepfather behind. And take me along, of course." Abby gave her a cheeky smile in the wavery reflection.

"That would leave Blake to deal with our stepfather by himself. I couldn't. His constitution is delicate, much like our mother's." Jessica fiddled with a pin before handing it to Abby to jab into her scalp.

"He didn't seem delicate on his last visit home. He was boisterous and happy."

"Exactly. He is happy and safe at Eton." Jessica handed over another pin. "Anyway, marriage may mean exchanging one hell for another. A gentleman could offer pretty words to lure me into marriage and turn into a monster behind closed doors."

"The duke isn't a monster."

Did Abby know? Heat flushed through Jessica's body and lit her cheeks on fire. She would need her powder after all. "Why do you say that?"

Abby lifted one shoulder, her attention on capturing any stray hairs with the next pin. "He's very popular with the Wintermarsh servants. They say he is kind."

It was no small endorsement, but then again, Jessica already knew he was kind to servants. Too kind. Her blush intensified.

"I can't imagine marrying a duke." Except in the recesses of her mind, hadn't she imagined sharing Simon's life and bed? Instead, she spoke an actual truth. "I'm not cut out to be a duchess, Abby."

Abby giggled. "It would be rather intimidating to be expected to be a hostess. You've not much experience there, I'm afraid."

Jessica had little experience with anything. She remained silent while Abby rubbed soot into the hair around her face to hide the red and leave it looking dull. Then she pinned on the hideous mobcap. Jessica closed her eyes and tilted her face up while Abby applied the creams and powders that sallowed her skin and blunted her features. The padding was next and then the dull gray dress of a poor spinster.

"How do I look?" Jessica stood and shook out her skirts, adjusting the padding so there were no suspicious lumps.

"Terrible," Abby said with a sigh of disappointment. "If you would allow me to—"

"No." Jessica turned away from the looking glass. "That will be all. I won't require you again until this evening. Can you keep yourself out of the way and anonymous?"

"Easily." Abby stopped at the door. "I'm going to need another novel to read though."

Jessica should have packed more than two books. Early into Abby's tenure as a housemaid, Jessica had caught Abby pocketing a book Jessica had finished reading. Knowing how important novels were for escaping everyday trials, Jessica had not only *not* punished Abby but had taken her on as a personal maid and encouraged her habit. "I'll acquire one. I'm sure Lady Drummond has a novel I can borrow."

Abby smiled and disappeared. It was Jessica's turn to leave the safety of her room for an exhausting day of deflections and ruses.

If she had timed things right, she had missed the hunting party and was early enough to avoid the late-rising ladies. She might even be able to enjoy a cup of tea and toast by herself. The door to the dining room was ajar, and just as she was about to push it fully open, she heard voices. Jessica froze.

"You are utterly scandalous. Anyone could walk in." While Jessica couldn't be sure, the voice sounded like it belonged to Lady Drummond.

"You think you can have your way with me this morning, make me miss the hunt, and then not allow me my turn?" The rough baritone most definitely belonged to Lord Drummond. Then in a sweetly cajoling tone Jessica was shocked to hear from the intimating man, he added, "I just want to kiss you, sweetheart."

"It's *where* you want to kiss me that would cause the ladies to swoon if they were to walk in on us." The sounds coming from the other side of the door were only too familiar after her experience in the stables with Simon. Getting caught eavesdropping on the couple would be beyond humiliating.

Jessica slid her foot back to take a step away as Lady Drummond said, "That's quite enough, you wicked man. I'm going to make you sit on the other side of the table if you can't keep your hands to yourself."

Lord Drummond's laugh was as warm as velvet. Jessica had rarely seen him without a scowl on his face.

"I can't wait for this little party of yours to be over so we can have Wintermarsh to ourselves again."

"You would prefer everyone to pack up and leave today. No one will accuse you of being the most congenial host," Minerva said pertly. The tinkle of silverware had Jessica's shoulders dropping. She could enter the room without causing anyone embarrassment now. She took a deep breath and pushed the door open another inch.

"By the way, what is wrong with your brother?" Lord Drummond asked.

Jessica stilled the swing of the door.

"Nothing is wrong with him," Lady Drummond said. "What's that look for? He's fine. Even better than fine. He's more relaxed than I've seen him in years. *Someone* enjoys my parties."

"He's been acting odd. The past two evenings, he's disappeared to God knows where. I've seen him more than once wearing a puppyish smile, and I heard him whistling last night —*whistling*, Minerva—and then he leaves me to deal with that ass Goforth when he's the one who wanted him invited."

Warmth bloomed in her chest and spread out, reaching to her toes, which had curled in her slippers. Simon's smiles and whistling were because of *her*.

"If I didn't know any better, I'd say he was in love." Lord Drummond's pronouncement landed like a cannonball. Shock reverberated through Jessica.

Silverware clattered on the other side of the door. "In love? But with whom? He hasn't paid any of young ladies marked attention whatsoever, except for..." A lull descended. "I did see Miss Danforth slip out to the garden yesterday evening soon after Simon went for a smoke."

"Miss Danforth?" A shudder of distaste entered Lord Drummond's voice. "That girl is trouble. I hope he's not taken with her."

"What about Miss Tremaine?"

"What about her?"

"Was he lying to us earlier? Could Simon be taken with her?"

"I've never seen him with anything less than a diamond of the first water. Who was that woman he took up with a few years ago? The widow, Lady Kate something or other. She was a stunner." A thick silence descended before Rafe tripped out words, "Not as stunning as you though. You know I love you."

"Oh, I'm not mad." Indeed, Lady Drummond sounded more amused than angry. "In fact, Delilah and I were just discussing how deliciously handsome Damien Northcutt is."

With a familiar belligerence, Lord Drummond said, "I rather like Northcutt. Don't give me a reason to rearrange his face, Minerva."

Wicked laughter from Lady Drummond followed his threat.

Mrs. Devlin led Henry Mitchell and another footman around the corner with chafing dishes. Jessica straightened and stepped away from the door, glancing up at Henry through her lashes, but he didn't spare her a glance. It was reassuring and settled her nerves somewhat.

She trailed the servants inside. Mrs. Devlin and Lady Drummond were discussing the dinner menu, but Lady Drummond noted her entrance with a quick glance. "Good morning, Miss Tremaine."

Jessica nodded as way of greeting and eyed the sideboard, bypassing the sausages and kippers for a piece of toast with butter and a cup of tea. She hesitated, wondering if she could make excuses to dine alone.

"Come join us, Miss Tremaine. Most of the gentlemen are off in the wilds tending to their primitive selves." Lady Drummond gestured to the chair at her right.

Politeness dictated she accept the invitation. Jessica slid into the chair, and Lady Drummond pushed a jar of jam toward her. "The blackberries are from the estate."

"Thank you," Jessica mumbled, concentrating on spreading the jam as if painting a masterpiece.

"My brother and his friend Mr. Northcutt missed the hunt,

and I haven't seen them yet this morning. I hope they didn't stay up all night playing cards." Lady Drummond exuded casual nonchalance, but when Jessica glanced up at the mention of Simon, she realized it had been a trap to gauge her interest.

"Oh." Jessica cursed herself roundly in her head and searched for something to throw Lady Drummond off the scent. Assuming a priggish tone, she said, "Gambling is an ignoble pastime."

In actuality, Jessica knew little about gambling except the fact Goforth spent considerable time at the tables when he was in town.

Lord Drummond merely chuckled. "Don't let Northcutt hear you say such. Although he regards gambling as more a profession than a pastime."

He rose and bussed his wife's cheek. Jessica had a difficult time squaring the affection and tease and heat they generated together. What was normal? The happy ease between her parents, the domination of Goforth and her mother, or something akin to what the Drummonds shared?

"What are your plans, love?" Lady Drummond asked.

"My only plan is to avoid—" He shot a wide-eyed glance toward Jessica, who couldn't stem a small smile.

"I believe our plans coincide, my lord," Jessica said.

With a bark of laughter, he strode out of the room, taking his palpable energy with him.

Lady Drummond smoothed the paper sitting next to her empty plate. "I was catching up on the news."

"Anything interesting?"

"Prinny will attempt to tie up Parliament in the next session to keep his wife out of the country. Poor Simon will be banging his head against a stone wall. None of his measures will pass given the current climate."

"That is a shame. Many would be better off if the duke could see his vision enacted."

Lady Drummond poured each of them another cup of tea. "Considering your stepfather's views, I am somewhat surprised to hear you say that."

Jessica thought it best to answer with a shrug.

Lady Drummond dropped a sugar cube into her cup and stirred. The *tink* of the spoon filled the silence. She didn't seem bothered by the quiet, studying Jessica over the delicate rim as she took a sip. "Have you considered my offer to help with your launch in the spring?"

"My stepfather has made no mention of a season as of yet. Anyway, I'm not looking to snag a husband, Lady Drummond. I plan to remain firmly on the shelf. I have my brother to see to." Jessica drank her tea black, the bitter brew helping to steady her thoughts.

"I've seen women bartered for land, money, votes. I have the feeling you'll be married by the end of the spring season, whether you wish it or not. If you'll allow me to help, you may be able to steer your ship toward a more favorable pairing."

Jessica took a bite of toast. Even though the sweet-tart blackberry jam was delicious, she had trouble swallowing past the lump of dread that had spouted. The reality of a forced marriage hung over her. No matter her protests, Goforth would use her to his maximum benefit.

The walls were closing in on her. She had nothing to look forward to but a few stolen moments with a man she could never have. But she could have him for now. Her earlier decision to avoid Simon at all costs was forgotten. She would go to the clearing as soon as darkness fell and hope he hadn't given up on her.

Jessica stood, the abruptness of the motion sloshing tea over the side of her cup. "May I borrow a novel? I believe I'll find a seat in the garden and read a spell."

"Of course. There is a stack in the drawing room, or if none suit, an entire shelf in the study. Enjoy the fresh air and sunshine before winter is upon us."

Jessica inclined her head and made good her escape. Something told her Lady Drummond was merely conceding and didn't plan on abandoning the issue of her introduction to society.

She made her way to the drawing room and peeked around the door. Empty. She sighed and went directly to the stack of books on a small table in the corner. Shuffling through them, she picked one that looked suitably gothic and hair-raising for Abby.

The clack of footsteps in the entry had her glancing to the door, her only means of escape, like a fox on the run. Goforth entered, shutting the door behind him. "Good. I caught you alone. We need to talk."

"Are you enjoying the party?" She parried with a dull question, inching her way toward the door.

"I would enjoy it more if your wardrobe and hair and lack of manners weren't such an embarrassment. You have been a disappointment." He blocked her and set his fisted hands on his hips. She kept her gaze on those fists. They could do damage. "Why have you squandered the evenings by retiring early? It's unacceptable."

"Surely you don't expect me to compete with the other young ladies for the few available gentlemen in attendance. The duke is the prime catch, and he wouldn't be swayed enough by my scintillating conversation to make an offer." A tiny sliver of hope invaded her voice.

Goforth made a sound of disgust. "Even if he did, I wouldn't accept. He is the one man I'd never countenance, duke or no."

"Your pride is worth more than his title and coin and political influence?" Goforth and Simon's first meeting had festered for years, but she was surprised Goforth's greed hadn't trumped his bruised ego.

"Political influence? Bah. I would rather see you wed to a man who could take the duke down a few pegs."

"It's neither here nor there, considering I have no prospects and am not likely to gain any."

"You aren't even putting forth an effort, and I'm beginning to wonder how much of that is deliberate."

Her heart kicked hard. How much did he suspect? "I'm afraid I'm a dull, unaccomplished lady compared to the present company."

He hummed and considered her for a long moment. "I see now I shouldn't have ignored you all these years. You need to resign yourself."

"Resign myself to what exactly?" She forced herself not to take a step away from him. He relished her fear, fed upon it.

"You will be presented in London in the spring. As the sister of an earl with an attractive dowry, you will receive offers. I will pick the one who will advance me the most, and you will marry him. Blake is still several years away from acting as my emissary."

"Your puppet, you mean. Once he comes of age, he'll be his own man, and you won't have power over us anymore." Anger and hatred had burned away her usual discretion. She wanted to stuff the words back in her mouth, but it was too late. She'd unleashed the monster.

Wearing a brutish expression, he rolled his shoulders and closed the distance between them. She backpedaled, her hip bumping the pianoforte. The keys jangled. Cursing her weakness, she forced her gaze to meet his. He grabbed her forearm and twisted her arm, forcing her to lean farther into the pianoforte, the edge biting into her side.

"You're hurting me." How she hated the tremble in her voice.

"Good." Instead of releasing her, he shook her even harder.

The pianoforte accompanied the violence discordantly.

It hurt. Tears burned up her throat. She blinked furiously

and didn't break their locked gazes, even though it would be wise to pretend she was thoroughly cowed and repentant. Surely he wouldn't hit her? Not with so many to witness her bruising. "Let me go."

He shook her hard enough to whip her head back and forth and then moved to whisper in her ear, "You will never have the chance to poison your brother. I give you three years before you go the way of your mother."

Cold swept through her, her fear transformed into fury. She spit in his face. The glob trailed down the side of his nose. His utter shock might have made her laugh if she wasn't instantly aware of how stupid she'd been to react in such a way. The game she played was long and complex, but it could be lost in an instant.

With a grunt, he swung her around and shoved her to the ground. The fall would leave a bruise on her hip even through her padding, and his fingers would be imprinted on her arm. She slowly rose from the ground, rubbing her side. Just bruised, and she counted herself lucky. No blood drawn today.

He wiped her spittle off with a handkerchief. They stood on opposite sides of the rug like two pugilists between rounds. Goforth conceded the field, tramping to the door and stalking out. She rubbed her sore arm and attempted to even out her shuddery breathing. Her chin wobbled precipitously, and she had to concentrate to keep the tears at bay.

She had played her role poorly and might have forfeited the game. Her future had taken a turn for the bleak, which was saying something. Picking up the book from the floor with trembling fingers, she held it close to her chest as if she could protect her heart from slings and arrows.

CHAPTER 12

Simon strode through the front door, his destination the study to hopefully pacify Rafe, who was understandably annoyed. The object of his brother-in-law's annoyance stalked out of the drawing room. Before Simon could pull up, their shoulders collided.

Simon stumbled to the side but caught his balance easily enough. The greater mass of Goforth spun into a table with festive decorations. A vase full of lilies tottered and sloshed water across the Goforth, wetting his jacket, shirtfront, and cravat, which wilted with the damp.

"You ass. Look what you've done." Goforth's voice was low and threatening, his anger not born of the shock of the accident, but of a deep-rooted hatred.

Fair enough. Simon had long detested Goforth as well. It was, however, a surprise to hear the semipolite veneer stripped away with so little effort. "If you had but taken a glance out of the door before dashing away, you might have avoided a soaking."

Goforth drew himself up, his shoulders more bull-like than ever. "I demand an apology, Your Grace."

Disrespect dripped from the title. Goforth seemed hell-bent on goading Simon into a confrontation. As much as he wanted to oblige him by planting a facer between his eyes, Simon merely bowed with as much irony as he could muster. "I didn't sense your imminent exit from the drawing room, sir, and happened to be making my way across the entry hall. I hope you accept my apologies in the spirit of their intent."

Goforth turned even redder, but the sound of encroaching female chatter stemmed a response. He turned on his heel and made his way toward the staircase and his room, presumably to change.

Simon didn't feel like making uninspired conversation about the weather and ducked into the nearest room to hide, which happened to be the drawing room. He stopped short. Miss Tremaine started. She held a book to her chest with wide eyes and a face even paler than normal.

His first impression was of a fox run to ground. Considering Goforth had recently vacated the drawing room in a state of high dudgeon, Simon could guess why. "Are you well, Miss Tremaine?"

"Why would ask? Do I look unwell?"

"Not unwell, but a bit shaken." Simon stepped closer and noticed her hands tightened on the book. He halted still several feet away. "If I may be so bold, I ran into your stepfather in the entry, and he was overwrought. May I assume the two of you had a disagreement?"

Her eyes narrowed. "You could say that."

Simon found the tartness in her answer strangely attractive. Miss Tremaine might look the part of a downtrodden spinster, but there was a hint of the fire he remembered from so long ago at the inn. "I realize our connection is... tenuous, but you can count me as a friend. I hope you know that. If there is any help I could offer—"

"No, sir. I mean, Your Grace. There's nothing you can offer to help me."

"But—"

"No." Her voice was firm. In a softer tone, she said, "Thank you, but no. I believe I'll retreat and find solace in my book."

She swept around him. He didn't stop her. He'd offered aid, and she'd refused. There was nothing more to be done. Except keep an eye out for trouble during the rest of the party.

He made it halfway to the door to make an escape himself when two ladies entered arm in arm and lit up when they spotted him. Miss Danforth and Lady Ester. Now he was the one who cowered like a fox run to ground. There was nothing for it but to allow himself to be caught.

The rest of the morning passed in a tedium of conversation about superficial topics that didn't interest him. After two hours in the company of the two ladies, he still had no idea what gave them joy or sorrow.

Rafe saved him in the afternoon for a spot of fishing. Marcus and Damien joined them. It didn't matter the sun was too warm to tempt fish to the surface of the river. The time was spent companionably with many laughs.

Simon and Damien found themselves fishing the same bend in the river.

"How do things proceed with your fair maid?" Damien asked.

"What if I told you I didn't seek her out?"

"I would say you are lying."

Simon grit his teeth. Damien was too good a card player to be bluffed so easily. Simon laid his cards on the table. "Miss Blackwell is fascinating. We're to meet this evening, after my obligations and her duties, but I'm not sure if she'll appear."

"Have you bedded her?"

"Of course not!" Simon wasn't entitled to any outrage at his friend questioning his intentions. He did want to bed her. And more. Much more. "We shared a kiss. It was..." How could Simon describe it without sounding like a melodramatic milksop?

Damien turned to watch his verbal fumbling with a raised brow. "Only a kiss?"

"Yes." Simon let out a gusty sigh. "Yet it felt momentous. Like a wildfire. Or an earthquake."

"You're saying it was akin to a natural disaster?" Damien asked dryly.

"It was earth-shattering." Simon caught a self-deprecating laugh in his hand. "Although Miss Blackwell did mention destruction could follow our association."

Damien didn't smile in response. "She is a maid. You are a duke. I can well understand her trepidation. Men in power tend to use and discard the weak without a thought to what might happen."

It was rare Damien spoke of his mother, even as obliquely as this. Simon sobered. "I'm not anything like your father. I would never—"

"You are a good man, Simon, and I know you don't intend to hurt this maid of yours, but dallying with her could cause unintended consequences. You can't wed her, so what are your intentions?" Damien flicked his rod with the grace and precision of a panther fishing.

"I know I can't wed her." He refused to admit he'd dreamed he'd done exactly that. "My other option would be to set her up as my mistress. I would offer a house and servants and a generous stipend."

"Do you think this little maid is the sort to toss away her respectability for such an arrangement? And what happens when you do wed and get children on your wife? What would happen to Miss Blackwell and her heart?" Bitterness flowed from a wound from Damien's past.

Nevertheless, his friend had a point. What was Miss Blackwell willing to trade for her respectability? And was it fair to even ask her to entertain the trade?

"All I can do is make the offer and let her decide for herself." Simon shrugged.

"You say it as if she has a choice. In the back of her mind, there might be the fear you would retaliate if she refuses you."

"I would ensure she understands there would be no repercussions if she refuses."

"For all your noble talk of bettering the lives of the poor and working class, you are still ignorant of their true plight and their lack of power in this cursed country." Damien set his pole aside and looked Simon in the eye while he delivered the rebuke.

One reason Simon appreciated Damien was because, unlike most gentlemen of Simon's acquaintance, he offered truths, no matter how unflattering.

"You're right, of course. Advise me."

"My advice would be to leave the chit alone. You live in different strata of society and will never cross paths again after this blasted party."

Simon swallowed hard against a rising denial. Seconds, minutes, *years* without seeing Miss Blackwell stretched out like a desert.

Damien barked a laugh and shook his head. "Based on your hangdog expression, I can see you do not acknowledge my wisdom. I don't understand. Miss Blackwell is a woman like any other. Why can't you walk away?"

It was a valid question. Damien had never had difficulty walking away and not looking back. Simon wasn't built that way. His attachments were few and far between. A woman had to be enjoyable in and out of bed for him to be interested, and even then, questions of her motives surfaced. His title hung like a black cloud over many of his relationships.

"I can't explain why I'm drawn to her. It's elemental and

undeniable. We have more in common than you might suspect, and she speaks to me like..." Simon ran a hand through his hair and looked up at Damien with a chuff. "Like you do. No false flattery. Honest and straightforward."

"Bloody hell, it sounds like you're falling in... *love*." The distaste Damien imbued in the word set Simon back on his heels.

"I don't know. Maybe I am. Would that be so terrible?"

"Love leads to disaster." Silence swelled between them, broken only by birdsong. Finally, Damien rolled his eyes. "Obviously, you plan to ignore my best advice, so allow me to offer my second-best advice. Put the power of choice in her hands and abide by whatever she decides."

Simon put his hand over his heart. "Yes, of course."

"And when everything goes to shit—which it will—I'll join you to drink away your sorrows."

Optimism and hope took flight in Simon's chest, and a grin came to his face. Damien snorted and shook his head. "Speaking of a drink, I'm ready for one now. Let's go."

AFTER CLEANING up and dressing for dinner, Simon and Damien shared a brandy at the cottage before entering the whirlwind in the drawing room. The conversation was light and the atmosphere gay. Dinner followed. Minerva had seated Simon next to Miss Danforth. The young lady had been taught to flatter and cajole and steer the conversation to him whenever possible. Her company was pleasant enough for an evening, but he couldn't imagine spending the rest of his days speaking of such mundane matters.

He couldn't help but flit glances at Miss Tremaine, who was sitting toward the end of the table between the vicar and Miss Danforth's father. Both men were in conversation with the ladies seated on the other side of them. As far as he could ascertain, she hadn't lifted her face, much less spoken.

An apple tartlet with fresh cream was being served. Miss Danforth cleared her throat, and Simon returned his attention to her. "What about you, Miss Danforth?"

"I would love to hear more about your stables. Do you have a favorite horse?" She gazed up at him through her long lashes and licked a dollop of cream off her spoon in a way that struck him as pure artifice.

"I would rather hear about your interests."

"Oh well. I play the pianoforte, of course, and dabble in watercolors. I embroider and am fluent in French. Mother has taught me to manage a household as well." Miss Danforth smiled at the recitation of her accomplishments.

"What brings you joy and makes you smile?"

Miss Danforth's gaze darted to her mother, who was several seats away and unable to do more than give her daughter an encouraging nod. "I enjoy all those things."

"There must be something that makes you laugh or sigh with pleasure. Do you read novels?"

She fiddled with a lovely cameo tied with a blue ribbon to match her dress. "No. I suppose I enjoy dancing. Especially the waltz. Perhaps you would partner me at the next opportunity." Her expression was one of relief she had managed to turn the conversation so easily.

"Yes, of course." His foot tapped, his impatience growing exponentially as dinner concluded. If luck was on his side, he'd be able to slip out while the gentlemen enjoyed their after-dinner drinks and prepare for his meeting with Miss Blackwell in the meadow. A pang of anxiety rose. What if she didn't come?

While her absence might solve his moral crisis, he couldn't accept all they would ever share was one kiss. Fate wouldn't be so cruel.

Minerva rose from her seat and clapped to gain everyone's

attention. "I'm sorry, gentlemen, but there will be no after-dinner drinks served here. Everyone's presence is required in the drawing room. We are playing charades." Her gaze narrowed and landed on Simon. "No excuses will be accepted."

He cursed his sister roundly in his head as the group filed toward the drawing room. Lady Wyndam had looped her arm through Miss Tremaine's. Miss Blackwell would not be free to meet him until Miss Tremaine retired. As long as she was forced to endure charades, he would not be risking standing Miss Blackwell up.

Simon joined Marcus and Rafe in the corner close to a sideboard with a variety of spirits. He poured himself a brandy and listened to Marcus and Rafe discuss horses.

Minerva directed the game. She designated teams and coaxed people up to perform clues they drew from a snifter. Even he couldn't help but be entertained watching the ladies and gentlemen play the fool with such aplomb.

Minerva cast about for her next victim, her gaze alighting on him with devilish glee. "Your turn, brother mine."

Rafe guffawed behind him.

Simon quaffed the remainder of his brandy and shot a dirty look over his shoulder at Rafe. "Laugh now, because your wife is going to drag you up there to perform like a dancing monkey next."

"Never." The grim promise and thundercloud expression on Rafe's face did much to soothe Simon's disgruntlement.

Not wanting to appear churlish, Simon smiled and weaved through the guests to pull a clue. He read it and tossed it on the table with the others. At least he'd gotten an easy one. Even though his sister had banned the after-dinner gathering of gentlemen, it seemed most of them had formed a cluster with their drinks and weren't paying attention to the game. The ladies, on the other hand, were raptly staring at him. Even though he was used to giving speeches in Parliament, the intensity made him feel like his collar had shrunk.

The sooner he started, the sooner the torture would end. First, he got his bearings and gestured north. Everyone turned to look in the direction he pointed.

"Flowers?"

"A novel?"

"Draperies!"

Simon merely shook his head and mimed exactly what he'd spent his afternoon doing. Angling in a stream. Damien stood in the back of the room with a diabolical grin. The bastard could put Simon out of his misery at any point.

"Northcutt? Would you like to hazard a guess?" Simon gritted out.

"I can't imagine what you could possibly be acting out, Your Grace." Damien played the innocent poorly.

"Shush, Simon. You can't speak. Anyone have a guess?" Minerva asked.

"Angling in Scotland?" Miss Tremaine asked almost too softly to hear.

Minerva clapped her hands together. "By Jove, that's exactly it, Miss Tremaine. How did you know it was Scotland in particular?"

Everyone shifted to look at Miss Tremaine. She shrunk at the attention. "The duke was pointing north, not to something in the room."

"I'm in your debt, Miss Tremaine. You saved me from further torment." He sent a warm smile and nod in her direction. "Who is next, Minerva?"

"It should be Miss Tremaine, shouldn't it?" When Miss Tremaine didn't move a muscle to rise, Minerva went to her, cuffed her wrist, and herded her to the front. Simon was halfway back to Rafe and Marcus when Minerva said, "Not so fast, Simon. Miss Tremaine has pulled a clue that requires two people. As you are in her debt, come and help her."

He turned slowly to issue his regrets, but the words caught in his throat at the sight of Miss Tremaine's abject terror at being on display. "Of course."

He rejoined her at the front of the room and turned his back to their audience to read the clue. Samson and Delilah. "Minerva was probably hoping to give this to the Wyndams."

"I'm no great beauty, and you don't have long hair. How are we supposed to act this out?" Miss Tremaine whispered.

"Stuff and nonsense," Simon said. "If you allow the presumption, I'll pick you up in a show of strength. You will then pretend to cut my hair, and I will promptly collapse to the ground like a milquetoast."

"I suppose that would work." She did not sound at all convinced.

"The only way through is to brazen it out. The sooner we begin, the sooner we finish, and the game moves on to someone else."

Her wide-eyed gaze met his. It struck him suddenly how pretty her eyes were. The brown richly swirled with caramel and was framed by long lashes. "Fine, but I'd rather you not—"

He swept her into a cradle hold before she could voice her protests. She was lighter than he'd supposed she would be. In fact, it felt like he was holding a pile of blankets.

"Put me down," she said through clenched teeth.

He did as she commanded but included a show of flexing his muscles. Then he sat in a chair and whispered from the side of his mouth. "Cut my hair."

Miss Tremaine smoothed her dress down, moved behind him, and delved her fingers into his actual hair. A shock passed through him at the pleasure her touch evoked. He jerked his head forward. Miss Tremaine took up the game and pretended to cut his hair. He then collapsed to the floor and held a hand up as if needed help.

"Samson and Delilah." Lady Wyndam's guess came accompanied by a roll of her eyes heavenward as if praying for patience.

"How astute, Lady Wyndam. Very nice job, Simon. Miss Tremaine. Take a bow," Minerva said.

Simon took Miss Tremaine's hand and performed the requisite bow as if they were on Drury Lane. Miss Tremaine performed an off-balance curtsy. She gripped his hand tightly. Simon steadied her and glanced toward their joined hands. The sleeve of her dress had risen a few inches during their game. Dark ovals marred her skin. His first though was ink stains. His sister had often had ink-stained fingers from her tally books.

But no… not ink. Bruises. His mind cast back to the morning and Goforth's fury. He controlled his expression as best he could. Miss Tremaine retreated not to her chair but the wall. He kept her within sight.

The charades continued with Lady Wyndam taking a turn. During the clue, Miss Tremaine inched closer to the door. Goforth was in conversation with Mr. Danforth. His face was florid from drink, his voice growing louder by the minute. Gesturing wildly while holding forth with Mr. Danforth, he shifted and put his back to Miss Tremaine.

She didn't dally and slipped out the door. Simon glanced around, but no one had even noticed. He shook his head and made his way out of the drawing room as well. He was not so lucky. Minerva's incinerating glare caught him halfway out the door. He ignored her.

He caught up with Miss Tremaine at the top of the landing, cupping her elbow and steering her into a slight alcove alongside a pedestal with a vase of flowers beginning to wilt, a scent of rich decay enveloping them.

"Is there anything you wish to tell me, Miss Tremaine?"

If possible, she was paler than usual, her eyes enormous. "N-no?"

He cursed himself for scaring her, not wanting to rouse any comparison to Goforth. Gently, he raised the sleeve of her dress. He'd only seen a small part of the bruise. The imprint of all four of Goforth's fingers was visible in purple against her pale skin.

"Oh, that." Sounding strangely relieved, she pushed her sleeve back down to cover the travesty. "It's nothing."

"Does this happen often?"

"No." Her answer was firm even as she didn't meet his gaze.

"I'll call him out." He surprised himself with the declaration.

"If you weren't aware, it's perfectly legal for him to treat me as he wishes."

"It's not honorable."

"While I appreciate your concern, I do not expect you to defend my honor, Your Grace. Good evening." She slipped around him and retreated to her room. The door closed firmly in his face.

Miss Tremaine had the right of it. It was not his place to defend her, but he could corner Goforth for a discussion on the morrow. But the evening was now his, and his mind turned from avenging the honor of one lady to possibly compromising another.

CHAPTER 13

Once Jessica was safely in her room, she covered her face and took a deep breath. She'd thought Simon had seen through her ruse. *Is there anything you wish to tell me, Miss Tremaine?* The cold fury in the question had set her knees to quivering.

Relief had poured through her when she'd understood the bruises on her arm were his focus. He'd offered to call Goforth out. For her. Miss Tremaine, not Abby Blackwell. Why? His intense dislike of Goforth was unmatched except by Goforth's hatred of Simon.

A scratch signaled the arrival of the real Miss Blackwell. Abby helped her remove her dress and stays, and then Jessica fobbed her off for the evening after giving her the book she'd promised.

It took Jessica another quarter hour to wash the paint off her face and the soot from her hair. After loosely braiding the thick mass and tying it off with a yellow ribbon, she pulled on the same dress she'd worn the past two evenings with Simon.

The sight of herself in the looking glass stopped her short. She did look like a different woman. Not so much because of her clothes or hair, but the spark in her eyes. It had been a long time since she'd felt such excitement and... hope.

Hope was a dangerous thing. Despair inevitably followed, the void deep and dark. Her mother had fallen inside and had been unable to climb out again. She was a warning. Yet Jessica couldn't stop herself from reaching for just a scrap of happiness.

She slipped down the servants' stairs and through the kitchen, keeping her head down to avoid Mrs. Potts and her knowing looks and well-meaning lectures. Once outside, she headed to the stables. The chuff of horses greeted her. No sign of Simon.

A young boy carrying a heavy pail of oats shuffled out of a storage area, his arms straining. "Hullo, miss. Are you needing something?"

"I was wondering if you'd seen the duke this evening."

"'Fraid not." He continued down the row of stalls. The disappointment was sharp enough to bring a sting of tears to her eyes. The boy made a sound of surprise. "But his 'orse is gone, miss. Not sure when that 'appened."

The whiplash of emotions was dizzying. Could she find the meadow? After thanking the boy, she set off. The full moon gilded the grass along the path. Leaves rustled as if whispering secrets of the universe. The water of a large pond rippled in the moonlight. Reality receded. She had stepped into a magical world, and anything could happen with the help of a bit of magic.

The nicker of a horse set her feet moving even faster toward her destiny. Simon stood in the middle of the meadow, holding a set of reins in one hand and stroking the cheek of a horse with the other.

He was hatless and coatless, but he wore the same waistcoat from dinner. The sleeves of his shirt were folded up his forearms. His hair gleamed gold, and the horse shone silver under the moon. Jessica wouldn't have been shocked to see the single horn of a unicorn.

One step into the meadow might take her straight into the land of the fae, where anything could happen. Did she dare? She shifted, and a twig cracked underfoot. Both man and beast swung their attention to her. The die was cast.

"I wasn't sure you would come," he said softly, as if the same spell affected him.

"I tried to stay away." She stepped farther into the meadow.

"What changed your mind?" He dropped the reins and met her halfway. His horse didn't move except to bend his head to snuffle at the grass.

The truth was entwined with her life. Her real life. "I suppose I'm a fool."

His smile flashed white in a shaft of moonlight. "Then count me the same. I haven't been able to stop thinking about you."

"Nor I you." It felt good to finally admit a truth. "I even dreamed of you last night."

Her confession galvanized him, and he moved to take her hands in his, rubbing his thumbs along the backs. It was too easy to cast the complications of the outside world aside in the moonlight with her hands in his.

Rising on her toes, she brushed her lips against his. He dipped his head to increase the pressure of the kiss, and she met him more than halfway, winding her arms around his neck. Only then did he crush her closer and deepen the kiss.

This time she didn't start when his tongue demanded entrance. She welcomed him. Their quickened breaths mingled, and her heart paced along, pounding hard against her ribs. Arousal streaked through her and incinerated the few inhibitions she had left.

Simon skimmed his hands to her bottom and squeezed before snugging her against his pelvis. His touch turned her bones molten. She let her head fall back, and he kissed down her neck, nipping the tendon where her neck met her shoulder. Tingles skittered through her.

The iron bar of his arousal pressed against her belly. It frightened her, yet her legs rocked apart instinctively. He swept her into his arms and carried her to the edge of the trees where the sweet scent of pines hovered. A blanket was spread out along with a basket.

He laid her in the middle of the blanket and draped himself over her, his leg notched between hers, his arms braced on either side of her. His weight anchored her, and his face hovered over hers, blocking the moon and casting his expression in mystery.

She closed her eyes instead of attempting to guess his thoughts. He swooped down and captured her mouth in slow, drugging kisses. He hiked his knee higher until it bumped between her legs. Sensation tremored through her, and he caught her gasp with another kiss and an answering groan.

He kissed across her jaw to nibble the sensitive skin behind her ear. "You are so sweet, love."

The endearment sent a warm flutter through her chest. She could never truly be his love, but in this moment, she felt cared for in a way she hadn't in a long time. Even more, she felt *seen*.

A tug on the front of her dress had her tensing. His fingers were at her bodice, slipping one button after another free until the night air caressed her skin. He shifted to slide his lips down her neck, peeling her dress apart as he descended until he laid a kiss at the edge of her chemise.

"May I?" His whisper was gruff.

She could refuse. She *should* refuse. He would stop, button her dress, and not touch her again if she so wished it. There was power in the knowledge that what happened next was her choice. How could she let the opportunity for a moment of happiness slip away? As long as she remembered the moment and the happiness were fleeting.

"You may." Her voice was reedy thin with anticipation and nerves.

He released a long, slow breath before tugging at the ribbon drawing the neck of her chemise closed. The loose cotton slipped away and left her vulnerable.

"Even lovelier than I dreamed." His words gave her the courage to look down.

A shaft of moonlight over his shoulder cast her bare skin in silvery light. Her nipples were budded against the gentle breeze and under his attention. Her breasts ached, and she arched her back, not sure how to ask for what she needed.

He cupped one of her breasts and squeezed. That's what she needed and more. "Yes, Simon. Please."

"Hearing my name on your lips is almost more than I can bear." He captured her nipple between his lips.

The action was so unexpected, she jerked. His laugh sent warm air across her nipple. Her shiver turned into spiraling pleasure. He sucked at her breast while his tongue worked wicked magic. She threaded her fingers through the soft strands of his hair and tugged. His hum of masculine pleasure sent vibrations traveling like an earthquake to between her legs. He pinched her unattended nipple.

Never had she imagined a man would behave so with a lady. Except… she wasn't a lady in his eyes. She was merely a maid to be used and discarded. Squirming, not knowing whether to push him away or clutch him tighter, she asked, "Is this how a gentleman acts with a lady?"

He raised his head to meet her gaze. "This is how a man acts with a woman. There are no distinctions when it comes to love."

It wasn't love. It was sex. Even knowing this, she didn't stop him when he flicked his tongue across her nipple. It felt too delicious. As long as she didn't completely lose her head, no one would know of this indiscretion.

She ran her hands over his shoulders, broad and flexed with

hard muscle. His collar was loose, and she slipped her hands inside to coast over the bare skin of his shoulder and upper chest. Coarse hair tickled her palm as her fingers glanced over his nipple. It was a flat disk with a barely perceptible peak. Still, she couldn't help but wonder if it was as sensitive as hers. She tweaked it.

He grunted and sucked her breast more strongly into his hot mouth. Although it seemed impossible, her pleasure ramped up to a new level, and the ridge against her thigh grew even harder. He shifted fully between her legs, and the iron bar pressed against her throbbing core.

He rocked once, twice, and she raised her knees to clamp his hips with a throaty moan she barely recognized as hers. With a curse, he tore his mouth away from her breast and came up on all fours, still over her. The sudden loss of his heat and hardness was like a dunk in cold water.

"What's wrong? Please, sir." She pulled at his flanks, beyond embarrassment at her begging.

"Sir?" he asked on what might be construed as a laugh, but it was a self-deprecating one. He rolled off her and sat at her hip, his arms propped on his knees. "I refuse to take advantage of you."

After pushing herself to sitting, she tied the ribbon of her chemise with shaking fingers and closed her dress with her fists, the buttons too complicated with her wits burned to ashes. Anger, humiliation, and despair crowded out her arousal.

He turned and brushed her hands aside. "Allow me this."

She hung her head while he buttoned her up like a child. "I'm sorry."

His hands stilled on the last button before finishing and smoothing his palms over her shoulders. "Why are you apologizing? I should be the one begging your forgiveness."

She glanced up at him through her lashes. "Why would I need to forgive you?"

"Because I am the experienced one, and you are the innocent. Not only that, but I am a duke, and you are a maid. I fear I was ready to take terrible advantage of you."

"I wouldn't have let you take me." Was that true though? Lost in the maelstrom, she would have let him do anything as long as it satisfied the ache plaguing her.

"Tonight was supposed to be about wooing and charming you."

"Was this not the point of wooing me?" She gestured to them and the blanket.

"Actually, no, it wasn't," he said on a slight chuckle. "Believe it or not, I had something slightly more gentlemanly in mind."

"Only slightly?" She shot him a wry smile.

"Very slightly." He kissed her softly on the lips. "But let's not discuss it now. I brought you here to ride, remember?" After a beat of silence, he burst into laughter. "That was awkward phrasing. I apologize."

Jessica shook her head, unwilling to admit she didn't understand what he meant. "The offer wasn't a ruse to get me under the moon on a blanket?"

"As a matter of fact, no. Would you like to ride or eat? I brought sweet buns and champagne."

"Getting tipsy before climbing six feet off the ground wouldn't be wise."

"As usual, you are correct. Your lesson then." He stood and held a hand out to her.

She reached for him and tried not to think about what that hand and those fingers had done to her body. He lifted her to her feet with little effort and led her to his horse. On closer inspection, the horse had lost its magical appearance. Its coat was more gray than silver.

Her knees quivered, partly from his attentions, but mostly at the thought of climbing into the saddle. "I'm not sure about this."

"Of course you aren't. It's a new, scary experience, but it's quite invigorating, I assure you. Trust me. I'll keep you safe." His solemnness made it sound like a vow.

Were they still discussing horses? "I do trust you." Except her voice had lilted what should have been a statement into almost a question.

His mouth firmed into a frown. Was he disappointed in her answer? Her head was well aware that trusting Simon would be a mistake. It was her heart that was ready to make any sacrifice for him.

He stroked her cheek lightly with the back of his hand. "I will attempt not to abuse your trust."

Attempting not to abuse her trust was not the same thing as not abusing it. She broke eye contact and petted the neck of the horse. "What is its name?"

"Moonlight."

An incredulous laugh escaped. "You are jesting."

"No, indeed. She is the progeny of Starlight, the jewel of Lord Wyndam's stable. I paid dearly for her and have never regretted it. She's intelligent and gentle and a joy." He cupped his hands for her foot. "You'll have to ride astride, so throw your leg over. Up you go."

"But I might dirty your hands." Would he notice her slippers?

He threw his head back and laughed. The deep, chesty rumble made her feel like wagging her tail like a puppy begging for a pat. "Believe it or not, I've mucked stables, built stone walls, and trimmed the hedges. I can handle a little dirt on my hands."

Unable to produce an excuse, she raised her skirts and fit her slippered foot into his hands. Then she had no time to worry over her footwear, because he launched her upward. She clutched at his shoulders for balance.

"The saddle. Take hold and throw your leg over." His voice didn't sound strained from holding her up.

She did as he commanded, and her weight shifted. Her bottom hit the saddle, and she panicked a moment when it seemed she would slide off the other side, but Simon had hold of her leg and steadied her.

Simon fit her foot into the stirrup and thankfully made no comment on her choice of footwear. She shook her skirts as far over her legs as possible, which was almost to her ankles. The dress was cut for a servant's ease of movement and not a ton ballroom. Simon handed her the reins and made his way around to adjust the other stirrup. His touch was deft and impersonal.

"What now?" She peered down at Simon and held the reins in a death grip.

"Now I'll lead you around the meadow." He took the bridle and walked to the right of the horse's head, glancing behind him to check on her. The moon cast dappled shadows over the ground. After three circuits of the meadow, the tension holding her ramrod straight in the saddle receded when it became clear the horse wasn't going to buck her off or bolt.

He gave her rudimentary instructions on how to hold the reins. "Now turn to the left toward the middle of the clearing."

It took the lightest touch for the horse to shift directions. "I did it!"

"See, not so difficult." He stepped back and propped his fists on his hips.

"You let go." She tightened her grip on the reins, and Moonlight stopped and tossed her head.

"Don't panic. Loosen your hands. She won't bolt. She's too well trained." Simon touched her knee. "Would you like to take a short ride through the woods?"

"It's too dark."

"I know the way. Kick your feet out of the stirrups and scoot forward."

She did as he instructed, and before she could do more than gasp, he mounted behind her, snugging her into his chest. She swallowed at the feel of him behind her. It was positively indecent and highly enjoyable.

He took the reins from her hand, and seemingly without giving her direction, Moonlight set off toward a path on the far side of meadow.

Under the canopy of trees, only faint light shone, but the darkness didn't bother Simon or the horse. Simon's arm banded around her waist.

"Will Queen Mab or Oberon snatch us away, do you think?" he whispered while his lips glanced over her ear.

She shivered and let her head loll back against him. "I would love to be spirited away from my life."

He tightened his arm. "You told me Miss Tremaine is kind. Is she not?"

Hearing her actual name on his lips was startling. "No, she's kind."

"It's Goforth then. Does he hurt you like he does his stepdaughter?"

Her breathing became constricted. She hadn't expected her realities to interconnect so starkly. "No. I'm beneath his notice." That was true for the real Abby, thank the heavens.

"I saw bruises on Miss Tremaine's arm from Goforth's rough handling. You must have seen the same."

She swallowed and stopped the compulsion to touch the bruises before he began to suspect the truth. "There's little I can do except comfort her."

"He's a bastard and deserves to be whipped." The outrage in his voice brought tears to her eyes. The last time she'd had such a champion had been... *him* years ago at the inn.

"I have to believe Goforth will get what he deserves," she said.

"You have more faith in the fates than I."

No, Jessica had faith in herself and her lust for revenge. A light shone through the woods. She blinked, wondering if they really had found a fairy's house. "What is that?"

"It's a cottage Rafe turned into a retreat. Damien and I are staying here for the party. It's been a godsend. I would be afraid of what might be waiting for me in my bed every night if we were staying at Wintermarsh."

She turned in order to see his profile. "Are you suggesting young ladies might await you in bed in order to seduce you?"

"Or to simply catch me in the parson's mousetrap."

"That's rather jaded." She faced the front.

The cottage was small but charming, and a lantern flickered through the windows. A man-sized shadow flicked the curtains aside. Damien Northcutt peered out. Simon merely raised a hand and continued along the path. Jessica relaxed in his hold. She hadn't been sure of his intent, but it seemed he was as honorable as he declared.

Needles and leaves softened the *clomps* of Moonlight's hooves. "You and Mr. Northcutt seem to be great friends."

"Besides family, of course, I would count him as my one true friend."

Surprise had her twisting to study his profile once more, but the shadows were deep under the trees and his expression remained a mystery. "You are friendly and amusing and kind. How could you not possess more friends than you could count?"

"You are the kind one." His laugh was rueful. "I used to have scads of friends. Or at least, I thought I did. One of them turned out to be unworthy of my trust, and as a result, my sister was almost irreparably harmed. Rafe saved her. And me, if you want to put a fine point upon it."

"You were betrayed."

"Indeed. It cut more deeply than I can describe." He was quiet for a moment, as if needing to gather himself. "Afterward, I cut the hangers-on out of my life. I quit drinking and gambling and chasing skirts. I became the sober statesman you see now."

"Not so sober if you are wooing a lady's maid, Your Grace." As soon as the teasing words were out of her mouth, the sympathy she felt was replaced by disquiet.

If she confessed and told him she was Jessica Tremaine masquerading as a maid, he would never forgive her. His trust had been badly broken long ago and healed like a poorly set broken leg, leaving him forever hobbled.

"And what of you?" he asked with a lightness that felt forced.

"What about me?"

"Has there been an event that shaped your outlook on life for good or ill?"

His question cut to the wound she carried. She should make something up, yet what came out of her mouth shocked her, for it was the truth. "My mother killed herself."

He tightened his arm around her and brushed his lips over her cheek. "I'm so sorry."

"I found her hanging from a rafter."

"How old were you?"

"Sixteen."

He whispered words of comfort, but it was his physical nearness that gave her the courage to continue. He was a rock to cling to in the tempest.

"I screamed for help and grabbed her legs, thinking to save her, but it was much too late." The regrets she had hoarded slipped out. "It was my fault. I should have done more."

"That's ridiculous. You were a child."

Anger she had tamped down for years bubbled out. "It's wrong of me, but sometimes I'm so angry with her for leaving. That's sinful, isn't it?"

"No. It's understandable. You have every right to feel anger and grief and regret."

His absolution meant more than she could put into words.

Taking his hand, she pressed a kiss into his palm. Moonlight shuffled to a stop. Simon cupped her face and brought their lips together in the gentlest of kisses.

Jessica wrapped her hand around his forearm. The sinewy strength reignited the need in her belly. He broke away first, and only her pride kept her from reaching for more.

"Thank you," he murmured.

"For what?"

"For listening to me and allowing me to listen to you. Our burdens lessen when we share them."

As a matter of fact, she did feel lighter. Not carefree—she would never qualify as such—but it was as if there was room for something more than anger and grief and regret.

He turned Moonlight down a narrower side path. Jessica closed her eyes and allowed herself to simply enjoy his closeness. The next thing she knew, he whispered in her ear. "Wake up, beautiful girl."

She started upright and popped her eyes open. "What happened?"

He chuckled. "You fell asleep in my arms."

"Oh. I'm sorry."

"I'm only sorry it was on the back of a horse and not in a feather bed."

A blush ignited. "Your Grace, you shouldn't say such things."

"Perhaps not." He dismounted and left her tottering on the saddle. But not for long. He took her waist, and she slipped into his arms like a rag doll. "Our picnic will have to wait. You have to rise early to take care of your mistress."

"The house party is nearly over."

"I thought the week would be interminable, and now I don't want it to end."

She didn't want to ask what was next. Nothing could be next.

"May I beg a favor?" Simon folded the blanket and gathered the basket with the uneaten tarts and uncorked champagne.

"Of course. Anything."

"Be careful what boons you grant, Miss Blackwell." A wicked smile flashed across his face before he became serious once more. He gathered Moonlight's reins. "Will you look after Miss Tremaine's bruises and let me know if things progress in a more violent manner between her and Goforth?"

"What would you do if the situation did progress?"

"I would act to protect her."

Jessica was beset by a myriad of feelings. Chiefly among them was a warmth she couldn't describe, but there was a green spike of jealousy underneath. Jealousy directed at... herself. Damn and blast. Her masquerade was growing more complicated by the minute.

But as she'd said, the house party was almost over. Her grasp at happiness would soon leave her empty-handed. She couldn't give him up now. Not yet.

"Shall we plan to meet again?" she asked tentatively.

"I would like that very much." He shot her a glance. "There is a gazebo at the edge of the gardens overlooking the lake. It would offer pretty views of the moonrise."

"And solitude." Jessica might be inexperienced and innocent, although less so after this evening, but she wasn't a fool.

"And solitude," he repeated with a ruefulness she couldn't help but find charming. "If you would rather, I could meet you in the kitchens under Mrs. Potts's eagle-eyed gaze."

She laughed. If his plan was to woo her, it was progressing splendidly. The evening had been a revelation. Her confession had lightened the yoke across her shoulders, and she was certain his admission of past regrets had been unusual for him.

Of course, his admission meant he could never discover her true identity. Their liaison must end at the conclusion of the house party. Tomorrow night might well be their last evening together.

The stables came into view. All was quiet. The house and its occupants slumbered. He stopped at the edge of the path and set the basket down. Taking one of her hands, he linked their fingers. "Will you be all right?"

He was referring to sneaking back into the house, of course, but the question resonated deeper. For the first time in a long time, she thought she might survive with a piece of her soul intact.

She leaned up to brush a kiss across his cheek, the first bristles of his night beard making an appearance. "Thank you."

He squeezed her hand before releasing it. "Until tomorrow?"

"Until tomorrow." She scampered toward the servants' entrance, unable to stop herself from pausing in the doorway and looking back. He hadn't moved. She raised a hand in farewell, and he threw her a kiss in exchange.

One fact crystallized. Her childhood infatuation had deepened until she felt like she was drowning. She loved a duke.

CHAPTER 14

There were advantages to being an early riser during house parties. Many of the ladies remained abed until luncheon after enjoying the late-night revelries, especially since the week of entertainment was coming to an end.

Voices had Simon pausing outside the drawing room doors. If necessary, he would tiptoe past and beg breakfast directly from Mrs. Potts. Minerva's husky laugh mingled with Rafe's deep voice. Simon sighed and entered the drawing room with a murmured greeting, not surprised to see the Wyndams had joined his sister and Rafe. Marcus tended to rise early to tend to his horses.

Simon was, however, more than a little surprised to spot Miss Tremaine tucked into the corner of the settee between the couples. Coffee, his preferred morning drink, was steaming from a pot on the table. He gratefully poured a cup and added a single cube of sugar.

"Dare I ask what the plans are for the day, Minerva?" Simon savored the strong brew, already perking up after his long evening with Miss Blackwell.

"A walk around the estate this afternoon if the weather holds and cards tonight. I expect you there to partner with the young ladies. And then tomorrow we will prepare for the dance. I've invited half of Lipton, so it should be a merry time."

"I suppose I'm grateful you aren't planning to auction my hand off as a parting gift," Simon said dryly.

"I might consider it if you were in the dun." Minerva sent a nakedly affectionate glance toward her husband. "I've been known to make bargains with the devil before."

Simon barked a laugh, drained his cup, and poured another.

"You're not hard on the eyes, as I'm sure you know. You could have your pick of ladies." Delilah tilted her head and studied him as one would a marble bust before turning to draw Miss Tremaine into the conversation. "What do you think, Miss Tremaine?"

It was obvious the conversation was the last thing she wanted to be a part of. Dressed in drab brown, she sank into the corner like a mouse hiding from a barn cat. "He's not ugly, I suppose."

Rafe choked on his sip of coffee. After regaining his composure, he wagged a finger at Simon and grinned. "Not ugly. That's how I'm going to describe you from now on."

Miss Tremaine looked mortified, and if possible, she curled in on herself even more. "I'm sorry. I didn't mean to offend."

"Don't pay them any mind. You are now a fast favorite with this bunch for putting me in my place." Simon smiled ruefully, hoping to set her at ease.

A comfortable silence fell. Or at least comfortable for everyone else. Miss Tremaine glanced around with wide eyes and obvious nerves. "I'm sure when you meet a lady of appropriate breeding, you will settle down."

"If only." Minerva poked him in the leg. "The house is full of ladies of appropriate breeding, and my brother shows no interest whatsoever. It's almost as if someone else has already garnered his affections."

Minerva tread too close to the truth for his comfort. He kept his face blank and his tone light. "I'm waiting for you to provide a ledger with notations for each. Width of hips. Condition of teeth. Family history of lunacy. Anything else I'm missing?"

"A copy of her bloodlines from Debrett's, Your Grace?" Miss Tremaine held a hand up to partially hide her smile, but her teeth were straight and in fine shape, he noted.

"I concur, bloodlines are very important when it comes to breeding." Marcus banged a fist on the arm of his chair like a gavel.

Delilah rolled her eyes. "Then why did you choose the daughter of a cit?"

Marcus leaned over to brush a kiss over his wife's mouth. "Because, unlike Simon, I needed the coin."

Delilah shoved him away with a laugh. Simon watched Miss Tremaine watch the couple. She stared as if observing a rarity in nature. While he couldn't be sure, he assumed her mother and Goforth's union had not been the model of a healthy, affectionate marriage. Then again, most ton marriages weren't. Simon was lucky, or unlucky, enough to be exposed on a regular basis to three such unions. His sister and Rafe, Delilah and Marcus, and Lily and Gray Masterson.

"You will face the gauntlet in the spring, Miss Tremaine. Will you be ready?" Minerva asked over the rim of her cup.

"I won't be sought after. I doubt I'll even be asked to dance. Which is a good thing as I am a dreadful dancer." Miss Tremaine let out a small little laugh, but no accompanying smile.

"The country dances can be complicated, but surely you can waltz? It's all the rage."

Miss Tremaine shook her head, her gaze on her lap. "I'm afraid not. Goforth didn't think the expense of a dancing master was necessary."

Minerva popped up. "That must be remedied immediately."

Rafe rose and was at the door in a blink. "On that note, I need to ride out to the west pasture."

Marcus was on his heels. "I'll join you."

Simon set down his cup with a clatter to make his own escape but Minerva cuffed his wrist. "Not so fast."

"But—" He pointed at the door, but he'd already been abandoned by Rafe and Marcus. "The bastards," he muttered.

"If Miss Tremaine is to learn to waltz, she requires a partner, and you are an impeccable dancer." Minerva pushed a chair aside to leave a cramped space on the rug. "Delilah, could you do the honors at the piano?"

"As long as your expectations are low." Delilah sat on the bench and arranged her skirts.

"Come, Miss Tremaine." Minerva crooked her finger playfully, but her voice had taken on shades of a general.

Not surprisingly, Miss Tremaine obeyed but with obvious reluctance. Simon stood back while Minerva taught her the count and basic steps.

Minerva snapped her fingers at Delilah. "Waltzing music, but keep it slow until she can pair the steps with the beat."

After executing the proper steps side by side, Minerva gestured him over. "Time to try with a partner."

Simon stepped in front of Miss Tremaine, placed one hand lightly on her back, and held his other hand out in the classic waltz position. She didn't lift her hand to join with his. Minerva chuffed, stepped behind her, and lifted her hand. Simon captured it, expecting a limp fish, but a strength was hidden under the threadbare lace of her glove. He gave her hand a quick, hopefully reassuring, squeeze. It must have worked, because she didn't require Minerva's help to place her other hand lightly onto his shoulder.

Her gaze remained on her feet, so his view was the top of her white mobcap. His fingers itched to snatch the hideous thing off her head, but he didn't. He was beginning to wonder if her mode of dress was a defense against Goforth's attention. As long as her stepfather dismissed her, she could remain unwed and in the country out of his reach, both physically and emotionally speaking. While it had worked thus far, it seemed her time was up.

While Delilah hit the occasional sour note, the music was lively, and Simon found himself swaying to the beat. "I'll count us down, shall I?"

A nod was her only response. She was as stiff as a tree trunk, and he hoped not as rooted in place. He counted them down and then took a step. Miss Tremaine stumbled in the opposite direction, her face bumping into his chest, her mobcap tickling his nose.

Under the fustiness of her clothes was a lighter scent. Pleasant and familiar. She smelled like Miss Blackwell. Not surprising as they might share the same soaps. Nevertheless, the strength of longing was unexpected. Memories of the night before with his nose buried in Miss Blackwell's hair and his lips gliding along her skin overwhelmed him.

"No, no, no. You must maintain the proper form, Miss Tremaine." Minerva peeled Miss Tremaine's face from his waistcoat, and he tightened his arms to keep their form correct. "Try again."

Simon counted them off once more. This time, Miss Tremaine stepped in the correct direction and managed a few steps before tramping on his foot.

She broke their form and covered her face. "I'm so sorry. I'm hopeless."

"Of course you aren't. You are merely inexperienced. Don't give up. You've almost got it." Simon took her wrists and pulled them away from her face. "Believe it or not, it would help if you looked up at me and not at your feet."

Slowly, she lifted her gaze to stare somewhere around his sternum. Her mouth was tight, her lips thin, and her face paler than normal. He gripped her more firmly in order to guide her with a stronger hand. He counted down and off they went. She stumbled over the edge of the rug, and he slid his hand toward her waist to keep her moving when she might have stopped.

Something was off, but he didn't have time to figure out what. She jerked to the side as if stung by a wasp. He did his best to right her, but his efforts only sent him stumbling after her. He might have saved them both if it hadn't been for the ottoman Minerva had shoved to the side.

He didn't have time to curse, much less call out a warning. He shifted in order to save Miss Tremaine from the brunt of the fall. Without being able to brace himself, he hit shoulder first, his head thumping on the wood floor.

Dazed, he closed his eyes and dreamed of Miss Blackwell. She was on top of him, her hands running over his body with a frantic need he mirrored. Her fingers sifted through his hair, and her scent blossomed around him. He wrapped a hand around her nape and drew her face to his.

His dreams were often lurid, but rarely did they seem so real. He could almost feel her lips against his, soft and inviting. He slipped his tongue to touch hers. For a heartbeat, she responded in kind, tangling her tongue with his. Then she vanished into the mist.

A sharp, unpleasant scent had him shaking his head and rearing backward to escape. Minerva squatted over him, capping a vial of smelling salts. Her eyes were wide with worry and something else. "Are you well?"

His head throbbed, and upon examination, a goose egg marked the epicenter of the pain. Miss Tremaine was being comforted by Delilah at the drawing room door. He tried to fit together the fragments of the past few minutes. He remembered falling and then...

He pushed to sitting and winced. "Is Miss Tremaine hurt?"

"Not hurt, but shocked and a little scandalized. You kissed her," Minerva whispered.

"I *what*?" His gaze darted toward Miss Tremaine.

Delilah sent him an exasperated look and led the apparently scandalized lady out the door.

"You kissed her," Minerva repeated and then arched her brows and added, "With gusto."

"No, I didn't." As soon as the denial left his mouth, doubts assailed him. "I was dreaming that I was kissing—" He bit his lip.

"Who?" Minerva pounced.

"No one." He pushed himself to standing, his head swimming before finding stable ground. "I should apologize. Was she terrified?"

Minerva shrugged. "At first, she seemed to welcome your attention and then she… didn't."

Delilah returned without Miss Tremaine. "That was interesting."

"How is she?" Simon asked.

"Although most men think their kisses are devastating, I expect her to survive," Delilah said with a spark of humor. "I stashed her in the study for the moment, but I should warn you that a gaggle of young ladies are making their way downstairs."

Simon turned to Minerva. "I can't smile and make polite conversation at the moment. My head is pounding."

"Of course not. Go rest in the cottage."

The echo of high-pitched voices had him slipping through the garden doors without delay. Guilt mixed with incredulity. He'd kissed Miss Tremaine and enjoyed it. How could his subconscious have been tricked into thinking Miss Tremaine was Miss Blackwell?

The indelible memory of his evening in the meadow with Miss Blackwell combined with the weight of a woman on top of him. Really, it could have happened to anyone. He almost believed it.

Facing Miss Tremaine later would be awkward. An apology would be required. The poor girl had never been kissed, and he'd gone and shoved his tongue into her mouth. Yet… He hadn't imagined the sweetness of her tongue tangling with his.

He rubbed his temples. He wouldn't dwell on the brief moment of insanity. Not when he had another liaison with Miss Blackwell to look forward to. A liaison he planned to spin into a long-term connection. It would require subtlety and deftness beyond his capabilities to envision at the moment. Instead, he fell into bed, landing halfway between wakefulness and dreaming, his thoughts tangling the two women until they were indistinguishable.

CHAPTER 15

Lady Wyndam returned and offered Jessica a cup of tea. "I debated whether to pour you a healthy glass of brandy, but it isn't yet noon."

Jessica took the cup, her trembling hands rattling the china. She set it down on the table next to the cozy leather chair. Her heart was ready to leap out of her chest and run back to Simon. "Thank you. You're being very kind."

"I'm sure His Grace meant nothing untoward. He did hit his head, after all." Lady Wyndam sounded concerned, but Jessica wasn't sure if it was for her or for Simon.

"Of course. A man like him would never kiss me." Jessica wished Lady Wyndam would leave her to let down her guard, but she seemed determined to assure herself Jessica was not traumatized.

"Oh, I don't know. You are an interesting person, Miss Tremaine."

"I'm not well connected, fashionable, or attractive." She wasn't fishing for denials or false compliments. After all, she worked hard to maintain all three attributes.

Lady Wyndam smiled warmly. In fact, Jessica had never seen

the lady looking less than friendly and welcoming. "My husband and I come to London often during the season to do business. We count on the young bucks around town to purchase our horses to show off. I hope to see you dazzling the ballrooms with your waltz."

"You may believe in miracles, but I do not," Jessica said wryly.

Lady Wyndam burst into a laugh so contagious, Jessica rested her forehead against the supple leather of the chair's wing to hide a smile. Lord Drummond's study was surprisingly warm and welcoming. The scents of paper and ink and cheroots was a comfort. She would love nothing more than to curl up in the chair with a book and while away the rest of the day.

The sounds of other guests carried from outside the door, and Lord Drummond wouldn't appreciate her invasion into his domain. She rose, her knees still weak. "I believe I'll return to my room to gather myself."

Lady Wyndam's smile faltered slightly, but she didn't mount a protest. "Don't let this little incident rattle you, my dear."

Jessica merely nodded and went upstairs to gather herself in solitude. When she entered the yellow room, a man was lounging on the window seat, a sardonic look on his face. She stood in the doorway, not sure whether she should enter or run in the other direction.

"You'd best close the door before someone spots us together and raises the alarm, my lady." Damien Northcutt lifted one of his black winged brows, his tone making it clear he would not be the one to suffer if caught.

Jessica closed the door and slowly turned to face the man, not sure if he was friend or foe. What sort of gentleman turned up uninvited in a woman's bedchamber? A gentleman didn't, which only made the situation more disconcerting and dangerous.

"What on earth are you doing in here?" She kept her voice low in case anyone might wander outside her door.

He rose, his movements languid even as his gaze sharpened. She understood how he made a fortune at the gaming tables. His gaze eviscerated her to her soul. He peered at her, judging every lie and truth. She let her gaze skate away, unable to bear it any longer.

"If you come a step closer, I'll scream." Unfortunately, fear strangled her voice, taking any bite out of the threat.

"Scream away. It's only yourself you'll ruin." Nevertheless, he didn't approach her, staying to prop a shoulder against the wall next to the window, crossing his ankles and fiddling with the curtain tie. His casual, comfortable pose made her less so.

He said nothing, but continued to examine her out of the corner of his eye. The indirect study made it easier for her to gather her wits and reassemble a facade. "Do you make it a habit to enter ladies' bedchambers and foist yourself upon them, sir?"

"I have no need to foist my attention on ladies." His aloof tone held an edge of humor that was too sharp to offer comfort. "I'm not here to make love to you. Unless you are asking me to."

Jessica spluttered a few words and settled on an embarrassed, "Goodness me, no!"

"I thought not."

No amount of powder could cover the heat reddening her face. "Why are you here? Did Goforth send you?"

"No." Northcutt cocked his head. "But interesting that would be your first supposition."

"Quit toying with me." Jessica was well aware she had little experience with the games men such as Damien Northcutt was an expert in. In fact, she wasn't even clear on the rules.

"I ran into your maid. Literally, considering her nose was buried between the pages of a book."

If there was ever a time to bluff, this was it. "Abby is a sweet girl. I try to feed her love of reading when I can."

"Yes, so she said. She also mentioned how much she has enjoyed the house party because of all the free time she has had."

"At Penhaven Manor, she is often expected to perform other duties outside being my maid."

Mr. Northcutt pushed off the wall. Jessica tensed, but he only proceeded to perambulate around the room, stopping briefly in front of the wardrobe to toss a glance in her direction. She forced herself not to react beyond a tightening of her fists in her skirts.

He didn't open the door and continued on to her dressing table. The powders and greases she used in her disguise were out, but he merely glanced in the looking glass and ran a hand over his hair to smooth the wavy dark locks from his forehead.

"Simon has told me all about Miss Blackwell." He turned, and her relief was fleeting. The ties of her deception were disintegrating before her. "And that little myopic maid with a Northumberland accent and crooked teeth is not the Miss Blackwell the duke has been dallying with."

"Abby has her charms." Her mouth had gone dry, and her knees were wobbly.

"I'm sure she does for some green stable boy, but she has not ensnared the soul of a duke."

Ensnared his soul? Even as her heart kicked its heels in delight, she dismissed Mr. Northcutt's assessment as an exaggeration. "It's not what you think."

He flipped the lid of her face powder off. A puff of white arose along with his brows. "You didn't arrive at Wintermarsh planning to masquerade as your maid?"

Denial was useless. "I didn't do it maliciously."

"What is your plan? Does your stepfather want to see the duke humiliated?"

"No!" Jessica shuffled forward. "He doesn't know about any of this. It's complicated."

When Jessica said nothing more, Mr. Northcutt's mouth

twisted in a wry smile that was not unattractive. "I'm not a simpleton, Miss Tremaine. I can understand complications."

"Simon—I mean His Grace—came across me in a pond some weeks ago. I didn't realize I was on Wintermarsh land. Based on my attire, he assumed I was a servant and inquired about me at Penhaven. An invitation was issued to me and my stepfather so the duke could further our acquaintance."

"And by *our* acquaintance, you mean him and who he assumed you were. Not Miss Tremaine."

She jerked her head in a nod. "Our paths crossed the first evening here. I didn't seek him out or intend to pursue him, but it happened anyway."

"Are you saying you believe in fate?"

"No, I don't believe in fate. Or luck, for that matter, unless it is of the bad variety." She chewed on her lip before adding, "Nevertheless, Simon gives me hope things will get better. I know I sound mad."

"No, I understand." Mr. Northcutt's obsidian eyes had softened to shale. "You are lying to him though, and he can't countenance a liar."

"As soon as I tell him the truth, he'll hate me." A quiver vibrated her voice, and she looked away to hide the sudden sting of tears. "Perhaps it was wrong of me, but I decided to enjoy his company for the length of the party. Afterward, I'll disappear from his life and he'll forget about me."

Mr. Northcutt grunted. "I'm not so sure it will be as easy as that."

She agreed it wouldn't be easy. In fact, even thinking about not seeing him again tore her heart asunder. "It's hopeless. Even if he somehow forgave me, my stepfather hates him."

"Why could you not forsake your stepfather, whom you seem to hold in great antipathy, and elope with Simon?"

Her frisson of hope died as quickly as it had struck. "Even if he did want me after he found out the truth, I couldn't elope."

"Why not?"

If she defied Goforth so openly, especially with his enemy, he would torment Blake in retribution and make sure she was aware of every indignity. She would never leave her brother as defenseless as her mother had left her. "It's impossible."

"I see." What he saw she couldn't imagine.

She rubbed her arms, not sure if the chill was from the weather or her heart. "What are you going to do?"

"Nothing. For now." Although his face was as bland as his voice, she could sense a threat behind the words. "Simon deserves your trust and the truth. He is a good man and a better friend than I deserve."

"I'll tell him who I really am tonight."

Mr. Northcutt sighed, his expression solemn and without a hint of his usual wickedness. "See that you do. Or I will."

Leaving the warning like a guillotine ready to fall, he slipped away with the stealth of a man used to sneaking into and out of ladies' bedchambers.

THE EVENING'S festivities seemed interminable. Lady Drummond had seated Jessica and Simon on opposite ends of the table. Jessica had only stolen one or two or a hundred glances of him. The conversation ebbed around her, stilted and uninteresting, and she stayed silent. It gave her the opportunity to plan her confession.

The group moved to the drawing room where Lady Drummond had arranged tables for cards or dice games. Goforth joined Damien Northcutt at a table in the far corner where the atmosphere was more serious than at other tables. After their confrontation earlier, Jessica had no doubt who would come out the winner.

Simon had been roped into playing a hand of whist with

Miss Danforth and two other young ladies, but as she watched him from the corner of her eye, he pulled out his pocket watch and checked the time. Was he impatient to see her? Or Miss Blackwell, rather. Dread warred with anticipation.

She begged off playing, and as she sidled toward the drawing room doors, Mr. Northcutt ensnared her in his intense black gaze from where he nonchalantly shuffled a deck of cards. He inclined his head slightly and raised his brows, his meaning clear. She gave him a grudging nod.

Only when she was climbing the stairs did she take a deep breath. In her room, she washed in the cool, clean water Abby had left for her in the basin. After removing the extra padding around her waist, she was able to reach the ties on her dress. Abby had cleaned the brown dress, and Jessica slipped it on. She unpinned her hair and brushed it until it shone, braiding it loosely.

She checked her reflection. The woman staring back was familiar in the way of seeing an old friend after a long absence. She wasn't ready to examine what that meant. Even dreading the coming confession, she couldn't stop her heart from leaping in excitement.

She slipped out of the manor and made her way through the shadowed gardens to the gazebo. Simon had not arrived. How long would it take him to extricate himself from the revelries?

She settled herself on a cushioned bench, drawing her legs up and wrapping her arms around them. The rising moon cast an arrow of light through the ripples over the water. She wished she could relax and enjoy the night, but her nerves rose with every minute of delay.

The fall of a footstep spun her around, and she grasped the edge of the seat. Simon climbed the three steps to join her in the heart of the gazebo. "I'm sorry I disturbed your contemplation."

He brushed a piece of hair torn loose by the breeze behind

her ear, letting his hand skim down her neck to wrap around her nape. The strength and warmth of his touch was a balm.

"I was worried you might not be able to slip away," she whispered.

"The revelries rage on. We have Damien to thank. He came to my rescue and spirited me away with the excuse of sharing a cheroot."

"You told him about me." It wasn't a question.

"I did. Does that bother you?"

She decided not to mention Damien's visit and threat. Simon was lucky to have a friend like Damien Northcutt. Jessica had bumbled her way through the past years without her mother to ask for advice. "The two of you are close."

"Indeed." He joined her on the cushioned seat, his thigh pressed against hers and his arm snaking around her waist. "But I'd rather not discuss another man during our time together."

"What would you rather discuss?" An opening yawned, but before she could tell him the truth, he captured her lips in a slow, drugging kiss that wiped her memory—and conscience—clean.

"I'd rather not speak at all." He coasted his mouth over her jaw to nibble at her earlobe. She clutched his arms, the muscles hard and flexing under her hands.

Delicious shivers tumbled through her, tightening her nipples. Now that she had a taste for the pleasure he could bestow, she ached for his touch. Did he ache for hers?

She slid her hands to his chest. The rise and fall quickened. The need to feel his skin was a compulsion she couldn't fight, and she attacked the buttons of his waistcoat.

"What are you doing, love?" He laughed softly, but she didn't care if he was laughing at her.

"I want to touch you and bring you the sort of pleasure you bring me."

He let out a low groan. "You are tempting me to madness."

She pulled away. "Was it mad for me to let you bring me pleasure last evening?"

His grin flashed before he pulled her in for another kiss. "Last night was only a small sampling of what we could share."

"A sampling?" She tilted her head so he could continue his trek down her neck. It was his turn to grapple with the fastenings of her clothes.

"Indeed. I would be honored to introduce you to a more intimate indulgence."

"Will I be ruined?" It was curiosity and not worry prompting her to ask. In the moment, she was willing to pay any price to discover more.

"Your maidenhead would remain, if that's what you mean, although you are already thoroughly compromised." He parted her gown and slipped her chemise off one shoulder.

"Only if we're caught." The night air kissed her bare breast right before he did the same.

He shifted her to his lap, arranging her legs on either side of his in a straddle, her skirts riding above her calves. "You are beautiful gilded by moonlight, but I want to see you shining in the sun. Or better yet, lit by a dozen candles with your hair spread over my pillows. Would I even recognize you? What shade of brown are your eyes?"

"Plain brown."

His laugh rumbled. "There is nothing plain about you, Miss Blackwell."

Hearing the false name on his lips galvanized her. "Simon..."

His mouth followed the path of his fingers, which trekked down her neck toward her breasts. He hummed, and the vibrations sent her confession skittering out of her head.

She located the words with some difficulty. "There's something I need to tell you."

His mouth covered her other breast with the swiftness of a hawk. He hadn't even bothered to pull her thin cotton chemise aside. She squirmed closer, the hard length of him tempting in a way she'd never thought possible.

He slipped his hands under her skirts to her stocking-clad calves. The warmth and weight notched her desire higher. But he didn't stop there. He slid his hands up, stopping to squeeze her knee, and then his palms caressed the bare skin of her thighs. All the while, he sucked and nipped at her breasts.

Her head spun, and she wrapped a hand around his nape, seeking stability but only succeeding in encouraging him to drive her harder. He grasped her hips and pushed her back on his lap. She made a sound of disappointment, but the feeling didn't last long. His fingers coasted to her mons.

She tensed. She was bared and vulnerable to him, yet she wanted to invite him in. The urge to close her legs against him warred with the need of her body. Her legs trembled. His lips nuzzled her damp chemise aside to expose her breasts fully to him.

"I'm frightened," she whispered.

"I'll take care of you, sweetheart. Let me touch you."

She was incapable of an answer beyond tightening her hold on his shoulders and leaning into his touch. And then… he was touching her folds, slick with desire, and she forgot to worry about anything except the pressure building low in her belly.

He was a magician. It was the only explanation. While his fingers traced and dipped and slipped through her folds, his thumb worked the epicenter of the building pressure. She gasped, and he captured her lips as the tension burst and sent pleasure flooding through her.

Time passed. It could have been seconds or minutes or hours, but when she lifted her head from his shoulder, the moon was still on the rise in the night sky.

In the aftermath of the maelstrom, he sipped on her lips. His cock was still hard against her. If she were braver, she would unbutton his fall and slip her hand inside to offer him the same satisfaction he'd freely given her.

"I had no idea such was possible." Her voice was hoarse. For all she was aware, she'd screamed her pleasure for all to hear.

"And now you do." He shifted her to sit crossways in his lap. Her bodice gaped open, but she was beyond modesty with him. "That was, in fact, my opening offer."

She raised her head and pushed her mostly unbraided hair over her shoulder. "I don't understand."

"I can't bear not to see you after this week. It's been special. *You* are special."

"It's impossible. You know this. I will return with Miss Tremaine to Penhaven, and you'll forget me before you even reach London."

He threaded his fingers through her hair, undoing the rest of her braid, and brushed soft kisses against her forehead and cheeks and lips. "No, I won't. I've never felt this way before, and I'm not sure I ever will again. I can't lose you."

"There's nothing to be done." She tried to keep her voice firm, but it wavered with emotion. "You can't marry me."

"No, I can't." His easy agreement made her feel like a bird hitting a window, dazed and hurt.

"But that doesn't mean we can't be together," he added.

"Do you want to keep meeting? Perhaps at the pond on the edge of Wintermarsh?"

His laugh was husky and slightly rueful. "I'm attempting in the most obtuse way possible to offer you carte blanche."

"What is carte blanche?" She stumbled over the French words. Yet another deficiency in her education.

Simon framed her face with his hands and forced her to meet his gaze. "I want to escort you to the opera, the theater, museums. I will furnish you with the wardrobe of your dreams and a lady's maid of your own. You will have your own town house with a bed outfitted with the finest linens."

She swallowed past a lump of disappointment. "You are asking me to become your mistress."

"Yes. A most cherished mistress." He rubbed his nose against hers with an affection that made her want to alternately agree to anything he proposed, no matter how scandalous, or plant him a facer.

Could she blame anyone but herself? In his eyes, she was a servant, and so far below his station as to make his offer positively benevolent. For a blink of time, she considered what it would mean if she accepted.

Her own house with servants to see to her needs. No Goforth to lord over her. Simon would be kind and do exactly as he promised. The price for the gowns and servants and house would be ready access to her bed. It wasn't like she was against the notion of Simon in her bed. She could envision long nights together without a stitch of clothing between them. How many times would he bring her to climax?

On the heels of such decadent imaginings was a cold shot of reality. He would eventually marry. He would be required to bed his lady wife. He would have children with his wife, not with her. And at some point in the not-so-distant future, he would tire of her, and she would be replaced with another wide-eyed country girl. The thought was the twist of a knife. A mortal blow.

Then there was her brother. What would happen to him in this selfish scenario? He would never be allowed to ever see her again. She would be well and truly ruined. The price for pleasure was too steep.

She scrambled off his lap and pulled her bodice together. "I can't be your mistress."

He rose, his person looking decidedly rumpled. His hair was disheveled by her fingers, his waistcoat open, and his shirt gaped at the neck, the tails hanging out of his breeches. She was in an even worse state.

He cupped her elbows and drew her closer. "The situation is not ideal, but I would do everything in my power to make you happy."

"For how long?"

"Pardon me?"

"How long would we be happy before you tired of me? What if your lady wife bids you to give me up?"

"I can't imagine ever tiring of you. And as for my future wife… This type of arrangement is not unusual in the ton."

His casual acceptance of having a wife and keeping a mistress set anger and disappointment kindling in her belly. "This type of *arrangement* is not usual where I come from, sir."

"If the future worries you, I'll have a contract drawn up."

"A contract." Her voice was bland with her shock. "And will this contract specify how many times a week I must spread my legs for you?"

He reared back but didn't release her arms. "Of course not. It would detail a monetary exchange in return for your… favors."

"Your offer would make me little better than a prostitute." She jerked out of his grasp.

"What would you have me do?" He ran a hand through his hair, his frustration tightening his voice.

What was she doing? She was supposed to be telling him the truth. "There's something I need to tell you. I'm not who you think I am."

A noise whipped their attention to the entrance of the gazebo. By the sound of it, several people tramped closer, their masculine voices pitched low.

Jessica fumbled with the bodice of her dress, panic and nerves causing her to make a hash of the endeavor. Simon cursed and tried to repair himself as well. It was useless. The moon cast its light over them, lighting every corner of the gazebo. The only other option was escape into the garden. She would find a hedge to hide behind.

She made it to the three steps leading from the gazebo to the path. Her escape was blocked by three men. The scent of cheroots wafted on the breeze. The braying laugh of one man froze her. *Goforth.*

Simon planted himself on the step below her and shoved her behind him just as the gentlemen spotted them and halted. She peeked over his shoulder, the height difference making the endeavor easier. Goforth was accompanied by Lords Drummond and Wyndam.

A gleeful expression lifted Goforth's lips around his cheroot. "Isn't this an interesting tableau? The high and mighty Duke of Bellingham, defender of the poor and disenfranchised, is caught taking advantage of a servant."

She ducked fully behind Simon, trying to make herself small. Panic made her palms dampen, and she clutched the silk of his waistcoat, probably ruining it forever. His jacket had been flung aside during their lovemaking. If she could maintain her masquerade until she was free of Goforth's focus, she would put things right tomorrow.

Simon's voice was cold and stern. "Allow the lady retreat to the house, and we can discuss matters."

"Wait until your sycophants in Parliament hear about this little tryst." Goforth's tone was mean-spirited, but that was nothing unusual. "Your reputation won't be worth a farthing once I'm done with you, Bellingham."

"You think anyone in London will care that I dallied with a lady's maid?" Simon's dismissive tone would only enrage Goforth more.

"A lady's maid, eh? She's dressed more like a scullery maid. To sink so low, Your Grace." Goforth's tuts dripped a familiar venom. "It will be quite the on-dit."

Jessica straightened her shoulders and fastened her bodice as best she could considering how her fingers trembled. She knew what she had to do no matter the cost to her. With her chin high, she stepped out from behind Simon's back.

"Stay behind me," he said quietly through clenched teeth.

"You will say nothing to tarnish the duke's reputation." Her voice came out clear and with more strength than her knocking knees could claim.

"And what do you have to say about it, girl?" Goforth whipped the cheroot out of his mouth and ground it under the heel of his shoe. "You are ruined. Once your lady finds out what you've been up to, you will be cast out with nothing but the clothes on your back and no reference from your master. That's no less than you deserve."

"No man is my master." She moved to the bottom step of the gazebo, putting herself at equal height to Goforth. "Especially not you."

"What an impudent tongue you have. Don't you know how to address your betters, girl?" Goforth's meanness was legendary among the staff. It's why few were loyal.

Simon joined to stand shoulder to shoulder with her. "Don't you dare speak to her disrespectfully, Goforth."

"I wouldn't dream of it, Your Grace. I'm sure you've *disrespected* her enough for both of us this evening." The salacious meaning was clear and ignited a blush in her cheeks.

She could not afford to be cowed and lifted her chin higher. "I'm sure Mr. Goforth didn't intend to impugn his own step-daughter."

It was almost worth the hell sure to follow to see Goforth's mouth hang open. Only too soon, outrage replaced the shock. "You little slut."

Simon grabbed Goforth by the linen and twisted. Jessica cried out but had no clue how to defuse the coming explosion of violence.

Lord Drummond grabbed Simon's arm before his fist made

contact with Goforth's face. "Let's retire to the library to discuss this like gentlemen over a glass of brandy, eh?"

Although phrased as a question, the command in the earl's voice brooked no argument. Simon shook Drummond's hand off and straightened his waistcoat. Goforth's face was red, and he was breathing hard, staring with unmitigated hatred at Simon. Yet he nodded.

Lord Drummond turned on his heel and strode toward the house with Lord Wyndam at his side, not even glancing over his shoulder. He expected to be obeyed, and surprisingly, Goforth followed with nothing more than a few unintelligible mutters.

Before Simon could do the same, she touched his arm lightly, unsure whether she should explain or apologize. Simon gripped her wrist and pushed her sleeve toward her elbow, holding her bare forearm up. The moonlight illuminated the dark bruises Goforth had left there the day before.

Simon cursed and dropped her hand. "You lied to me."

"No!" She shook her head. "Well, yes, but not with the aim of hurting you. I intended to tell you. My real name, that is."

He made a scoffing sound, shrugged his jacket on, and brushed by her. She tried to keep pace with him, but he only walked faster and faster until she was breathing hard by the time they entered Wintermarsh through the front doors.

Lord Wyndam exited the study and sent Jessica a nod she interpreted as sympathetic. Or was it scathing? He disappeared up the stairway. What would his wife and Lady Drummond think of her once they heard about her deception? She deserved to be given the cut direct and worse.

Simon stopped in the middle of the grand entry and raised a brace of candles to study her from head to toe in the light. "How could I be so blind?"

"You weren't. I disguised myself with padding and paints and powders."

"Your accent."

In her panic, she had slipped back into her quasi-American accent. "I have a good ear and can go back and forth."

"Why did you do it?"

"I started years ago to avoid Goforth's machinations. He plans to use me to his own ends." The desperation she fought on a daily basis under Goforth's thumb infused her voice, but Simon seemed unmoved.

Lord Drummond stepped into the doorway and jerked his head in an unmistakable get-in-here gesture. He was as protective of Simon as Jessica was of her little brother. Would Lord Drummond rail and curse at her?

Simon stalked into the library, and Jessica had no choice but to follow. It was time to pay for the pleasure she'd stolen with Simon.

As soon as the door closed, Goforth grabbed her upper arm in a grip so tight she couldn't stem a small cry even though her reaction provided a satisfaction she wanted to deny him.

Simon shoved Goforth's shoulder hard enough to loosen his grip on Jessica. She backed away and rubbed her arm, although she was more shocked Goforth had shown his colors in front of the two men than physically hurt.

"Look at you," Goforth said accusingly. "You aren't an ape-faced hag after all. You've played me for a fool."

"It was hardly a challenge." Jessica didn't break eye contact with Goforth even though she wanted to judge Simon's reaction.

"Did you take up with him as revenge on me?" Goforth pointed at Simon.

"You give yourself too much credit." She was afraid of what she might see on Simon's face. Disgust. Hatred. "The duke is kind and easy to talk to. He understands me."

Goforth turned to Simon. "Did you dally with her knowing she was my stepdaughter?"

"No." Simon bit the word out as if the fact she'd fooled him as well was physically painful.

"The duke was under the misconception I was Abby."

"Was that simpleton party to your fraud? I'll have her out on her ear this very night," Goforth said.

"No! She's entirely blameless. It's all my fault. All of it." She turned her attention to Simon, but he gazed at the ceiling, his jaw tight. "I'm so sorry, Simon."

"Naturally, I will make an offer for Miss"—Simon tripped over her name—"Miss Tremaine's hand in marriage."

"Did you take the girl's maidenhead?" Goforth's crude question set Jessica's cheeks on fire.

"I did not, but she is ruined, nevertheless. I will do what's honorable." Finally, Simon dropped his gaze from the ceiling to her. None of the warmth and teasing she was used to radiated from him. His blue eyes were as cold as a January snowfall.

"There is no bloody way in hell I will allow you to marry her." Red crept up Goforth's neck.

"You would rather see her disgraced?" Simon asked.

"I would rather see her dead than form a connection with a man like you." Goforth's voice rose, and he stepped toward Simon, the threat clear.

Two paths came into focus. One would see her a duchess, married to a man she loved who would never forgive her, much less love her in return. The other would see her wed to a man of Goforth's choosing. Either path seemed intolerable, but if she chose wisely, only one of them would suffer because of her poor judgment. She refused to be the instrument of Simon's unhappiness.

She stepped between the two combatants and held her hands up. "There is no need for such a grand gesture as marriage. No one knows what occurred beyond the people in this room and Lord Wyndam. I assume we can count on your discretion as a gentleman, my lord?"

Lord Drummond gave a single nod. "Of course. Marcus will gladly keep your secret."

"You are refusing my offer of marriage?" Simon's gaze had sharpened, but the iciness had melted. "Wasn't that the aim of this great deception?"

"Whatever you may think of me, Your Grace, trapping you in marriage was never my intent." Oh, but she had dreamed of marriage to Simon. Blissful days—and nights—spent laughing together and sharing their burdens. In him, she'd found someone who listened and understood her. Or at least, it had seemed that way. At the moment, he looked at her as if she were a schemer of the worst sort.

"I expect no word of this incident to circulate in London to ruin Jessica's entrance into society. In return, I will not besmirch your name, Bellingham." As grudgingly as the promise emerged, Goforth offered his hand to seal the agreement.

Simon hesitated, throwing Jessica a glance she refused to meet, and then shook Goforth's hand. "Fine. This little indiscretion will be forgotten."

"Could you call for our carriage, Drummond?" At Lord Drummond's reluctant nod, Goforth took her chin in a tight pinch and examined her face and hair with the satisfaction of a man receiving an unexpected gift. "You are a conniving little thing, but your game is up. Your London season just got more interesting. Pack your things. We're leaving at once."

"Won't running away in the middle of the night cause more gossip?" she asked.

"No one will be sorry to see you go. I doubt anyone will even notice." His words stung with a truth she wanted to deny.

Once in her room, she sank down on the edge of the bed and covered her face. She was hollowed out of hope and happiness, the emptiness vast and forbidding. She laid a hand over her chest, but her heart was still in there somewhere, beating. After all, she was a survivor.

A series of regrets swirled. What if she could have told Simon the truth before being caught? Would he have been more understanding to her plight? Or would he have turned away from her no matter what?

Abby came into the room, her eyes wide. "Are you well, miss?"

She was as far from well as she could imagine. "We're to leave immediately."

"So I was told." Abby started packing away her dresses but hesitated. "Should you change?"

Jessica nodded. She refused to skulk out in disgrace. "I'll wear the blue gown."

She'd brought the dress on a whim, fueled by fantasies of dancing with Simon. Now she would wear it as she retreated to her personal purgatory. Once she was fastened in the gown without her usual padding or powders, she had Abby pin her hair into a loose twist, tendrils escaping to frame her face.

A footman arrived to claim her trunk, and Abby trailed him out. Jessica took a moment to take stock of her changed appearance in the looking glass. Her color was high and her eyes glittered with fury and grief. The blue of the gown sparked the red in her hair and the cut displayed her figure to its best advantage.

She wasn't a maid or a wallflower. She was a woman whose mettle had been tempered in the fire. The battle was lost, but there was a war to be waged. Lady Drummond's advice came to mind. She had weapons, and she would have to learn to master them before the season got underway. All was not lost.

All except for her heart. That would always belong to Simon.

CHAPTER 16

Simon paced the study. Sipping on a brandy, Rafe half sat on the front of his desk, his leg swinging, pity and sympathy playing equally across his face. "Are you sure I can't get you a drink?"

"How could I be so blind?" Simon muttered to himself.

Rafe took his nonanswer for an affirmative and pressed a tumbler with three fingers of brandy into Simon's hand. "In the shadows, I would never have guessed she was Miss Tremaine either, if it's any consolation. Did you always meet at night?"

"Yes. It was the only time she was free." Simon cursed internally. She had been busy not because she'd had to see to her mistress, but because she had been committed to the same social niceties he'd been caught up in. "I'm an imbecile."

"If you are interested in my opinion, I don't think she intended to play you for a fool. She seemed rather devastated by the turn of events."

Simon turned to glare at his brother-in-law. "She lied to me. She tried to trap me."

"She did lie, I'll grant you that, but she had you trapped and released you anyway. If Miss Danforth had been in the same position, the banns would be read this Sunday."

That was much true, at least. "Still, she is a deceiver."

"May I ask how the mix-up between Miss Tremaine and her maid occurred?"

The story showed Simon in a poor light, but Rafe had seen him through worse humiliations. Once he was done with the telling, Rafe said, "Minerva did wonder at your sudden interest in Miss Tremaine."

"I can't believe I never suspected…" But he had, hadn't he? At least subconsciously. Their waltzing lesson had devolved into a kiss. A kiss Miss Tremaine had welcomed. Simon had put the literal slip of his tongue down to her scent, but it had been more than that. He recalled the glittering defiance in her eyes when he'd confronted her about the bruises Goforth had left.

"Miss Tremaine has taken great pains to disguise her beauty, and from what I inferred from Goforth's comments, this little deception has been going on long before this house party." Rafe raised a brow and took a sip.

Shock had held Simon in its grasp for most of the exchange, and he'd been focused more on his own grievances and hurts. "Tell me your impression of the situation."

"Goforth was as surprised as you at Miss Tremaine's transformation. After everyone agreed to hush up the indiscretion, he turned almost gleeful. He is planning to use her, which is exactly what she was attempting to avoid, if you ask me." Rafe peered at Simon from under his lashes with a wry smile. "And indeed, I predict the transformed Miss Tremaine will attract much notice in London during the upcoming season. The right match will garner Goforth a foothold plus power."

Simon tried not to care Miss Blackwell—no, Miss Tremaine—would be bartered off for Goforth's gain. She had lied to him. *Lied*. It was a sin he could not forgive.

A commotion came from outside the library. Simon put his brandy glass down and went to investigate, Rafe on his heels.

Minerva was pacing Goforth down the stairs, a flower-patterned brocade dressing gown cinched tightly about her waist. "But, my good sir, it would make more sense to wait until morning. Travel will be slow in the dark."

"The moon is full and high. I expect we'll make it back to the manor house before dawn breaks." Goforth caught sight of Simon. "I refuse to spend another night under the same roof as that devil."

Minerva shot them a questioning, exasperated look. Rafe slipped his arm around Minerva's waist and drew her out of the way of the footman who was carrying down a trunk, his wig askew from being roused to duty.

"Let them depart," Rafe said quietly.

"But what about—" Minerva gasped. "Is that Miss Tremaine?"

The woman descending the staircase was indeed Miss Tremaine, but she looked nothing like the dour-faced oddity skirting the edges of the party. Neither did she embody the Miss Blackwell Simon had come to know. She was both of those women, and yet someone else entirely.

She had molted and emerged as a butterfly. No, not a butterfly. Her spine was steel and her aura that of a warrior princess sans her sword.

Her frock was a cornflower blue with a scooped neckline edged in white. The thin cotton emphasized the curve of her bosom and trim figure. Her brown hair glinted red and was pinned up in a style popular with the ton ladies. He'd sifted his fingers through her hair and grasped it as a lover would. He caught glimpses of her well-turned ankles. Ankles he had grasped in his hands as she writhed on his lap.

Goforth waited at the door, impatience and aggression his calling cards. Cuthbertson, Wintermarsh's elderly butler, wisely gave Goforth wide berth and stood to the side in his dressing gown and with his white hair standing on end.

Miss Tremaine paused for a moment in front of Simon, Rafe, and Minerva, but she didn't face them. Her profile was strong and her chin firm. She had even altered her features to play the wallflower. Simon shook his head, attempting to square her motivation with his resentment.

It wasn't to him but Minerva she directed her words. "I apologize for the uproar of our departure, Lady Drummond. I hope you'll forgive me. For everything."

"My dear, there is nothing to forgive." Minerva stepped forward to take Jessica's hand. "I'm not sure what has happened this evening. I presume a great deal that I'm unaware of, but I hope you know you can count me as a friend."

"That's very kind of you, Lady Drummond, but you should speak with your brother before offering such a boon." Jessica extricated her hand and swept her gaze to Simon.

The spin of his world slowed. He forgot about his sister and Goforth and the hovering servants. *Jessica*. Her name sifted through his head, taking the place of any other. In her eyes, he saw his own pain reflected. He recognized the woman he'd wooed every evening, but he could also see her veneer of awkwardness wasn't fake.

The vulnerability unpinning her undeniable strength distracted him from climbing onto his high horse, and he had a difficult time remembering why he was angry.

"Be well, Si—Your Grace. You shan't be troubled by me again. I would ask you to forget me and seek happiness elsewhere." She walked away and didn't look back, disappearing into the night, dragging his heart in her wake whether she wanted it or not.

The door closed behind Jessica and Goforth, but no one moved or said a word until the crunch of gravel under carriage wheels faded.

Minerva whirled on Simon. "What on earth happened?"

Rafe gestured for them to repair to the study for a modicum of privacy. "Get yourself to bed, Bertie," Rafe called to the butler. "I don't expect any more nighttime exits."

Minerva paced in front of the desk, and Simon took up his half-finished brandy glass to down the contents in one swallow. The burn did little to cauterize the wound inside his chest where his heart formerly resided.

"Someone start talking." Minerva stopped, propped her hands on her hips, and darted searing glances between him and Rafe.

Rafe, the coward, retreated to the sideboard and presented his back to pour another drink.

Simon opened his mouth, closed it, and then settled on a vague truth. "It's complicated."

Rafe returned, pressed the drink into Minerva's hand, and guided her to a chair. "Sit, listen, and don't judge, love."

Simon almost apologized for thinking Rafe a coward. His brother-in-law was a saint among men. In a halting voice, Simon laid out the story from the moment he spotted Jessica in the pond earlier in the summer to her closing the door with a painful finality.

When he was finished, Minerva blinked and sipped at the brandy. "Everything makes much more sense now."

"How so?" Simon asked.

"There were moments I saw flashes of a very pretty woman under Miss Tremaine's costume. She put on the act of a dullard and mostly succeeded unless one looked closely. You sensed she wasn't as staid and dour as she put on too, didn't you, Simon?"

"Yes, but I didn't connect her to the woman I thought was her maid. I'm a fool."

Minerva shrugged. "Every man—and woman—in love is sometimes a fool, brother."

"I'm not— I can't be— The woman lied to me." Not only had

she lied about her name and circumstances, but now Simon was questioning the tales about her father and mother and brother. Was any of it true?

"A sin, yes, but is it so unforgiveable considering her circumstances? Her path crossing with you in such a way was probably more than she could resist. You would have never paid her any attention whatsoever as the Miss Tremaine you met in the glare of my drawing room. As a simple maid, however, she could enchant you in the moonlight."

His confusion was an unusual and uncomfortable state of being. Even as he longed for what his sister and Rafe enjoyed, he had avoided messy entanglements. Until now. "There's something I neglected to confess. Quite full of smug benevolence, I offered to make her my mistress."

Minerva groaned and covered her face. "Did she plant you a facer?"

"Shockingly, no. In fact, she seemed to consider my offer with the seriousness in which it was delivered."

Minerva dropped her hand to her lap. "That's interesting."

"Is it?"

"It means her situation is more dire than we are crediting. Goforth has a temper and could do something rash." Minerva twisted in her seat. "What do you think, Rafe?"

"Goforth may be a brute, but he is an ambitious one. Now she has been revealed to possess beauty, her worth has risen exponentially, and he will want to keep her hale for her debut."

"What do you wish to do, Simon?" Minerva asked gently.

"I wish to go to sleep and forget this blasted night ever happened." He crossed to the door and paused with his hand on the latch. "And then tomorrow, I'll ride for Penhaven and offer my hand to Jessica once more."

CHAPTER 17

Six Months Later...

Jessica sipped on a glass of lemonade and swayed slightly to the music being played by an eight-piece orchestra from a squat balcony over the ballroom. A quadrille was in progress, and after her dancing lessons, Jessica could complete the steps with her eyes closed. She could also waltz and reel and perform any number of country dances.

Her frock was made of sheer white muslin heavily embroidered around the bodice and hem with looping flowers and vines in a matching white. The neckline was low, and the sleeves puffs of the same shear white. The only color breaking the unrelenting white was a dark blue ribbon under her bosom to add emphasis to the display of flesh above it. The dichotomy of the virginal white with the expanse of her décolletage had given her pause, but as all the young women were on similar display, she didn't feel out of sorts.

In fact, she was so like all the other young debutantes, it was a simple thing to hide herself among them. If it weren't for her stepfather, that is. He was determined to see her on display like she was a mare to bid on at Tattersalls.

For the moment though, she had escaped and taken refuge behind a faux pillar. A white-wigged butler in black-and-yellow silk livery stood at the entrance of the ballroom and announced new arrivals. The crush had grown to the point where the volume of voices layered on top of the music made it difficult to hear him, but she could see all the entrance.

When Lord and Lady Drummond stepped through the door, she wearing a smile, he a scowl, Jessica's heart pounded faster. Would Simon accompany them? She ducked behind the pillar until her sense came back. It was foolish to become excited by the thought.

Simon had no desire to see her. She'd seen to that. It had been months since the debacle at the Drummond's house party. While Simon had made a determined effort to see her afterward, she'd rebuffed him just as determinedly. Her final note had been more than brusque. It had been heartbreakingly rude, in fact. She'd had to rewrite it twice, because her tears had smudged the ink and spotted the paper.

Her note had worked. Simon's visits ceased. She spent the winter reassembling her heart and focused on navigating her London debut. The game had changed, and she had to adjust her strategy.

Blake had come home at the end of Michaelmas term. While his company had been welcome, Goforth had used the visit to remind Jessica exactly what her cooperation was buying—a continued education for Blake at Eton away from Goforth. If she balked at his plans, Goforth threatened to pull Blake home and personally take him under his wing.

No doubt Goforth's education would include corporal punishment for any slight or infraction. Blake was a sweet boy, with their mother's dreamy disposition. His interests ran toward poetry and literature over political aspirations. Jessica would not allow Goforth to corrupt him as he had their mother.

A throat cleared behind her, and she whirled around. Sir

Benedict Pennington stood awkwardly, his eyes wide and blinking. "I believe I have claimed the next dance, Miss Tremaine. You didn't forget, did you?"

"Oh yes. Of course. I mean of course I didn't forget." She tried to imagine the man as her husband and shuddered.

Sir Benedict was one of Goforth's cronies and thirty years her senior. His figure was gusseted and corseted to disguise the creep of middle age. Thinning hair couldn't hide the shine of his pate under the glow of the hundreds of candles lighting the room.

She put her hand in his, thankful for the barrier of their gloves. The last time she had received him in their drawing room, he had taken her bare hand in his sweaty palm and pressed a sloppy kiss on the back before she could react.

Jessica lay a hand lightly on Sir Benedict's forearm and allowed him to lead her to the floor. She took her spot across from him in a line of similarly white-clad young ladies. While the first strains of music lilted from overhead, Jessica's gaze clashed with Lady Drummond's.

All her lessons flew out of her head, and she stumbled over the first steps of the dance. Instead of looking at her partner like she'd been taught, she stared at the Drummonds. Were they furious with her? Not only had she brought embarrassment down on their house party, but she'd treated Simon terribly. She deserved to be given the cut direct.

But that's not what she saw in Lady Drummond's expression. She wore a slight smile and regarded Jessica with a warmth she didn't deserve. She snapped her attention back to Sir Benedict. Apparently, he had asked her something and was currently expecting a reply.

"Erm... Yes, of course," she said, hoping it was something about the weather.

"Excellent! I'm happy to hear it." Sir Benedict broke into a grin that highlighted gaps where teeth had once resided.

Thankfully, the dance spun her out of his immediate sphere, and she made trite conversation with a gentleman who briefly claimed her hand before she was returned to Sir Benedict. She spent the remaining long minutes of the dance smiling and nodding and wondering what she had agreed with. Nothing so serious as her hand in marriage, she prayed. At the conclusion of the dance, she dipped into a curtsey.

Between the last strains of music and the start of chatter, the butler intoned from the doorway, "His Grace, the Duke of Bellingham."

Simon stood on the threshold, adjusting his cuffs and scanning the crush. The sea of young debutantes on the dance floor seemed to take a coordinated step toward him. Except for Jessica. She was desperate for an escape.

Could she plead a megrim or a tummy ache? Goforth would never allow her to leave early. Not at her very first ball. The musicales and routs she'd attended thus far had been practice for tonight. He expected her to expand her connections through dancing and flirting. Neither of which she could do from behind her faux pillar. Yet that's where she headed.

Simon looked exceedingly handsome in a dark green velvet jacket, silver striped waistcoat, and black breeches. His shoulders were as broad as ever and his hair burnished to the same gold. Yet he did look different somehow. It took several minutes of furtive study to decide where there used to be a spark of humor was only a dull coldness.

Damien Northcutt approached Simon from the crowd and drew him into the scrum and out of sight. She took a step back and trod on a foot.

"Oh dear. Pardon me." Jessica made her apology while turning, freezing when she saw who she'd stepped on.

Lady Drummond smiled through a slight wince. "It is I who should apologize. I sneaked up behind you to see who the object of your attention might be."

The heat rushing into Jessica's face was like running up the flag of surrender. Any denial now would look foolish. "I hope your brother is doing well."

"He is barely tolerable." Lady Drummond cocked her head, her voice warmly sympathetic. "And how are you?"

"I am… barely tolerable as well." Jessica blinked hard to stave off the rising tears. She thought she'd prepared herself for the eventuality of seeing Simon again, but the reality was a punch to the chest.

Lady Drummond pressed her lips together and appeared to want to say more on the subject, yet she only asked, "Who was the gentleman you shared a dance with?"

A shallow shuddery breath returned a small portion of her composure. "A friend of my stepfather."

"A suitor for your hand?"

"It appears so." Jessica tried to sound nonchalant, but it came out defeated. Even though she was far from giving up, her options were narrowing at a rapid pace.

The music of a waltz coursed through the room, and ladies and gentlemen rushed to the floor. Lady Drummond's attention shifted over Jessica's shoulder, and her mouth tightened. Curiosity had Jessica shifting around to see what had caught Lady Drummond's ire.

She stepped closer to the dance floor, forgetting about her need to hide. Simon waltzing was a mesmerizing sight. He was graceful but led with an undeniable strength. It took a circuit around the room for Jessica to notice the woman he whirled in his arms.

The skirts of her low-cut dark red gown swished against his legs. The curves of her décolletage were pale and creamy. In contrast, her hair was black and sleekly arranged off her graceful neck. The lady was several years older than Jessica and beautiful in a way that made her feel more gauche than ever.

As they made a turn close to where she stood, the lady

laughed throatily at something he whispered close to her ear—a sensuous, inviting sound. Jessica had no doubt the lady would be happily waiting in his bed tonight if he so desired. And it appeared he desired her very much.

The lung-crushing jealousy made her feel light-headed. That fact she had no right to the emotion only made it worse. The tart lemonade burned a path up her throat. Dear Lord, she was going to cast up her accounts in the middle of a ton ballroom.

"Excuse me," she mumbled to Lady Drummond and pushed her way through the melee.

The doors at the back of the ballroom beckoned like air to one being suffocated. Slipping to the gardens, she gulped in the cool night air. Her stomach thankfully left her throat.

A cluster of three men stood smoking at one end of the balustrade, but they were easily avoided on her flight down the stone steps and into the solitude of the garden. An alcove of vines offered a respite. She sank onto a bench, the seeping cold of the stone a welcome balm. Anger and grief and love warred in her heart.

A figure blocked the entrance to her hideaway. The man stepped forward. "Here you are. I thought we were meeting in the library, my dear." It was Sir Benedict.

"I was seeking solitude, sir." Would he take the hint? Doubtful.

"Don't play coy with me, my lady." He wagged his finger playfully. When she didn't reply, his voice took on an annoyed edge. "You agreed to our assignation."

Oh dear. That must be what she'd inadvertently agreed to on the dance floor. "I'm sorry to disappoint you, sir, but I am feeling overheated and ill." Not untrue. She was heartsick at watching Simon smile at another woman.

He advanced, putting him within an arm's reach and blocking her exit. "I have just the medicine."

He fumbled with the fall of his silk breeches. It took a few astonished blinks to understand what he was implying. While she wasn't a woman of experience, her time with Simon had left her more knowledgeable than most debutantes. Or so she assumed.

"Sir! Step aside this instant." She rose, which unfortunately put her only inches from Sir Benedict's person.

"Goforth gave his blessing, considering I made an offer."

"My stepfather gave you leave to accost me?" She gestured toward his breeches.

"He told me you might protest, but that you had expressed your admiration for me in most specific terms. Come and let me give you a little tickle."

He took her stunned silence as acquiescence. His arms came around her, and she did her best to squirm away but only managed to turn so she could see the exit but not break free.

"Get away from me, sir. I do not wish to give you any of my favors." She managed to push one of his arms away, but he merely tightened the other.

"I like a little fight in my women, but do keep it down. We don't want to bring the ton on our heads."

Panic dried her mouth. If she screamed, she might be saved, but at what cost? Would she be forced to marry Sir Benedict? Yet if she did nothing, she would be truly ruined, not just of reputation, but of soul. That she couldn't allow either.

He planted a kiss on her neck and the squelchy feel of his lips sent a shudder through her. It also gave her a jolt of strength born of desperation. She put both hands on his chest and shoved.

He released her to catch his balance. She didn't hesitate and stumbled out of the alcove. What she had first viewed as a sanctuary had turned into hell. Her only thought was to escape the demon on her heels.

CHAPTER 18

"I'm expecting to see lightning and hear thunder at any moment." The darkly amused voice of Damien Northcutt came from behind Simon.

Simon continued to scan the dance floor and the chairs set along the back wall, but Jessica had disappeared. "What are you talking about? I'm not in the mood for your joshing this evening."

"No, I can see you are not. You look positively murderous." Damien moved to stand shoulder to shoulder with Simon. "Am I to assume your sinister mood lies at the feet of the lovely Miss Tremaine?"

"Why would you think that?" Simon clipped out. "Where the devil did she go? The ladies' retiring room?"

"Yes, why *would* I assume such a thing?" Damien asked in fake bewilderment. "So silly of me. Are you rekindling your affair with the beauteous Lady Herriot as consolation for losing your true love?"

Finally, his attention caught, Simon turned a scathing, deadly glare on his best friend. "That's preposterous. Miss Tremaine is not my true love. She lied to me."

Damien made an exaggerated sound of disgust and rolled his eyes. "Not that trite excuse again. You judge her too harshly based on your past. The more I learn of her stepfather, the more I believe she had due cause for her masquerade."

Simon hated Damien's smugness, even more so because he was absolutely right. "I realize my initial reaction was too harsh. Don't think I didn't try to see her many times in the aftermath, but she gave me the cut direct." The note had been a rapier straight into his heart.

"Ah, so that's why you've thrown yourself to the wolves this evening. If I wasn't at your side as the resident blackguard bastard, you would be overrun by women in white muslin."

"I'll admit Minerva informed me of Jessica's presence this evening. How she came by that information, I haven't a clue."

"She is the wife of a former spy and a formidable woman in her own right. She's frankly rather terrifying. She mostly likely threatened Eversham's bollocks to obtain the guest list on your behalf."

Simon found himself chuckling. "By the by, what are *you* doing here?"

"I heard the card room will have some highfliers with more coin than sense. I've come to relieve them of the former so they might gain the latter." Damien's smile was wicked. "By the way, I saw Miss Tremaine slip out to the veranda as you and Lady Herriot were dancing."

Simon shot him a look that promised retribution at a later date. "Why the devil didn't you lead with that information?"

"I thought you didn't care."

Simon took off toward the doors leading to the gardens, leaving Damien's teasing laughter in his wake. Navigating the throng on his way to the door involved a delicate dance to avoid offending anyone, but he finally made it and flung himself outside, expecting to find her alone on the balustrade. In his endless dreams, she always appeared limned in moonlight.

Usually with considerably less clothes than she wore this evening.

He'd spotted her on one of his spins around the dance floor with Lady Herriot. Her gleaming brown hair was braided elaborately and strung with a length of pearls. Her white dress was delicate and skimmed her figure attractively. The joys of what was underneath had haunted him for months. So much so, he had eschewed any other woman's company, even though Lady Herriot had insinuated her bedroom door would forever be open to him.

Standing at the top of the stone stairs, he scanned the garden, but it was full of tall hedges and draping vines. A rustling drew his attention, and he jogged down the steps and into the garden.

A warm body crashed into him with an *oof* of exhaled air on both their parts. A familiar scent tickled his nose. He grabbed Jessica's arms and rebalanced her. She glanced over her shoulder with a panic that set his own heart sprinting ahead.

"What's the matter?" he whispered.

"I have to get away before he finds me." Her voice was reedy.

He took her by the hand and pulled her in the opposite direction. After tucking her between a pair of tall evergreens, he blocked her from view. "Is it your stepfather?"

"No. Not him. One of his cronies." She was pale and her chin wobbled.

Whatever had happened had shocked her. If the situation were different, he would be tempted to take her in his arms and offer comfort.

"Where are you, you little tease?" A man's voice carried to them, anger overriding the attempted cajoling in the words.

Jessica tensed and grabbed the lapels of his jacket, pressing closer to him. He would gladly protect her and would be more than happy to grant the man a lesson in manners with his fists. Alas, his aggression remained untapped. The man bypassed them and climbed the stairs, stopping briefly at the top to scan the gardens before disappearing inside.

"What were you thinking?" The question emerged with more vitriol than he intended. Mamas whispered warnings to their young daughters to never be alone with Sir Benedict. He was an aging rake who could no longer attract pretty, young ladies through his looks or charm and so resorted to other means. "Did he hurt you?"

She shook off his hands. "Why does it matter to you? Whatever happened is my fault. Isn't that right?"

Simon took a step away from her and ran a hand through his hair when he'd prefer to check her for bodily or emotional injury. "I apologize if I implied his scurrilous behavior was your fault, but I must know... Did he *hurt* you?"

"If you mean rape, then no, he did not."

He let out a long sigh. "Why did you accept his invitation into the gardens?"

Her chin firmed, and her eyes flashed. "Again I ask, why does it matter to you? I'm surprised you dragged your nose out of that woman's décolletage."

The accusation cut deeper than he'd expected. He had been living like a monk because he couldn't stop thinking about her and self-flagellating with regrets. His exasperation flared into anger, and with a snide twist of his lips, he asked, "Were you jealous?"

She held his gaze for a moment before letting it slide to rest somewhere over his shoulder. "Yes," she said curtly.

Her answer doused whatever resentment he carried about her deception.

As he searched for something to say that didn't make him sound like a halfwit, she continued. "It made me sick to see you with her. I came outside to gather myself, and Sir Benedict followed me. Is that what you want to hear? Does my suffering somehow make up for my lies?"

He swallowed past a lump, but his voice was hoarse with emotion anyway. "Was it all lies? You told me your mother…"

She ran a hand over her forehead, hiding her face from his searching gaze. "That was true. No one else knows. Except for Goforth and Mrs. Hamish."

"I suppose Goforth bribed or threatened the magistrate to rule it a natural death."

"Yes." She dropped her hand but kept her focus on the middle of his chest. "That was the only decent turn he gave her. Although I'm certain it was more to save his reputation than hers. I was glad to see her buried in sacred ground. She deserved that."

"And your brother is away at school, isn't he?"

She gave the slightest of nods. "Eton, of course. I'm doing my best to see that he remains there."

"Does doing your best require you to kowtow to men like Sir Benedict?"

"I must keep Blake away from Goforth's influence until he reaches his majority."

"And how do you plan to do that? Subject yourself to more abuse? Barter yourself for your brother's freedom?" An incredulous huff escaped his throat. When she didn't respond, he took her arms and gave her a slight squeeze. "You aren't going to allow Goforth to sell you for votes or influence."

"Allow him?" Finally, she raised her eyes. Fury blazed through a sheen of tears. "I am merely a woman, and he is my guardian. I have no say in the matter. If Goforth wishes to promise my favors to men like Sir Benedict, then what recourse do I have to deny him?"

"Is that what he's done?"

"Based on Sir Benedict's insinuations, yes, but—"

Simon turned on his heel and stalked away. A wrathful spirit had invaded. He took the steps to the balustrade two at a time and reentered the ballroom. He cut a path through the crowd, ignoring the niceties this time. No sign of Goforth.

The man wasn't the type to cultivate relationships with the matrons and their eligible daughters. He wanted to form connections with gentlemen of influence. Where better to do that than the card room? Simon followed two young men up a staircase and down a hallway to where a cacophony of laughter and male conversation emanated on a waft of smoke from numerous cheroots.

He paused in the doorway to get his bearings. Goforth was seated at a table of four men playing whist. Notes were piled in the middle. Goforth appeared slightly sweaty and rumpled. A tumbler stood empty at his elbow.

Simon focused on Goforth with the intensity of a hound and didn't answer any of the calls of greeting that went up as he pursued his prey. Goforth spotted him when he was less than six feet away. A smirk crested his face.

Before the bastard could open his mouth to say something as equally repugnant, Simon's fist made contact with Goforth's nose. Blood spurted onto Goforth's white linen cravat and down his cream-colored waistcoat. He tumbled backward, along with his chair, and lay stunned. The other three gentlemen at the table leaped to their feet and backed away from Simon.

"You are an utter bastard." Simon pointed at Goforth and stepped close enough to apply a swift kick to his ribs if so inclined.

"I should call you out for this." Goforth's voice was muffled behind the hand he pressed to his face to staunch the blood.

"It would be my pleasure to put a bullet through your heart. If you have one, at any rate."

"Ah, I know what this is about then." Behind his hand, Goforth's lips curled cruelly. "It's that—"

"A duel won't be necessary, will it, gentlemen?" A hand

gripped Simon's arm and pulled him back a few steps. "You can discuss your differences over a brandy once cooler heads prevail."

If it had been anyone but Damien interfering, Simon would be tempted to throw another punch. But Damien was an expert pugilist and could put Simon on his back with the same ease as he had put Goforth down.

"I'll expect an apology, Your Grace." Goforth scrambled to his feet with the help of another player.

"Excellent. I'll be sure to offer one and will even tell you where you can put it." Simon tried to inject coolness into the words, but they came out harsh.

A faint rumble of laughter had Goforth sending a glare to locate the offending parties.

Damien leaned in to whisper. "It would be best to depart."

"But—"

"No. If her name comes into it, she will be ruined." Damien didn't need to specify who he was referring to.

With a curse, Simon allowed Damien to lead him to the door. Rafe met them at the top of the stairs, his manner brusque but with a steadying calm Simon found reassuring. "What's the situation?"

"We need to get Simon out of here before he makes more of a spectacle of himself than he already has," Damien said softly while sending a smile and nod toward a cluster of ladies eyeing them at the foot of the stairs.

"It will take a half hour at least for me to gather our carriage in this crush," Rafe said.

"I called for mine earlier, prepared for a quick getaway after fleecing poor Kinnock." Damien collected his hat and coat. Simon and Rafe did the same.

"I feel as if you're sending me to my chambers like misbehaving child." To make matters worse, a rather childish resentment flavored his tone.

"Your behavior has been foolish, ill-advised, and at least adolescent, if not indeed childish." Damien led them outside, and sure enough, his black carriage bearing no family crest waited at the curb.

"What about Minerva?" Simon asked Rafe.

"She knows I'm seeing to you."

"How did you even know what was going on?"

"Gossip flies faster than the quail from the bush." Once the three of them were loaded in Damien's carriage, Rafe sat back and crossed his arms. "Who in the devil did you punch?"

"Goforth."

"Of course you did." Rafe let his head fall back and muttered a string of highly colorful curses. "Are you half-sprung?"

"No, I'm as sober as a vicar."

"I don't find that particularly reassuring."

Damien twitched the curtains open. "Goforth might deserve a thrashing, but why in the middle of a ball? Didn't you consider the talk it would cause? Especially if Miss Tremaine's name becomes involved."

Simon hadn't been able to focus on anything except the fury and overwhelming need to teach Goforth a lesson. "Goforth is basically selling access to Miss Tremaine for votes or influence or coin. Word of that will eventually make the rounds and leave her with few options."

"That is dire news," Rafe said. "Are you sure it's true?"

"Miss Tremaine had a run-in with Sir Benedict in the gardens that left her shaken." Simon shrugged. "I believe her."

Damien rubbed his chin. "Goforth has been amassing gambling debt. He's not so far in the dun to cause gossip, but he's been bitten by the bug and doesn't know when to fold and walk away."

Rafe tapped his fingers on his knees, the only sign he was agitated. "Does he owe you coin? Can you exert pressure?"

"He refuses to play with me after the thrashing at the table I gave him at Wintermarsh last fall."

"That's a shame," Rafe said.

Damien took a chit from his waistcoat pocket and deftly turned it in his fingers. It was a long-standing habit of his when he was plotting. "What is your plan, Simon? Arrive on Miss Tremaine's doorstep hat in hand to make Goforth another offer? He would be more likely to put a bullet between your eyes than agree. You should have played the game and bided your time."

"It's not a game for me, Damien."

Damien ceased his fiddling and nodded. "I know, but the fact of the matter is Goforth will never accept your suit. He has hated you since your first meeting, and tonight is not likely to have changed his feelings."

"I understand the antipathy he feels for you, but he is mad not to want to align himself with a duke through marriage." Rafe twitched the curtains open to check their progress.

"Not really," Simon said. "If I wed Jessica, I may become Lord Penhaven's guardian. I would be in a position to mentor and guide him, thereby weakening Goforth's connection to society and influence in the upper House once the young earl takes his seat. He wants Lord Penhaven as his puppet."

"Then he has much to lose if you win Miss Tremaine's hand," Damien said. "I suggest you retreat, regroup, and approach the situation with a bit more planning and exponentially more cunning."

"I must see her and verify her well-being." Fear churned in Simon's gut now the ramifications of his actions reverberated.

"That would be extremely foolish." The warning in Damien's voice was almost a growl.

Simon bounced his knee, impatient to do *something*. Even something foolish.

"Talk some sense into him, will you, Drummond?" Damien

nudged Rafe's knee with his own in the tight confines of the carriage.

Rafe rubbed his jaw and grunted. "In Simon's position, I would have broken Goforth's jaw, but then again, I've always been a hot-tempered son-of-a-bitch. I would want to whisk Miss Tremaine to Gretna Green as soon as possible. However, the question is how to gain access. A morning call is not an option."

"I'll sneak inside." Simon crossed his arms.

Damien threw his hands up. "And when you're caught by Goforth? He's a regular at Manton's and known to be a crack shot. Most of those Americans are. I fear these tender feelings you hold for Miss Tremaine will be the death of you."

"Or his saving grace," Rafe said.

"Dear God, not you too?" Damien sounded aggrieved. "For a man who's rumored to have killed a half dozen men with your bare hands, your wife has turned you into a milquetoast."

"Don't believe everything you hear, Northcutt." Rafe's deliberate pause sent a chill through the carriage. "It was many more men than that."

The carriage came to a stop outside the Drummond town house. Rafe hopped out, but when Simon went to follow him, Damien tugged on his sleeve. "Can I count on you to not do anything romantically suicidal this evening? I have an appointment to keep."

"I won't do anything rash." It was a promise Simon wasn't sure he could keep.

He exited to the curb, but before he closed the door, Damien called out, "Tell my uncle I'll be by for tea soon."

Simon nodded. "I'll do that. Thank you for not letting me get myself killed tonight." It was a weak attempt to convey his feelings of gratitude toward his staunch friend.

Damien merely raised one brow and rapped on the ceiling. Simon watched the black carriage turn the next corner and disappear. He trudged up the steps. Northcutt, the Drummond's butler in town and Damien's uncle through his mother, was not there to greet him.

Simon divested himself of his hat and cloak, laid them over a chair in the entry, and made his way to the study where he knew Rafe would be waiting. And waiting he was with two glasses of brandy already poured.

"What now?" Simon asked.

"We see what insight Minerva's gleaned once she's returned." Rafe sat behind his desk and propped a leg over the corner of the gleaming mahogany in a stance of total relaxation.

Simon couldn't locate even a sliver of his calm. He paced the room like one of the caged lions at the Tower. An agonizing hour passed before Minerva appeared. Simon peppered her with questions.

"Goodness, Simon, let me catch my breath." She took the small glass of port Rafe offered and collapsed in the nearest chair. "What an evening!"

"You're making me daft. What news?" Simon resumed his pacing, this time in front of his sister.

Minerva took a sip and tracked him with her gaze. "Goforth railed against you, of course. Called you a madman. The ladies tittered behind their fans. Luckily for you, Goforth is not particularly well liked, so the gentlemen paid him little mind, and I'm afraid the ladies might be even more entranced with you now that you've gained an air of danger."

Simon waved away the suggestion. "And Miss Tremaine? Did you see her? Speak with her?"

"Only very briefly. Goforth bundled her home not long after you departed. She was quite upset, both with you and for you." Minerva twirled the crystal stem of her glass between her fingers and added in a slightly chiding tone, "You acted quite rashly."

"So I've been told multiple times. I don't know what to tell you except that I saw red. Goforth is a bastard who deserves more than a thrashing."

"I have no doubt. Still..." Minerva cocked an eyebrow but added nothing more, to his already growing chagrin.

"How damaging will the gossip be?" Rafe asked.

"It depends on how soon another scandal breaks. If a debutante is caught in a rake's embrace tomorrow night, then we need not worry." Minerva's tone made Simon think the possibility was unlikely.

"What course of action do you suggest?" Simon asked his sister.

"I will make some calls tomorrow and subtly hint at a political disagreement between you and Goforth. That shouldn't be a difficult story for the ton to swallow. The fact is, most ladies find politics dry and uninteresting. As long as you stay away from Miss Tremaine for the time being, I predict the incident will be forgotten in a week." Minerva finished her glass of port and set the crystal glass on the side table. When she turned to face him, her expression was stern. "Can you manage that?"

A week? Considering he wanted to tear through the streets of London this very moment, he had a difficult time grinding out a reluctant agreement. "I can try."

Simon let himself out and walked the short distance to his own London home. Goforth had rented a town house in a semi-fashionable area of London known for housing well-off cits and high-ranking members of the judiciary. Simon could be there in twenty minutes.

But Minerva was right. If his name was attached to Jessica's so soon after his scuffle with her stepfather, the talk would escalate and sully her reputation. As much as he railed against the plan, he needed to take Damien's advice and play not to win a trick, but to win the game.

He would retreat. For now.

CHAPTER 19

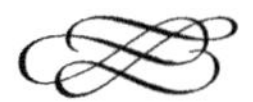

The week passed in fits of excruciating nerves and worry for Jessica's well-being. Simon attended every function he was invited to and some he wasn't. He'd promised Minerva not to approach Jessica, but until he clapped eyes on her to verify she was hale and hearty, he wouldn't rest easy. Neither Jessica nor Goforth put in an appearance.

As Minerva predicted, the gossip died a quick death once she ascribed the disagreement to politics. Now he was worried less about her reputation and more about her person. Why was Goforth keeping her locked away? Had he hurt her because of Simon's rash actions? The thought was turning him into a madman.

Which was why he had sent a desperate note the evening before and was standing outside the Drummond town house at an ungodly early hour. A dignified white-haired butler answered the door and took his coat and hat.

"Good morning, Your Grace."

"Northcutt. I apologize for the early hour. Are the lord and lady of the house still abed?"

"His lordship is in his study if you'd like to go up. And how is my scapegrace nephew? He hasn't been by for tea in a fortnight or more."

"He's been occupied with a new venture. One he's been tight-lipped about, as a matter of fact," Simon said.

"A venture of the female variety?"

"Honestly, I'm not sure, but he did give me a message to pass along to you. He promised he'd stop by for tea soon."

"I'm not sure if he's the pride or the scourge of the family," the butler intoned in the way only a good, solemn butler could but with a quirk of his lips.

"I'd say both, depending on the day." Simon headed to the study and paused in the doorway.

Rafe was lying on the rug in front of his desk playing toy soldiers with Christopher.

"You can't do that, Papa!"

"'Course I can. See, this knight is me, and I'm worth ten of your weak-kneed men. Make that twenty," Rafe said teasingly.

"This knight is me, and I'm worth thirty of your chicken-hearted men." The boy knocked all Rafe's men over with gusto.

"Ouch. Chicken-hearted, are they? I'd best beat a hasty retreat in that case."

Christopher caught sight of Simon and launched himself off the floor for a hug. Simon picked the boy up, spun him around, and then plopped in the nearest chair with the boy on his lap. Christopher prattled on about a trip to Covent Garden, his excitement making his words trip over one another.

The chimney sweeps had particularly caught his attention, and Simon held his tongue, letting Christopher think the boys led a merry, carefree life without parental oversight. The bleakness of the world would eventually touch the child, but Simon wouldn't be the one to make the introductions. Eventually, Rafe sent Christopher up to tickle his mother awake.

"Minerva's still abed?" Simon asked.

"Indeed. She's increasing," Rafe said with worry-tinged satisfaction.

Her confinement with Christopher had been difficult. She'd been heartily sick, and the delivery had left her weak. "Congratulations. I can't wait to be an uncle again. She's seemed well. Has she been ill?"

"Not like last time, thank the Lord. Everything is progressing smoothly." Rafe took the armchair flanking Simon's before the grate. "I assume you're here about your situation and not mine."

"It's been a week with no sign of Jessica. Damien tells me Goforth has been frequenting one gaming hall after another, winning just often enough to keep him coming back. Goforth might be beating Jessica or starving her or worse. I can wait no longer. Will you help me?"

"Even before your note, I had set a plan in motion. I dared not mention it, as I didn't want to get your hopes up, but"—Rafe glanced at the clock—"our secret weapon will be arriving any moment."

As if waiting for the pronouncement, an arrival echoed through the marbled entry. Simon tensed and shifted to see the study door.

A disreputable-looking man in coarse woolen breeches and a patched jacket slunk in, his shoulders hunched. His hair was dark and lank, and he wore a filthy, wide-brimmed cap on his head. It wasn't until the man straightened and tipped his hat back with a smile that Simon recognized him.

"Gray Masterson!" Simon couldn't stifle a bark of surprise.

"Northcutt refused to touch my hat." Gray dropped his filthy hat on Rafe's desk.

"I can't say that I blame him. I hope it's mostly bluster and not actually vermin-ridden." Rafe exchanged a handshake with Gray and then poked the hat to the far corner of the desk, away from his ledger.

"Why are you dressed like a rag-and-bone man?" Simon asked.

"Rafe confided your troubles the other evening. I offered to discover what I could about Goforth and Miss Tremaine."

Simon's shoulders tensed. "Did you see her?"

"Unfortunately not. She and Goforth had a row after returning home the evening in question, and since then, Miss Tremaine has been confined to her room. The hired footman is rattled and was only too willing to air his troubles after a pint or two." Gray leaned against the desk, stretching his legs out in front of him and crossing his worn boots at the ankle.

"That tells us nothing about her physical and emotional state of well-being." Simon's frustration heated his words.

"I also discovered her room is on the third level facing the mews, which is rather convenient." Gray didn't seem at all perturbed by Simon's attitude.

"That calls for a bit of reconnaissance tonight. What say you, gentlemen?" Rafe asked.

"Yes!" Simon wasn't sure how he was going to be able to wait until the evening.

"The moon is waning, and the rain should hold off until the wee hours." Gray pointed at Simon. "You'll need something more practical to wear."

Comparing his tailored Weston jacket and scuff-free Hobby boots to Gray's unmatched patchwork clothes, Simon gave a rueful laugh. "I'll have to borrow something."

"We're of a size. I'll send something over." Gray's smile flashed like lightning before his expression turned serious. "Let's meet at the Laughing Goat at midnight."

"Is that really necessary?" Rafe asked with a slight eye roll. "We're hardly on the hunt for royal secrets."

"Don't spoil my fun, dammit," Gray said with the same petulance as five-year-old Christopher earlier. "It's not often I get in the field anymore. Since taking over for Hawkins, I've been forced into shuffling papers and giving orders."

"Good Lord. Fine. Midnight, it is." Although Rafe spoke with his typical gruffness, an undeniable spark twinkled in his eyes.

Simon, on the other hand, fought nerves and anxiety for the rest of the day. After dismissing his valet and sending his servants to bed with instructions not to wait up for his return, he dressed himself in the borrowed clothes. While they were approaching threadbare, they were at least clean.

He tied the black neckerchief around his collar in a simple knot, put on the hat, and examined himself in the looking glass. He could be any working man walking the streets of London. It was a reminder how only an accident of birth separated him and the rest of his ilk from the common man.

Simon walked until he could hail a hack to take him the rest of the way to the Laughing Goat. It was easy enough to spot Gray and Rafe in the sparsely filled pub. Midnight was late for all but the most hardened, dedicated drinkers.

Gray and Rafe rose from their corner table and led Simon out the back of the establishment into a narrow alley speaking in gestures. Once they were outside, Simon whispered, "Aren't you two taking the skullduggery to extremes?"

"Better to be safe than dead, I always say." Rafe grinned.

Gray shushed them and motioned them farther into the shadows through the alleys and mews that ran behind the town houses. The chuffs of horses sounded over the occasional rattle of carriage wheels on the main streets. The occasional groom went about putting their charges away after a long evening.

The three of them moved like wraiths. Or at least Gray and Rafe did. Simon felt as if his every boot strike would bring a yell for the night's watch.

Finally, Gray halted and pointed. "Here we are, and there is Miss Tremaine's room, if my source was correct."

No light shone from any of the windows, and the curtains

had been drawn on Jessica's room. The town house might as well be deserted, except for the frisson of awareness that heightened his senses. She was close.

"What now?" Simon asked. "Should I throw pebbles at her window?"

Rafe ignored the suggestion. "I could watch the house for a day or two. Note the routine of the servants and sneak in. No one would be the wiser."

"It's not a large town house, and you are a large man and out of practice. Wait here." Gray slipped over the low wall into the garden, lost behind a line of sculpted evergreens. He returned in less than two minutes. "The door is locked and bolted."

"We could bring back the tools we need to cut it." Rafe turned to Gray, shutting Simon out of the deliberations.

"Neither one of us can be tied to a break-in. What if I get myself taken on as a footman?" Gray asked.

"Aren't you getting a little long in the tooth for that? I doubt you'd make it past the first interview." Rafe rumbled a soft laugh.

While the two of them quietly argued, Simon looked up and studied the bricks and pipes and ledges that made up the back of the town house. In his misspent, dissolute youth, he'd had to take alternative exits more than once to escape wrathful husbands. It was a skill he hadn't put to use in some years, but hopefully, it was like riding a horse.

"I can't wait for your subterfuge, gentlemen. I'll make a direct assault." He jumped the garden wall and grabbed hold of a downspout with one hand while he wedged his booted foot into a crack in the mortar.

His progress was slow but steady. As he pulled himself to a squat on the narrow outcropping of her window, holding precariously onto the narrow stonework at the top, he looked down to see Rafe and Gray watching him intently.

Rafe cupped his hands around his mouth and called out

barely loud enough for him to hear, "Nice job, Romeo. I assume you'll be occupied for some time?"

Perched like a gargoyle, he lifted a hand to wave them off, immediately regretting the move when he almost tipped backward. He clamped the ledge tighter and pressed his cheek against the top of the wood sill, praying Gray's sources were correct and this was Jessica's room.

He rapped on the window and waited. If Goforth's red-faced visage appeared, Simon might as well jump to his death.

CHAPTER 20

Jessica awoke with a start, her heart pounding. Had she been dreaming? Maybe, but not the same nightmare that usually stalked her. She lay in bed with her cover clutched to her chin. A rap at her window had her gasping and sitting up, her gaze fixed on her curtains.

Was it a bird or a rat? She was being silly. Animals didn't knock. She slipped out of bed and opened the curtains just enough to poke her head through. She nearly screamed. The wavy figure of a man was perched on her window ledge.

A duke was at her window. Her third-floor window. Perhaps she really was dreaming.

The apparition pointed to the latch, his words barely penetrating the leaded glass. "May I come in? Please?"

Her sleep-addled mind cleared, and she fumbled with the latch, finally able to fling the window open. The edge caught Simon in the shoulder and sent him careening to the side. She let out a little scream and grabbed his jacket.

A cold breeze with scattered rain drops whipped around them and snatched his hat. She watched it tumble a long way to the ground. Her hands on him became more frantic as she imagined him following it to a sure death. Between her pulling and him scrambling for his footing, he managed to get one leg inside.

He ducked through the window and closed it behind him. It was dark in her chambers, the only light coming from the dying embers in the grate. His ragged breathing slowly calmed in the ensuing silence.

No, she was the one who was breathing hard and whose heart was ready to explode. He had risked life and limb to see her. Throwing herself in his arms would not be an appropriate greeting.

How else did one welcome a duke to their chambers in the wee hours? A curtsey? She stifled a spate of inappropriate, panicky giggles. It was simply unbelievable he was standing an arm's length away when she hadn't been sure she would ever see him again.

"Why are you here?" she whispered even though Goforth's chamber was on the floor below and at the front of the house.

She feared what Goforth might do if he caught Simon in their town house. Goforth had grown positively zealous in his hatred for the duke. Blood would be spilled, and she didn't want to see Simon hurt or in Newgate for murder.

"I was sick with worry. As far as I can ascertain, you haven't been allowed to leave since the ball. Have you been mistreated?" He approached her with the care one would give a wounded wild animal.

"I'm well enough. Bored mostly. Except for Abby, I've seen no one. Goforth was very angry with me." A vast understatement she wouldn't elaborate on for fear Simon would haul Goforth out of bed and do something rash. "He is making plans for me, but I don't know what yet."

"Marriage?"

"Perhaps. Or something more humiliating." Embarrassment

kindled a blush. After what Sir Benedict insinuated, she would put nothing past Goforth.

"Wouldn't anything but a respectable marriage bring censure down upon him?"

"I'm not sure he cares anymore. He is a man possessed." While her stepfather had never loved her—or even liked her, for that matter—he had never regarded her with the level of disgust and hatred he directed at her now.

"Any idea when he will make his move?"

"Soon. He visited me this afternoon and was practically vibrating with excitement. Yet when I asked, he put me off."

Simon hummed and began to pace. She tugged him to a stop. "If you're going to do that, you should at least remove your boots before the clomping draws attention."

He covered her hand gripping his jacket and smiled down at her. "I would be happy to remove whatever clothing you deem appropriate."

He sat on the only chair in the room and pulled off his boots. Seeing his stockinged feet was strangely intimate. It was at that moment when she became aware of her own state of dishabille. While her night rail covered her from neck to toes, it was an older garment, the fabric worn soft and thin.

"I should retrieve my dressing gown?" Why had she turned what should have been an emphatic statement into a question?

"Or not. I'm here to check on your well-being." Simon rested his hands on her shoulders, the warmth and weight a steadying force. But then his hands trekked down her arms, his touch setting her heart to quaking. The slight friction of the soft muslin between her skin and the heat of his hands started a delicious ache in her belly. One she recognized.

"As you can see, I am perfectly fine." She had become breathless, lending her voice an unintentionally provocative quality.

"I fear I must assure myself you are unhurt before I can take my leave." A wickedness lightened his words and made a thrill zip down her spine.

"How can I assure you?"

He left her to light a brace of three candles in the remains of the fire. While the wavering circle of light was soft, it was a shock after spending so much of their time together in the shadows.

A slight laugh burst out of her. His attire would be better suited for a dockside worker. "What on earth are you wearing?"

"Courting clothes." He set the candles on the stand by the bed, took her hands in his, and drew her closer. She didn't protest in word or body, and even tangled their fingers to hold him tighter. He lifted their joined hands for an examination.

"Such delicacy and strength." He proceeded to kiss the tip of each finger one by one. The sweetness of the gesture was nearly her undoing.

"I feared you'd never be able to forgive me." It was hard to get the words past the lump of tears in her throat.

He dropped one of her hands but retained the other to press against his heart. "I was angry—very angry—but I'm old enough to understand not everything is black and white. Speaking of forgiveness, I'm surprised you didn't wallop me for asking you to be my mistress."

"I'm surprised I considered the offer. If it hadn't been for Blake, perhaps I would have." She gave a little laugh and looked at their joined hands. "Since we're being perfectly honest now, escaping Goforth and putting myself in your care sounded heavenly."

He tugged at the ribbon drawing her sleeve closed at her wrist and pushed the loosened fabric toward her elbow with the slide of his hand. His calluses from riding rasped erotically against her skin, inciting a shiver of goose bumps.

"I can say with equal honesty that I have dreamed of taking care of you in and out of my bed every single night during and since the house party." He raised her arm and kissed the inside of her wrist. Could he feel the flutter of her heart?

"I have dreamed the same," she admitted on a gasp as his lips found a particularly sensitive spot in the crook of her elbow.

"I am thrilled to hear it. Would you like another of my confessions?" He moved to finger the ribbons holding her night rail closed at her neck.

"I would hear it with an open heart." Her entire body trembled in anticipation, yet he didn't unfurl the ribbons.

"I love you, and I would make you my wife. If you will have me, that is." He dipped his head so he could catch her gaze.

The wavery candlelight reflected only his honesty. The shadows of the night stripped away all the pretense and complications of their lives and stations, just as it had at Wintermarsh. She was his equal, and if she said no, he would abide by her decision. She didn't want to say no though.

"I love you too." Her voice was thick with emotion. "In fact, I think I've loved you since the first time we met at the inn."

"You didn't even know me then. Not really." He wrapped his hand around her nape and stroked her jaw with his thumb, tilting her head back so he could search her eyes.

"I knew you were honorable and brave. You stood up to Goforth to protect a stranger. I never forgot what you did. I followed news of you for years. When we finally met, you far exceeded any of my girlish fantasies."

"I was a cad. A duke shouldn't pursue, much less dally with, a lady's maid." His guilt was palpable.

She popped to her toes and planted a brief, hard kiss on his lips. "Please don't feel guilty. I could have walked away, and you would have let me."

"As much as it would have hurt, I would have let you go."

She smiled up at him, feeling lighter than she had in weeks, months, years. A tiny seed of hope had worked its way into her heart to bloom. He *loved* her.

He wrapped an arm around her waist and snugged against the length of his body. "Will you marry me, Jessica?"

"Of course I will." Her happiness dimmed along with her smile.

"I sense a *but*. What's wrong?"

"How can you even ask that? Goforth will never give his blessing."

"Then we'll elope. Tonight, if you wish. I'll procure a special license first thing in the morning, even if I have to wake the archbishop, or we can make a mad dash for Gretna Green."

She wanted to beg him to sweep her away like a fairytale prince. Instead, she said, "I can't."

"Is it your brother?"

She nodded wordlessly.

"I'm a duke and not without influence, my love." When it was clear she was unconvinced, he added. "If you won't leave with me tonight, will you trust in me to find a solution to the problem of your brother? Then we can marry."

She wanted to trust him, but deep down she worried there might not be another chance for them. What if this night was their only night?

Rain pattered against the window. "It's raining," she said inanely.

"Indeed."

"You should wait for it to pass."

"Should I?" He treaded his fingers through her hair, fisted his hand, and tugged her head back. "What should we do to pass the time until the weather clears?"

She gasped at the prickly pleasure in her scalp. "You have promised to wed me, have you not?"

"On my honor, I will see it done."

"I want you to bed me."

He blinked, and his lips parted with a sharp intake of breath.

His shock made her laugh. She had a feeling it wasn't often he was caught flatfooted.

"It would be my pleasure. Literally." He daubed his tongue along his lower lip. "Are you certain?"

"I was certain the night in the gazebo. I was ready to bed you then. Please don't make me wait any longer." She would wring as much joy from the experience as possible.

"If you weren't next to your bed in a night rail I can see straight through in the candlelight, I might have the strength to deny you." He shifted her until he sat on the bed and drew her between his legs.

"You can't see—" She looked down at herself. Dear Lord, he could see everything.

Her nipples were peaked shadows against the thin muslin. She crossed her arms over her chest even though he'd seen her breasts and suckled and squeezed them. Realizing how silly she was being considering her most recent request, she dropped her hands to rest on his thighs. His muscles there twitched at her touch.

He rumbled a laugh and went to work on the ribbons at her neck, this time not pausing until they were unfurled and the edges of her night rail parted into a vee ending a few inches above her belly. The inside curves of her breasts were on display in the wavering candlelight. A flush heated her and pinkened her skin.

"We only had the moon all the times we met before," she said softly.

"How many times I cursed the shadows." He ran his fingertips along the edge of the night rail until he reached the undersides of her breasts. The gentle touch nearly took her out at the knees. She clamped his thighs tighter.

"You should have thanked the darkness. It was the only way I could have met you. Otherwise, you were sure to recognize me."

"I was a fool for not realizing long before who you really

were." He tugged her closer and nuzzled the night rail to the side until her right breast was exposed.

His eyes were half closed as his lips found her nipple. A honeyed ribbon pulled taut in her lower belly, the feeling decadent yet faintly uncomfortable. Simon had the ability to appease her appetites, yet he appeared in no hurry to satisfy her as he had in the gazebo.

She shuffled closer and skimmed her hands farther up his thighs. He gasped around her nipple. A niggling sense of power accelerated her breathing. His experience gave him the advantage, but he wasn't immune to her touch. She claimed another inch of his thigh and another until her thumbs grazed the hard length of him pressing against the wool of his trousers. His head fell back with a groan.

If she was going to her ruination, she didn't want to merely submit to him. She wanted to bring him equal pleasure. With trembling fingers, she slid his trouser buttons free until his fall did just that.

He lifted the tails of his shirt out of the way and leaned back. The candles were bright enough for her to see him. The hard length of him jutted from a thatch of blond hair a few shades darker and coarser than the hair on his head. The thick staff boasted a flanged end with a glistening slit across the top.

"May I touch you?"

He blew out a slow breath before responding on a raspy laugh. "I have craved your touch for too long. I hope I won't embarrass myself."

"How could you possibly embarrass yourself?" Her gaze rose from his intimidating staff to his eyes. "You have done this before, haven't you, Simon? I assumed based on our past interactions that you understood the basics of what we are about to engage in, because—"

The affection in his laugh this time kindled a different sort of fire inside her. One she hoped would burn forever. "I have done this a few times over the years, yes, but never with someone I wanted to please so badly."

She had the feeling he'd done this more than a few times with more than a few women. "With Lady Herriot?"

He cupped her cheek with his hand, his smile rueful. "Since I spied you at the pond, I haven't even thought of another woman, much less been with one. I worry I'll spend before I satisfy you."

While he didn't directly answer her question, her spike of jealousy dissipated like mist. Too many unknowns riddled their path. Instead of worrying about the past or future, she would enjoy the moment. Thoroughly enjoy it.

She ran a finger from the tip to the base, the skin velvet over iron. "Oh, I see. Your staff isn't always so robust, or you wouldn't be able to conceal it in your trousers."

His eyes twinkled with a devilish tease. "It would be quite awkward to walk around with a cockstand all day and night."

"I can only imagine."

"My trousers are smoldering from the look in your eyes, my love."

"I wouldn't complain if they burned to ash."

"That would make my walk home rather embarrassing. Why don't I simply remove them instead?" He stood, and Jessica shifted back to give him room and, if she were being honest, to have a better view.

Jessica had never heard her mother and Goforth engage in flirtation even at the beginning of their courtship. While she did not know—and didn't want to know—anything of the state of their marriage bed, she couldn't imagine them engaging in the sort of banter she and Simon were enjoying.

He peeled off his stockings and then stood to shuck his jacket, neckerchief, and shirt. The veneer of a ton gentleman was stripped away with every item of clothing he removed until he stood before her with only his trousers between him and his natural state. So slowly she decided he was teasing her on purpose, he hooked his thumbs in the waistband, stripped his trousers off, and kicked them aside.

She didn't know where to look first. His shoulders were broad and muscled. His upper chest was furred with blond hair that thinned into a sparse line leading to his gravity-defying cockstand. The differences in their bodies were stark and arousing.

With a small smile tipping his lips and a hooded, sensual look around his eyes, he was silent, waiting for her judgment.

"You're beautiful," she said breathlessly.

"That's not a compliment I've ever been paid before. Your turn." He grasped the top of her night rail and peeled it off her shoulders.

Turnaround was fair play. Still, she tensed as the soft muslin caressed its way down her breasts to flutter around her feet. She kept her gaze lowered yet could feel the touch of his eyes down the length of her body. Amazingly, his staff jerked and stood even higher. Was it because of the sight of her body? Her mortification faded in the heat of her arousal.

He wrapped a hand around her nape and an arm around her waist and pulled her flush to him. Her lungs forgot to do their duty, and she grew breathless. He didn't give her time to acclimate to the feel of his hard, hairy body against her. He kissed her.

Not a gentle, wooing kiss, but an aggressive domination. She gave herself permission not to think or question his actions or her responses. She moaned into his mouth and wrapped her arms around his neck, her aching breasts against his hard chest granting her gratification.

He clasped her bottom and shifted her to her toes. Cradled against her belly, his cock throbbed a matching beat to her own needs. She was wet and ready for him. He pushed her to lie crosswise on the bed, her legs dangling off the edge. He shifted her knees apart and lowered himself over her. The tip of his cock slipped over the sensitive flesh between her legs.

Her breathing hitched, and she closed her eyes. This was it. He would breach her. Claim her. A moment's trepidation at the thought of his impossibly thick, long cock stretching her made her tense up.

Instead, Simon claimed her mouth in a long, drugging kiss. Her hands found their way to his flanks to explore the ridges and dips. He loomed over her, propped on his forearms, seemingly in no hurry.

"Aren't you going to finish things?" she asked when he broke away to look down at her.

His eyebrows cocked. "Sweetheart, we've barely gotten started."

He slid down her body only far enough to flick his tongue across first one nipple and then the other. She arched her back and weaved her fingers into his hair. Her experience with the final act was nonexistent, but she was intimately familiar with this pleasure.

She raised her legs, set her heels on the edge of the mattress, and clamped him around the hips with her knees. After sucking her nipples until they were hardened points begging for more, he trekked farther down her body, laying kisses along the soft curve of her belly.

She raised her head when he reached the downy hair of her mons. "What are you doing?"

He merely smiled wickedly and licked her right between the legs. He continued his ministrations at her core, sucking and nipping and driving his tongue inside her.

Tremors rocked her until she was unmoored. Embarrassment didn't exist in the new world he'd unlocked, only need. She drove her hips higher into his mouth, begging him in harsh whispers. He pressed a finger inside her, and then another. A noise in her head like a million butterflies beating their wings drowned everything else out.

Pleasure splintered her. She searched for a stable force, her hands finding and clinging to his shoulders as her body writhed. He withdrew his fingers, and she gave a mewling cry of distress at the sudden emptiness. He shifted her farther up the bed with ease and knelt between her spread legs. She forced her eyes open, any fear subsumed by her climax.

He was a sight to behold. His face was thrown half in shadow by the bed curtains, the planes and hollows emphasized. Candlelight sparked off the blond hair peppering his muscular chest. He fisted the base of his cock and guided himself to her entrance, rubbing the head through the slickness welcoming him.

"Are you sure you want this?" He raised his gaze to hers. "There's no going back after this."

The intensity in his blue eyes was like the hottest part of a flame. She would gladly sacrifice herself to the blaze if he asked. Afraid she might beg, she shifted her hips to take the head of his cock. The slight burn was drowned out by the pleasure of fullness.

He didn't hesitate and pressed his hips forward an inch, watching her intently. "How do you feel?"

"Fine." She almost laughed at the inadequacy of the word. The weather was fine. Horses were fine. This was *not* fine. This was… "Primal. I feel like an animal. I want more."

The chesty noise he made was an equally animalistic grunt. He gave her another inch and another, until his pelvis was seated against her.

She scored her nails across his shoulders, and his hips bucked like a horse being given spurs. He pulled almost all the way out and pressed back inside her, slowly, almost gently.

"Don't be gentle with me, Your Grace."

He barred his teeth, the cords of his neck tight, and

answered by pumping faster and harder into her. A sheen of sweat broke over his shoulders. With every stroke, her own pleasure spiraled tighter. She curled her pelvis toward him, and his next stroke dizzied her. It was the same, yet different, as earlier. Could she possibly reach her climax again?

Yes, she could. The tumult was harsher and yet more satisfying than before. After a half dozen more hard thrusts, Simon pulled out and rubbed his cock with a sure hand. Fluid spurted out of the end onto her belly. He threw his head back on a low groan and collapsed at her side as if shot, his arm heavy under her breasts.

The fluid on her belly cooled, but she was in no hurry to move. The weight of his arm and the heat of his body against hers was comforting in a way she couldn't describe. Their breathing slowed together, and her heart seemed to find the same rhythm as his.

As the rain continued to patter against the window, two of the candles guttered and extinguished themselves. What time was it? Sometime between midnight and dawn was as close as she could guess.

Simon levered himself up with a noise of regret and retrieved a square of linen from the pocket of his jacket. Still naked, he sat on the edge of the bed and cleaned his spend from her body. Without his heat, she shivered, and he tucked her in bed, pressing kisses along her bare skin as he pulled the covers up.

His hair was tousled. The rigid edge of propriety he used to keep society at bay had been cast aside. When he shifted to rise, she propped herself on her elbow and caught his hand. He met her gaze with a quizzical expression. She wasn't sure what she wanted to know or how to ask. Hesitantly, she tried to put her query into words. "Is it always like that?"

"You mean coupling between a man and woman?"

"I never knew my mother to enjoy the act. She seemed to dread sharing a bed with Goforth, even at the beginning."

He crumpled the soiled linen in his fist even as he gently stroked her cheek. "It has never been so intense for me, but then again, I've never been in love before."

All she could do was smile through a sudden haze of tears. Was it exhaustion or the fact he had stripped away all her defenses to leave her intensely vulnerable?

He retreated to pull on his trousers and shirt, tucking in the tails while he gazed through the streaks of rain to the outside world. The few remaining candles still burning wavered light over his face, but no hint of dawn lightened the veil of darkness.

"The rain has abated," he said.

"When must you go?" she asked with increasing dread. Why couldn't they stay cocooned together forever?

"Soon. Too soon. I don't want Goforth to suspect anything. Not until I have a chance to solidify plans on how to extricate you while keeping your brother safe." He turned to her. "It might take some time."

"Yes." Or it may never happen. She understood the realities.

While her experience with matters of the flesh had very recently been expanded, she had too much experience with disappointment and loss. Losing Simon would be yet another devastating loss, but one she would survive.

"You must string Goforth along and make sure he doesn't do anything rash," Simon said.

"I will do my best."

Simon slipped on his jacket and sat on the edge of the bed to pull on his boots. He leaned over her and touched his forehead to hers. "I love you."

"I love you too."

With that, he opened the window, letting in damp, chilly air and a scattering of raindrops. She wrapped the coverlet around herself, her heart taking the scary plunge out the window with him. Carefully, he lowered himself over the ledge and deftly scaled to the ground with catlike agility. He turned to look up and blow her a kiss.

She raised her hand and watched until he disappeared into the misty dawn. Exhaustion swamped her, and she returned to bed to hopefully dream of Simon. Instead, she was plagued with nightmares of Goforth and Sir Benedict Pennington.

CHAPTER 21

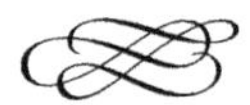

A pounding on her chamber door woke her from a restless sleep. What an odd way for Abby to announce her arrival. She sat up with her covers tight under her arms. Where was her night rail? Her mind was fuzzy from sleep.

"Just a moment, Abby!" Unless she wanted to answer awkward questions about her state of undress, she needed to find the garment.

Before she could rise, the door burst open. She let out a little scream and burrowed under the covers. It wasn't Abby who entered, but her stepfather. He was in high dudgeon if his ruddy face and the set of his mouth were any indication. Abby hovered in the doorway, wringing her hands in her apron.

"Sir! You must leave at once. If you wish to discuss something, I will have Abby help me dress and be down shortly." It was difficult to sound imperious when she was at such a disadvantage.

His gaze swept over her. He stalked to the puddle of white that was her night rail, lifted it, and waved it about like a flag of surrender. Except she feared she was the one who would lose the battle ahead.

"Are you in the habit of casting off all proprieties when not under my gaze?" His snide tone set her hackles up but also shot fear through her.

He couldn't know anything. Could he? "My personal habits are none of your business, sir. Please take your leave."

Goforth spun to the door, and Jessica let out the breath she'd been holding. He didn't leave, but slammed the door shut in Abby's face. They were alone. Her mouth dried, and she found it difficult to swallow, much less voice a protest.

Still holding her night rail in one fist, he walked not to the bed to accost her as she feared, but to the window. He knelt and pulled a length of black cloth from where it had been lost under the curtain.

Simon's neckcloth. She tightened her grip on the covers, fighting the urge to bury herself underneath them altogether.

"I don't even have to ask who was here." Goforth rent the cloth in two.

The sound made her flinch. "That is nothing. A scrap of cloth Abby dropped."

"Do you think I'm a fool!" Spittle flew out of his mouth. "You sneaked the bloody Duke of Bellingham into your room and gave yourself to him."

As it wasn't a question, she didn't bother answering.

"At least you aren't stupid enough to deny it. A stable boy saw him scaling out of your window. You allowed him to take the only thing of worth you possess—your virtue."

"He is willing to wed me. Think of the social and political benefits of having a duke as your relation. It would be a coup. A feather in your cap. Your invitation to any function would be assured." Her cajoling was born of nerves. Her palms were damp and her hands shaky.

He threw down the torn pieces of cloth and tossed her night rail on the edge of the bed. "He fed you the pretty words you wanted to hear to get between your legs, stepdaughter. Just like your mother when she wooed me. If I'd known I'd have to deal with her slut of a daughter for the rest of my life, I might have denied her my name and protection."

Anger loosed her tongue. "Protection? Is that what you call your constant belittling of her? I blame you for her death."

"I loved your mother." At her huff of disbelief, he gripped the post of her bed, his knuckles turning as white as the night rail he held. "Why else would I marry a widow with two brats in tow? I did love her. I only realized later how little regard she held for me."

Jessica's mind whirled through memories set askew at his declaration. "Why would she marry you if she didn't hold you in her affection?"

"Because your father left her penniless. Destitute." He leaned forward with such aggression she worried he might do her harm. She pressed back into the pillows. Even though she was covered, her nakedness left her feeling vulnerable.

"My father did not die destitute." Her defense of a man she remembered only in vignettes was reflexive, but did she know that for certain? She had been a child, only concerned with childish things.

"Oh, but he did, and once your mother discovered Blake was the heir to a title and fortune, her true feelings became clear. She no longer needed or wanted me." His pain had made him hateful.

Forgiveness didn't rise, only a numb understanding. "Did she attempt to leave you?"

"I owned her. There was nowhere for her to run." As her husband, he was correct. His power over her mother was absolute. "Have you asked yourself why you and Blake were not enough for her to live for?"

The sharp breath she took tightened the already painful hold her mother's death had on her heart. Of course, she had asked herself the question and felt like a traitor to her mother's memory every time. How did Goforth manage to discover her wounds and drive a stake through them?

"I stand by my word. You will not marry the duke. He cannot be allowed to win."

"He wounded your pride a decade ago, and your pride is more important than my happiness. Is that about right?"

"I vowed to make him pay for his insolence. I never thought the instrument of my revenge would be you, but here we are. You have been a thorn in my side since the moment you came into my life. I could throw you into the streets to earn your living on your back without a moment's regret. That would be beyond the pale, I suppose."

His cruelty was a cold thing. It was calm and calculated, and she wondered not for the first time if he had gone a little mad. She pulled the covers up another inch, wishing she could don her disguise and disappear once more.

"What do you plan to do with me? Marry me to Sir Benedict Pennington for a vote, I suppose?"

"No, he desires an unsullied bride, but he would be more than pleased to pay me to enjoy the same favors you gave to the duke for free." Goforth tapped his lips. "Or could there be men who would pay even more than Sir Benedict to enjoy a night between your legs?"

"You wouldn't dare. The gossip would ruin you."

"Not among the set of men I circulate with, my dear. They have the coin to spend but are not bound by the rules of the ton. You would be a conquest for them to boast of in the common houses. A night with an earl's sister." The self-satisfying smile on his face shot terror through her. He turned on his heel and slammed the door behind him.

Surely he was merely attempting to frighten her. Unfortunately, like her mother before her, Goforth had absolute power over her. If he chose to marry her to one of his cronies, he could. If he chose to send her to an asylum on charges of impurity, he could. If he decided to sell her body to the highest bidder, he could.

Unless Simon kept his promises. He *would* keep his promises. She ignored the niggle of worry.

When Abby didn't rush in to check on her well-being, a sinking feeling came over her. Goforth would make certain she couldn't contact anyone before he was ready to put his plans into motion. Time was running out. What if Simon didn't discover Goforth's plans until it was too late?

THE WEEK CREPT by for Jessica. Not even Abby was allowed in her room. Basins of water for her ablutions and trays of food were set outside her door by a dour, unsympathetic footman. Her attempts to cajole him into posting a note for her went in vain.

She contemplated leaving the same way Simon had, but her stepfather had posted a man outside her window to keep her in, or perhaps to keep Simon out. Dread and anticipation built until she could take no more. She grabbed a pillow and screamed into it. Another day of this and she might welcome an extended trip to an asylum.

The sound of locks being turned on the outside of her door —another new addition—had her tensing. It wasn't the usual time for her meals. Her stepfather entered and calmly closed the door behind him. She would have preferred his anger or agitation as it might have meant his plans for her had been dashed. His smile of oily smugness settled a knot in her stomach.

"I'm sending Abby in shortly to ready you for an evening at the theater." His announcement surprised her. She'd expected something more sinister.

"Why the theater?"

"So you can be seen beforehand. You must look your best."

He opened her wardrobe and riffled through her frocks, pulling out one she had not yet had the occasion to wear.

He'd chosen her most extravagant, daring gown. Its golden hue took on a metallic gleam in candlelight, as if it had been cast in bronze, and the lace train rippled like molten metal. The theater would provide the perfect backdrop for its drama.

"What happens after I am seen at the theater?" She took the gown from him and laid it on the bed. There was no use arguing. Anyway, her only chance of escape would be outside this room.

"You will find out." The flick of his gaze made her skin crawl.

The endgame was upon her, and without any word from Simon, she must save herself.

Soon after he left, Abby entered, followed by two footmen with a tub. The two women were silent while pitchers of water filled the tub. Once they were alone, Jessica couldn't control herself and gave the girl a quick hug. The complete solitude had worn Jessica's nerves to the quick.

"Do you have any idea what his plans are for me?" She dashed away a sudden spate of tears at having a sympathetic ear.

"None, miss." Abby chewed her bottom lip. "But he's ordered a valise packed for you."

Not her trunk. Would she be taking a journey only to return to her prison? Was his plan to barter her to the highest bidder still in motion? She couldn't dwell on the possibility lest the encroaching panic make her unable to act.

After having only basins of tepid water for her ablutions all week, the bath was a luxury, but one she couldn't enjoy. Too many scenarios, each one more dire than the next, scrolled through her imagination. The hours crawled by. It was impossible to make plans when she had no idea what fate awaited her.

After Jessica's hair had dried, Abby returned to sweep the mass up into an intricate style and thread her hair with a chain of plated gold. After donning her gown and slippers, Jessica pulled on matching gloves of the finest satin. Abby produced a necklace fitted with an amber stone surrounded by a delicate filigree of gold.

Jessica recognized her mother's necklace immediately. She had searched for it after her death to no avail. When she'd found the courage to question her stepfather about the piece, he had claimed to have pawned it. The news had added another crack to her heart.

A coal of fury she kept banked in her soul flared. Goforth had known how much she desired the necklace as a keepsake of her mother, and he had kept it from her out of spite. Why did the depths of his antipathy toward her still have the power to surprise?

Once the necklace was clasped around her neck, she held the stone in her hand and gathered strength from her mother's memory. She would not give the necklace up again.

The sun had yet to set when a footman scratched on her door to escort her downstairs. Goforth waited in the entry, rocking on his feet and fiddling with his tall black hat. Could his impatience and nerves be used against him?

His gaze widened when he spotted her. "I must say, you are nothing like the ape-faced wallflower of six months ago, my dear. Drury Lane is a possibility after our business is concluded."

Even though a profession on the stage was considered a short step up from prostitution by many in society, it would be preferable to the ruination facing her this night. After they were ensconced in the carriage, Goforth flicked the curtain aside and watched the passing scenery. "I rented a box for the evening."

"That's rather extravagant, isn't it?"

"I plan to recoup my investment in you many times over."

"And if I don't cooperate?"

Goforth shrugged. "Some of the men prefer a bit of fight. It might even drive the bidding higher."

Even though it wasn't unexpected, hearing him confirm her fears was shocking. "You are intent on this plan?"

"There is no way out now."

Neither pleading nor arguing would change his mind, so she remained silent. The carriage came to a stop in front of the theater. Goforth exited first and offered her his arm. She ignored it and took the step without assistance, sweeping past him and handing her cloak off to an attendant. Grandly gowned ladies and dapper gentlemen crowded into the grand saloon.

The ceiling was beautifully arched, and a rotunda rose at the far end with two grand staircases leading to the private boxes that ringed the stage. Since her arrival in London, she had been looking forward to attending the theater, but not like this.

Was it her imagination, or was she the focal point of too many gazes? Gazes that took liberties and made her long for her cloak. All she could do was hold her head high and formulate a plan of escape. Would word reach Simon of her presence? Hope flared.

As they worked their way toward the rotunda and the staircases, Goforth introduced her to a dozen gentlemen. Some of them were familiar, like Sir Benedict Pennington, but most were strangers. None besides Sir Benedict possessed a title beyond a simple mister, and only one made an indelible impression. It wasn't favorable.

"Mr. McKelvey, is it?" Goforth asked, his brow furrowing.

"That's correct, sir." Mr. McKelvey wasn't ugly, but his face was stark and possessed not a whit of softness or humor. His shoulders stretched his black evening jacket to the limit of its seams. While his clothes were finely made, he did not give the impression of a gentleman. The shiver skating down her back was born of fear.

Goforth seemed as taken aback by the man as Jessica. "How did you hear of our enterprise?"

"My tastes are well known around town. Don't worry, Mr.

Goforth, I have the coin." The man's gaze licked down her body as if he had already laid claim. "You'll not regret having me present at your *enterprise*."

"Very well then. You are welcome to join us." Goforth passed McKelvey a sealed note. "The details are here."

Mr. McKelvey's slight bow conveyed more animus than respect, but Goforth was too distracted to notice. He took her elbow and led her on, but she couldn't stop from looking over her shoulder. Danger hovered around Mr. McKelvey like a cloak. If she ended up in his hands at the end of the night, what might befall her?

Her knees quivered on the climb to their rented box. It was situated to the left of the stage in the middle of the second tier. Goforth positioned one of the chairs to put her on perfect display and then excused himself, leaving her to settle in alone.

The green velvet chairs and curtains provided the perfect frame for her gold dress. Ladies and gentlemen alike held opera glasses and searched the crowd. After all, people came to the theater to see and be seen as much as to enjoy the show.

She decided to do the same and pulled her glasses from her reticule. It didn't take her long to find who she was not so subtly searching for. Simon was indeed in attendance. But he wasn't alone. Next to him sat the beautiful woman from the ball. This evening she wore an exquisite lavender gown covered in sparkling beads of glass.

Her beauty was lush and extravagant, her dark coloring the perfect foil for Simon's burnished Adonis-like handsomeness. He smiled as the lady whispered in his ear, surely closer than was strictly necessary, but what stopped her heart was the hand caressing his thigh. Simon made no move to end her intimate touches.

As if sensing her regard, he raised his gaze to meet hers. Jessica whipped the glasses into her lap. *Fool.* She had been a fool to trust him, and an even bigger fool for hoping he would ride to her rescue like a white knight.

Goforth returned and took a seat behind and to the right of her. It wasn't long before he too spotted Simon and his new ladylove. His chuckle was mocking. "I see the duke cast you aside easily enough for his old paramour, Lady Herriot. Can't say that I blame him. She is a pretty piece of baggage and very experienced in pleasing a man, or so I've heard. You must have been quite the disappointment."

Heat rushed through her, anger and humiliation in equal parts. She refused to turn and give Goforth any more power than he already had over her.

Had Simon used and discarded her? Had all his words and declarations and touches been false? With trembling fingers, she raised her glasses again. Simon was no longer looking in her direction, but fingering a curl of Lady Herriot's hair. A sob threatened to choke her. It was clear no salvation would be forthcoming. If she was to be saved, she must do it herself.

CHAPTER 22

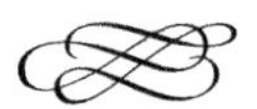

Lady Herriot looked at him quizzically, and Simon cursed internally. He hadn't been listening, which was boorish considering how shamefully he was abusing her kindness. "I'm sorry, Kate. I'm rather distracted this evening."

Her throaty laugh held no censure. "While I was hoping to be your current distraction, I can see the beautiful young lady in gold has gained your full attention. Who is she?"

"Miss Jessica Tremaine. Her younger brother inherited the Penhaven title."

Kate held up her opera glasses and casually glanced over the row of boxes across the theater. "Who is that with her? Not their father, obviously."

"Edward Goforth. Her stepfather."

"A mushroom."

Simon stifled a strained laugh. He was too tense to find anything truly humorous. "Lord Drummond voiced a similar opinion not long ago."

"Oh dear, I do believe she caught me staring." She lowered the glasses to her lap and shifted to Simon. "I value honesty, Your Grace, and thought you did as well."

"I do. Of course I do." The back of his neck heated. He sighed. "I should apologize."

"Yes, you should," Kate said lightly. "You shouldn't be using me to make another lady jealous, although I am flattered."

Simon gaped at her before composing himself. "That was not my intent."

"Miss Tremaine looks as though she wants to shove me into the Thames. If not to make her jealous, then why are you here with me? Most people will assume we have become lovers once more."

Simon's collar shrunk at least two sizes. He tugged at it with a finger. "Miss Tremaine knows my heart is hers."

"Does she?"

The skepticism in Kate's voice gave Simon pause, and he glanced in Jessica's direction. Without glasses, her expression was a mystery, but her rigid posture gave credence to Kate's opinion.

He could soothe Jessica's tender feelings after Goforth's scandalous game was finished this evening and she was safe. Although he wasn't sure he would truly relax until he put the special license burning a hole in his pocket to use.

Too many things could go wrong, and as Simon couldn't appear at all interested in winning Jessica, he had to rely on others to carry out their plan. The level of trust required of him was proving difficult.

As he watched surreptitiously, several gentlemen—and he used the label generously—stopped by Goforth's box to offer greetings. The pattern was the same for each. Goforth would introduce each man to Jessica, a short chat would ensue, and then Goforth would take the man aside for a conversation. The more men who showed interest, the more difficult it would be for Simon's plan to succeed.

The lights dimmed. Shakespeare's Macbeth was being performed with gusto. It was impossible to enjoy the tragedy being played out on the stage when the ending to his own life could be just as dismal. He was impatient for the interval. Damien was to meet him and pass along an update.

As the lights came up, he excused himself from Kate's box and weaved his way through the throng to procure a glass of champagne. Damien cut through the crowd like an apex predator. Simon was heartily glad Damien was on his side.

Damien took a glass of champagne from a circulating footman and joined Simon. Their tête-à-tête was less conspicuous among the crowd. "She is here?"

"Yes. At least twenty men have shown interest."

Damien's eyebrows rose as he took a sip. "More than we'd hoped, but she is a lovely woman."

Even lovelier than normal. Simon wasn't sure if it was the dramatic gold gown or his carnal knowledge of what was underneath making her appear positively iridescent.

"What have you learned?" he asked.

"It seems Goforth's gambling debts are mounting by the day. He is spread thin and will be desperate for this evening to go well."

"Gray's man is in place?"

Damien gave a brusque nod. "Let's pray he's trustworthy."

As Goforth would never allow Simon or anyone associated with him into the auction, Gray had offered up one of his contacts who'd agreed to pose as an interested party in return for payment. The bargain did not settle Simon's worries in the least. If the man could be bought by Gray, then he could be turned if more money was offered from a different quarter.

Damien looked over Simon's shoulder and cleared his throat. "The lady approaches with her stepfather. You must not give us away."

Simon closed his eyes for a moment to gather himself before forcing a bland smile and turning. Goforth had Jessica's hand tucked firmly on his arm. Some might see it as a protective gesture in such a crowded room, but more likely, he worried about her attempting an escape.

Damien slipped away, the coward. Simon inclined his head. "Miss Tremaine. Goforth. How are you enjoying the production?"

"A bit boring, if I'm being honest." Goforth patted Jessica's hand, which had pulled into a fist around his jacket. "I'm anxious for our next engagement to begin."

Simon nodded at a passing acquaintance and forced a note of disinterest into his voice. "I suppose you have grand dinner plans?"

"More like a grand experiment." Goforth's smile was mocking. "You wouldn't be interested considering you've already enjoyed the experience."

Simon tamped down his rising fury and did his best to mimic Damien's perpetual air of insouciance. "Indeed. Why pay for something I've already enjoyed for free?"

Jessica's sharp intake of breath gutted him. Hurt flashed across her face, but she schooled her features quickly. She had to know he was playing the cad as well as any Drury Lane actor.

He proffered a small inclination of his head. "I wish you luck with your experiment. If you'll excuse me, I must return to my friend."

Before he could make good his exit, Jessica spoke. "Do you mean Lady Herriot?"

"That's right. She and I are old friends." He imbued the last two words with as much insinuation as he was able. Which was quite a lot considering they had indeed been lovers.

"I see," she said in a small voice.

She didn't see at all. Reassuring words were ready to trip off his tongue until he caught sight of Damien shaking his head in warning behind Jessica and Goforth where he was eavesdropping.

Simon met her gaze straight on and hoped she could see the

truth of his heart. "I hope the evening concludes to everyone's satisfaction."

It was the height of irony he was now the one forced to deceive her.

However, if everything went to plan, the deception wouldn't last long, and he would spent the rest of his life making it up to her.

Goforth grunted and led Jessica away. She glanced over her shoulder at him once, and he took a step toward her without thinking. He could snatch her away and make a run for Gretna Green.

Damien grabbed his shoulder. "You mustn't."

His friend was correct. Simon had to let the evening play out, or else Blake would become Goforth's new pawn. He returned to Lady Herriot's box, only to be tortured by a rotation of men meeting Jessica.

Finally, the interval ended. Every moment built tension until the penultimate scene of Macbeth's beheading. Simon hoped there were no lessons for him to be found in the bloody ending.

When the lights came up, he stole a glance toward Jessica and started at seeing the box empty. He rose, frozen in a moment of indecision and panic. How long had they been gone?

"She left a quarter hour ago." Kate rose and gathered her wrap around her.

Courtesy dictated he see Kate to her carriage. He owed her that much at least. His impatience to be gone earned him an exasperated look from Kate. "I can see myself home. I don't want a man who wants another."

"I'm sorry, Kate." He meant it sincerely.

"I am too." Kate gave him a smile, albeit a sad one. "Begone with you. I hope matters of the heart go better for you than they have for me this evening."

He kissed her hand and pushed through the crowd for the door, praying everything was going as planned.

It wasn't.

As soon as he walked through the door of his sister's town house, Rafe met him in the entry with a tight mouth and crinkled brow. "We've hit a snag, I'm afraid."

"What sort of snag?"

"Goforth changed the place of the auction. Or perhaps this was always the original plan and he put forth a dummy location to avoid undesirables from attending. In short, we don't know where they went."

Simon ran a hand through his hair and cursed roundly. Minerva, who was pacing the rug threadbare, didn't even chastise him. Gray was seated at Rafe's desk, his head down as he dipped a quill in ink to continue scratching out a message.

"Does Goforth suspect something?"

"We hoped you might have learned something at the theater about their change in venue." Minerva looked at him hopefully.

"No, I bloody well did not learn anything. If you'll recall, you people"—he pointed from Minerva to Gray to Rafe—"told me to make sure Goforth left with the impression I no longer wanted Jessica."

Gray finished his missive, sanded it, folded it, and applied a wax seal. "I realize this is not ideal, but I have faith the man I have in place will not betray us."

"He's an honorable man then?" Simon asked.

The look Rafe and Gray exchanged did nothing to settle his rising panic. "He has his own code of honor," Gray finally said. "Most likely, Goforth suspects nothing and the change is not a change at all. Our man either has not had time to get a note off or is confident of his success."

"Not reassuring, Masterson," Simon said through clenched teeth.

"In endeavors such as these, one must adapt to the changing tides." Gray rose and tucked the letter into his jacket. "I will ferret out the new location and send news once I have any."

"You are mad if you think I'm going to sit here and idle away the hours while you search for her." Simon beat Gray to the door. "I'm coming with you."

Gray didn't argue, and Simon followed him into the unknown.

CHAPTER 23

Jessica sat in the carriage and waited. If it wasn't for the man guarding the door, she would have bolted. Except, if she were being honest, it wasn't only the thick-necked man stopping her attempt. She had no clue where she was or where to go even if she did escape.

It was clear Simon was not an option. He might help her out of guilt for what he'd taken with no care. Not her reputation or her maidenhead, but her heart. And what if she found Lady Herriot warming his bed? Her pride balked at the thought of throwing herself on his mercy.

She had few other friends. The only one who came to mind was Lady Drummond. Yes, she was Simon's sister, which made things deuced awkward, but she had been kind and offered her help. Something Jessica required badly at the moment.

Jessica peeked out the window. They were in a narrow alley barely wide enough for the conveyance. Horse hooves striking stone echoed around her. She could hear the calls of men and women and the clack of carriages moving on distant lanes. The building was soot streaked but respectable. They weren't in Mayfair, but neither were they in Clerkenwell.

Night blanketed London. The darkness was accompanied by an ominous sense of doom. Her opportunities to escape her fate were diminishing.

A stranger emerged from the building. The man was dressed in black and had the unmistakable pompous airs of an upper servant. He murmured something to her guard. The thick-necked man said nothing, only opened the carriage door and stepped to the mouth of the alley. His bulk blocked any chance of escape.

"My name is Bishop, miss, and I'm to escort you to a waiting area." Bishop gave a perfunctory bow and gestured toward the side entrance, his tone bordering on rude. "If you please."

She didn't please but had no choice in the matter. After taking her cloak, Bishop deposited her in a windowless receiving room and left her without even offering her a drink. Her hands were trembling too much to handle a delicate teacup, but she wouldn't have turned down a tumbler of liquor.

A brace of three candles cast a circle of light not bright enough to banish the shadows lurking in the corners, but she could see enough. The distinctly masculine room held an aura of shabby disuse. The colors were dark blues and the lines stark with no ruffle or flower pattern in sight. The chairs were wooden and stiff-backed without even a cushion.

She was too nervous to sit anyway, so she searched the room for something of use. The only feminine touch was a small escritoire with a lattice of interlocking curves sitting in the corner like a lady left without a dance partner.

She placed the candles on the scarred top, opened the desk, and riffled through blank sheets of paper. What if she wrote a note begging help? While she had no coin, if she could find a willing scullery maid or a groom, she would promise them a great reward to see it delivered. Her hands shook with a shot of hope. She found an ink well tucked into a cubby, but when she dabbed the quill, it came up dry.

The disappointment was sharp. The urge to collapse in tears was there, but so was an abiding anger. She snapped the quill and dashed the contents of the escritoire to the floor. The *plink* of metal on wood drew her to a squat to sort through the mess.

A tarnished silver letter opener peeked from under a pile of faded parchment full of sums. It wasn't a dagger, but the point was still sharp. The sound of a lock being turned had her fumbling with the ties of her reticule. She stuffed the opener inside just in time.

The door swung open, and Bishop stood on the threshold. He flicked a narrowed glance toward the open desk and scattered papers but only gestured for her to follow him. Releasing her held breath, she touched the outline of the letter opener and considered stabbing Bishop in the back.

But what if he was merely earning a living to support a family? Before she could wrestle her conscience into submission, the dark corridor widened to accommodate a set of stairs. He led her up them and opened a plain door with a brass handle at the top to reveal an opulent hallway lined with rooms. Two men in conversation at the far end turned to cast them curious glances. Bishop ignored them.

The buzz of masculine conversation muffled through doors pulsed around her, giving the impression she was the only woman on the premises. Was she in the hallowed halls of a gentleman's club? Not White's obviously, but one of the lesser known clubs?

Bishop rapped on the door directly across from the servants' hallway and waited. It cracked open and revealed her stepfather, his face wreathed in a smile and his eyes glassy with too much drink. He pushed the door wide upon seeing her.

"Here she is, gents." Goforth gripped her arm and dragged her to the front. A cheer went up among the two dozen men gathered. Bishop departed, closing the door in his wake. Was it locked?

In a half panic, she scanned the room. Was there anyone who would intervene and help her? Sir Benedict Pennington was sitting front and center, his smile friendly enough, but his gaze oily. The rest were the cits she'd met at the theater, including Mr. McKelvey. He was not leering or cheering, but staring intently from the far corner. She shuddered and averted her face.

"Do a turn around the room, Jessica. Let the men see what they're buying." Goforth tried to maneuver her toward the scrum of men.

She slapped his hands away. Anger flashed across his face. An anger she recognized. Unfortunately, she didn't duck quickly enough. His palm found her cheek in a slap that silenced the laughter. She cupped a hand over her throbbing cheek. His handprint would remain for hours.

He smirked and turned to the men. "She is as feisty as a wild mare. Who will be the lucky man to break her?"

The feeling in the room shifted to something darker as the men murmured to one another, their smiles turning to leers. The moment took on a nightmare-like quality. Surely she would wake at any moment.

But no, her senses cataloged the scent of cheroots and brandy, the taste of her own blood where the inside of her cheek had cut along her teeth at the slap, and of course the pulse of pain from the blow.

"How closely can we inspect the goods, Goforth?" a man called out.

Humiliation swamped her. She kept her gaze focused over the men's heads and on a watercolor of the sea and cliffs. It was hardly a masterpiece and had been hanging in the room long enough to become discolored from smoke. If only she could walk through the frame and be gone from this place.

The men circled like a pack of wolves readying for a kill. She hated being the defenseless doe in the tableau. She clutched her reticule, the hard length of the letter opener giving her a welcome measure of courage.

The last wolf to circle her was Mr. McKelvey. There could be no doubt he was the alpha. If he wanted her, he would win her. The thought turned her knees to water. He slipped a finger under her chin and forced her to meet his gaze.

"Will you come willingly to my bed, sweeting?" His voice held a gravelly quality that was strangely soothing. Did he use it to lure unsuspecting prey closer?

"No." She intended the word to come out as cutting as a knife, but it wavered on a faint whisper.

"Good." The man's silver eyes were arresting, and it took all her power to break their hold. Jessica's only hope was the man did not have the coin to keep up with the well-heeled cits in the room.

But he more than kept up, he bettered every bid. Finally, the last man standing, Sir Benedict, bowed out with a disgruntled curse. Her honor had been sold for one hundred pounds. A fortune for some, but it felt miserly knowing it would cost her her soul.

McKelvey rose from where he'd been negligently sprawled in his corner seat with a brandy.

Goforth did not seem pleased, but he hesitated less than a heartbeat before sticking out a hand for a bargain-sealing shake.

The man tapped his lips, regarding her but addressing her stepfather. "What if I wish to keep her longer?"

"What do you mean?"

Jessica stared at Goforth, but he ignored her as if she were a piece of furniture.

"Let me have her for a week. She—and you—would be well compensated, I assure you." The man flicked a gaze over the men drinking away their failure. "I assume you plan to offer her again once I'm done with her."

Goforth licked his lips. "It would cost you more."

"I'll double my offer."

"That would buy you three days. And nights. No more." Although Goforth attempted to sound firm, his excitement vibrated.

"Three days then. I'll begin teaching her what pleases me immediately." Even the man's smile was wolfish.

His confident aggression stamped out any protest her conscience might attempt. She would bide her time and seek the opportunity to escape through fair means or foul.

"Take her then, but bring her back unmarked." Goforth turned away. His dismissal stung more than she'd anticipated.

"That's all you have to say?" she called after him.

He spun back around. "Would you have me speak words of love and good wishes? Very well then. Good luck to you in this man's bed."

"What about Blake?"

"Your brother is an earl. You are a fallen woman, and consorting with you would be beyond the pale. The boy is gullible and will swallow whatever Banbury tale I concoct." Goforth offered her a chilling half smile. "I will toughen him and make sure he understands his responsibilities to me and to his station."

What terrors would he wreak on Blake? She couldn't allow it to happen, but she could do nothing to save her brother until she saved herself.

McKelvey led her out of the room with a firm hand on her elbow. When she tried to tug free, his grip tightened. "Let's not, shall we?" he murmured.

They exited the way she'd come in, through the servants' door across the hallway. Once they were descending the narrow stairway, he whispered, "Listen to me, miss, I've been—"

"What's this then?" Bishop stood at the bottom, arms akimbo, voice affronted.

"I apologize, Bishop, but I didn't want to feed the gossipmongers by taking the lady out the front. Could you see my horse brought around, if you please?"

Bishop's mouth was pinched, but he snapped for a young boy to do as requested.

The man guided her outside and around to the street where a handsome bay horse was led up by the young boy. Jessica looked around for a carriage but saw none waiting for her. "Do you expect me to ride? With you?"

"Indeed I do. Now quit quibbling." He mounted and took the reins from the boy who cupped his hands to help her mount.

"Are you quite mad?"

"Mad, bad, and dangerous. Now come on. We must be gone as quickly as possible." He held out a hand.

Taking surreptitious glances up and down the street. She had no idea where they were, and the sparse lanterns did little to enlighten her. The buildings lining the narrow lane were well maintained although narrower than their counterparts closer to fashionable Mayfair. Light and noise spilled from the windows of the establishment they'd left.

What if she ran? Could she evade the man on the horse long enough to seek help from another quarter? She had no coin for a hack, but she was hardy and enjoyed walking the hills and woods around Penhaven Manor. Except this wasn't the country, and she was in slippers and an evening dress in an unknown area of town.

"Don't even think it." His gaze seemed to chisel straight to her thoughts.

"Think what, sir?" Even as she asked, she knew her bluff would fail.

"I would ride you down in less than a dozen steps. I promise you won't regret accompanying me."

She didn't see of a way out. Not yet.

With help from the boy, she mounted in front of him and

held herself as stiff as a board. His hand settled on her waist, and she jerked around ready to slap him.

"Whoa," he said with an equanimity she couldn't claim. He got them moving at a fast walk. "Trust me, everything will be fine."

"Trust you? Ha!" Her voice was bitter with derision. "How did you hear about my stepfather's plans?"

"A business associate." It was clear she wasn't going to get useful information out of him. Did it really matter who he was or why he had paid an exorbitant amount for three nights with her?

Once he had her behind lock and key, she would be at his mercy. Now was the time to act, but she would only have one chance.

"I want to trust you, I do, but this entire evening has been quite distressing." It took embarrassingly little effort to squeeze tears to her eyes. She slumped into him, a bit intimidated at how muscular he felt. Pretending to fumble in her reticule for a handkerchief, she gripped the letter opener. The satin of her gloves made the hold precarious.

"There, there. You'll be right as rain soon enough." He shifted the reins in order to awkwardly pat her shoulder.

She felt almost bad. Almost. She drew the makeshift weapon from her reticule and stabbed him in the thigh with all her strength. The slide of metal into flesh made bile rise in her throat. Whether from pain or surprise, McKelvey dropped the reins and jerked away from her, his seat precarious.

Her original intent had been to leap from the horse and run, but without hesitation, she shoved him. He floundered for a long, heart-stopping second, his hand catching the neck of her dress. Fear careened through her, and she batted at his arm. The delicate fabric ripped, and the man plunged backward.

The horse tossed its head and slowed without guidance from a steady hand. One of McKelvey's feet was stuck in the stirrup.

It was his wounded leg, and he clutched at his thigh and cursed. Blood welled between his fingers, the opener still deeply embedded. The horse dragged him along, and she could only imagine how painful the position was.

She leaned over and shoved the toe of his boot free, nearly toppling on top of him. She groped for purchase, fisting her hand in the horse's mane and righting herself. Her heart kicked into a gallop, but thankfully, the horse only walked a little faster now it was free of the man.

She took up the reins and swung her leg over to ride astride. Her slipper flew off, but she dared not retrieve it. McKelvey had pulled himself to standing. He took three steps toward her before stopping to probe at his wound.

Her skill on horseback was nearly but not completely nonexistent, thanks to Simon. Still, she would be lucky to avoid being tossed. The stirrups dangled several inches too low for her to use. Thankfully, the horse was well trained and docile and didn't balk at her awkward handling of the reins or the tight grip of her legs. What now?

A chilly breeze rushed over her, but she had no cloak, and there was little she could do about her exposed limbs. The sleeve and seam along her flank had been rent, making the bodice gape indecently. She could only hope darkness cloaked her state of undress.

McKelvey had lost his investment and his horse and sustained an injury. What would the heights of his fury lead him to do? His first action would be to retrieve the bank notes he had given Goforth and demand recompense for his stolen horse.

Goforth would blame Jessica—rightly in this case. He would want to hurt her, but she wouldn't be there. Would he begin an immediate search for her? Or would he retrieve Blake, knowing that would lure her home? At least Blake was out of his reach at Eton. For now. She had time to make a plan.

Jessica looked around, desperate for a landmark she recognized. Was she even headed in the right direction? What if she was riding toward the docks or into Seven Dials?

The street grew wider and the town houses larger and more prosperous-looking. Did the garden square she was passing look familiar? Had she seen the square on her way to a ball or rout or on her way home? Impossible to tell.

Exhaustion born of the late night and the stress of the evening swamped her. She slumped in the saddle, her legs trembling from trying to keep her from sliding off. Another more prosperous square came into view. The horse halted, stomping its feet and tossing its head, and she realized she'd tightened her hands on the reins.

Simon's town house was on the other side of the square. Out of curiosity, she had directed the coachman to take her there her first week in London. It was grand and beautiful and intimidating. She had not exited the carriage but rapped on the door to tell the coachman to move on. And now she was faced with a decision.

He'd made it painfully clear he had moved on with Lady Herriot, but fate was intervening. Righteous indignation had her steering her mount toward his town house. When the horse plodded by the front without obeying her tug on the reins to stop, she panicked, tossed her leg over the saddle, and jumped to the ground.

Her legs buckled like rotten twigs. She went down on her hands and knees, tearing her gloves and bruising more than her pride. The horse nudged her shoulder and chuffed wetly against her neck.

Jessica fought the urge to throw her arms around the beast. At least someone seemed to care about her. Using a stirrup strap, she rose and hung on to the saddle until she was reasonably sure she could walk without falling on her face.

Her knees were weak from more than just the ride. Would

anyone answer at this time of night? Would Simon turn her away? No, he wouldn't. He might not love her, but he would help her. She had to believe that much at least.

The steps were a challenge for her knocking knees, but she made it to the top and rang the bell pull. She didn't have to wait long. Locks turned on the other side of the door. She held her bodice together as best she could and raised her chin.

An older, dignified man stood in the threshold in a dressing gown. "Yes?"

"I'm a friend of the duke's. Is he home?" Her question landed like a shovelful of horse dung.

The butler's gaze flicked down her person. She didn't follow it, knowing she must look a fright. She curled the toes of her bare foot and tried to tuck it under her hem, but the butler had seen. He seemed a man who missed nothing.

"His Grace does not receive friends such as yourself at this house, madam." His imperiousness would have done a king proud.

Desperation trumped her gauche embarrassment. "My name is Miss Jessica Tremaine. Please, may I see the duke?"

"He does not receive visitors at this late an hour." The butler stepped back and the door swung closed.

Jessica grabbed the edge and pushed it back open. The butler stumbled backward to keep his balance. Her boldness surprised them both. "I must see His Grace."

"He is not receiving."

Jessica took a shaky breath. "I realize I'm dressed oddly to pay a call at such an inopportune time, but His Grace will most certainly want to see me. In fact, he will be most upset if he learns you have turned me away. Now go wake him."

The butler pursed his lips as if weighing the consequences. "I was not telling a polite untruth, madam. The duke is not at home. What would you have me do?"

Her head swam with the implication. She knew exactly

where Simon was spending his evening. Lady Herriot's bed. What should she do now? She'd seen no hacks about this late in the evening, and she had no idea where Lord and Lady Drummond lived, even if she wanted to try her luck back on the horse. Not that she would be able to mount on her own.

"I will wait for his return in the drawing room." Her pride barely put up a fight. She had nowhere else to go.

"But, madam—"

"Miss Tremaine, if you please." If she couldn't appeal to the butler's better nature, she would bluster through, using her position as precarious as it might be. "If you could send a groom to care for my horse, I would be most appreciative."

"You... You can't wait here for the master's return. It would be unseemly." While he might not have a hair out of place, his dignity was decidedly rumpled.

Jessica bypassed him and picked a random door. A sitting room opened to her. The opulence struck her dumb, but for all its beauty, the room was cold both in temperature and temperament. It was not a well-loved or well-used room.

"I will wait here for the duke's return." Doing her best to mimic Lady Drummond's imperiousness, she glided to a settee covered in cream-and-blue striped silk and lowered herself to the edge.

The butler winced, probably as worried as she was about her leaving a grimy outline on the fine upholstery. "I'll not wake the maid to start the fire. Or bring tea," he said with defiance.

"I'm content to wait without either." The sense of safety was enough.

The butler harrumphed and exited the room, softly closing the door behind him. Not even the undignified arrival of a fallen woman could ruffle him enough to slam it. She stifled a laugh twined with relief and hysteria.

Jessica rose and meandered across the thick rug to the window, her nerves unspooling to exhaustion. The room faced the street. The butler's reluctance to extend hospitality to her thankfully did not extend to her horse. Well, not *her* horse, but best not inform the butler of that fact or he'd bring Bow Street down on her head. A young groom was leading the horse away while patting its neck.

Even though Simon might toss her on the streets, for the moment, she could breathe without the crushing fear. She settled on the settee and found herself listing to the side. Surrendering, she lay down and curled in on herself to ward off the chill of the room. For once, it wasn't Goforth but the hard-looking man who'd bought her and fear of his impending revenge that stalked her dreams.

CHAPTER 24

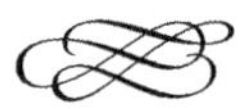

"Just pull the bloody thing out, Masterson." Selwyn McKelvey gritted his teeth.

"You've been dealt worse." Gray ripped the man's trousers, removed a flask from the inside of his jacket, and poured liquor over the wound.

McKelvey jammed his fist against his mouth, not quite stifling a low groan. "Not recently. I'd forgotten how much it hurts to get stabbed."

"I'd guess it hurts worse coming from a lady who you top by a good eight inches and outweigh by at least six stone." The tease in Gray's voice settled Simon's churning stomach. Surely he wouldn't be so cavalier if McKelvey was in danger of expiring in his kitchen.

"Give me the blasted flask and do what you must. Why I agreed to take part in this madcap scheme is beyond me." The man took a long swig from the flask and grimaced.

"Because you need the coin," Gray said baldly before yanking the weapon out.

The man hissed and writhed a moment before bending over to examine his leg. Blood welled, but it didn't appear excessive. "You owe me a horse, by the way. The woman stole it."

Gray muffled laughter. "No one will believe it when I tell them the fearsome Wyn McKelvey was bested by a slip of a woman."

"Women can be the most devious and dangerous of all creatures." McKelvey took the object Gray had pulled from his thigh and let out a bark of laughter. "A letter opener. The woman is resourceful, I'll give her that."

Simon paced the length of his town house's kitchen. They were doing their best to stay quiet and not rouse the servants. Not only did they deserve their sleep, but Simon didn't relish having to explain why a man had been stabbed and was receiving treatment at the servants' table.

Gray finished dressing McKelvey's wound, and the man rose and took a tentative step. He drained the remaining liquor in the flask and raised his brows at Simon. "Why don't we retreat to your study for a real drink and a discussion on the next steps?"

"Good plan," Gray said, already moving toward in that direction.

McKelvey followed with only a slight limp. "Better than the one you two laid this evening."

Simon took up the rear. "It was coming along fine until you got yourself stabbed."

"Sir! Sir, I need to speak with you." Peters, his butler, popped out of a chair that had been placed next to a small seldom-used receiving room and intercepted him in the middle of the entry.

"I told you not to wait up for me, Peters. You look exhausted. Go to bed."

"A woman arrived, sir." Peters pointed to the receiving room.

The butler's pronouncement startled all three men to stillness.

The butler's gaze darted from one man to the next. "I-I

didn't know what to do. She forced herself inside and refused to leave."

Simon leaped at the door, his heart hammering. A dark chill hovered in the room. Gray was close behind him, holding a taper. A woman lay on the settee with her back to them, her gold gown shimmering in the candlelight.

Simon wanted to fall to his knees and thank the gods she was here and safe. It was a bloody miracle she'd made it past Peters. He was of the old guard and more formal and dictatorial than any duke.

His relief unknotted the guilt he'd hauled around since the theater. She'd sought him out even after the dreadful evening. He dropped to a squat next to the settee and found one of her hands. It was frozen even in her dirty satin glove.

"Ask Peters to have the fires stoked in my chambers, would you, Masterson?" Simon didn't look around to see if his command was being followed, but he heard Gray retreat.

Jessica shifted to face him but didn't open her eyes. Her gown was dirty and ripped, exposing a scandalous expanse of bosom.

"Is she hurt?" McKelvey asked in his gravelly voice behind him.

The sound roused Jessica like a bucket of cold water on her head. Her eyes popped open, and she let out a choked scream, shrinking into the corner of the settee. "No! How did you find me? Don't touch me, or I'll put a dagger into your heart. I swear it!"

She hadn't even seen Simon in her terror. He sat on the edge of the settee and bent over her, blocking her view of McKelvey, who he would have stern words with later for frightening Jessica so thoroughly. "You're safe, love. I promise. You're safe."

Her expression changed as soon as his identity registered. She threw herself at his chest, rocking him back, and clamped her arms around his neck with the strength of a constrictor.

"I'm safe?" she whispered.

"Always with me. I'm so sorry for earlier at the theater and... and everything," he finished weakly. "I asked you to trust me, but I didn't know what that would mean at the time. I had to make sure Goforth didn't suspect I'd make a move to extract you from the situation."

"Lady Herriot is not your mistress?"

He hesitated a moment. Only the truth would do. "Lady Herriot and I were lovers years ago, but we parted as friends, and that's our only connection now. Honestly, I feel guilty for using her as I did tonight."

Jessica pulled away, glanced over his shoulder, and tensed. "Why is that man here?"

Without turning, Simon said, "Go help yourself to the brandy in my study, would you, McKelvey?"

"Where's my horse?" McKelvey asked brusquely.

"In the duke's stable. It's a gentle creature." *Unlike you.* Jessica's unspoken qualifier seemed to hover in the air.

McKelvey's lips twitched, and he performed a small bow. "Thank you for taking care of her."

Simon knew he was gone when Jessica relaxed against the cushion. "You sent him?"

"McKelvey was one of Masterson's colleagues during the war. The aim was to have someone intimidating who Goforth wouldn't recognize as anyone associated with me do the bidding."

"A word of warning would have been appreciated. He nearly scared me to death."

"If you'd known, you might have given the game away. It was too important. McKelvey had to win you without raising Goforth's suspicions that I might be financing him."

Jessica jerked straight. "I stabbed him."

Simon's lips twitched in spite of the situation. "You should apologize to soothe his ego, if nothing else."

"But—"

"The wound was clean and will heal." Simon pulled her to his chest and rocked her slightly. "I'm proud of your quick thinking though. It seems you didn't need saving after all."

"What happens next?"

"Next is a bath and a rest."

"Goforth is threatening to pull Blake from school. I can't allow it."

"We have time. Goforth is under the impression McKelvey has you for three days."

Jessica picked at the ripped fabric of her glove. "If Goforth discovers we took him for a fool, he will retaliate. It's his nature."

"We'll figure everything out." He lay a kiss on her nose. "Together."

Jessica shook her head, not meeting his gaze. "Do you regret I'm not a simple maid with simple problems?"

"I regret nothing. Least of all your complications." He rose and held out a hand. "Will you come with me?"

She didn't hesitate. Knowing how precious her trust was, he swore to himself not to take it for granted again. Hand in hand, they exited the receiving room. He instructed Peters to rouse two footmen to ready a bath for Jessica.

Gray emerged from the study as Simon and Jessica made their way to his chambers on the second floor. He nodded with an unusual solemnity. "Are you well, Miss Tremaine?"

"Dirty and sore, but alive and safe. Thank you for standing by us during this endeavor." Her voice was strong enough, but she sagged against Simon.

The flash of a smile made Gray's green eyes spark with life. "Love can be a dangerous adventure. Sometimes we need a little help from our friends to win the day."

She let out a little chuff. "It's a good thing Simon has friends, because I have none to call upon."

Gray tutted. "I wouldn't be so sure of that. Lady Drummond and Lady Wyndam have both pleaded your case."

Jessica's intake of breath was small but noticeable. "I hope to thank them for their kindness soon."

"Jessica needs rest. You're welcome to pass the night here. You and McKelvey both."

"I'll drag McKelvey home with me. Lily enjoys hosting the brute. She finds his stories of derring-do exciting. When would you like to reconnoiter?"

It was still dark out, but dawn crept ever closer. "Come back this afternoon. I'll ask Rafe to be here too. The more heads we have, the better."

Behind him, two footmen carried a tub up the stairs. Simon led Jessica on to his chamber. She went straight to warm her hands at the stoked fire while the footmen left for hot water. After stripping off her dirty gloves, she balled them up and tossed them into the flames. Sparks crackled as the satin burned.

He came up behind her and laid his hands on her shoulders, kneading the tight muscles. Her beautiful gold dress would be good for nothing but the rag bin. Grime marred the torn fabric. She lifted her skirts before letting them swish around her ankles. "I have nothing else to wear."

"You seem to be missing a slipper as well."

"Lost off the side of the horse."

"How did you manage to ride from there to here?" He chuckled slightly until the realities of what could have befallen her on the trip triggered his imagination.

"Without your lesson, I would never have found the gumption to even attempt riding."

"You must have been terrified and unsure of where to turn."

Her chin wobbled, and a tear trickled out. He gathered her in his arms. Her sobs were muffled in his neck cloth. The footmen returned with buckets of hot water, well trained enough to ignore the waterworks from the woman in the room. She cried through the trips needed to fill the tub. Finally, he dismissed the footmen and locked the door behind them.

Her eyes were swollen and red, and her nose was running. He offered her a kerchief from his pocket. She turned away to blow, a sound that made him smile.

"I must look a fright," she said.

"You look lovely as always."

She chuffed and glanced over her shoulder with a smile. "You're lying."

"Come now, your bath is ready. You'll feel better after you're warm and clean." He began unfastening her gown.

She spun away, holding her tattered bodice over her breasts. "What are you doing?"

"Taking care of you."

"I'm not a child."

"Indeed not. I'm well acquainted with your womanly attributes." He imbued a hint of dark tease into his words, but lightened his tone. "Let me take care of you, love. I must make amends for my earlier caddishness."

"Yes, you must," she said tartly and presented her back to him once more.

Her hair was a half-pinned mass, and he plucked out the remaining pins until the thick waves tumbled over her shoulders. Next he divested her of gown and stays with deft hands.

Her chemise was of the finest, thinnest cotton. Blood rushed to his cock. A brace of candles on the stand next to the bed cast a soft light around the room. He could see the outline of her bottom through the garment, and his fingers itched to explore the lush curves.

He controlled the urge and instead knelt. He removed her one slipper and then skimmed his hands up her calf to the ribbon holding her stocking in place. He made quick work of the first one, only allowing his hands to wander as far as the delicate skin at the back of her knee. With her hand braced on his shoulder, she trembled under his touch. The other stocking was peeled away and discarded over his shoulder.

He stood facing her and slipped the strap of her chemise over her shoulder a slow inch at a time. She grasped the fabric before it could fall to the floor.

"The water will cool if you don't get in." He kept the smile off his face, but it imbued his words.

"I'll be naked."

He laid a kiss on her bare shoulder before sliding his lips over her collarbone. "It's generally how baths are accomplished."

"Some young ladies bathe with their underthings on." Her voice was growing more breathless with every kiss he brushed over her bare skin.

"But you are a lady of knowledge, lest you forget the night we spent together in bed." He brushed her lips with his. "You needn't worry, I'll not take advantage of you this night."

"It's not worry but modesty I'm struggling with at the moment."

"No need to be modest with me. I've seen every beautiful inch of you." He tugged on her chemise.

She let it fall to the floor. He didn't let his gaze linger, even though he longed to chart her every curve. He helped her into the bath. She sank into the water with a hiss of pleasure.

He stripped to his shirt and trousers and took a seat next to the tub on a stool, rolling his sleeves to his elbows. Water clung to her lashes like tiny jewels. "Are you here to make sure I don't drown?"

"As you are lacking a maid, I will play the part and wash you." He took up a cloth, lathered it with soap, and lifted her hand. He took his time, cleaning each finger before kissing the tips. Next came her forearm and elbow, finishing with a kiss to the inside crook. He glided the cloth up her biceps and washed her shoulder and neck, the motion more a massage than a scrubbing.

As he hoped, she relaxed into his touch, her muscles growing slack. He walked around the tub and performed the same with her other arm and shoulder. By the time he dipped the cloth over her collarbone, her protest was limited to a gasp on parted lips.

As the cloth circled lower, she arched her back, her peaked nipples breaching the water. "I'm not sure what you imagine in your moments of depravity, but I can assure you my maid does not wash me in this fashion."

The invitation was one he couldn't refuse. He cupped her breast and thrummed her nipple with his thumb. "Your actual maid has never made an appearance during one of my moments of depravity."

"I'm glad to hear it." Her eyes were languid, and her voice dreamy. "It was an odd feeling to be jealous of myself, by the way."

"I thought I was going mad after our fall in the drawing room. After I hit my head, I was certain you were… *you*—the weight of your body, your scent, the taste of your mouth—but after Minerva roused me, I was just as certain it had been a trick of my imagination. I was very confused."

"I was just as certain you had figured out my ruse."

"If I had been thinking more with my brain and less with my cock, I might have done." After giving her nipples a last pinch, he trailed the cloth down her belly until his fingers brushed her mons. She parted her knees and tensed.

Hiding a smile, he withdrew his hand and circled to the end of the tub, resoaping the cloth. "Give me a foot."

Her eyes flashed annoyance, but she obliged, lifting a foot out of the water. He grasped the heel and proceeded to wash off the grime. After propping her foot against his stomach, his attention switched to her leg.

"I'm getting you wet." Her breathlessness made him smile, but he tipped his face down to hide his amusement.

"I don't mind as long as you don't mind me getting you wet."

"But I'm already— Oh. You are incorrigible, Your Grace." Her already flushed cheeks grew pinker.

Holding the linen in one hand, he trailed both hands up and over her calf, past her knee, to her thigh. Her muscles quivered. He advanced another inch and then another until he was a hair-breadth away from touching her core. Retreating was difficult but worth the effort when she huffed out a frustrated breath.

"Why are you teasing me so?" Petulance flavored her voice.

"I promised to not take advantage of you."

"Giving me what I want is not taking advantage of me. You are being cruel."

"What is it you want?" He returned her leg to the tub and took up her other foot, repeating his ministrations.

"I want... I want..."

He washed her other leg and again drew close to her core but stopped to hold her gaze. "We must be honest with one another from this moment to eternity. I'll start. You did look ghastly after your cry earlier, but I loved you even more."

A tentative smile played around her lips as she shoved his chest lightly with her foot. "Liar."

"I love you more every second of the day, Jessica." He met her gaze straight on, all teasing deserted in the face of his truth. "Now tell me what you want."

"So many things," she said in a whisper.

"Concentrate on what you want this instant."

Her gaze trailed down his body to where his hands dipped into the bath water. "Right this instant, I want you to pleasure me with your fingers."

"Yes, I want that too," he said with satisfaction. It was enough. For now. There would be time for earth-shattering confessions later.

He returned her leg to the water, pressed her knees to rest against the sides, and leaned farther over the tub to claim a kiss. Then he settled on the stool while she watched him through half-lidded eyes, drawing her bottom lip between her teeth.

Her breasts bobbed at the surface, her nipples hard nubs. His cock throbbed. Had she any notion of her power over him? Not yet, but she would learn quickly and keep him on his knees. He wouldn't squander the opportunity to be in charge.

He grazed his hand down her mons and into her folds. She was slick, not with bath water, but her arousal. He ran the tip of one finger along the delicate outer tissue before finding her bud.

Her exhale bordered on a moan, and her eyes closed. She gripped the sides of the tub, her knuckles white. He'd planned to tease her, but she didn't allow it. Her hips bucked and sloshed water onto his shirt and trousers. Before he could tease her off the edge, she fell into bliss. Her knees clamped his hand between her leg, and she reached for his nape to pull him in for a kiss so hot he was surprised steam didn't rise around them.

With a satisfied smile on her face, she went lax and slipped fully under the water. He grinned and loomed over the tub, his hands braced on the sides, enjoying her playfulness. He had a feeling she had not been able to embrace that part of herself for a long while. She emerged and dashed water out of her eyes.

"Your hair still needs washing." He moved behind her, hoping the mundane task would blunt his arousal. If anything, washing her hair only made the uncomfortable situation in his trousers worse. The task was intimate in a way he couldn't describe. Even more so than bringing her to climax.

She tilted her head back for him to rinse her. The water had cooled while they'd played, and she squealed in reaction. She sat up and wrung the water from her hair. Her hard nipples begged him to bend down and take one in his mouth, but he resisted.

Instead, he retrieved one of his dressing gowns and a length of cloth. She stepped out of the tub, and he wrapped the cloth around her, rubbing her dry. After replacing the wet cloth with his dry, too-big dressing gown, he settled her in front of the fire and positioned himself behind her with a brush. He took his time, taking care with the tangles, and she relaxed between his legs, propping her arms on his knees.

"You are exhausted." He could brush her hair for hours from the sheer enjoyment of touching her, but she needed to rest. Obstacles awaited them. "Let me tuck you into bed."

He rose, moved in front of her, and held out his hands. She didn't take them.

"You are aroused." She ran her tongue over her bottom lip, and his cock twitched.

The state was so enduring, he'd almost forgotten. "Yes. I can't seem to help it around you."

"What do you want?" She cast a look at him through her lashes, a half smile hovering on her lips.

"I want you to be happy."

A huff signaled her displeasure. "That's not what I meant, and you know it. Have you already forgotten your promise of honesty?"

With slow, languorous intent, she ran a finger down the length of him. Her touch was light, and the fabric of his trousers was thick, yet the trail of sensation made him groan deep in his throat.

"You've had a difficult night."

She tutted and cupped his erection. "Honesty, Your Grace. Tell me what you want in this instant."

He surrendered. "Unbutton my trousers."

Her hands jumped up to comply. While she fumbled with the buttons, he pulled his water-splotched shirt off and tossed it aside. As soon as his trousers were loose, he shoved them down his thighs, freeing his cock.

He was ready to burst before she even touched him. This

was going to last an embarrassingly short time. He fisted the base with one hand and cupped her head with the other, guiding the tip to her mouth.

She made a little sound of surprise and glanced up at him. The picture she made was erotic. His cock was tantalizingly close to her lips. Lips she daubed with her tongue as if knowing he was slowly going mad. Her hair was loose, and his dressing gown gaped to reveal the top curves of her breasts.

"I want you to suck me off." He barely rasped out the words, but he knew she understood when, with their gazes locked, she opened her mouth and engulfed the head of his cock.

His knees wobbled, and his hips flexed, pushing deeper into her hot mouth. He wrapped her hair around his hand and held her, pumping gently into her mouth and making sure not to go too deep even as he wanted to feel her throat catch and squeeze him.

As predicted, he didn't last more than a handful of minutes, erupting in her mouth. She gamely tried to swallow his spend, but some dribbled down her chin. The picture etched itself into his memory to be revisited even as embarrassment at his rough handling rushed through him.

He tucked himself back in his trousers. She sagged backward into the chair, her lips swollen and her eyes heavy. He wiped her chin clean with his thumb and picked her up in a cradle hold. She rested her head on his shoulder, boneless in his arms. His selfishness knew no bounds.

"I'm sorry, Jessica."

"For what?"

"For using you so dreadfully."

She stifled a yawn with the back of her hand. "Was I dreadful at it? I'll get better with practice."

"That's not what I meant." He lay her on his bed and climbed in next to her. She cuddled into his side like a contented cat. "You are innocent and—"

"Not so innocent anymore." She patted his cheek absently. "Stop worrying so. I enjoyed taking you in my mouth."

And with that pronouncement, she fell asleep. He could only shake his head and stifle laughter. Gray light seeped through the curtains. It was a new day, and he had much to do, but he could not bring himself to leave her. Not yet.

CHAPTER 25

Jessica came awake with a start, pushing up on an elbow and clutching the covers to her chest, unable to fit herself in time or place for one heart-pounding moment. With the rush of a dam breaking, the events of the past hours flooded her, including her bath and the aftermath. Blushing, she flopped back to the impossibly soft pillows in the bed. Simon's bed, although he was no longer next to her.

Light pierced the curtains. How long had she been asleep? Hours or days? She slipped out of bed, still in Simon's dressing gown, and peeked through the slit. The window overlooked a large private garden. Two gardeners worked on planting spring flowers and pruning dead limbs. The slanting sunrays pointed to afternoon.

The sound of voices in the hallway spun her around, and she tied the dressing gown tighter. The door opened without preamble, and Lady Drummond popped her head inside. Seeing Jessica by the window, she threw the door wide and grinned.

"My dear girl. What a gauntlet of challenges you've faced. My brother doesn't deserve you, but I'm so pleased you're to be my sister." Lady Drummond approached and took Jessica's hands in a strong hold that seemed to transfer a bit of strength.

Jessica stood up straighter, and while her worries didn't disappear, they seemed lighter. "I'm pleased to see you once again, Lady Drummond."

"I insist you call me Minerva." Minerva's gaze flicked over her.

Jessica curled her bare toes in the thick rug and braced for a setdown. "I can explain. You see, last night—"

Minerva held up a hand and winked. "No need to explain. Rafe and I were young and impetuous. We are still rather impetuous on occasion."

Jessica let out a puff of breath. If Minerva hadn't stopped her, Jessica wasn't sure exactly what explanation she would have offered. The truth was entirely scandalous. "Simon asked me to be his wife."

Minerva's smile was all knowing. "Yes, he told me. That's why I'm here. To prepare you."

Jessica opened and closed her mouth, not sure how to respond. Her mother had died long before discussing what was expected in the marriage bed, but considering Jessica was wearing nothing but Simon's dressing gown, she did not need a tutorial on the finer points of the wedding night. At least, she didn't think she did.

Minerva raised her eyebrows. "Please tell me Simon mentioned he acquired a special license. Although there was talk about whisking you off to Gretna Green if necessary."

"No, actually, he didn't. He did say some time ago we should marry quickly to head off Goforth's plans."

"I should ring the peel over his head, but he has much on his mind." Minerva rolled her eyes before settling her gaze on Jessica. "No doubt he would have you both sign and make the marriage legal while you wear his dressing gown, but I put my foot down."

Jessica fisted the lapels of the gown together. "Are you saying he wants to wed me this very day?"

"That's exactly what I'm saying." Minerva patted her arm. "If the situation were different, I would insist he wait and read the banns, but you and your brother need the protection a duke can provide as soon as possible."

Jessica swallowed, casting her head around the matter. "I have nothing to wear. My dress from last night is a shambles."

"I have an assortment of dresses you can choose from. Come with me." Minerva led Jessica out of Simon's chambers, up a floor, and down a long hall. Portraits of Bellingham ancestors marked her progress with serious expressions and censorious eyes.

The town house was at least five times as large as the one Goforth had rented for the season. The furnishings were tasteful and elegant, but the stillness gave an impression of stasis. Even though it was where Simon lay his head while in London, it wasn't a home.

The chambers they entered were distinctly feminine. Blues and golds overlay rich creams. The furniture had elegant lines and was delicate yet sturdy.

"My old rooms," Minerva announced. Two maid were already at work. One arranged dresses on the large bed, while the other hung one from the wardrobe door, fluffing the skirt.

Jessica ran her hand over the rich satins, silks, and muslin fabrics. "They're all lovely."

"A few seasons out of fashion, I'm afraid, but thankfully, they should need minimal adjustments. We are of the same size and height. Or at least, we were." Minerva cupped her hands under the outline of a bump at her belly. It was obvious she was well pleased with the news.

Jessica gasped and smiled. "Congratulations to you and Lord Drummond."

"Indeed. Our families have much to celebrate." Minerva

moved to finger a beautiful claret-colored dress hanging on the wardrobe. Elaborate gold embroidery detailed the skirt. "This one is too dark for spring."

A butter-yellow dress on the bed drew Jessica closer. It was simple and fresh with long sleeves, a high collar, and modest ruffles at the shoulders. "You told me once yellow is Simon's favorite color. What do you think of this one?"

Minerva whisked the dress up and pressed it to Jessica, examining her with a tilt of her head. Her smile filled Jessica with much-needed confidence. "The color suits you. A beautiful spring flower. It's perfect."

Minerva bustled her behind a dressing screen and handed over a set of undergarments. Jessica slipped on the chemise, and one of the maids helped her into a set of stays. All the while, Minerva kept up a stream of chatter.

"Simon has done little to the town house since I married Rafe and moved to Wintermarsh," Minerva said.

"He told me once he considers Wintermarsh his home." Jessica adjusted the sleeves while the maid fastened the hooks of the dress in the back. The clothes fit exactly as if they were made for someone else. The bodice was an inch too tight and the hemline an inch too short, but it would do in a pinch.

"I'm sure you'll make many changes to this house as well as to the primary country estate. After all, the two of you will want to make your own home and fill it with children." Minerva handed over two delicate silk stockings and ties.

Jessica's head spun. She would be a duchess in charge of not one, but many households.

Her panic must have shown plainly on her face, because Minerva took her by the elbow with concern wrinkling her brow. "Whatever's the matter, my dear?"

Jessica plopped into the nearest chair, the cream velvet soft under her hands. "I'm not... I don't... I have no idea how to be a duchess. I know nothing of managing a household or being a proper hostess."

"Pish. You're hardly a dunderhead. You'll learn. The housekeeper is excellent. A no-nonsense Scottish widow I hired myself. I'll introduce you."

Jessica wrapped her arms around her waist and leaned over until her forehead nearly touched her knees. "I wasn't raised a lady. I was never meant to be a duchess. I'll be a disappointment."

Minerva dropped to her heels and set her hands on Jessica's knees. "Stop it right now. I hear Goforth's words coming out of your mouth. It is an easy thing to denigrate yourself. Simon isn't marrying you for your skill and experience in menu planning, for goodness' sake. He loves you."

"And I love him," Jessica whispered.

Minerva patted her knees and stood. "Trust me, that's all that matters. The rest will work itself out. I promise."

Feeling marginally better, Jessica pulled on the stockings and slippers Minerva provided. She stood and did a turn for Minerva, who hummed. "It will do for now, but I assume your old wardrobe is now out of reach. We need to call on the modiste tomorrow."

Disquiet slipped through Jessica. While marrying Simon was a dream come true, she couldn't forget her promise to keep Blake safe. "Do you have a traveling dress I could borrow in case I need to fetch my brother on the morrow?"

Minerva's brows twitched down, but she turned to the wardrobe and riffled through what was left, pulling out a navy-blue habit with gold braiding. The severe cut was elegant and military inspired. "It's woefully out of fashion, but you are welcome to it."

"Thank you." It wasn't a matter of if, but when Goforth discovered their subterfuge.

Minerva sat Jessica down in front of a looking glass for the maid to style her hair into an intricate braid that suited her well. "You look lovely, Jessica. Are you ready?"

A pang of longing formed a lump in her throat. "I wish my mother and brother were here."

Minerva's bright smile faded into one of sympathy. "I know, but Rafe and I are here, and we're your family now too."

Jessica could only manage a nod.

"Let's make it official then."

The walk to the drawing room seemed a long and winding path, not unlike the events that had brought Jessica and Simon together in the first place. The drawing room was marginally more welcoming than the cold receiving room of the night before. A colorful rug or two and new curtains would add warmth.

A young man in black robes and holding a Bible hunched on the edge of a settee, his eyes round. Deep in conversation, Simon and Rafe stood at the mantel, each holding a tumbler of liquor, neither noticing their arrival.

Simon was dressed in dark, formal breeches and a dove-gray frock coat. Not a hair was out of place, and his stock was crisp and elaborate. In short, he looked nothing like the man in shirt sleeves with rumpled hair who'd tended to her so sweetly the night before.

Jessica tensed on the threshold as Minerva cleared her throat. "Gentlemen."

Both men's heads swiveled toward her, but Simon might have been the only one in the room. He straightened and made his way to her, depositing his glass on a table on the way.

He took her hands and leaned down to buss her cheek. His lips were warm, and his breath was sweet with brandy. In her ear, he whispered, "You look like a lemon twist I'd like to unwrap."

Leave it to him to lighten the moment and put her at ease.

While the trappings were more formal, the man she loved was underneath. She smiled.

"Ah, there comes the sun." He crooked his arm, and she lay her hand on his forearm. "Are you ready?"

"I'm nervous."

"So am I." Simon turned to the man of the cloth to perform an introduction. "Mr. Jones is a curate of Saint Mary's."

"I've never performed a wedding." His voice was barely past the point of breaking.

"You're in luck, Mr. Jones. My lady and I have never been married before, so we don't have anything to compare it to. You'll do fine, I'm sure."

The young man let out a braying, nervous laugh. The ceremony commenced without delay. The young curate didn't opine about the sanctity and gravity of marriage. He dived into the usual recitations, probably because he had no intimate knowledge of the union.

Jessica repeated her vows, and Simon did the same. She might have promised to wash his feet every evening for all she could remember of what she said. What would happen next? There was no happily ever after possible with Goforth threatening her brother.

Finally, they both signed to make things official, and Rafe took the document with promises to see it delivered to the appropriate authorities.

The moment verged on the unreal, but the gold ring on her finger anchored her. "So that's it. We're married?"

"We are." He dipped his head to catch her gaze, his smile tottering on the edge of uncertain. "I hope you aren't already harboring regrets."

She grabbed his hand for a squeeze. "No regrets, only worry for what comes next."

"I wish I could whisk you away for a proper honeymoon." He was silent for a moment as if grieving the loss. "We still have two days—and nights—before Goforth expects you to return."

Her smile was tremulous. "Another night together would be lovely."

As if her pronouncement angered the devil, the butler rapped on the door. "A message was delivered, sir."

A prickling sense of foreboding turned to outright terror when she recognized the wax seal on the missive. Simon ripped it open, muttering curses as he read. "Goforth is aware we duped him. He suspected correctly we would wed at the earliest opportunity."

He handed the parchment to Jessica, and Rafe and Minerva gathered closer, as if they could protect her from its contents. The letter slipped out of her fingers to float to the floor. "It's too late. He has Blake."

"We'll retrieve your brother." Simon took her hands between his and chafed them.

"Right now?"

Simon firmed his mouth and nodded. "I'll order the carriage brought around. If the weather holds and we can manage decent stock during the changeovers, we can be at the Penhaven estate by midnight."

"I can change and be ready in a quarter hour." Jessica took off toward the stairs, her hands and knees shaking. The culmination of all her fears pressed on her chest until she was gasping back tears when she entered Minerva's old chambers.

The maid helped her out of the daffodil-colored dress into the somber military-style riding habit. Apropos, considering she was going to war. The maid packed a valise for her, and Jessica resisted the urge to hurry her.

Simon paced the entry. He too had changed into traveling clothes. Buckskin breeches and boots topped by a simply tied neckcloth and serviceable frock coat. Minerva bustled out of a side hallway, followed by a footman bearing a hamper.

"Nothing fancy, but as you won't get a wedding feast, this will have to do." Minerva picked at Simon's jacket. "Be careful. Desperate men act irrationally."

Simon put his arm around her shoulders. "We'll be careful. Thank you for everything. You and Rafe."

Rafe stepped from the shadows, fingering the scar that ran down the side of his face. "I don't like this. I should come."

"No. You should take care of my sister. Our marriage is legal and binding. Once Goforth faces reality, he will be more amenable to negotiation. I can make things deuced uncomfortable for him in London, especially if the rumors of his gambling debts are true."

Jessica shot him a look. Gambling debts? No wonder Goforth had been willing to sell her off. It wasn't merely her reputation at risk but his own. Debtor's prison would ruin him.

The carriage waited outside. Jessica cast a look at the sky before entering. Clouds were massing on the horizon, blotting out the setting sun. Progress was slow until they got out of London where the roads were more sparsely trafficked.

Simon set the hamper on his lap and went foraging. "We should eat. It's bound to be another long night."

Jessica choked down a piece of bread with jam but waved away the succulent chicken he offered, her stomach protesting violently.

"What's the matter?" he asked and then let out a dry chuckle. "Beyond the obvious, of course."

"I keep imagining what he could be doing to Blake."

"Goforth has had Blake in his custody less than a day, sweetheart."

"How long does it take to beat someone or humiliate them? How long does it take to break one's spirit?"

Simon took her hand and pressed a kiss to the gloved back. "Forever wouldn't be long enough to break your spirit, my love."

"I'd like to believe that is true, but if he had managed to sell me to Sir Benedict or a man like him, I might now be damaged beyond repair."

Simon wrapped her close and said nothing for what might have been minutes or hours. Finally, he said, "We need to make a plan."

CHAPTER 26

The remainder of the trip passed with Jessica alternately napping and arguing with Simon. His plan had them separating on arrival at the manor. Even worse, he was going to confront Goforth alone while she was to locate Blake. She preferred to keep Simon in sight at all times.

His harrumph was one of exasperation. "Do you truly believe Goforth can best me in a fight? I'm not some ton dandy, you know."

"Goforth won't fight like a gentleman. He won't go easy on you just because you are a duke."

Simon cast her a narrowed glance. "You should be more worried about his well-being than mine, wife."

"I'm more concerned about my husband's life, especially considering we haven't consummated the marriage yet," she said tartly.

His expression softened. "I promise to remedy the deficiency as soon as possible."

Rain pattered on the roof of the carriage. Not a fortuitous omen. A call from the coachman set her stomach diving. She flicked the curtains open. They were on the final approach, passing under the trees lining the carriage drive. It was late, but light bloomed behind several windows. Goforth could be torturing Blake even now.

The lovely lines of the house were in contrast to the evil deeds it had witnessed over the generations. Was it cursed?

The carriage pulled to a stop at the main doors. Simon smoothed his hair back and straightened his jacket. Blond hair stubbled his cheeks. The hours of travel had left him looking unusually rumpled.

"You know what to do. What must be done." Simon waited for her nod before pressing a quick, hard kiss on her mouth and hopping down.

She lost sight of him when the carriage rounded the corner. The coachman did not climb down to help her disembark. She needed to stay as invisible as possible. Goforth needed to think Simon had come alone to defend her honor.

She ducked out of the carriage and scurried through the kitchen garden to rap at the door. Mrs. Hamish opened the door, spotted her standing in the rain, and goggled. Jessica held a finger up to her lips.

Mrs. Hamish swallowed audibly before nodding. She almost closed the door, turned, and clapped her hands. "Head to bed, girls. I'll finish the bread."

Jessica shivered and shifted on her feet, impatience and fear colliding to her chest. Finally, the door opened, and Jessica stepped in out of the rain and into a floury hug from the cook. Jessica closed her eyes and leaned into the warmth.

"You can't be here, lamb. It's not safe for you. Turn around and run for the woods. Seek help at Wintermarsh." The unexpected plea had Jessica rearing back.

"I can't leave without Blake."

"Blake was bait to lure you home. Your stepfather. He's..." Mrs. Hamish struggled for words. "He's not in his right mind."

"Where is Blake now? Has he been hurt?"

"Your brother is well enough." Mrs. Hamish's lips clamped together, and her gaze slid away. Her hands twisted in her apron. "I think."

Not exactly reassuring. Trying and failing to keep her voice calm, Jessica asked again, "Where is he?"

"Locked in the turret room," Mrs. Hamish said with a heavy dose of dread.

Jessica rocked back a step. It was the room where their mother had taken her own life. The room Jessica had been unable to enter since. "I must go to him."

Mrs. Hamish grabbed Jessica's arm in a grip made strong from kneading. "Goforth brought two men with him. Bruisers. One is guarding Blake, and the other is patrolling the house."

Fear stomped on Jessica's lungs. Simon had walked into a trap. She grabbed the edge of the table to steady herself and corral her panicked thoughts. Did she go to Simon or to Blake? Simon's reassurances he could handle himself weighed against the surety Blake could not.

"I'm not alone. The duke is here. I'm..." The state of matrimony was a new, fragile bud she was afraid might wither before taking root. "I'm his wife."

Mrs. Hamish held one of her chapped, work-worn hands over her mouth. "My dear, that's a most welcome bit of good news."

She paced, feeling time slipping through her fingers. She needed to act. "I need the key to the turret."

"Goforth confiscated the housekeeper's key to the room. I know of no other."

An old memory clawed its way to the surface. Her mother had a key and kept it under the baize lining in her writing desk. Could it possibly still be there? Her mother's rooms had remained mostly untouched since her death. Even Jessica had avoided them, finding no solace among her things.

"I might know of another key. If Goforth asks, you haven't

seen me." Jessica took a candle and scampered out of the kitchen without waiting for a response.

Her mother's rooms were on the second floor and connected with Goforth's through an inner door. She tiptoed past her stepfather's door to her mother's. The door didn't open. She tried it again and put her shoulder against it. It was locked. For all Jessica knew, the door had been locked for years.

Her only option was to enter through Goforth's rooms. She held her breath, but the door opened on a squeak. She paused, but no one jumped out of the shadows, so she stepped inside, leaving the door cracked.

The room had a musty scent, and she held up the candle, her shaking hands casting changeable light around the room. The covers on the bed were in disarray, and the washstand was dirty with disorderly shaving implements. The curtains were drawn, but she could hear the ping of rain on the windows. The storm had settled over Penhaven in earnest.

She tiptoed to the connecting door as if the room were an extension of his mind and he could sense her invasion. The connecting door opened, and she entered her mother's rooms for the first time since choosing the gown she would be buried in.

It was immaculate. No dust covers protected the long unused furniture. She ran a finger over the dressing table. Perfectly clean. The bed was neatly made, but a niggle of unease sent a shudder down her spine. Something was eerily wrong.

Then she noticed the indentation in the pillow and the faint outline on the coverlet. Someone had slept on the bed recently. It could only be Goforth. She swallowed past a lump, unsure what it meant. Did Goforth battle guilt? Did her mother haunt him?

Those were questions she didn't have time to unpack. She turned her back on the bed and set her candle on her mother's writing desk. Saying a little prayer, she lifted the edge of the baize. At first, she saw nothing, but then a gleam of dark iron caught her eye in the top corner. She pulled out the familiar key.

A yell had her clutching it to her chest and blowing out the candle. The darkness was both a comfort and a terror. Footsteps echoed loudly down the stairs, growing fainter by the second. Her fear transposed to Simon. What was he facing downstairs?

Without light, she made her way back through the connecting door and out of Goforth's room, only hitting her shin once. As soon as she sprang Blake and made sure he was safe, she would help Simon however she could.

Thankful she was familiar with the servants' passages, she slipped into the narrow stairway from the panel door in the hall and crept upward to the top floor. She barely opened the door and saw no one guarding the corridor. She scurried up the stone staircase and rapped on the heavy wooden door, trying to make as little noise as possible.

"What do you want now, you ninny-headed arse? I'm happy to discuss your whore of a mother some more." The voice on the other side of the door was unmistakably her brother, but a version she had never encountered. He didn't sound timid or dreamy or scared. He sounded furious and mocking.

"Blake! It's me."

"Jess! I'm locked in." It sounded like he was ramming his shoulder against the door.

"I've got a key. Hang on." She had to use both hands to steady the key. Even though she knew it was the right key, she still tensed until the mechanism turned.

Blake threw the door open and wrapped her in a hug. "Thank you. I was considering climbing out the window and edging along the ledge. You've kept me from splatting on the lawn."

His tone was upbeat and bordered on amused. She pushed him back. Even the shadows couldn't disguise his battered face.

His right eye was nearly swollen shut, his bottom lip pooched out, and his nose was most likely broken. Yet, he grinned at her.

"This is not funny. Goforth is dangerous."

"He's more than dangerous. He's gone completely queer in the attic." Blake grabbed her hand and looked around. "Where's the whoreson who's been on guard?"

"I'm not sure, but there was a ruckus downstairs. Simon is confronting Goforth. We need to help him."

Blake paused and tossed her a glance. "Are you referring to the Duke of Bellingham?"

"Yes. He's my husband." Her ring bit into her fingers where her brother clasped her hand tightly.

"You bagged a duke? Way to go, sis." Blake's attitude flummoxed her. She had expected to find him beaten and broken. Instead, he was beaten and defiant. Nothing like their mother. More like... her. Had she underestimated his strength?

She allowed him to lead her to the main stairway. Pounding footsteps had them scrambling to the opposite end of the corridor from the servants' stairway. Her stargazing platform was the only choice. She climbed the ladder and shouldered the trapdoor open. The rain lashed at her. Once up, she pressed herself to the stone side of the manor to allow Blake room to climb up. He shut the trapdoor and squat on top of it.

"This won't fool anyone for long, considering we left a puddle in the hall." He had to raise his voice to be heard over the wind and rain. "Does this lead anywhere else?"

Jessica had trapped them as surely as Blake has been locked in a room.

A bang sounded on the trapdoor, and it bucked up even with Blake's weight on top. Jessica hopped up next to him, and the door flopped back down. A ledge led back to the turret room, but Goforth or one of his minions could simply lock the door, and they'd have captured themselves. If they could scoot to the rainwater drain running up the side of the manor, they could possibly shimmy down to the floor below. It would leave them in the old nursery.

She told Blake her harebrained plan.

"Jolly good! I've become quite skilled at climbing in and out of my room at Eton. I should be able to manage fine." He looked over the edge. "We'll have to make a go for it quickly though."

"Yes. You go first." She gave his shoulder a little shove. "I'll be right behind you."

"I'm the man. You should go first so I can protect you."

She let out an exasperated breath. "I'm the oldest. Go before I decide to put you over my knee. You can enter the nursery and help me from there."

Although he didn't look pleased, he scampered over the rail and onto the ledge with the agility of a red squirrel. How was she to manage in her skirts? She would because she had to. Without Blake's added weight, the door lifted a few inches once more. She stood and jumped on it, slamming it back down.

Blake had moved out of sight. It was her turn. She stripped off her riding jacket and hitched her skirts as high as possible for ease of movement. She scrambled over the railing with less grace than her brother and scooted onto the ledge. The rain chilled her to the bone and numbed her fingers. Her skirts were sodden and heavy around her legs.

The cracks in the stone provided handholds as she made her way inch by inch to the drain. She dared not look down, but the top of Blake's head was in her periphery several feet below her.

The trapdoor banged open like a crack of thunder. Unable to stop herself, she stole a glance. Goforth emerged like a wrathful devil, his teeth bared. Rain streamed over her eyes, blurring him. Her only hope was to put distance between them, but her nerves were fraying and the trembles in her hands and knees weren't helping her odds of escape.

She risked a glance down. Blake was almost to the ledge below.

"Get back here, you cunt!" Goforth yelled.

Jessica took another step away.

"Did you think to escape me? I'll crush you the way I crushed your husband."

Jessica faltered. "What did you do, you monster?"

"What I've wanted to do for years. What he deserved for humiliating me."

It was all she could do to cling to the stone with her heart shattering in a million pieces. Her fault. It was all her fault.

Goforth grabbed the wooden rail and leaned toward her with his hand outstretched. His fingers caught the sleeve of her shirt and held. A primal urge to survive had her screaming and attempting to shake him loose. He tugged her backward, and she tightened her grip, pressing her cheek against the rain-slicked stone.

A crack sounded. The rotten railing snapped. Their gazes held, and Goforth's eyes widened. He blinked once, twice, and then he was lost to the darkness and rain. Time stretched into years before she heard a dull thud through the storm.

A cry, this one closer, shot terror through her. Blake had lost his foothold and was dangling from the edge of a stone. His bravado was gone, and his fear turned him back into her little brother.

She crouched lower on the ledge. It was wide enough that she should be able to lie prone and reach him. Her wet skirts clung and hampered her movements, but she managed to reach her knees and then pitch forward to her belly. Scooting backward, she anchored her hand in the stone, her fingers pinched and her nails broke as she reached for her brother with her other hand. She gripped his wrist.

"Jess!" Blake's voice trembled.

"I've got you. I won't let go," she yelled, with more desperation than promise. If he fell, his weight would pull them both over to join Goforth.

"Jessica!" Her name was yelled again over the storm, but this time in a deeper, beloved voice. "Let go, sweetheart. I'll catch your brother."

She looked down and blinked what might have been rain or tears out of her eyes, unable to let go of the stone wall or her brother. Simon hung partway out of the nursery window, his arms outstretched. He was very much alive. She let out a sob.

"Let him go, sweetheart. If he pulls you over, I can't catch you both. Trust me."

Trust him. Her heart pounded furiously. Without a doubt, she did trust him.

She looked down at her brother and her husband. "I love you."

The declaration encompassed both of them. Then, ever so slowly, she pried her numb fingers apart. Without her added strength, Blake's grip slipped. The ledge seemed to sway under her, and she closed her eyes, unable to witness the outcome. No thud answering to Goforth's reached her.

What felt like seconds later, a warm hand gripped her leg. "Love, it's time to come in."

While she couldn't see him, Simon's voice was reassuring and solid. "Blake?"

"Surprisingly chipper. I sent him to the kitchens."

She clung to the ledge with the knowledge her brother was safe. She, on the other hand, remained in a precarious situation. "I don't know what to do."

"Can you get on your hands and knees?"

Her knees were like water, and the thought of letting go of the stone set her body to trembling. The combination of cold and fear had wilted her mettle. "I don't think I can."

"Do you feel my hand?" He gave her leg a squeeze. "Now scoot backward like an inchworm. A little at a time. You can do that, can't you?"

She nodded, even though he probably couldn't see her. She

did as he asked, moving toward him an inch at a time. Finally, Simon circled her waist with his hands, anchoring her until her feet hit the wide platform. He lifted her backward into his chest and twisted them away from the edge where the railing had broken off.

"Goforth said he killed you." She turned, wrapped her arms tightly around his neck, and buried her face in his chest.

He snorted. "Hardly. He left his hired lackeys to finish me off. Terrible decision as it gave me better odds. Of course they expected me to fight like a toff. Rafe taught me long ago how to fight dirty."

"Goforth fell." She felt like a simpleton, unable to formulate complex thoughts.

"Yes. Let's get out of the rain. You're shivering and soaked through." He moved toward the trapdoor, but she made things difficult for him, unwilling to let him out of her reach.

He helped her down the ladder and joined her. The trapdoor shut out the noise of the storm, and her ears rang in the silence. They stood in one another's arms.

"I love you," she whispered into his neck.

"I love you too. Everything will be fine."

She wanted to believe him. "I don't feel anything at all about his death. Shouldn't I feel *something*?"

"You're in shock. When you're ready, we can talk about everything. I'm here to share your burdens. But right now, we both need to get out of these clothes and into a hot bath." Simon led her down the stairs and into the kitchen.

Her brother's cheeks were rosy from the kitchen fire, and he had a dollop of red-current jam in the corner of his mouth. He smiled at her, but it was tinged with the same numbness invading her. She went to him and gathered him in for a hug while Simon and Mrs. Hamish conferred.

"Everything will be fine." She repeated what Simon had told her. If she kept saying it aloud, maybe she would believe it.

"Of course it will be fine. You're married to a bloody duke!" A spark of his earlier bravado twinkled in his eyes. "I'll return to Eton without having to worry about Goforth planting a facer on the majordomo and dragging me away."

"That must have been terrifying." Jessica ruffled his damp hair.

"I can't wait to get back and tell the boys about it." He took another jam tart and bit into it with gusto. His resiliency was a revelation.

Simon interrupted them. "Baths are being drawn and fires started in your rooms."

"Thank you, Your Grace." Blake extended his hand.

The corner of his lips twitched, but otherwise, Simon maintained a serious expression as he shook her little brother's hand. "My pleasure, my lord. Although, as your sister is my wife, we are family now and I insist you use my given name. Call me Simon."

"Then you must call me Blake." Her brother ruined the effect by taking off at an adolescent lope to his room and a warm bath.

Simon turned to her. "You as well, my love."

"Will you come with me?" She fisted her hand in his shirt.

"The magistrate has arrived. I left two men unconscious and tied up in the drawing room, and your stepfather's body must be dealt with. There will be an inquiry."

She shuddered and listed into him. "Compared to that, a bath sounds lovely."

He pressed a kiss on her forehead and handed her over to Mrs. Hamish.

As Abby was in London, Mrs. Hamish helped her undress and climb into the tub. Her fingers tingled with feeling once more, and the bliss of being warm helped drive away the ghosts. But as soon as she was tucked into bed in an old night rail, she found herself reliving Goforth's final moments on the ledge. What had he been thinking?

Finally, Simon slipped into the room. He had bathed and was wearing a dry set of clothes.

"Is it resolved?" She sat up.

"The magistrate will need to question both you and Blake, but I expect it to be perfunctory." He climbed into bed and turned her back to his front, his warmth subduing her anxiety. "I thought we might repair to Wintermarsh on the morrow for a few days."

"Yes, please. We should close up the manor until Blake comes of age and decides what to do with it. I never want to see this place again." While that was true, she couldn't imagine leaving everything—or everyone—behind. "Mrs. Hamish will need a new situation."

"Agreed. Her tart recipe is too valuable to let go."

Jessica elbowed him and found a laugh, albeit a weak one. "Do you have any ideas?"

"In fact, I do. While I love Wintermarsh, we can hardly live there with Rafe and Minerva and raise children."

His casual mention of children stole her breath. "You own a multitude of estates, don't you?"

"Not a multitude." His pause was rife with gloom. "None have ever felt like a home. I suppose we should settle at the family seat. It's where Minerva and I grew up."

"What's it like?"

"Dusty, drafty, and damp." Almost grudgingly, he added, "The gardens are pretty, and it's situated with a lovely view. If you'd rather—"

"All it takes is love to make a home, and we have that to spare." She grabbed his hand and pressed a kiss to the back.

He laced their fingers. "That we do, my love."

EPILOGUE

Simon raised Jessica's hand to press a kiss to her palm. Her head was tucked under his chin. He was enjoying the sight of her lithe leg tangled in the white sheet and draped over his. Between the inquiry into Goforth's demise and seeing to the closing of Penhaven Manor, Simon had despaired of enjoying a night alone with his wife to finally consummate their union.

Rafe had pulled him aside after the magistrate had left the evening after the incident and suggested use of his cottage in the woods. It had proved a respite from the chaos of Wintermarsh. They had been able to enjoy one another numerous times in bed and out without fretting about anyone hearing them.

The freedom was something he wasn't accustomed to as a duke. Servants and hangers-on seemed to trail him like a bad odor. He was already plotting to refurbish the folly by the lake at his estate as a similar escape for them to enjoy, but that was for the not-so-distant future. At the moment, he planned to thoroughly enjoy his present.

He rolled until he was the one draped over her. Brushing her hair back from her flushed face, he asked, "Are you well, darling?"

A complicated smile twisted her lips. He not only enjoyed her complications, he appreciated them. "I am more than well. I am happy. And that is no small thing. I never expected happiness."

"I hope I am the cause of at least a portion of your happiness." He pressed a kiss to her lips to ensure his tease didn't completely mask his understanding.

"I'd say you're responsible for at least half of my happiness."

"Only half?" He playfully tickled her sides, and she squirmed and giggled beneath him, dislodging the sheet. His body reacted predictably in contact with her bare skin. "You must recalculate once I'm done with you, my love."

He slid down her body, his shoulders bracing her legs apart and imparted great happiness with his tongue on her tender flesh if her moans and encouragement were any measure.

Panting, she dug her nails into his shoulder and drew him over her. He entered her with a sharp thrust and they both gasped. He held himself still inside her, enjoying the aftermath of her climax.

Nuzzling his lips along her temple, he whispered, "I despaired of ever finding this sort of happiness either. I love you."

She clutched him tighter with arms and legs. Clutched him with an intensity that spoke more than words. He began to move inside her. Their earlier lovemaking had been playful and exploratory and sweet.

This was different. Elemental and true and stripped of any artifice. He was not a duke in her arms, but a man. A man well-loved. And she was no duchess, but a woman whom he loved beyond measure.

THE END

~

I HOPE you loved Simon and Jessica's story as much as I loved writing it! Next up in the Spies and Lovers world is a Christmas story. Do you like Regency bodyguards? How about the old "Uh-oh, there's only one bed!" story? This has both! Plus, a little unrequited love thrown in. Watch Victoria and Thomas discover love on the run in A SCANDALOUS SECRET!

AS THE DAUGHTER of England's spymaster, Miss Victoria Hawkins is no stranger to secrets. Her biggest secret is the tender feelings she holds for Thomas Garrick, her father's personal guard. As the pressure to choose a husband at an upcoming Christmas house party mounts, Victoria grows desperate. When circumstances trap them together in a cottage with a single bed and a bottle of brandy, her infatuation with the gruff Garrick might cause the scandal of the season...and give Victoria exactly what she wishes for this Christmas.

LEARN MORE

Read on for an excerpt of A SCANDALOUS SECRET!

Garrick swallowed. He should look away. Their banter earlier had been in jest. Victoria's life was not in any danger. His sanity, on the other hand, was being held at gunpoint. Victoria remained facing him as the girl worked the length of buttons in the back. The bodice began to gape and reveal more delectable skin and the gathered edge of a white shift.

Victoria ran her hands along the skirts, then looked up with a smile when the girl gently tugged one of the sleeves down. Her gaze swept over the slit in the curtain, and he pressed himself back against the wall out of sight.

If he'd been in the field, the possibility of exposure would have signaled his immediate retreat. A wise agent knew when to give up a position, no matter how tempting the information gleaned could be.

All wisdom deserted him. He peeked through the slit once more, expecting her to have turned and shielded herself from the inappropriateness of his spying, but she hadn't. His position hadn't been compromised.

The girl had tugged both sleeves off and was helping

Victoria step out of the heavy skirts. Her posture offered a tantalizing view of the shadowy valley between her breasts. She straightened on the dais, her shoulders back, her gaze finding its way unerringly to his, unflinching and brazen.

He had been outflanked. Not only was she aware of his attentions, but she welcomed them. Her breathing paced his, shallow and rapid, the movement drawing his attention downward along the tempting curves of her body. Her stays pressed her full breasts high. The rise and fall of her chest against the thin fabric of her shift was decadent. Her nipples were barely covered, and he ruminated on their shape and color.

Her waist dipped above the curve of her hips, and the looking glass reflected her pert bottom. The shadow of her mons was visible through her shift. He allowed his gaze to wander all the way to her stocking-covered feet and then back up. In his mind's eye, he lifted her shift higher and higher, exposing her calves, her knees, her thighs until…

"Anywhere else you would like to visit, my dear? We won't be back until after the new year." Lady Hawkins turned to Victoria while the modiste took the dress and disappeared into what Garrick assumed was her workroom.

Victoria blinked once, then shifted to face her mother while the shop girl helped her back into her yellow dress. "I should like to visit the milliner next door."

Lady Hawkins hummed thoughtfully before saying, "This will be our fourth visit to the milliner in as many weeks. You have shown an unusually keen interest in bonnets lately, yet you never seem to have one on in the garden. Why is that?"

Garrick didn't hear Victoria's reply. He backpedaled toward the door, flummoxed by his lack of control and positively dumbfounded at Victoria's boldness. He tried to summon shame or regret or some emotion that would blunt the arousal humming through him but failed.

ALSO BY LAURA TRENTHAM

Historical Romance

Spies and Lovers

An Indecent Invitation Book 1

A Brazen Bargain, Book 2

A Reckless Redemption, Book 3

A Sinful Surrender, Book 4

A Wicked Wedding, Book 5

A Daring Deception, Book 6

A Scandalous Secret, Book 7

Spies and Lovers Boxset

Contemporary Romance

Sweet Home Alabama Novels

Slow and Steady Rush, Book 1

Caught Up in the Touch, Book 2

Melting Into You, Book 3

Christmas in the Cop Car, Novella 3.5

The Sweet Home Alabama Collection

. . .

Highland, Georgia Novels

A Highlander Walks Into a Bar, Book 1

A Highlander in a Pickup, Book 2

A Highlander is Coming to Town, Book 3

Heart of a Hero Novels

The Military Wife

An Everyday Hero

Cottonbloom Novels

Kiss Me That Way, Book 1

Then He Kissed Me, Book 2

Till I Kissed You, Book 3

Christmas in the Cop Car, Novella 3.5

Light Up the Night, Novella 3.75

Leave the Night On, Book 4

When the Stars Come Out, Book 5

Set the Night on Fire, Book 6

Fieldstones Adventure Novellas by Leah Trent

An Impetuous Interlude, Fieldstones Adventure Book 1

A Naughty Notion, Fieldstones Adventure Book 2

A Mysterious Masquerade, Fieldstones Adventure Book 3

A Dangerous Desire, Fieldstones Adventure Book 4

The Fieldstones Adventures Boxset

I love to hear from readers! Come find me:

Laura@LauraTrentham.com
www.LauraTrentham.com
Sign up for Laura's Newsletter
Join Laura's Facebook Squad

Are you interested in receiving a FREE book?!

Join my newsletter! There will be links in your Welcome Email for TWO free books!

Sign up for Laura's Newsletter

ABOUT THE AUTHOR

I hope you enjoyed *A Daring Deception*! If you have a chance please leave a quick review! Although, many readers know me from my Southern-set contemporary romances, the first books I wrote were the Spies and Lovers series! I grew up reading the historical "bodice rippers" of the late eighties and early nineties along with wonderful gothic romances. Now that I have the opportunity to publish all of the Spies and Lovers series, I'm so excited! The Spies and Lovers world will be expanding soon with a new series called, Laws of Attraction!

I was born and raised in a small town in Northwest Tennessee. Although, I loved English and reading in high school, I was convinced an English degree equated to starvation! So, I chose the next most logical major - Chemical Engineering- and worked in a hard hat and steel toed boots for several years. Now I live in South Carolina with my husband and two children. In between school and homework and soccer practices, I love to get lost in another world, whether it's Regency England or small town Alabama.

My first two Falcon Football books received TOP PICKS from RT Book Reviews and a STARRED review from Library Journal. KISS ME THAT WAY, Cottonbloom Book 1, won the Stiletto Contest for Best Long Contemporary and finaled in the National Readers Choice Award. THEN HE KISSED ME, Cottonbloom Book 2, was named an Amazon Best Romance of 2016 and was a finalist for the National Excellence for Romance Fiction. TILL I KISSED YOU, Cottonbloom Book 3, is a finalist in the Maggie contest. LEAVE THE NIGHT ON, the latest Cottonbloom book, was named an iBooks Best Book of the Month and a Recommended Read from NPR. AN INDECENT INVITATION and A BRAZEN BARGAIN were both finalists for the 2014 Golden Heart® Award.

I love to hear from readers! Come find me:
Laura@LauraTrentham.com
www.LauraTrentham.com
Sign up for Laura's Newsletter
Join Laura's Facebook Squad

NOTE: This is a work of fiction. All of the characters, organizations, and events portrayed in this novel are either products of the author's imagination or are used fictitiously.

A Daring Deception

Cover by Angela Waters

Edited by Heidi Shoham

eISBN: 978-1-946306-13-5

Printed in Great Britain
by Amazon

43729754R00182